Families of
AMBER HOUSE

Compiled by Fiona Campbell Warren in 1933

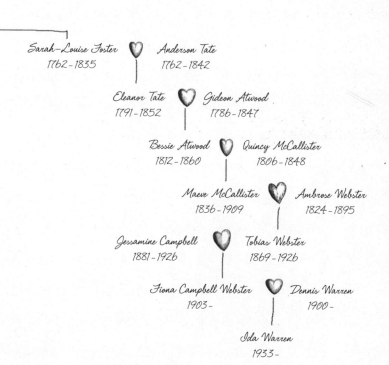

Sarah–Louise Foster
1762–1835

Anderson Tate
1762–1842

Eleanor Tate
1791–1852

Gideon Atwood
1786–1847

Bessie Atwood
1812–1860

Quincy McCallister
1806–1848

Maeve McCallister
1836–1909

Ambrose Webster
1824–1895

Jessamine Campbell
1881–1926

Tobias Webster
1869–1926

Fiona Campbell Webster
1903–

Dennis Warren
1900–

Ida Warren
1933–

A spider the color of amber spun a web before me. Her threads formed a maze I knew I must unravel to find the treasure hidden at its heart.

I followed the twisting path, running lightly in autumn gold slippers, the night held back by candle lanterns, the leafy branches of the walls plucking at my gown. The hedges grew into a forest all around, but I knew which way the spider's web had revealed.

Right, skip, right, left, skip, left.

A little girl in white observed me, her eyes — green eyes — filled with hope.

At the center of the maze, I found the chest inside the spider's house, wrought in curlicues that told words that whispered. The spider or the little girl tempted me: "Don't you want to look inside?"

I knelt on the black-and-white floor before the puzzle of the box, shifting the panels to solve the secret of its opening. But when the catch at last came loose and the box cracked open, black miseries scuttled out on eight legs.

The dark creatures ran for the people frozen in the heart — Sam, Mom and Dad, Maggie, Jackson, Richard. I used a broom to sweep the things away. Then I picked up my people and put them in my purse.

But the creatures swarmed over the little girl in white and she disappeared before me, one spider bite at a time.

I watched and wept tears that fell from the hem of my dress.

I could not have the treasure yet. I had to try to solve the puzzle again.

Chapter One

I was sixteen the second time I had my first kiss.

Maybe we all have more than one first kiss — maybe an infinite number — and we just don't remember. First kisses. First loves. First sorrows. Until we get it right. Until we become who we were meant to be.

But this first kiss I wish never to forget.

So I make myself remember it all. From beginning to end. My grandmother's stroke in mid-October. Her funeral, when we buried her beside my grandfather in the family plot on the hill above the river. My parents' hidden conversations that I eavesdropped on — about whether they could go back "there" now, to Maryland, whether things had changed enough. The events that took us back, and threw us forward. Again.

The home I'd grown up in — a sweet yellow Victorian that sat on the water's edge on the west side of Seattle — sold just two weeks after the realtor posted her sign. Thirty days later, my father, mother, brother, and I were on our way to my grandmother's house. *Amber House*. Now ours.

That first day — when we drove up in our station wagon, with me asleep, wedged in the backseat — I felt the place even before I saw it. I woke to the sensation of all the little hairs on my arms standing on end. Dad turned in the front gate, carving a solitary pair of tire tracks in the snow-smooth drive. The house sat on a bluff above the Severn River at the distant edge of wooded pastures. It waited there under the gray sky of late afternoon, its blank eyes regarding our approach.

The estate was famous — one of the oldest in North America, owned by a single family, *my* family, since the 1600s. Dormant gardens surrounded the house, which was all white clapboard and pillars, brick and green trim. Not stately so much as solid. Filled with time.

My grandmother used to tell me how three hundred and fifty years of my ancestors had added to Amber House — a wing here, a porch there, a balcony, a turret. Decade after decade. Generation after generation. Century after century. As a child, I'd had a hazy notion of the house having slowly shrugged up out of the earth.

A beautiful place. A remarkable home. No question. I just didn't want to live there. I remembered once wandering its hedge maze, thinking with gladness about becoming a part of Amber House — but that day in December when we took possession, I no longer remembered why.

It wasn't simply that I was homesick, though that was a part of it. It was as if something was out of place, missing, but I was the only one who noticed. A phantom limb with pain I couldn't numb.

The feeling had grown as I'd entered the front door. I'd stopped still, looking at all of my grandmother's familiar things now made unfamiliar because she was gone. It was like the first time I'd ever seen them for what they were — not just my grandmother's *stuff*, but *her* grandmother's, and *her* grandmother's before her. As if some kind of thread, spun of place and possessions, tied us all together down through the generations in both directions. A lifeline. A chain.

I saw the past in everything. The gleaming stretch of the golden-hued floor polished by the feet of centuries. The Windsor chairs built wide to hold hooped skirts. The tall-case clock with stars painted on its face, still numbering the minutes between then and now. Candlesticks, leather-bound books, china as fragile as dried leaves, the sea chest that had been around the Horn, and some part of me with it, in the man who brought it home to Amber House.

All of it pulled on me somehow. As if I *owed* the House something. As if the oil-painted faces of my ancestors, staring down at me from every wall, were waiting. And day by day, as we settled in, the feeling grew.

Outside was no better than in. The stable with its sweet-sour smell of horses; the tree house hidden in the limbs of the ancient oak; the dock on the river where my grandparents' sloop, the *Liquid Amber*, rested on blocks until spring; the silence-drifted corridors of the hedge maze — they no longer felt like the places I had always loved playing during all my visits from the time I was small. Yet they hadn't changed. So I must have. I just didn't fit. I felt incomplete, deficient.

Beyond the fences bounding the estate, however, that feeling ebbed. So I developed a need to escape. The Saturday after we moved in, I was trying to coax my little brother, Sammy, into walking once again to Severna, the only town we could reach on foot.

"Nope," he told me. "I'm busy, Sarah." He was sitting in front of a disemboweled radio, most of its guts arranged on the tabletop. He'd turned six the month before; this more grown-up Sammy didn't have the same endless enthusiasm he used to for my various plans and propositions.

"I'll buy you an ice cream," I said.

He sighed and pointed out the obvious: "It's snowing."

"Hot chocolate, then," I begged. "You like hot chocolate."

He finally consented. Not because he wanted the cocoa but because he'd heard the begging.

As we shuffled out the front door, my mother appeared in the arch to the living room. "Going into town *again*?" she said.

Apparently my obsession with being elsewhere was worrying her. So I shrugged. "I need something," I said.

"What?"

I considered telling her I needed to get out, but I knew I wouldn't be able to explain it. "Chocolate," I said. "I promised Sammy hot chocolate."

Her lips pursed a little. Ever since Sammy's diagnosis, she'd honed "concerned parenting" to an art form. It was almost a supernatural talent. I could tell *she* could tell I was withholding information, but she decided to let it slide. "Make sure to take Sam's hand —" she started, with her usual rising note of anxiety.

"— take his hand on the main road," I finished, nodding. I pulled the door closed before she could think of some other advice to give.

It was a fifteen-minute walk, mostly across parkland that spread between Amber House and town. When we reached Severna, I paid Sam back for his kindness in coming with me by taking him to the hardware store. Sammy had a deep appreciation for hardware stores. He was all about connecting things, so the million parts and pieces were like treasure to him. He wandered the aisles the way other people wandered a zoo, staring at the strange things, occasionally reaching out to touch one. This trip, he came to rest in the plumbing department. I stood and watched him for a few minutes as he made a road map of copper tubes and elbows on the floor.

Across the aisle from the bins of pipe, a dozen Sarahs in a dozen vanity mirrors considered me. Each surface held a slightly different girl — taller, wider, sharper, pinker. One mirror was gold-veined, its Sarah caught in a metallic web. I stared at the images. For the past couple months, something about my reflection kept surprising me.

A voice spoke from just behind me. "This is not a toy store."

I turned, startled, embarrassed. It was the owner. "Sorry," I said. "I'll get all the pieces put back in their correct bins right away."

"I'm sure you will," he said, leaving us to it.

We cleaned up and slunk out, emerging into a moving crowd — the sidewalks had filled with people heading toward the center of town.

"What's happening, Sarah?" Sammy asked.

"I don't know, bud."

Someone called my name. "Parsons!"

I searched through unfamiliar faces and then finally spotted Richard Hathaway zeroing in on me. Wheat hair over bronze skin; blue topaz eyes; square-cut features that framed a square-cut smile, just slightly crooked. He was without a doubt the best-looking boy I had ever met. Plus, athletic, funny, charming, and smart. The son of my parents' old friends, who were also our neighbors. As far as I was concerned, Richard was maybe the only real benefit to living in Maryland. "Hathaway," I answered.

"Needed nails?" he asked.

I must have given him one of those uncomprehending looks, because he nodded in the direction of the store. "Oh," I said, "no, Sam just likes hardware stores."

"Hey! No kidding?" he said to Sam. "Me too!" And Sam beamed.

I couldn't think of a single thing to say, so I turned Sam in the direction the crowd was moving, and started to walk. The main street of Severna, a short stretch of older, mostly wooden commercial buildings, was a block north. "We're going to the drugstore."

"Candy counter?" Richard guessed as he fell in alongside us. "Congrats, by the way, on your admission to S.I."

S.I. — Saint Ignatius Academy — was the incredibly exclusive prep school he attended to which my parents had absolutely *insisted* I apply. I shrugged a little. "I don't think my mother gave them much choice."

He smiled. "I don't think my dad did either."

The senator is pulling strings for me? I wondered why. I knew, of course, that an A-list prep like S.I. had to have some good reason to accept a B-list student like me, but nobody'd told me it was the senator. *That would do it.*

The flow of people just ahead had pooled into a crowd eddying on the sidewalk and spilling over into the street. Everyone seemed to be staring at something happening below the marquee of the Palace Cinema. As we neared the drugstore on the corner, I heard chanting, and the buzzing voice of someone speaking into an amplifier.

Richard halted us by the entryway to Lane's Pharmacy. "You're not headed into that mess, are you?" he asked.

I smiled, because his voice had that same well-intentioned rising note of worry my mother's always had. "No," I said. "Going inside to get my chocolate fix."

"Addict." He grinned and backed away, waving, heading off to join the "mess" he'd just warned us against. Sam and I stood in the pharmacy entrance and watched him melt into the crowd.

Then Sam said, "I wanna see." He started walking and I followed after. I wanted to see too.

At the back of the crowd, Sammy pulled one of his signature weave-through-the-legs disappearances. "Sam, stop!" I ordered, but missed snagging the hood of his coat by millimeters. I began to apologize my way forward, squeezing around the bulk of winter coats and scarves: "Sorry, can I get past? Have to catch my little brother."

I found him at the very front, his toes hanging over the edge of the curb. I got a firm grip on that hood. "Sam. You can't go running off like that."

He was pointing at the scene across the street. "See him, Sarah?"

"See who?" I lifted my eyes to look just as a policeman stepped directly in front of me, his back a solid wall. Black-booted, helmeted, and uniformed. Massive in what I guessed was a bulletproof vest. His right hand gripped a shiny black baton. "Who, Sam?" I repeated, leaning to see around the policeman's body.

Sammy pointed again. "There!"

A man came running down the street in front of the crowd then, shouting words I could only partially hear — *something, something* "move" *something something* "pepper cans." The policeman took a half step forward, and I was actually afraid for a moment that he was going to strike the man with his baton. But the man continued past, still yelling.

"What did he say?" I asked aloud, feeling I should take Sam and go. "What's happening?" The officer swiveled his head to look at me, anonymous inside the chitinous shell of his helmet.

"Protest." His voice squeezed from his helmet electronically. "A young lady shouldn't be here."

I hated that kind of *you're-not-doing-what-a-nice-girl-ought-to* stuff. "If I see any young ladies," I said brightly, "I'll let them know." I could feel his eyes narrowing behind the black face-plate; it gave me a queasy sensation in my stomach, but I continued to smile up at him. Fortunately, Sammy gave me an excuse to look away.

"Jackson! Jackson!" He was making little leaps, waving an arm in the air.

The crowd surged left to make a path for a mounted police-man, and I finally got a look at what everyone was staring at:

Two lines of people stood with interlocking arms across the entrance to the theater. I scanned the faces until I found Jackson near the right-hand side, between two other men. The man to his left looked terrified. I saw his warm breath pulsing in fast clouds from his mouth, his clenched fist mashing an incongruously cheerful yellow handkerchief. Jackson was calm, determined.

"JACK-SON!" Sam called with all his might.

Jackson's head jerked. He looked around, confused, worried, trying to track that bird voice. His eyes connected with mine and widened.

The sounds of the crowd grew louder, higher pitched. I heard snarling and spotted three German shepherds straining against their leashes. Little pops sounded; round metal objects arced overhead, leaking trails of smoke and landing in the street to spew a thickening cloud.

That's when people started screaming. And running.

All around me, the crowd churned, scattering in every direction. I lost my grip on Sammy's hood. The edges of the smoke reached us. My eyes burned. I started coughing, doubled over, the spasm going on and on until I was choking on it, unable to catch my breath.

A hand caught my wrist. I looked up through tear-filled eyes to see Richard holding Sammy on one shoulder, up above the worst of the gas. "You two shouldn't be here," he said. "Come on!"

He tugged me into motion as a wave of black-suited police ran down the street. Two officers held the nozzle of a fire hose gushing water at the lines of protestors in front of the Palace. I stumbled after Richard, wondering why anybody thought these people deserved to be hosed down in the below-freezing December weather.

I staggered the long block back toward the hardware store. There I had to stop. I leaned against a blank wall and threw up.

A handkerchief appeared in my line of view. "You gonna make it, Parsons?" Richard said.

"I think so," I said. I waved the hanky off. "I can't take that from you."

"Yes, you can," he said. "It's fresh from my drawer, where I have five hundred more."

He caught my hand and pressed the hanky into it. I wiped my eyes and mouth. "What was that?" I managed between fits of coughing. "Why'd they do that?"

"Protest," Richard said. "The police chief takes it personally." He set my brother down and put Sam's little hand in mine. "You take your sister home, all right, Sammy? I've got to go back."

"What were they protesting?" I asked.

"The Palace still restricts blacks to the balcony."

I felt nauseated all over again. Severna might look like any small town in Astoria, but it was part of a society that was completely alien to me. I was in a country that still justified "separate but equal" facilities for the races. Not that "separate" had ever actually been "equal."

I hadn't ever seen the full depth of its ugliness before — not this starkly, this violently. It was hard for me to believe that there were still places in the world that practiced institutionalized racism in the twenty-first century. That it still happened in this place, my family's homeland. My home now. The American Confederation of States.

Chapter Two

The walk home was a misery. The cloud of gas had triggered a monster headache all up the back of my skull. My eyes burned and my throat felt like a skinned knee. Plus, my feet, hands, and ears were going numb in the cold.

Most of the distance, we followed a path that wound through the park on the southwest side of town to a point just across the road from the northeast corner of the estate. There, a tree-hidden gate let us inside the fence, where another coughing jag sent me stumbling. I stopped to bend over and wheeze.

Little mittened hands cupped my face. "You all right, Sarah?" Sam's eyes were wide.

"I'm fine," I gasped. I'd been coughing so hard, tears were leaking down my cheeks. I caught my breath, brushed the tears off. "Thanks."

"You're welcome." He smiled. He had a thing about *thank-you*s and *welcome*s. One social ritual he'd definitely mastered. I noticed the tip of his nose was pink and his cheeks looked chapped. I wanted to get him inside, someplace warm. And safe. Someplace back home in Astoria.

"*You* all right, bud?" I mentally cursed myself for not being more concerned about him before this.

"Didn't you see?" He spun around, suddenly excited. He held his arms straight up. "That boy who likes hardware stores lifted me way, way high. He was so strong, Sarah. That ol' smoke didn't get me."

I pulled his hood back over his head. "Thank goodness for that boy, then, huh?" Sam nodded and trotted ahead a little to crunch through an ice-crusted puddle. He turned and waited for me to catch up with him so we could walk together on the narrow dirt trail that cut across a pasture toward the stables.

"Sarah, why were all those people so *mad*?"

"It's kind of hard to explain, bud, maybe even harder to understand. A lot of people around here think people who aren't white aren't as good as the white people and don't deserve the same rights, the same respect."

"Even *Jackson*?" he asked, his voice tight with outrage.

"Even Jackson, even Rose. Even Dr. Chen and Mrs. Jimenez back home."

"That's crazy, Sarah. Why d'they think a crazy thing like that?"

"I don't really have an answer for that. You know that the South fought a war a long time ago against England so they could keep owning slaves? And that they had slaves in this country till just before Gramma was born?" He nodded. "I think maybe when you force another person to be a slave, you have to make up a reason why you're so much better than he is that you get to *own* him. You have to believe that there's something the matter with *him* that makes him less of a person." I shook my head. "They thought that for such a long time around here, they just — they just can't stop thinking it. It's like part of who they are. They won't give it up."

Slavery had been abolished for less than a century. The South's infamous "black codes" — official limitations on black citizens' basic liberties — weren't repealed until the 1980s. In the thirty years since, the races had continued to be kept separate and very much unequal. It wasn't easy to make people change their beliefs; generations had to die and carry the old hatreds with them to the grave.

"They're pretty stupid, Sarah."

I laughed. It wasn't often that Sam criticized anyone, but when he did, it was a straight shot. "Yeah, bud. They are. And, you know, they sort of think that way about women too — that women aren't as smart or as good as men."

Sam, God bless him, just shook his head, disgusted. "That boy who likes hardware stores doesn't think that, does he?"

"No, I'm pretty sure he doesn't. And neither does his dad. Not everybody around here thinks that way. But too many people still do."

Sam stopped still a moment, a puzzled furrow in his brow. "Why is it so much worse now, Sarah?"

The question hit me with peculiar force. For half a moment, I had some sense he wasn't talking about Astoria. I shook my head, lifted my shoulders a little. "I don't know, bud. The place we came from was just better."

"But Maggie's here. And we love Maggie."

"Yeah," I agreed, "we love Maggie."

He nodded and started walking again.

Sam hadn't really known Maggie before Gramma's funeral. She'd been in South America for several years, working as a teacher at a school that specialized in helping to mainstream teenagers with cognitive disabilities. So the first time she and Sam had met since he was a baby was at the funeral, and it had been typically Sammy-odd. "This is your aunt Maggie," Mom had told him.

Sam looked at Maggie with really wide eyes and said, "Oh. You got big."

Which made me think that Mom maybe shouldn't have referred to Maggie as "my baby sister" quite so often. But Maggie just nodded seriously and said, "I got big."

Then Sam had tucked his hand into hers and said, "But we can still be friends."

And Maggie smiled and said, "We can still be friends."

Which — they had been. They'd clicked instantly. Made me kind of jealous, really. Sammy had always been my best buddy.

We walked out of the little woods just northeast of Amber House. I paused for a minute, eyeing my new home. Winter-bare trees and shrubs formed a barricade of spider legs around it. In its place above the river, the house stood silhouetted against the southern horizon as if it were the last solid structure between us and what lay forever beyond.

When we went inside, my dad was in the front hall, winding the grandfather clock. "How was Severna?" he asked, smiling.

I contemplated telling him that Severna was the kind of place that sicced attack dogs on protestors and gassed little kids who were just innocent bystanders, but my throat hurt too much. I'd tell him later.

"Fine," I answered.

Sammy added with excitement, "We went —"

"Let me guess," Dad interrupted. "To the hardware store." Sam nodded. "Sounds like you had fun, then. You two have been making a lot of trips into town. Isn't that four times in three days?"

"Nothing else to do around here." In the interest of avoiding a longer conversation, I nudged Sam up the stairs. "Why don't you show me that radio you took apart, bud?"

Mostly I really liked my dad — always good-natured and unassuming, even though he was a pretty famous surgeon who'd made changes to the way medicine was practiced all over North America. At the moment, however, I thought he was incredibly irresponsible for dragging Sam and me away from Astoria.

At the upper landing, I followed Sam into his bedroom, full of antique sailing gear and various disassembled electronic devices.

The Nautical Room, it was called. Which was another one of those weird pretentious things about Amber House — a lot of the rooms had names. Not regular names, like "the den" or "the dining room," but capital-letter-type names like the "White Room" or the "Chinoise Room." I felt I ought to be wearing pink chiffon whenever I brushed my teeth in the Primrose Bath.

"Thanks for coming with me today," I told him.

"You're welcome," Sam said. "You really want to see my radio?"

So I looked at the gutted thing, picking up a couple of pieces, returning them carefully to their places. "Not much of a radio anymore. You going to be able to put that thing back together?"

He made a dismissive face. "I'm making something *better*. Something that will listen to *different* places."

I almost asked him, "what places," but thought better of it. I just nodded. "Really cool, Sam."

He selected a screwdriver, and went back to his work.

My room was through the arch to the east wing. It was the Flowered Room — a fairly recent naming, because my mother had done the flowering of it. She'd been eleven or twelve when she'd decided to transform the room, covering its pale green walls with a child's fantasy garden. Roses, hydrangeas, wisteria, irises, even bees and snails.

I judged every other bedroom in the world against my mother's Flowered Room, with its crewelwork canopy bed and heirloom quilt, its window seat, its bookshelves of first editions that flanked a doll-sized Amber House faithful in its every detail, right down to the furniture and the tiny compass rose inlaid in the floor at the top of the stairs.

I saw that Sam must have been playing with the dollhouse again, because its catch was undone and the two hinged halves of its front rooms left slightly ajar. I swung them fully open to make sure the contents were all present and secure. The only things he appeared to have moved were the little china dolls — the daddy and the little blond girl had been put together in the front bedroom, while the mama and two dark-haired children had been seated in a circle upstairs in the nursery. I left them as he wanted and swung the front rooms closed.

Dinner wouldn't happen for an hour or two, so I got out some notepaper, thinking I could dash off a letter to Bethanie back home. I loved Bee; I loved her family. They were the type of people who recycled, only bought products from American nations, and picketed the German Embassy for the full truth about what had happened to the Jews of Europe. They were true-blue Astorians. I missed them.

I sat at the desk and started scrawling:

Dear Jecie —

I stopped to stare at what I had written. *Jecie? Who's Jecie?*

Disturbed, I balled up the piece of paper and started again. As I struggled down the page, I became aware of humming.

It seemed to come from the far side of the bed, but no one was there. It was a sweet, high-pitched voice, singing six or seven notes with no particular rhythm, as if someone was keeping herself company while she concentrated on a task. As I stood there, staring at the empty corner, confused, the sounds faded away.

My eyes settled on the heating grate in the wall. The humming must have been coming through that, probably from Maggie in her room directly below mine.

I went back to my letter. I told Bee a little about the Amber House exhibit my parents were putting together. Practically as soon as we'd moved in, they'd started collecting stuff from the entire life of the house relating to "women and minorities of the South," for a show the Hathaways, Richard's parents, had helped them arrange at New York's Metropolitan Museum. The whole thing was faintly embarrassing to me — I didn't think my family was all that interesting. Still, I knew Bee would be as surprised as I was that my folks were getting into the whole activism thing. Pleased, because she thought *everyone* should be an activist. But surprised.

A little tap caught my attention. I jumped, even though I knew the sound: a pebble on glass. I smiled.

From the window, I spotted Jackson on the flagstones below. He was getting ready to make another toss but saw me and interrupted himself. He waved and I waved back. He pointed toward the other end of the house.

I nodded, turned, and headed for the west wing.

Chapter Three

Amber House was an odd place at any hour, but it was oddest when the darkness started to fill it at the end of a day. Especially in the rooms and halls that were hardly ever used anymore, like the entire second floor of the west wing.

My mom had told me when I was small not to pay attention to the house's "creepies," as she called them. She said Amber House was old the way people get old — their knees start to pop, and they groan a little when they settle into a chair. She said the sighs of an old house can make you start imagining things — hear voices in the creaks, turn shadows into shapes. I had to try to ignore it. Shut it out. So I learned how to do that. But I still didn't like Amber House in the dark.

I hurried down the west wing's hall, past the six doors to four bedrooms and two baths — all mercifully closed this evening, though sometimes they weren't. It was too easy to imagine people half hidden in the deep shadows of a room. I tried to keep the doors shut; I didn't know who was forever opening them.

At the end of the hall, I burst out through the French doors that opened onto a lacy metal landing at the top of a spiral stair. I stood there a moment, trying to catch my breath and calm myself down. I didn't want Jackson to see how panicky I'd let myself get — he'd tease me for it.

The tops of small trees formed a leafy cloud between me and the frozen world outside the glass walls of the conservatory. This had always been my favorite spot in Amber House — built in about 1920 as a sixteenth-birthday present for my great-grandmother Fiona. It was a web of iron framework that rose from ground level to the peak of the west wing, filled with trees and flowers too delicate to survive a Maryland winter. Above me, outside, large white flakes materialized from the darkness to settle on the transparent ceiling, but inside the web, birds sang and orchids bloomed.

Jackson and I had claimed it as our own many winters before. We'd played every kind of game there, from hide-and-seek to imaginary adventures. We'd even made up a friend to play with us, a little girl we called Amber. I wondered how old I'd been when we finally stopped pretending her.

I found Jackson waiting by the koi pool, standing below the stone statue who guarded it: a blind-eyed Pandora who wept tears that trickled soundlessly down her gown.

I went and sat on the stone edge of the pool and Jackson joined me.

"Saw you at the protest," he said. "Wanted to make sure you and Sam were all right. What the heck were you thinking, Sare, bringing him to that?"

He was scolding me. Again. Seemed like he was always scolding me lately, but it hadn't used to be like that, before Gramma died.

"I didn't 'bring' him there," I said. "We were going to the drugstore. He just slipped away."

" 'Just slipped away,' huh? And your own curiosity didn't have anything to do with it?" He said it with a smile, but it stung because it was true. I couldn't fool him — he knew me too well. My parents, maybe, but Jackson, never.

He shook his head. "This isn't Astoria. Sam could have been seriously hurt. You could have too. You've got to —"

"Sam's fine," I said shortly. I crossed my arms and legs. "Look, you're right. I should have taken Sam home as soon as I saw what was going on, but —" I felt like I was talking to my dad. I didn't like him lecturing me, acting like he was so much older. We were practically the same age. "Sam's fine. I'm fine. I got a sore throat, but I'm fine."

"I forgot." Like magic, Jackson reached into his pocket and produced exactly what I needed — a purple cough drop wrapped in foil. I rolled my eyes and gave him a small smile — he was forever doing stuff like that. I took it, unwrapped it, and popped it in my mouth.

"I know you don't like it when someone tries to stop you or tell you what to do, Sare, even me. And in general, that's a good thing. More people ought to challenge authority. But that kind of attitude can get you into serious trouble around here. You have to be careful. You have to be *responsible*. People are counting on you."

"Got it," I said. I noticed then that Jackson's skin had a bluish cast to it. He looked half made of ice. "Where the heck is your coat?"

"One of the ladies was drenched. I figured she needed it more than I did."

I went around to the benches on the other side of a screen of bushes, and came back with a lap blanket. I shook it out and swept it around him. "I could not *believe* that fire hose," I said, remembering. "That was like something the Nazis would do."

"Fire hose is standard. Hurts *and* humiliates. We expected it."

" 'We'? Who?"

"Oh," he said, shaking his head, "the people who were there. The people who showed up."

That was another thing he'd started doing since Gramma died — not answering questions. Getting all *secretive*. Not like the way we used to be. I wondered about the yellow handkerchief tied to his belt loop. I'd seen several other yellow handkerchiefs at the demonstration. I thought it might have something to do with who "we" were. But if Jackson didn't want to explain, I knew better than to ask.

"Listen," he said, "can you do me a favor and not mention to Gran you saw me at the protest?"

"Sure, J," I said. I was a little angry, to be asked to keep a secret I wasn't part of. But of course I would. I'd always kept Jackson's secrets, like he'd always kept mine.

I didn't remember much from when I was really small, but I remembered meeting Jackson. Twelve years earlier, he'd come to live on the Amber House estate with his grandmother, Rose Valois, my grandmother's housekeeper. He'd hidden halfway behind her as she introduced him to us — a quiet boy covered in bandages. His parents had died in a car accident that had burned the left side of his body and made him have seizures. But I didn't know all that then. I just knew he was sad. So little-me took his hand the way Sammy might have done and we went outside to play.

He'd been sort of a part-time big brother to me ever since, showing me which trees were the best to climb and where to go crabbing, guiding me to all the special places he found around Gramma's property. Spending time with him had been one of the best things about visiting my grandmother. Until her funeral.

When I finally realized that Jackson wasn't really like a big brother at all.

That had been such a weird day. I'd wandered around the reception after the service, with this feeling that there wasn't enough air to breathe. Like the space between this world and the next had grown thin somehow and the oxygen was leaking out. I'd had a constant feeling of déjà vu too. And then I'd bumped into Jackson and —

It was like I could see for the first time that he wasn't just this nice older boy I could always count on. He was . . . well, he was almost a man. All the long, thin angles of his frame — the lankiness most boys go through, but which had been worse for Jackson because he grew so tall — had rounded out with muscle.

His face had changed too; his features had gotten stronger somehow. Firmer. He was — attractive. Handsome. It left me feeling really off balance.

When I'd found him that day, while I was talking to him, he'd touched a tear on my cheek. And I'd wondered for a moment, with this uncomfortable feeling in my chest, what it would be like if he slid his hand along my chin, and tilted my head, and stepped in close —

Like I said. I'd felt really off balance.

I realized he was watching my face as we sat there by the pool, as though he had some idea of what I was remembering. So I made that thought go away, just like I did with the creepies. I widened my eyes to innocence: *No thinking going on here.*

"You don't like it much at Amber House," he said. A question posed as a statement. Yet another thing he did without fail.

"Definitely liked the place better as a visitor. But I won't be here that long. I'll probably go back to Seattle for college."

He shook his head and looked down, as if I'd just disappointed him again. *Honestly,* I thought irritably, he was only fourteen months older. He didn't have to treat me like I was such a child. I'd grown up too.

"You don't feel you owe something to this place?" he said. "Not many people have a home like Amber House."

"It's not my home," I said, matching his tone. "I'm Astorian, remember?"

He shrugged a little with just his face. I felt judged. Again. It was frustrating. Why couldn't I connect with him the way I used to?

"Truth is, I don't want to stay here either," he said. "I don't *fit* here. I don't belong. But I don't know how to get to where I do belong."

He'd said the same words I'd used in my head to describe myself. *Odd.* Impulsively, I reached out. "If I can help you somehow —"

But it was the wrong move. I'd touched his scarred hand. He pulled it back, shoving it into his pocket. Then he noticed what he'd done and lifted his eyes to mine, smiling a little, sadly.

"I don't really think it's possible to get to there from here."

A voice inside my head said: *It is possible.* A line I'd heard in a movie, maybe. Or something from a dream.

"I gotta go," Jackson said. "I want to have some supper ready for Gran when she gets home."

I pinked up and was glad he couldn't see it in the darkness of the conservatory. His gran would get home after she got off work — making dinner for *my* family, a dinner she didn't eat any part of. He started to slide the little blanket off his shoulders. I shook my head severely. "You'd better just wear that home and bring it back tomorrow, mister," I said.

He smiled and pulled it closed around him. "Thanks, Sare." And it almost sounded the way it used to, when we were best friends.

"See you, J," I said.

The ground floor of the west wing stood between me and the rest of my family, a tunnel of night. I fumbled for the light switch. I wasn't going to walk through the dark. Bad enough I'd still have to walk past all the gaping mouths of unlit doorways.

At its end, the hall bent right and joined up with a gallery that ran the width of the main house. The library's rear door opened into the gallery, as well as the passage that led past the kitchen's swinging door and on into the entry. I ducked right into the kitchen, softly lit and fireplace-warm. Rose was dishing up dinner plates.

I felt another twinge of embarrassment. It had never bothered me much that Rose had worked for Gramma — Gramma had hired Rose as a cook and housekeeper after Jackson's grand-father died, and I had the impression there was some story there I'd never been told. But when Gramma passed, Mom had sug-gested Rose might want to retire on full pay — we simply weren't the kind of people who were used to help in our own home. Rose had refused. Said she wasn't taking charity.

"Can I carry something in, Mrs. Valois?" I said.

I could almost see her mentally shaking her head. She was impatient with our Astorian compulsion to help "the help." But she said, "Sure, Sarah. Just give me a second." She picked up a spoon and started ladling green beans onto each plate. "You go into town again today?"

"Yeah," I said, instantly anxious to avoid saying what Jackson had asked me not to. Which was a mistake. Rose had a grand-mother's near-psychic ability to pick up on anxiety.

"You didn't go anywhere near the cinema, did you?"

"*No-ope*," I said, accidentally adding an extra *o* to the word. "I took Sam to the hardware store."

"You see Jackson?"

"Nup." That one was too abrupt. "What I mean is, I didn't see him in *town*, but I did just see him a few — a little *while* ago, when he stopped into the conservatory to say hi."

She was looking at me squirm, her skepticism plain on her face. But she let the subject drop. "Can you carry in these two plates?"

"Sure," I said, happy to get out of there.

She picked up another three. "Thank you, child. You're a good girl." She turned for the other swinging door that led to the dining room. "Sometimes a little distantly connected to the truth, but a good girl."

She backed through the door, and I made myself follow.

Mom was going around the table with a pitcher, filling water glasses. She smiled at me as I entered. I loved my mother's smile.

It was a part of her gracefulness — the way she moved, the tone of her voice, the shape of her words, the ever-present hint of smile. I almost smiled back. But then I reminded myself how angry I was about being in this house and this country.

The fifth place set at the head of the table was empty. Sammy said, "She'll be here in a little moment."

"She" meant Maggie. "I thought she was already here," I said.

"Nope," Sam said.

I wondered who'd been humming in the room below mine. Rose, probably, or maybe Mom, or even Sammy.

I seated myself and started picking at my food. Mom sat down opposite Sammy. "I am enjoying Maeve's photographs so much," she said in my direction. "She really captured what it was like to be alive and breathing in the late 1800s. You should help me, honey. It's fascinating."

Maeve McCallister was my great-grandmother's grandmother, who'd achieved a certain postmortem fame for the thousands of tintypes she'd taken of everyday life — women, children, servants, and slaves. Subjects most other photographic pioneers didn't deem worthy of capturing for posterity on expensive metal plates. Mom was searching through Maeve's life work to cull the best pieces for the Metropolitan exhibit.

"Not interested in the twisted history of the ACS, Mom," I said with a tight smile. "I'm Astorian."

She blinked, a little surprised by my brittle tone. Dad, ever perceptive, asked, "Something happen today, Sare?"

"There was a big crowd on the main street of Severna. Sam dashed over to see what was happening, and by the time I caught up with him, the police were lobbing gas canisters and hosing down a line of protestors in front of the movie theater."

"Oh, my God," my mother said, her face going pale.

"We got out of there as fast as we could," I said, adding, "and Sam wasn't hurt."

"The boy who likes hardware stores lifted me way up above the gas," Sammy contributed cheerfully.

"Who?" Dad asked.

"Richard Hathaway," I explained.

"Well, thank God for Richard," he said. "You shouldn't have been there."

"No," I said, "*We* shouldn't be *here*."

I didn't know how my father could stand living in the ACS. Mom at least had grown up here. But Dad was from New England, born in Nova Scotia. He'd met Mom while he was at Johns Hopkins — she was attending the all-girls college of Notre Dame in Baltimore at the time. After Dad finished his residency, they'd both wanted out of the South. But Mom refused to go north, because she didn't want to live in a country that still recognized royalty. The two of them had instead headed west, to the nation built on the bones of John Jacob Astor's trading posts. A country of free thinkers who'd emigrated from all over the Pacific Basin and North America. My real home. Astoria.

My father started to reply, but Maggie finally made her appearance, smiling, removing her coat and gloves. Mom jumped up, real happiness lighting her face. She hugged her sister so hard she squeezed an "oomph" from Maggie. "Magpie," Mom said, "so happy you're here."

Maggie made the circuit, returning Sam's enthusiastic hug, reaching up to kiss Dad's cheek, then coming around to hug me. "Sarah too," she said.

After Gramma's funeral, Maggie had gone northwest into Louisiana, to the area just below the New English province of Ohio, to oversee the use of the family foundation's resources to help fight an outbreak of meningitis. We were all happy and relieved to have her back again.

There was something about Maggie, something fragile, that made you want to keep her safe. She was a lot like Sammy: sweet and generous and gentle. She fell in the autism spectrum too, only she fell a little deeper in than he did. She was beautiful and fine-featured, like my mother, but where Mom was all drive and channeled perfectionism, Maggie had this hint of tenuousness that was almost like sorrow. She'd nearly died when she was young — she'd fallen from the tree house in the old oak on the front lawn and hovered in a coma for several weeks. Maybe that accounted for the slightly dreamy and faraway quality she had.

The dinner ran more smoothly after that, since my lack of participation became less noticeably obvious. As Mom cut up the huge chocolate cake Rose had left on the sideboard, Sam went to fetch the Advent calendar he'd been diligently opening every day.

"Look, Maggie," he said, "the special day is almost here." He graciously let her break the seal on the day's window, revealing a tiny plastic compass. "Great!" he said with enthusiasm. "I needed that."

Maggie looked into my eyes over the top of his head and smiled. It was hard to stay angry around her and Sammy, but I kept working at it. After I polished off my cake, I cleared my plate and disappeared upstairs. I thought I'd force myself to crack open one of Mom's old books.

By nine, the house was mostly quiet. I could hear the ticking of the clock in the entry and the faint, faraway sound of voices rising — the television still babbling in the sunroom. It was only six-ish my time — Pacific time — but I got into my PJs anyhow. I wanted to put an end to my misery for the day.

And I was evidently pretty tired. My eyes were playing tricks on me — making shadows in the corners, giving me double vision as I walked down the hall to the bathroom. I had the strangest notion that the girl in the mirror, brushing her teeth, was moving just a fraction of a second slower than I was.

Maybe I needed glasses.

Back in my room, I slid in under the heavy Tree of Life quilt that covered my bed and shut off the little table lamp. Outside the window, caught in moonlight, fat snowflakes were still falling, making me feel cozy and warm. I wished I could like this place. But it just didn't feel right.

Amber ran ahead of me, down the green corridors of the conservatory. I caught glimpses of her pale dress flashing behind the leaves. She slowed to let me catch up. "Let's play a game," she said.

"Hide-and-seek?" I asked.

"Nope," she answered, pushing farther through the branches. "Let's hunt for treasure."

She disappeared into a hedge hall lined with doors. It went on and on, and I gathered up my gold skirt and ran faster. I knew I had to choose. But which door was the right door?

I stopped and opened the one on my left. Amber was waiting for me inside. It was a library with no ceiling, built around a single tall tree that had one withered side, blasted by a long-ago catastrophe.

She held out her hand, and I took the thing she gave me — a gilded walnut. I hated to break such a pretty thing, but some things must be broken. I set it on the floor and stepped on it, and it cracked in two. Curled inside was a scrap of paper.

There were words written on it, but I could not read them. I had to concentrate. I had to make them swim into focus. And then they said to me:

Seek the point where past and future meet.

CHAPTER FOUR

At seven the next morning, before dawn, my mother stuck her head through my door to wake me. "Get up and get a move on, sweetie." She pushed the door open a little farther, letting in more of the hall light. I pulled my pillow over my head. "Come on. Look alive. Church, and then we've got a ton of work to do before our solstice party tomorrow. With Gramma gone —" Her voice broke. She took a breath and blew it out. "The Christmas decorations are so far behind. You have to help."

I unburied my face, rubbing my eyes with my knuckles. And stared, amazed, at what Mom was wearing. She stood there with her hand on the door, lit from behind, in a severe, sleek charcoal suit, its skirt tailored Astorian-style above the knee. "*Where*'d you get that outfit?" I said.

"It was packed," my mother said, a little confused, tugging down the hem of the jacket. "With all my other clothes. You're not going back to sleep now, are you? Cover your eyes — I'm turning on the light." She flipped the switch.

I went temporarily blind as my eyes adjusted to the sudden glare. When my vision returned, I saw that Mom had on her usual pale pink, square-cut, conservative suit. Not a stunning black one. Transformed in an eyeblink. Like in a movie, where the guy in charge of making sure everything stays the same from one shot to the next made a major error. Or maybe like my brain got carried away with wishful thinking. I rubbed my eyes again. "I'm — never mind," I said. "Trick of the light."

"Get a move on," she repeated. And turned to go.

"Um. Mom?" I dropped my feet over the side of the bed so their weight would pull me vertical. "Have you ever had a black suit?"

"Black?" She wrinkled her perfect nose a little. "So grim. You know I like happier colors. Besides, I don't look good in black."

I didn't know if I agreed.

Twenty minutes later, I was almost ready to go except for the jewelry I wanted to wear. Instead of the necklace I was looking for, I found a scrawl on a piece of the stationery I'd left out on the lamp table. I guessed I must have made it during the night, while I was half asleep. The words were nearly illegible, but I puzzled out what they were supposed to say.

"Seek the point where past and future meet."

I stared at the little piece of paper in my hands, reading and rereading the words. *Where past and future meet? Some kind of existential advice about living in the moment?*

Impulsively, I tore the phrase out of the full sheet of paper it was written on, reducing it to a slip the size of a Chinese fortune. I opened the dollhouse and set the words inside its tiny library. I could not say why I felt they belonged there.

"Sarah?" My mom called up the stairs. "We're all waiting on you, honey."

"Coming," I yelled, spotting the missing necklace and grabbing it and my wool coat. I clomped down the stairs, shoving my arms into the sleeves. Dad, Mom, Maggie, and Sam were already in their coats. My mother and aunt both looked neat and polished in their complementary suits, with pillbox hats pinned just so. Sam was tugging unhappily at his collar, trying to loosen the grip of his striped tie. He hated anything tight around his neck.

My mother picked a hair off my collar. "What are you wearing on your head?"

I pulled a lace doily thingy out of my pocket. It was a little wrinkled, but it would have to do. I hated hats as much as Sammy hated ties. Mostly, I hated how the church required only *female* heads to be covered during Mass. The little circle of lace was as far as I was willing to go.

Annapolis stood at the mouth of the Severn River, just off the Chesapeake. A port city precious to the Crown before the Confederation's secession in the 1830s, it wore a mix of northern and southern influences — lots of the straight-laced lines of the Puritan North, with some of the soft colors and curlicued details of the decadent South. The earliest houses were built in the mid-1600s, and most of the government buildings dated to the colonial era. The Confederation was home to many beautifully preserved communities full of gracious homes and marble-faced public buildings, but Annapolis was its own kind of gem. I had to remind myself not to let its loveliness distract me from the issues hidden behind the immaculate façade.

We made our way down toward the old harbor, where St. Mary's Church sat on a hill. The Hathaways had arrived before us and saved a spot for my family, which was fortunate, since I'd made us all a little late and St. Mary's was crowded this last Sunday of Advent. We hurried up the aisle to the front pew Senator Hathaway had chosen. Mrs. Hathaway — Claire — motioned silently for me to sit beside Richard. She was all long, blond elegance, wearing a suit very like the one I had imagined on my mother, sleek and sophisticated in a very unconservative way. She evidently didn't think she looked too grim in black. And neither did I. I couldn't help but admire Claire's sense of style, but there was something about her manner — something I couldn't quite put into words — that always made me uneasy. Maybe I just felt frumpy beside her.

Richard seemed genuinely happy to see me. He leaned over and whispered in my ear, "I like your doily, Parsons." I rewarded him with a dirty look; he grinned.

I found it uncomfortable to be squeezed in next to him. I noticed too much when he brushed up against me — a kind of pins-and-needles feeling. I pulled myself into the slimmest person I could manage and worked hard at not thinking about Richard at all.

I shifted my focus to the church, an edifice in which every detail was designed to draw the eyes up. The altarpiece with its five lacy gold spires; the soaring pointed arches endlessly repeated; and at the top, above all, a starry ceiling suggesting the vault of heaven. I was contemplating that vault, imagining the scaffolding they'd put up to get it painted, when Richard leaned in to deliver another amused whisper: "You're making Father Flaherty mad."

I snapped to and focused as Father Flaherty worked his way toward the conclusion of his homily: ". . . teaches us that Advent is a season of new beginnings, a time of hope and promise. We — all of us — have an opportunity now to embrace change, and to help a new president bring about a vital new beginning for our nation and for our continent." The priest then nodded meaningfully toward Senator Hathaway, seated a few places down from me. As all eyes turned toward our pew, I was glad — *very* glad — I was no longer staring at the ceiling.

After Mass, most of the congregation headed over to the Carvel Hall hotel for brunch. Richard fell into place beside me on the way to the doors. "Want to walk?"

"With you?" I said stupidly.

He chuckled and nodded. "Yeah. With me." He was giving me one of his patented smiles. He bent his head down, as if he were a little uncertain, then lifted his eyes, locking them with mine through a heavy fringe of gold lashes. I wondered if he had any idea how irresistible he looked. *Probably.*

"Sure," I said. I was wearing heels and too-bare legs, so it would be a cold, uncomfortable walk. But I was prepared to be stoic.

We walked up Main Street, window-shopping. An aproned man leaning against the doorway of the tobacco shop — smoking, of course — nodded to Richard. "When's your father announcing?"

Richard smiled. "As soon as he tells me, I'll be sure to let you know."

"I bet Jimmy Nealy a bottle of the good stuff that he'd do it at the exhibit opening." The man grinned. "Nice piece of politicking, that is. *Amber House: The Women and Minorities of the South . . .* Pull in the liberal votes. Soften up the allies."

I didn't really have any idea what the man was talking about — this was the first I'd heard that Robert Hathaway anticipated some kind of political benefit from my parents' exhibit. Even so, I didn't like the cynical way he talked about it, like my parents were part of some sleazy propaganda ploy.

Richard didn't like it either. He frowned slightly. "This is Sarah Parsons," he said, gesturing toward me. "The daughter of the owners of Amber House."

The man gave me an embarrassed look. "I meant to say," he amended, "how — smart the whole idea is, putting Senator Hathaway into the international spotlight that way. We're all so grateful to your folks."

I gave him a small, brittle smile. "I'll tell them."

He pretended he didn't notice the brittleness. Beaming, he said, "Can I borrow this gentleman for just a minute?" Without waiting for an answer, he beckoned for Richard to follow him inside. "I have something for your dad — new Cubans. Will you take them for me?"

Richard politely looked to me for permission; I nodded that I would wait. Because of course a sixteen-year-old young lady was not welcome in the tobacco shop. Some places were still considered male territory.

"Be right back," he promised, and mouthed at me silently, *Sorry*.

I stood there, in the cold, stamping my feet a little to force warm blood into them. A lot of holiday shoppers were on the street — moms and dads holding the hands of Christmas-hyper children. Much the same kind of frenzy I might have seen back home, in Seattle, but for the fact that there the crowds would have been a mix of Hispanic and Asian and Caucasian. Here, everyone was white.

The street ended at the harbor's choppy gray waters, where boats of all types and sizes bobbed. But my eyes fixed on the plain blue building sitting on the water's edge that served as the local yacht club.

A wave of déjà vu smacked me so hard I was dizzy with it. My vision actually rippled.

I *knew* what the club looked like inside — blue carpeted with golden wood accents. I could see in my mind a beautiful two-masted ketch framed in the lobby's sheet glass window. Could imagine the old man in a captain's hat who managed things. But I'd never been inside that building. Never. It was like having a memory of something I knew I'd never done.

I stopped, bent over; the heels of my hands pressed against my eyes.

"Are you all right?" Richard said beside me.

"Yeah," I said, straightening up. "You ever been in there?" I pointed at the club.

"Sure," he said.

"What color is the carpeting?"

"No carpeting. Wood floors with area rugs. Nautical themes."
Huh. "You sure you're all right?"

"Just — need to eat, I think. Let's get to Carvel before all the hash browns are gone."

He grinned. "A girl with an appetite. Points, Parsons."

Points? I thought. He was keeping score?

"I shouldn't have left you waiting. I'm really sorry. Took longer than I thought. And I've never liked that guy — he's the kind who thinks everybody's as crooked as he is. It's part of my job description, though — running errands for Dad."

"It's fine," I said. "What was he talking about? Is your father actually going to announce at the exhibit?"

"Hey," he said, "don't ask me — just the errand boy. Nobody tells me nothing."

I shot him a mock-exasperated look. "Come on, Hathaway. You left me standing in the cold. You *owe* me. Cut me in."

"All right, all right," he said. "But you have to keep this quiet. Dad has been working for years on building relationships with political heavyweights from all over the Americas, and a lot of them are going to be at the opening gala. So yeah" — he leaned in to whisper — "he's probably going to announce then. The exhibit's the perfect occasion, with the perfect theme. It was a brilliant idea — Dad was so grateful your folks came up with it. It'll help cement my father's image of someone willing to push the Confederation into the twenty-first century."

Wow, I thought. *Hathaway's announcing at my parents' exhibit.* That was — kind of impressive. Helped explain why my mother was so obsessed with it.

No hash browns, as it turned out. When Richard and I walked into the banquet room, my mother intercepted me. "What took you so long? I was worried." She handed me a doggie bag. "I ordered some eggs to go for you, hon," she said. "We have to get a move on." Which apparently was the operative phrase for the day.

When we got home, Jackson was in the main hall, helping another man — I guessed the tree-delivery guy — brace a towering fir in the U formed by the stairs. The grandfather clock, a table, and a couple of wing-back chairs had been removed to make room for the tree.

As soon as my mom hit the threshold, she flipped into party-dictator mode. Though she hid it pretty well most of the time, my mother was a die-hard perfectionist like her mother before her. Something I hadn't inherited, thankfully. With her arm linked in mine, tugging me to keep pace with her, she directed, "Throw on some work clothes, eat that breakfast, and then come back and start covering the wires holding the swag with bows of that ribbon." She pointed to a stack of spooled red velvet. "Three-foot lengths. Sound good?"

"Sounds perfect." I sighed.

She nodded and headed off toward her room briskly, her heels clicking on the hardwood floor.

I staggered like a condemned woman up the stairs, my head lolling back, my eyes closed. Every year, when we'd come to visit my grandmother, most of the house's Christmas decorations had already been taken care of. My family had only ever had to help with the tree trimming. This year, we were working double-time to get caught up. It was looking to be a long day.

"Suck it up, Sare," Jackson said, eyeing me with amusement. "It's Christmas. Most wonderful time of the year."

"I'm pretty sure I hate Christmas," I said, catching him in the corner of my eye on my way past and giving him my tiniest smile.

When I returned with a pair of scissors and a yard stick, the men were gone, but Jackson was still there, busy unraveling strands of tiny white lights for the tree. There were a lot of them. "Jeez," I said, "that's going to take a while."

"An hour." He shrugged. "I've had a few years' practice."

"Sounds like you'll be finished before I will, then," I muttered. I unwound a three-foot length of ribbon and cut it. Then I tied my first bow over the wire on the lowest newel post.

"Sare," Jackson said.

"What?"

"The bows" — he shook his head a little — "they should be level."

I looked at my unfortunate product, hanging drunkenly to the side, one dangling leg showing nothing but ribbon back. I wasn't sure I cared. "You think *any*body is going to notice my cruddy bows?"

He squinted a little at me. "Come on. Why are you even asking me that? You do a job, you do it right and see it through."

"You read that in a book somewhere?"

He smiled at my sarcasm. "What's the matter? They don't teach kids that in the fancy private schools?"

He untied my bow, readjusting its knot. "See," he explained as he worked, "make the top piece a little longer, then use the lower piece to make the first loop." I watched his fingers, his hands. They were long fingers and square hands. Like my father's. "Come *over* and then under with the top piece, twisting it as you go to keep the velvet-side out —" He pulled his loops tight; a perky *level* bow now hung on the newel, with nothing but velvet showing. "Scissors," he said, holding his hand out like a surgeon awaiting a scalpel. I slapped them in his palm. He made two quick snips. "Finish by trimming the ends into matching points. Your grandma was pretty particular about that."

He looked up at me and smiled his old smile, the gentle and generous smile I had come to expect and rely on. I wondered again why he always seemed to be irritated with me now.

I was standing so close to him I could smell all his scents: the strong clean soap Rose favored, the fir tree resin on his arms, the trace of summer hay from the stables, where he must have gone before coming here. I thought as I stood there that the sense of smell, more than any other, had a way of erasing time. That a fragrance could carry you back to another moment with such force, such drawing power, that you felt you should be able to open the door to that moment and step into it again. The past pressed in all around me, almost tangible, as I stood above Jackson and breathed in his scent, and I wanted it. I wanted the way Jackson and I used to be.

"You awake?" he said.

I snapped back. I rolled off another three-foot length of ribbon and held it out. "Could you show me one more time, please?"

We carried on a friendly, if superficial, conversation as we worked our way upward — he on the tree and I on the stair rail. I felt awkward, but it helped that I had bow-tying to focus on — my bows improved as I rose.

"Gran said Saint Ignatius accepted you?" he asked.

"They didn't want to, but Hathaway made them."

"The senator?"

"He and Mom are old friends. I think he might be my godfather, actually."

"I guess it might be handy," he observed, "to be the goddaughter of the next president."

I guessed it might. "How do you like . . . ?"

"Severna High? It's decent. It's been integrated since the eighties."

"You're graduating this year. What'll you do next?" I wondered why I had no idea what Jackson wanted out of life.

"I don't like to talk about the future," he said.

"It isn't the future anymore," I said. "It's the next step. It's where you're applying right now."

He hesitated, as if considering whether he wanted to tell me. It hurt that he didn't trust me. "I want to do premed at Hopkins," he finally answered quietly.

"Hopkins?" I shouldn't have sounded so startled, but it was as if he'd said he wanted to go to the moon. A poor black kid from nowhere admitted to Johns Hopkins University? The school had an international student body composed of the best and brightest, but when it came to diversity, its stats skewed heavily white and male. This was the Confederation, after all.

"Your dad said he would try to help me get in."

"Wow," I said, making myself sound enthusiastic. A recommendation from my dad, a Hopkins alumnus, a respected member of its faculty, and an internationally renowned surgeon, *might* help overcome the prejudice Jackson would face. *Might.* "You must have crazy-good grades. You want to be a doctor?"

"I'm going to be a doctor," he said firmly. "Some time." But he looked down and inside as he said it.

"You'll do it, J," I said, meaning it sincerely. "Hopkins ain't gonna know what hit it."

His eyes softened into a tiny smile. "Thanks." He stood there silently for a half beat, as if there was something else he wanted to say. But then he brushed his hands on the legs of his pants and said briskly, "Got to fetch the ladder. Catch you later."

I was just finishing the bows when Maggie and Sam arrived with a basket of four-inch stuffed bears and an armload of dried baby's breath. Gramma's stair swag was *always* decorated with her antique bears tucked among a "snow" of tiny blossoms.

I wanted to stay and help, because this was the fun part, but Mom had different ideas. She handed me a bundle of mixed evergreen boughs and directed me to deck the dining room table and mantel. I set to work layering the branches down the length of the table's red brocade runner, while I listened enviously to Sam, Maggie, and Jackson talking and laughing in the entry. I was just finishing up when Maggie and Sam came in with an ancient Noah's Ark filled with small wooden animals to set amidst more baby's breath. Gramma's dining table was *always* decorated with three dozen pairs of animals trouping across the evergreens to Noah's opened boat.

As I reached for the giraffes, I had the sense of generations of hands making the same motion. Generations of my family standing here in this same spot, doing this same task. I wondered if they'd wondered too — about the ones to come who would stand where they stood. Family. Part of me resented the burden of that history. But part of me realized it was something venerable. Primal.

"Sarah?" Mom's voice. She came in with more boughs for the table next to the front door, and both the living room and library mantels. I sighed again. It was only one o'clock and I was already exhausted.

But it was beginning to look a lot like Christmas.

After that, we had to get going on the tree. The four of us — Jackson, Maggie, Sam, and I — headed up to the storeroom on the third floor to fetch Gramma's mountain of neatly organized ornament boxes.

I'd avoided going up to the third floor when I was young. Most kids believe that "the monster" lives in some part or other of their house. I had always had that hinky feeling about the long garret room at the end of the stairs.

There were two smaller rooms off the third landing. The first room on the left had been my mother's studio when she was a girl. I spotted a fresh canvas clamped in an easel, marked with Mom's usual bold charcoal strokes. She painted in a style I thought of as heightened realism — her colors were all a bit more vivid than anything real life had to offer, creating a kind of dream effect. Sometimes I wondered if she actually saw the world that way. Tucked slightly behind my mom's canvas was a smaller, quieter work of a cat licking her paw. Maggie's. My aunt didn't share my mother's obsessive appetite to paint, but she did have talent. She contented herself with doing some of the illustrations for the children's books she wrote.

The room on the right was a deserted office with a writing table and a glassed-in cabinet. I could see that a woman had once worked here; small bits of comfort and beauty — a flowered pillow, a gold-framed mirror, a portrait of a dimpled child — testified to that. I had the impression this was where my great-grandmother Fiona had retreated to write her strange poetry.

The last room took up most of the level. It was dedicated to storage now, but Gramma had always called it the "old nursery." Our target mountain of boxes stood in the center of the room.

I stopped in the doorway for a moment, reluctant to step in.

I could feel the little hairs on my arms prickling into vertical. I wasn't a kid anymore, but my monster still lived in this attic. Chinks and gaps in the walls let the wind through, so that the whole room seemed to sigh. Even Sam and Maggie had fallen silent. Jackson was the only one unaffected.

I walked in and quickly picked out the smallest box for Sam to carry, since I wanted him to be able to see his footing on the way down. "Here, Sammy."

He came to take it from me, his head down. He was humming something so quietly I almost didn't hear. A simple variation on a handful of notes. It seemed familiar to me. *The tune through the heating vent.* "What song is that, bud?"

He shook his head without lifting his eyes. "A song I used to know. I don't sing it anymore."

Maggie took that moment to swoop in and scoop up her own stack of three boxes. "Come on, Sam, let's get out of here."

"Me too." I sounded a lot more anxious than I'd meant to. I picked up my stack of three and saw there would still be another half dozen boxes left after Jackson took his.

He saw my face and chuckled the smallest bit. "I'll get the rest. I'll make two trips."

"Really?" I said.

"Really," he said. We started down the stairs. "As long as I've known you, Sare, you've always hated the third floor. I guess some things never change."

Some things? I thought to myself. *Nothing* ever changed at Amber House. Except him.

One of my ancestors had been obsessed with angels, so her father, a world traveler, had always brought one home to her. From every continent, from dozens of countries. From jeweled and ornate to primitive wood carving. Having every shade of skin color and every shape of eyes. When Christmas trees came into style sometime in the late 1800s, my family had pulled out the angel collection to decorate the very first Amber House tree. And of course, every generation had added to the flock. I stared miserably at all the opened storage boxes. The entire host of heaven, and we had to hang every single one.

Jackson came down the stairs with the last of the boxes, and I went to help him unload. "You staying?" I asked hopefully.

"Nah," he said. "I can't."

"Why not?" I was used to him helping us with the tree.

"We — I — have to do something."

"Yeah?" I said, waiting for an explanation.

He didn't offer one. Or the true one, anyway. "Gran . . . asked me to do something for her at home."

"Oh," I said.

He said good-bye to everyone and slipped out the front. I walked to the window to watch him turn — not west, toward his house on the river, but north toward the road to town. Jackson was not only keeping secrets from me but lying to me as well.

"Sarah?" Mom called. "We have to —"

"— get a move on," I said. I turned away from the window.

CHAPTER FIVE

We managed to finish the hall tree before dinner — "Sunday supper," Rose called it, serving up a Southern feast, right down to the fried chicken and grits.

That whole thing with Jackson had left me short-tempered. "So," I asked, passing the basket of warm rolls to my father, "when were you going to tell me?"

"Tell you what, sweetheart?" he said, passing the basket on.

"Tell me that this whole Amber House exhibit is a really big deal. Tell me that Hathaway is actually *announcing* his candidacy at your gala party. You think I can't keep a secret? Why is it nobody thinks I can keep a secret?"

"*Perhaps,*" my mother said, "we worried you might start talking about it in front of your younger brother, who really shouldn't be asked to keep a secret this big."

Sam put his head in his hands. "Not *another* secret I have to keep."

"*Perhaps,*" I said, "if you had told me privately when you *should have*, I would have known not to bring it up. I'm not a little kid anymore. I shouldn't have to hear these things about my own family from an outsider."

"We're doing what we —" my mother started, but Dad raised his hand a little, and she stopped mid-sentence. Dad hardly ever weighed in on the whole parent-child relations thing, so I guessed Mom was as surprised as I was. He took a moment to order his thoughts.

"Your mom and I had good reasons for moving to Astoria when I finished at Hopkins." He looked at me. "You were already on the way. We wanted you to grow up someplace where women were expected to" — he searched for the words — "to partici-pate fully, to define them*selves*. A place, by the way, that had just elected a woman president when we moved there. But I want you to know, honey, that part of me is ashamed for having gone." He looked it. It pained me.

"I'm glad I grew up in Astoria."

"We shouldn't have run away," he said. "We should have stayed here and fought to make things better. That's what good people have to do. Even when it's hard. Even when you have kids. Maybe especially then. So you can teach them by example how to do the right thing.

"Maybe things would be better now if we hadn't left. Maybe the things we're trying to accomplish at the last minute, at the eleventh hour, would be more possible." He looked at my mother, and she smiled a little sadly.

"Senator Hathaway is trying to do something really necessary," my mom said. "He's trying to speed up change in the South so he can unify the Americas. The South is key, because we have a common language and customs with New England and the west, but we are also a bridge to Louisiana and Mexico, and through them, all of South America."

"We came back to try to help him," my dad said.

My history teacher had talked about something like this — a Unification movement for the Americas. So that we'd be a world power as big as the Reich or the Empire. I was a little boggled at the concept that my neighbor and parents were working together to try to make that real.

"Do you remember when the Hathaways came to Gramma's funeral?" Dad asked. I did remember them, standing off to one side because they'd arrived a little late — the three of them handsome and solemn in matching black. Another surreal detail in that bizarre and disturbing day. "They didn't stay long, but Robert had come to talk to us. He asked us to return to the ACS. We discussed it with Maggie."

"I told them to come back. The house belongs to your mom anyway."

Mom looked at Maggie fondly. "Big enough for all of us."

"So we came," my father concluded.

"Why would Senator Hathaway want your help?"

"He thought that we could be useful to the movement. It wasn't just because our family and Amber House are prominent in this area — Robert also knew I had ties to the president's advisors in Astoria." I think my mouth must have dropped open. Dad smiled a little bit. "I helped the surgeon general establish new guidelines for surgical procedures, and oversaw a few things for the Disease Control Department." He shrugged.

I had no idea my dad had ever done anything for the government. I mean, I knew he saved lives — he was a doctor. But big-time political connections? It was one of those moments when I was forced to see my parents as wholly separate people from me. *Interesting* people. People who would *be* interesting even if they hadn't had the good sense to give birth to me. And the thing that was really impressive was not that Dad was important but that he'd never said anything about it before. He didn't feel it was something to broadcast. It was just part of his job description.

I was a little ashamed, then, that I'd been so miserable about moving. "I wish you'd told me before," I said.

"I guess we should have," my mom said.

Christmas was definitely more enjoyable when I wasn't trying to punish my parents. We decorated the smaller family tree in the parlor, the one Gramma had always saved for us when we came for our winter visit. The parlor tree was all about traditions too, but traditions that belonged just to my little family. Not to Amber House. There was a comfortable feeling in that.

Mom and Maggie draped the tree with spiraling chains of glass beads while Sam and I unpacked ornaments. It was a completely random collection, new and heirloom mixed, but they were all old friends. When the chains were finished, the five of us hooked the ornaments into every available space. The tree became a glittering froth.

I was poking through the packing material in the bottom of a box, when I found a last little glass walnut, so old its gold paint was wearing thin. The front of my brain throbbed with another wave of déjà vu.

I could almost see a different pair of hands picking up the same ornament and holding it out, light refracting off its surface as it spun on its ribbon. I heard voices, far away but growing louder: She, laughing — "Mistletoe, Edward? It's not supposed to be mobile, you know," and he — "If the lady won't come to the mistletoe, Fee, then the mistletoe must come to the lady." My vision was frayed at the edges, like something was trying to possess it, trying to squeeze into my head. And then, near my ear, so close I was embarrassed, the unmistakable sound of a kiss.

I gasped as the ornament slipped from my fingers and fell. It hit the wood floor and shattered, in a single, sharp note.

"Oh, Sarah," my mother said sadly, "please be more careful, hon."

I nodded silently and went to fetch the whisk broom and dustpan from the kitchen closet. *What was that? What just happened to me?* A bubble of panic was rising in my throat, and I struggled to swallow it down again. *Is that what happens to schizophrenics? Made-up stuff in their heads just starts blotting out reality?* My great-grandmother had spent time in an asylum. *Maybe I'm losing my mind.* I bent to sweep up the pieces.

In the largest chunk of glass, I spotted a yellowed slip of paper curled against the inside. I pulled it loose. It was brittle with age, shaped into a permanent O, its back pocked with the walnut pattern of the dead ornament. Someone had slipped it inside the uncapped top of the gold glass long ago. I managed to flatten it enough to read the pretty, spidery script that ran across it, spelling out four words.

Make all good amends.

"What is it, honey?" my mother asked.

I realized I was staring, holding my breath. I said lightly, "Just a piece of paper," and dropped it in the dustpan.

But I took it out again on the way to the kitchen trash.

We all headed for bed after Dad lifted Sam up to crown the tree with the star. I smiled and joined our cocoa-mug toasts to "a good job well done" as if everything was normal, as if I was not doubting my sanity. Then I hugged everyone good night, but I waited behind a little so I could fish the curled slip of paper from the drawer I had tucked it into. Upstairs, I put it with my other scrap of paper stowed in the library of the miniature Amber House. I didn't know why, but it seemed to me that the two phrases belonged together. They *pulled* at me somehow. As if there was something I was supposed to understand. I swung the dollhouse closed. I didn't want to think about it.

On my way back from the bathroom to bed, I detoured out to the second-floor landing. I stood at the balcony railing, inhaling the Christmas-scented air, looking and listening.

My family was all tucked into their rooms. I could hear Sammy snoring softly already. Amber House was lit now only by the tiny lights glowing warmly in the trees and evergreen swags. Hand-carved Magi adored a baby nestled in cedar branches on the front hall table. Pineapples crowned the evergreens on each mantel, in colonial style. Candles stood flame-ready everywhere.

My gramma's traditions living on without her. Christmas, the way it had always been, the way I remembered.

But it felt — *wrong*, somehow.

Amber House was dressed to the teeth, but, I thought to myself a little queerly, it was all on the surface. The house seemed hunkered down beneath the greenery and glitter. Separate. Patient. Waiting.

She — I — sat in the corner with my knees drawn up under my night-gown. Papa came in with the new maid, Lizzy, who was carrying a little Christmas tree. I could see she was frightened of me. They were all fright-ened of me. The girl set the tree on the trunk at the foot of the bed and hurried out.

Papa bent down to pick up a few of my wadded papers. He pulled one smooth. "Choose it all again," he read. He smoothed out the next one. "Choose it all again." He opened a third. "All of them exactly the same?" He sighed. He shook his head, his voice a mix of anger and grief. "You must stop this, dearest."

"I want to stop it. I'm trying to stop it, Papa, only I don't know what went wrong."

" 'What went wrong'?" He was perplexed.

"With time," I said. Obviously. "How can I stop it when I don't know what went wrong, what changed?"

"Nothing went wrong, child." He wadded my papers back up and threw them in the fire. "Everything's just the way it's supposed to be. That's the only way it can be."

I shoved up onto my feet, shaking my head, my back still in the corner. "No," I said. "Can't you feel it? This isn't the way it's supposed to be. Something went wrong and that little girl has something to do with it."

"What little girl?"

"The little girl who is half dark and half light. I need to find out who she is and when she came from."

He looked so sad. I knew he thought I had lost my mind, and I could not prove otherwise. How could I prove the truth of something only I could feel? Yet even if I alone in all the world knew the truth, how could I stop trying to make it right? But I was afraid.

He stepped closer and stroked my hair. "You've got to try to take hold of yourself, Fee. Or we'll have to go on to the next step. Please try, honey."

I looked for words to explain. "Everything feels so wrong, Papa, it's like ants inside my skin. I need to make her fix what happened. To choose it all again."

"The little girl?"

"No, no," I said impatiently. "The one who is always listening."

"No one is listening! Nothing went wrong!" His face crumpled into unhappy lines. "I'm sorry, child," he said, and left.

I could feel her then. Could feel her listening to my thoughts. Maybe I was not alone in all the world. Maybe she would understand.

I went to the tree and plucked a golden walnut from its branches. I pulled off the ornament's little tin cap, held in place by two metal prongs. I rolled a slip of paper into a tiny tube and tucked it in the opening. Replaced the cap. Rehung the ornament.

Then I sat before my mirror and looked for her in my eyes.

"Do you see?" I — she — asked.

CHAPTER SIX

I woke remembering the dream, remembering the strange, familiar feel of it. Almost like I'd been there. I had dreamed myself Fiona Campbell Warren, my grandmother's mother. Slightly mad Fiona. I'd dreamed I left that paper in the walnut ornament for someone — *me?* — to find. What would a dream interpreter say about that? Maybe that the chaotic part of my subconsciousness was trying to tell me to — what were the words? *Choose it all again.*

I wrote the new phrase on another slip of paper and put it with the scrap from the walnut — "Make all good amends" — and my scribbled phrase from the other night: "Seek the point where past and future meet." All three safely hidden in the dollhouse library. The phrases floated around inside my brain as though they should come together in a rhythm, like a poem or a song. *Something I heard before?* Fiona had been a poet — maybe I had read or heard something of hers and kept a memory of it in some hidden corner of my mind. I wondered what missing words would transform my phrases into the poem I imagined was there.

Perhaps that was what my dream was trying to say — that I was like my poem: assembled with a few things left out. The missing words were missing pieces. Perhaps the pieces Jackson so obviously wished were there. Responsibility. Maturity.

I smiled at my self-betrayal. Maybe even my subconscious agreed I needed to grow up.

At eight o'clock, Mom, Maggie, Sam, and I piled in the car and set off for an all-day trip to Baltimore. Mom had a long list of errands that included everything from taking care of stuff for the exhibit to helping with a "Santa" party for some of the young patients at Johns Hopkins. Sam was lucking out — he was meeting up with Dad for part of the day and then heading to the Anchor Bay Aquarium for the rest. I was stuck following Mom around the entire time.

Our first stop was the gallery where Mom was dropping off a bunch of Maeve's old tintypes to be mounted.

Near the Old Harbor, in the part of Baltimore known as Fell's Point, we drove down a narrow cobblestone street lined with nineteenth-century brick commercial buildings. The area had been transformed into one of those ultra-hip art districts: antiques shop next to café next to art gallery. Mom parked in front of a place so understated it didn't even have a name, just a large three-digit number in brushed stainless steel. Which I figured was the owner's way of saying, "If you don't know who we are already, you don't belong inside."

A tall, slim man in casual but expensive clothes greeted Mom at the door, gave her many air kisses, directed an assistant to give her and Maggie each an espresso in a tiny cup, and gushed over the box full of Maeve's photos. "I am so honored to have the chance to do this for you, Anne — McCallister was such an important pioneer in photorealism." He led Mom and Maggie to an interior office. "You *must* see the shipment of paintings I just got in," he said. Sammy and I followed along, apparently invisible.

My mother gasped as she walked through the door. Maggie said quietly, some awe in her voice, "A Klimt!"

The painting they'd fixed on was pretty: pastel colors with lots of gold and these sort of Byzantine geometric things worked in all over. The rest of the stuff was "modern" and beyond my ability to appreciate, but my mother gushed, "Oh, Oskar.

Pechstein. Dix. Schiele. Beckmann. Where in the world did you find these? So many banned artists!"

I knew from my mother that the Nazi government had a long-standing policy of destroying the works of Jewish artists and anyone else they found "depraved" or "subversive." The life's work of many of her favorite painters, guys with names like Picasso and Braque and Miró, mainly existed only in photographic reproductions.

"Who knows how they found their way off the continent?" Oskar said. "But a private collector in New York offered them to me. He needs to liquidate, raise funds."

"Send me your listing when you have them priced," my mom said. "I'm very interested."

Our next stop was Johns Hopkins. We met Dad in the lobby just as a tour guide was concluding her biography of the hospital's founder: "We are all the beneficiaries of the hardships Mr. Hopkins endured and surmounted. In some sense, we are the children he and his beloved Elizabeth never had."

The tour group headed up the stairs while we turned down the hall, heading for another building. "It's kind of crummy when you think about it that way," I commented.

"What?" Mom said.

"Well, that Johns Hopkins had to suffer so the rest of us could benefit."

"That's what makes someone a hero," my father said. "Summoning up the strength to sacrifice for somebody else."

I thought to myself that it kind of sucked to be a hero.

Dad and Sam went off "in search of trouble," as Mom, Maggie, and I found our way to the hospital wing named after Gramma: the Warren Neurological Research Clinic. Part of the work done there was studying and providing therapy for children who had neurological abnormalities. Some of them were like Maggie and my little brother — autistic — except a little more trapped inside themselves by their odd neurological wiring.

The wing was named after Gramma because family money had paid for it. Gramma had been able to make the kind of enormous donation it took to build this facility thanks to two of our seafaring ancestors — a man named Dobson who'd built a fortune in the slave trade, and his son-in-law, Captain Joseph Foster, who'd also dabbled in slaving but went on to accrue even greater wealth and power through positions of influence in the colonial government. I'd always figured that along with the ton of money she'd inherited, she'd got a ton of guilt to go with it. This research facility was just one of her charitable causes, all of which *we* had now inherited, together with the responsibilities that went with them. Like attending the Warren unit's holiday party for its youngest patients. Senator and Mrs. Hathaway were also making an appearance.

I wasn't surprised to see Richard had come along too. He was clearly a valuable part of the whole Hathaway package. I watched him work with the kids, getting down on the floor with them, helping them open packages and find something to enjoy inside. Which wasn't always easy with these kids — they didn't necessarily "get" the intended purpose of a toy.

He was something of a mystery to me. I really didn't expect extremely good-looking people to be generous and empathetic — it was too easy for them to get by on charm. But Richard seemed willing to go the distance. I couldn't imagine any guy more perfect. So why did it feel like I was always waiting to discover his secret flaw?

Near the end, he pulled me aside to ask me if I wanted to drive back to Severna with him. I had to shake my head — the errands weren't done yet. "Mom and I need dresses for the New Year's Eve gala."

"Come on, Parsons, don't tell me your mom still helps you pick out your clothes?"

I refused to let him ruffle me. "Of course not, Hathaway, I help her pick out hers."

He laughed and excused himself — his father's aide had beckoned. I was left staring up at the brass letters that declared the building the F. C. Warren Research Facility. I was confused. "F. C.?" I asked out loud.

And a silky female voice answered, "Fiona Campbell." Claire Hathaway had snuck up behind me.

"But I thought Gramma built it, after Maggie's coma."

"Oh, no," she said. "The building's several decades older than Maggie. It seems Fiona was quite interested in neurological anomalies." Claire gave me her usual small smile.

What kind of "anomalies" had my great-grandmother been interested in? I wondered.

"Did you know she was treated here? Well, not 'here' exactly," Claire amended. "She had the building that stood here before razed to the ground, and most of the staff fired, as a precondition to the very generous endowment that made this facility possible."

"I guess," I said, "she *really* didn't like the way they'd treated her."

Claire rewarded me with a small musical laugh. "I guess she really didn't," she agreed, "and who could blame her? Psychiatric medicine was still so barbaric in the thirties. Primitive drugs. Electroshock treatment. Lobotomies. I'm under the impression Fiona was given a little helping of everything."

The girl in my dream, I thought, *who'd pleaded for her father's belief.*

"She must have been an amazing woman, don't you think?" Claire said. "After all she suffered, she still had enough gray matter left to build this hospital wing. I never met her myself, but my father knew her. He said she was very beautiful and remarkably cogent for someone reputed to be completely out of her mind."

"Why did people think that?"

"She seemed to have been somewhat delusional," she said. "Maintained all her life that time had" — she shaped her fingers into little air quotes — " 'gone wrong.' She was also obsessed with a purported relative who apparently didn't actually exist." She pointed to a small plaque below the brass letters: "In memoriam: A.M."

"Who was A.M.?" I blurted.

Claire lifted her eyebrows. "Exactly. No one knows."

"Sarah?" My mother's voice. It held a climbing note of concern. As if she knew, somehow, that Claire was dishing gossip about Mom's grandmother. "Time to go, honey."

I said to Claire, to excuse myself, "Nice talking to you."

"Yes," she agreed with her same little smile, "very nice."

I left to trail after Mom and Maggie, on their way to the year's last board meeting for Gramma's foundation. Or was it Fiona's? Which was now Mom and Maggie's. And was one day expected to be *mine*. Whether I wanted it or not.

The head of the board, Mrs. Abbot, seemed pretty anxious to settle the question of who was going to be in charge now that Gramma was gone. "We worked so long and intimately with Mrs. McGuiness, you can rest assured that we are doing everything possible — all that she wished — for the patients of her foundation."

"Students," Maggie said.

The woman turned, a condescending smile on her lips. "What, dear?"

"Students," Maggie repeated. "The children we help are not sick. They are not 'patients.'"

Mrs. Abbot widened her eyes and said tolerantly, "Isn't that just a question of semantics?"

My mother spoke up then. Firmly. "It isn't, actually. My sister is making a very important distinction. Our clients are not ill and not in need of medical care. They are students learning skills that will help them cope with the world. I think that shift in attitude will be one of the improvements my sister and I bring to this foundation."

She'd surprised both me *and* Mrs. Abbot. I didn't know Mom could be so calm and polished. And implacable. Gently letting Mrs. Abbot know *exactly* who was going to be in charge now that Gramma was gone.

After the meeting, Maggie slipped away to find Sammy for their trip to the aquarium down by the harbor. Mom, in her standard overanxious mode, delivered herself of several parting bits of advice about getting around the city before she let her little sister escape, as if Maggie hadn't traveled alone to a half-dozen different countries. Seemed like Mom just couldn't stop herself from being a nudge — I'd always figured it was a reaction to her little sister's near-fatal accident. Maybe I'd have the same compulsion to micromanage my loved ones if I'd almost lost Sammy.

But Maggie accepted all of Mom's suggestions with a smile. I wished I was going with her and Sam. But Mom and I were headed downtown to Stewart's Department Store. A local business, but similar enough to what I was used to in the Northwest that I nursed some hope of finding something suitable to wear to the gala.

We took a copper-and-glass elevator up to the ladies' department and made a beeline for the formal wear. A sales associate materialized when it became clear my mother and I were browsing through the selection of designer gowns. She guided my mother from one option to another — lots of cinched-waist, corset-requiring satin numbers. Typical Confederation stuff. But then I noticed a familiar-looking silhouette. A lipstick-red chiffon creation that swept down in clean, curving lines to the floor. More fitted in front, fuller in back, strapless with a sweetheart neckline.

"Is that a Marsden?" I asked the clerk.

"You have an excellent eye, miss. That dress is one of our newest arrivals. Imported."

Yes, I thought, I knew a Marsden when I saw it — the fluid blend of vintage and modern, the mind-boggling attention to minuscule detail. Her designs regularly graced Astorian red carpets and showed up in our magazines. And they reflected our current trends, no corset required.

"I'll take it," I said.

My mother made an involuntary movement, as though she wanted to physically stand between me and the dress. "Don't you worry . . . you'll get cold?"

My mother's code for too much shoulder and décolletage. I just smiled innocently and opted to take her literally. "I'll be fine. I saw a velvet cloak when we walked in, in a crimson that will go great with this. It'll be perfect."

My mother knew not to argue. When it came to clothes, I was every bit as opinionated and stubborn as she.

We picked up Maggie and Sam at a café near the aquarium. It was dark when we set off home. The light rain-become-snow that had been falling since we arrived in Maryland was dusting the windshield with white feathers. We stopped at an intersection in a worn-out neighborhood and saw the flashing lights of several police cars across the way.

I leaned forward to see what was going on, but my mother put up her hand. "Don't look." Which of course made me try even harder.

The police were clustered around a black man on the ground. One officer seemed about to hit the man with a nightstick. But something stopped him.

Materializing out of the darkness, appearing one by one at the edges of the red-blue pool of light, people came to stand witness for the beaten man. Some held the hands of their children. Many of them, I saw, wore some bit of yellow. They stood silently, a ring of dark faces, bitter and determined.

The police seemed to reach some unspoken agreement. The man was lifted and put in the back of a police car. The ring of watchers parted slightly to let the police retreat.

I held Papa's hand tight as we walked along the dock on Spa Creek. The sailors and dockworkers all stopped what they were doing to nod and back out of Papa's way. Papa owned both the ships tied up here, and many more besides. He was the boss of all of them.

And of the greasy man who walked with us, Mr. Carruthers. I did not like Mr. Carruthers.

"Sold an even dozen already for top dollar," Carruthers said, as though Papa should pat him on the head. "Clean the rest up for auction. Lost twenty-three in the crossing. Still have —"

Papa held up a hand, stopped him. He opened the book he carried tucked under his him. He made careful notes in his beautiful handwriting. I loved Papa's handwriting — like a pea vine growing and curling across the paper. "Still have eighty-seven bucks, seventy-one females, and twenty-six children over the age of five," Carruthers finished. "We will make a good profit."

At the dock's edge, amongst a stack of crates and barrels, a raggedy pile of worn sailcloth moved ever so slightly. I let go of Papa's hand and went closer. There was an unpleasant odor that grew stronger as I drew near.

"Here, come away from there," Mr. Carruthers told me, but I merely looked at him coldly. I did not take directions from him. "'Scuse me, Missy, begging pardon, but you don't want no part of that there."

Had it been aught but Mr. Carruthers, I should have minded him, but instead, even under Papa's watchful eye, I bent quickly and threw back the cloth. "Merciful Lord!" I said, horrified, and crossed myself to ward off evil.

A female slave lay there, a tumble of limbs, her face battered and bloody.

"Now see there, Missy. You shoulda oughter've listened to me." Mr. Carruthers was pleased with my horror. "That one's dead, Capt'n Dobson, sir."

"I saw the cloth move," I said, my eyes narrowing.

"'Twas the wind," he said.

Her arm flopped out; her fingers brushed my boot. Swollen eyes opened to slits and I saw that she saw me. Her split lips moved and a word sighed out, so soft that only I heard. "Dee-da-ra," she said. My name.

She had touched my boot and knew my name.

"I want her, Papa," I announced.

"Deirdre, I will find you a healthy girl, a smiling, pretty girl," Papa said reasonably, coaxingly. "This one is beyond our help."

"I want her," I said, stamping my foot. And Papa sighed and made it so.

They loaded her onto a makeshift pallet in the back of our skiff. When we arrived home, I told Absalom to handle her gently, and he smiled and said he would. I insisted they take her up to the small room beside mine. "I want to make sure she is cared for properly." And Papa sighed and made it so.

CHAPTER SEVEN

I woke haunted by the image of that woman on the docks. I was ashamed I had ancestors who had been slave traders. One with a daughter named Deirdre. Odd that I should dream of her so specifically.

Teeth brushed, hair combed, I headed for the stairs. Just before the balcony, I noted a rectangle of sunlight where there shouldn't have been one — someone had left open the door to the Captain's suite again. It was irritating. I didn't know how many times, over the years, I had asked everyone to *please* leave that door closed.

I strode for the open door, brisk steps that got slower and slower. An unpleasant feeling grew in me that I was trespassing, that I should go no farther. I stopped near the opening, looking in.

The Captain had been one of my two slave-trading ancestors, married to the woman that the little girl in my dream had grown up to become. The room was suitable, somehow, to be the bedchamber of a slaver. It was decidedly masculine, dressed with dark green and oxblood fabrics. An oil painting of a ship in a storm hung over a fireplace. The walls were hung with a collection of swords, sabers and scimitars amassed from all over the world. And every flat surface was littered with scrimshaw — the teeth of slaughtered whales carved by the sailors who had harvested their oil.

I stood, wavering, wanting to tug the door closed, but unwilling to put my hand out. And then I heard a *thunk* that sounded like it came from the middle of the room. Then heard it again. Metal on wood.

Thunk.

I changed my mind. I had no inclination to go a step further, to reach inside the room for that knob. I would leave the door be.

I headed for the stairs. But a flicker of movement caught my eye. A golden spider scuttled across the hall carpet. It was a Good Mother. She ran under the door of the next bedroom.

I shuddered, slightly nauseated. I hated all bugs and creepy crawlers, but I hated spiders more, and hated Good Mothers most of all. They were poisonous and their bite never really healed. I was Sammy's age the first time I'd encountered one. Jackson and I wanted to go puddle-stomping up Amber House's front drive. I'd found my boots and stuck my hand inside one to make sure I hadn't left a sock stuffed in the bottom. My fingers brushed against some crackly straws that I started to fish out, when Jackson shouted at me to drop the boot. It hit the ground and a Good Mother plopped out. I could still remember the sick feeling little-me had, watching the spider try to drag herself away on broken legs before Jackson smashed her under his shoe.

If I let this little monster get away, then maybe the next day I'd find it in my shoe or bed — or, worse, in Sammy's. I pulled off a slipper and made myself open the door she'd run under.

The room was another one I rarely entered. It was plain compared to the rest of Amber House — a bed, a chest of drawers, a crucifix centered over the bed, a painting of two children. The room always felt cold to me, perhaps because it was so sparsely furnished. No one used it. It waited in shadows, its curtains always drawn.

The spider sat centered in the fan of light that fell in through the doorway, poised and ready to run. I held my breath and lifted my slipper.

As if she could sense my intentions, she was off and scuttling, freaky-fast. I went after her, bent over, smacking the floor with my slipper, missing, missing again, clenching my teeth to keep from shrieking. She darted under the darker shadow of the bureau, then dashed out into the open space beside the bed. I swung the slipper again, but she leapt up onto one of the legs of the bed's headboard and ran up its curves. At the top of the bed-post, almost at eye level, she paused. Staring at me.

I raised the slipper again.

The spider jumped onto the wall and scrambled up, ducking behind the wide wooden crucifix hung over the bed. Standing as far away as I could, I nudged the bottom of the cross with my slipper.

Two things fell loose and down behind the bed's headboard. One was the Good Mother. I crouched and saw her running for the far side of the bed. I darted around the end of it, only to spot her scuttling up the wall into the window curtains. I gave up then. I wasn't poking around the curtains in search of a poison-ous spider. I'd probably find a few.

I stopped on my way out the door. Doubled back to the bed. Bent down to look for the other thing that had fallen from behind the crucifix.

And found a slip of paper with a familiar spidery script.

Fate is in thy hands.

I stared at it. A fourth sentence fragment.

Again the sense of a poem tugged at my mind, like a singsong nursery rhyme I couldn't quite hear. *"We chase . . . drawn on . . . toward mystery . . . hushed . . . wake"* and *"rise to meet."* It seemed like my fragments should be in it too. I could almost hear it.

I went back to my room and opened the little dollhouse. I spread out the slips of paper already there, nudging them into a column, adding the one from behind the cross. I changed them up, and changed them up again, until I was satisfied with my ordering:

seek the point where past and future meet
Fate is in thy hands
Make all good amends
choose it all again

It was missing pieces. They hovered like a name on the tip of my tongue — almost ready to be spoken, but somehow always slipping away. Why had all these fragments come to me? It couldn't be just a coincidence, could it? There had to be some meaning there.

But then I rolled my eyes. *Are you out of your mind? Someone is sending you a message? Get a grip.*

I latched up the little house and headed for the kitchen. And noticed that now the door to the Captain's rooms had been closed.

The walk down the stairs and through the entry was oddly silent without the constant tick of the grandfather clock, banished to the east wing. As if the house was missing its heartbeat. The more I listened, the more the silence massed around me, like the world had emptied while I slept.

It's just the house and me, I thought irrationally.

I paused at the kitchen's swinging door, my hands pressed against the wood, hoping Sam was on the other side.

Then the door bumped into me and I screeched. "Lordy, child," Rose exclaimed, jumping back a little, "don't stand behind a push-through door."

"Sorry," I said, recovering myself.

She held the door open for me. "Come in. Saved you some johnnycakes." She went to the oven, pulled out a plate, and put it on a mat on the table.

"Thank you," I said. "That was really nice."

She snorted. "Didn't want you making a fresh mess in my clean kitchen."

"I try to clean up after myself, Mrs. Valois. I hope I'm not —"

She shook her head and leaned against the counter, not looking at me but speaking with sudden gentleness. "You do fine, child. You always have. I shouldn't have suggested otherwise."

It was another one of those moments — seeing a person from a whole different perspective. Like the prickly Rose I thought I knew wasn't who she was at all. Like everybody had entire casts of characters inside them, but only showed most people one or two.

I didn't know what to say. Feebly, I settled on shifting the subject. "Where is everyone?"

"Your folks went down into Annapolis to get the last things they need for the party tonight. Sammy's out with your aunt."

I nodded. "Thanks." I dug into the pancakes, immersed in jealousy: *Sam is always with Maggie.*

A crash startled me. Rose had dropped the plate she'd been drying. I jumped up. "Can I help?"

She bent over the mess as if she had a stitch in her side, with tears rolling down her face. I felt dazed, helpless. The outside door opened, and Jackson came in with an armload of firewood. When he saw Rose, he dropped the wood on the hearth and took her around the shoulders, trying to guide her toward a chair. "Sit, Gran. I'll clean it up."

Embarrassed, she brushed him off. "I just need to rest a spell. Make sure you get after the slivers with a wet cloth." She averted her face and pushed through the swinging door.

He stood there a moment, watching the door make smaller and smaller arcs. Then he went to the closet for the whisk broom and dustpan.

I bent down to pick up the biggest pieces. He crouched beside me. "I got it."

I went back to my chair and awkwardly shoved into my mouth a bite I didn't know if I could swallow. The pieces of china shrieked as Jackson swept them together into the dustpan.

"It wasn't the plate, was it?" I asked.

He shook his head. "December twenty-first," he said. "The day my grandfather — died." The broken pieces shrieked again as he dumped them in the trash.

"Oh," I said.

He stood there a moment, contemplating the dead plate. "Your grandmother used to get so upset when something got broken. She'd say, 'Every little thing has its own story to tell, even if we can't hear it. When it's broken, those stories are gone forever.'" He put the trash can back under the sink. "Anyone ever tell you how my grandfather died?"

I shook my head.

"He was part of the Equality movement back in the seventies. He'd lived abroad most of his life, so he was used to being treated with respect. He couldn't live by the rules around here."

"Why'd he come back?"

"He told my grandmother it was payment for a debt he owed Ida's mother. It was when your great-grandfather took ill."

"A debt?"

"That's all Gran knows. That's all he ever said."

More secrets, I thought. "What happened to him?"

"He spoke too loud and said things people didn't want to hear. Gran saw him hauled off into the night by a white mob — she couldn't do anything to stop it. She never saw him again. Then, with him gone, she and my mom didn't have anyplace else to go. Turned out Fiona had transferred the title to our piece of the estate to my grandpa a decade before, on the one condition that it remain in my family — it couldn't be sold. So Gran stayed, and your great-grandmother gave her work."

The pancakes sat heavy in my stomach. I'd heard about lynchings, of course, but had never been able to make that kind of brutality real in my head. And here it was. Very real. "Horrible. Unbelievable that things like that actually happened."

"Things like that are still happening," he said. He shook his head a little, as if trying to understand. "Something went wrong."

The same words Fiona used in my dream.

He was watching me speculatively. "How — how's the house treating you?"

It seemed like a nonsense question, but I knew it wasn't. It had some meaning for him I couldn't make out. *Too many secrets.* "It's fine. Everything's fine."

Maybe that was the wrong answer. He seemed disappointed. Abruptly he said, "Your mom left a list of things I'm supposed to take care of. I'm earning money for college. I'll see you later."

I cleaned up carefully after my pancakes, making every effort to leave the kitchen spotless. Somewhere in the house, I thought I could hear Rose weeping.

CHAPTER EIGHT

Mom and Dad got back not too long after that. Mom was full of excitement at the prospect of trotting out so much family history at tonight's "pre-exhibit" and at the museum itself in ten more days. Sam and Maggie also wandered in, their cheeks rosy from being out in the cold air. I remembered it was in fact the first official day of winter — the solstice — the shortest day and longest night.

"Where'd you guys go?" I asked.

"Visiting," Sam said. "And we played with the little girl."

"A little girl? A neighbor?"

Maggie nodded, smiling. "She's from around here."

"Well, I wish you guys had let me tag along," I said wistfully. "Next time, wake me up and take me with you."

Sammy said, "If the little girl says it's all right." He slipped his hand into our aunt's then, and tugged her away.

I trailed along after them, trying not to sound too pathetic: "Where're you going?"

"Wrap presents," Sam said.

"Can I help?" I said.

The pathos must have leaked through because Sam agreed generously, "You can help." But first he had to get my presents "hided," he said. He ran ahead of us up the stairs to his room, and I heard the sliding of a drawer before he poked his head back out into the hall. "You can come in now!"

I sat and admired the remainder of Sam's presents: a pillow for Mom that bore a painted wreath made of Sam's little handprints; a framed photo of Sam and me for Dad's office; four handwoven pot holders for Rose. I picked up a stethoscope, clearly from a much earlier era. "Who's this for, Sam?"

"That's for Jackson," he said. "Maggie helped me find it at a shop of old stuff."

"Huh," I said. "How'd you know he wants to be a doctor, bud?"

"I just remember," he said unhelpfully. "You wrap that, all right?"

"Sure, Sam. It's a great gift," I said a little enviously. "And I think I have the perfect box for it. I'll be back in just a sec."

I made a nice job of wrapping the old stethoscope, lining a long box with tissue, getting all the folds of the paper crisply and exactly creased. I let Sam choose the ribbon, then set to work making a flawless bow, in accordance with the bow-making instructions of the intended recipient.

"It's weird not having Gramma with us this year," I said.

"Yes," Maggie said with a twist of sorrow. "Weird."

I wished I hadn't said it. Thoughtless. Of course Maggie missed Gramma more than I. "Did you know *your* grandmother?" I asked her.

"Yes," she said. "But she was white-haired by the time I came along, and she'd been changed. She wasn't the way I think of Fiona, an auburn beauty full of fire."

I recognized that I too thought of Fiona as a young woman. It was a little strange. She was already an old lady when she asked Rose to stay on at Amber House. "Were you friends with Jackson's mom, like I'm friends with him?"

"Cecelia?" Maggie smiled a little and shook her head. "She was years older than your mom and I. And we were just in awe of her — she was so sure of herself."

"Did you know her very well?"

"A little, not well. Rose never let her work here at the house — said Cece's daddy would turn over in his grave. And Cece was always busy training anyway — she knew she would become a dancer."

"In New York," I said.

"Yes." Maggie nodded. "Where she belonged. She was the most graceful girl — she taught your mom how to carry herself like a princess. Annie was such a klutz when she was little."

"Mom?" I was incredulous.

"Oh, yeah," Maggie said. "She hit one of those ugly duckling phases when she was ten or eleven. She curled inward. Cece made her stand up straight and believe in herself."

"I never knew. You guys never talk about her."

"Well," Maggie said, "after the accident, Rose never did, so we just sort of followed suit."

That was too bad, I thought. I bet Jackson would have appreciated seeing his mother through others' eyes. Like I had just seen mine. An ugly duckling once. Not always a swan.

"You settling in all right?" Maggie asked. "At Amber House?"

. I came back to the moment. "I'd really rather be back home," I confessed, realizing too late this was probably rude for me to say about Maggie's home. I rushed on. "I miss my friends and my school, you know?"

"I know." She nodded. "You feel all right? Nothing — weird?"

"No," I said, smiling, "nothing too much out of the ordinary. Been having some intense dreams and a lot of déjà vu. Must be the time change. Messed with my head."

"What is 'daisy-voo'?" Sam asked.

"Day-zha-voo," Maggie corrected him. "Some people say it's a glitch in your brain, when you think you remember something that hasn't happened. But some people say that maybe you're remembering something that everyone else forgot."

We'd finished wrapping all the gifts on the table. Sam gave me the eye. I was a little slow on the uptake. "You need to go now," he said patiently. *The present in the drawer*, I realized.

"Gotcha," I said. I wandered out, still feeling at loose ends. I wanted to sit somewhere quietly, preferably by a fire. I slipped into the library, thinking I would curl up in one of the wing-back chairs.

After the conservatory, the library was my favorite room in Amber House. It was exactly what a library should be. Book-filled shelves stretched up out of reach, with sliding ladders to take you to the tops of the stacks. Small brass plaques on shelf edges identified subject matters. Near an ancient globe, a heavy Oxford unabridged dictionary lay open on a stand, with more reference books on a shelf underneath — thesaurus, atlas, directory, almanac. I sat on the floor next to the stand and pulled out a book of quotations.

It took a few minutes to figure out how to use it, but then I got the hang of it. I searched through the index, hunting down key words from my paper scraps upstairs. But I didn't find a single one of the phrases. If they were familiar to me, it was not because they were famous.

I spotted Mom across the entry in the dining room, setting out silver punch cups on the sideboard. I wandered over. The table was already laid with silverware, plates, and serving dishes for the party, awaiting only the food that would be brought out just before.

"Mom, where's Jackson?"

"Jackson," she said, making a puzzled face. "How would I know?"

"Wasn't he doing some jobs for you?"

She shook her head.

Huh. Another lie. I didn't think I could take much more of this. *Maybe*, I thought, *I'll track him down, find out why all the mystery.*

When Jackson and I were little, hide-and-seek had been our go-to game. When everything else had gotten boring, we'd go outside or into the conservatory and take turns hunting each other down. I never knew how Jackson had always been able to find me. Whenever I'd asked, he'd just shrug and say, "I know where you'll be."

But I'd always found him with my secret trick. I called it "Hotter, Colder." It only worked for people I knew really well, like Mom or Dad, or Jackson, or Sammy. First, I'd fix an image of the person in my mind, and then I'd fill it with the right thoughts and feelings, until the image built up into a whole person, until it had *heat*. Then all I had to do was follow that heat. *Warmer, warmer, warmer* — I always found them.

It had been years since I'd tried it with Jackson.

I imagined him. Gingerly. It was an oddly uncomfortable thing imagining him so completely as a young man, full-grown and muscled. I imagined what he was thinking and feeling — his earnestness, his determination. I saw his face, listening, concentrating, with the smallest frown between his brows.

Ah. There. The heat.

I went to the front hall, pulled on Mom's galoshes, grabbed her gloves, and shoved into her coat. "Going somewhere?" my mother called.

"Just a walk. Be back soon."

"Well, be careful," she said, evidently unable to produce more specific advice on short notice. "And make sure you leave yourself enough time to get ready for tonight."

It was cold out, the air tattooing my face with a flush. The sun was already sinking toward the western hills — nightfall would come by five. I pulled on Mom's leather gloves and flipped up the coat's hood as I considered my route.

Like the day before, Jackson had not turned left toward the river but right toward town. I could see his long footprints in the slushy snow. I followed them past the stables and across the field to the small side gate at Amber House's northeast corner. There the prints disappeared in general mush along the road. But the feeling of warmth drew me on.

On the outskirts of Severna, I was pulled toward the west side of town, not where I expected. I found some more of Jackson's long footsteps crossing an empty field to a narrow street without sidewalks. I had wandered into a black neighborhood. Residents were staring, as if I must be lost. But I kept going, pretending that I knew exactly where I was headed.

I zeroed in on a small white clapboard church. Its frosted, close-cropped lawn was planted with a neat sign: GOOD SHEPHERD BAPTIST CHURCH.

I climbed its front steps eagerly. I was finally going to get some answers.

But whatever it was I had come to see was over. As I swung the front door open, I saw a door in the rear of the church swinging closed. The handful of people left in the pews were buttoning up coats, slipping on gloves, exchanging good-nights.

I spotted Jackson. Getting a hug from a pretty Asian girl who then hurried out, looking me up and down when she was most of the way past and thought I wouldn't notice.

Oh, I thought, with a queer uncomfortable feeling in my chest. *His secret.*

He walked up to me, his face mild, but his voice lightly accusatory. "What are you doing here, Sarah?"

I think I turned a little red. An older man in a clerical collar joined us. He smiled and held out a hand. "I'm Pastor Howe."

"This is Sarah Parsons, Pastor," Jackson said as I shook the offered hand.

"You looking to join a Bible study, Sarah? We meet once a week, and all are welcome."

"No, um, I was only looking for Jackson."

The pastor looked at me intently — still smiling — but his eyes were sizing me up. "And how did you know to look here?"

I just stared at him a moment, no proper answer in my head. I saw Jackson hiding the hint of a smile, waiting for me to find words. Not helping.

"I — followed his boot prints. Then asked a couple people. They pointed me here."

"That's fine, then," the pastor said. He invited me again to join the Bible study, and said good-bye.

Outside, Jackson gave me the eye. "Hotter, Colder still works?" he guessed.

"Yeah."

"Did you think maybe you shouldn't be prying into my business?"

I realized then just how rude and invasive I'd been. "Um," I said. "No. Not really."

He laughed at that, but shook his head. "Maybe, Sare, you ought to give that one some thought. Promise me you won't do this again."

I nodded, and he didn't scold me any further for it. We started back toward Amber House. I wanted to ask him about the girl — the hugger — but I held it in. I resolved to try to be less curious and more respectful of Jackson's privacy — after all, he didn't belong to me just because we used to be friends. The thought, I noticed, was painful.

When he pulled his gloves from his pocket, I saw him tuck a flash of yellow back in. Then I remembered that the pastor had had a yellow kerchief folded in his shirt pocket. Which was kind of an odd note of color for a pastor dressed all in black. Yellow handkerchiefs at the protest in Severna. Yellow handkerchiefs in the crowd in Baltimore.

Instantly, I forgot my resolution. And wondered.

CHAPTER NINE

My gramma had always operated on the premise that any holiday and every family occasion — engagements, weddings, births, baptisms, even funerals — was an opportunity to schmooze with members of the community and further one or another of her charitable causes. Consequently, most of the old-money crowd between the Potomac and New England's border, and plenty of the new-money folks as well, were accustomed to gathering at Amber House each winter for a solstice celebration and dessert buffet.

This year's official raison d'être was to preview a small portion of the items that had been selected for the Metropolitan Museum exhibit in New York. It included period fashions, textile art, paintings and photographs, framed poetry and samplers, furniture, folk art, portraits — and more. Mom had spread small displays of the items throughout the ground-floor rooms and halls of the main wing so that people could meander.

The rest of the celebration followed all of Gramma's rituals for the event. Guests trickled in a little after eight. Each carload of arrivals was greeted at the door, where my mom accepted gifts as she handed off packages of her own — a Christmas ornament and a dozen beeswax candles hand-dipped in the colonial manner, to invoke (in solstice tradition) the return of the light. Desserts weighed down the trestle table in the dining room, second door to the left, with champagne and eggnog set on the sideboards.

I stood out of the way on the staircase and watched this year's receiving line — Mom, Dad, and Maggie, and Senator and Mrs. Hathaway. Beyond them, the sweep of car lights through the glass on either side of the front door foretold a constantly renewed stream of guests.

I had another one of those moments — a slipping-sideways moment of déjà vu — as I stood there with my hand on the banister. I thought helplessly and disconnectedly that I should have been wearing a long gold dress instead of a short black one, and that I should have been standing next to my mother. And then the moment was gone, and the smiling face of Richard Hathaway rose into my line of view.

He stopped on the step below mine. Which put me pretty much on a level with him. "Still adjusting to the time change, Parsons?" he teased me. "Or have you been sampling too much eggnog?"

Evidently I'd let my face go too slack. I chased away the remnants of the confusion I'd felt a moment before and lifted all my features with a small smile. "That depends, Hathaway," I said, raising my eyebrows innocently. "How much is too much?"

He grinned. "You watching my old man work?" he asked. "He's pretty good with people."

"No," I said. "He's pretty *amazing* with people." Which was the absolute truth. It helped that Robert Hathaway was being pegged as the next president, but his charisma had more to do with the way he seemed to make people feel. Like he was charmed to see each and every one of them. Like they all, to a man and woman, *mattered* to him. He *needed* them on his team. Together, he and they could accomplish *great things*. It also didn't hurt that he was really handsome and athletic — qualities he wore with shrugging modesty. It was all pitch-perfect; people adored him. "Really. Amazing."

"Yeah," Richard said. "Wish I'd inherited some of that." He stood there in his golden perfection, his head tipped a little ruefully, shaking his head with aw-shucks humility, and I just started to laugh. "What?" he said.

"I think you got your share, Hathaway." His eyes narrowed with pleased calculation, so I excused myself before he could run with the compliment. "I gotta save Sammy," I said. "A couple old ladies have him trapped." Then I scooted.

I pulled Sam away from the two elderly women who were listening to him with some befuddlement. Probably a monologue about dinosaurs, I thought. He had a near-encyclopedic knowledge. "Hey, bud," I coaxed him, "how about we get you a few of the best-looking desserts to sample and set you up in front of the TV?"

"That would be good, Sarah," he said gratefully. "Talking to these people is pretty hard work."

I loaded up a plate with a half-dozen desserts — fruit tarts, little cheesecakes, gingerbread cookies, a scoop of trifle.

"Too much," Sam protested.

I leaned down and whispered in his ear, "Save half for me. I'll sneak away and join you as soon as I can."

When I returned from the west wing, I wandered the crowd, listening. My dad always told me that eavesdropping was a bad habit of mine, but it was really more like an instinct. Maybe it wasn't entirely ethical, but I wouldn't have learned half of what I knew about the important stuff in life if I hadn't eavesdropped every once in a while.

Our guests seemed slightly adrift at a celebration that was, for the first time ever, occurring without its original hostess. Very few paid attention to the displays Mom had put out; mostly people grouped and regrouped to gossip and speculate. Some of the guests remembered Gramma; some talked about the house and its reputation for ghosts. Most people were wondering about

Robert's candidacy and when he would announce. I liked that I had that piece of insider's knowledge.

A few raps from the door knocker signaled a late arrival. Maggie was closest and went to greet the newcomers. But when she opened the door, she stepped back, away.

An older couple entered, smiling, followed by a handsome blond man in a black wool overcoat that had two small silver figures on its collar points. I stared, confused. The man looked like —

Claire Hathaway rushed over to hug and air-kiss the couple: "Agatha, Harold, so good to see you." She extended her hand to the third member of their party. "Reichsleiter, a pleasure to meet you."

— a Nazi.

My mother trailed in Claire's wake. "Mr. and Mrs. Wexler, welcome. And —" She paused awkwardly, waiting for someone to fill in the blank.

The Nazi held out his hand, with a little bow of his head. "Karl Jaeger, Mrs. Parsons. Attaché from the German Socialist Republic. Please forgive me for intruding on your festivities. I have been staying with the Wexlers, and they insisted you would not mind an extra guest." All in perfectly accented English, accompanied by a humble smile.

My mother's voice was tightly cheerful. "Of course not, Mr. —"

Mr. Wexler interrupted: "Reichsleiter Jaeg —"

But the Nazi interrupted him in turn. "Karl," he said, bowing slightly again, "please. It is easiest."

I realized my jaw was locked, my back teeth clenched together. I was incensed — *incensed* — to have him in my grandmother's house. In seventy-five years, the Nazis had wiped out all the Jews, Gypsies, homosexuals, and disabled people in Europe, except those who had escaped to the Americas. They'd taken over every country on the continent but a small remnant of

Russia. Just twenty-five years before, they'd bombed London to a hole in the ground, finally forcing the rest of the nation to surrender.

For the past two decades, they'd been working hard to put a human face on the "new" German Socialist Republic, but no one I knew was ready to forgive and forget.

Except, evidently, the Wexlers.

My mother excused herself, and I could see by the pinched lines of her mouth that she was not happy with this addition to her party either. I wondered why she hadn't asked him to leave — perhaps it would have been just too rude. Claire continued to chat with the Wexlers' guest, and then led him to her husband for an introduction.

I surveyed the rest of the room. Some people looked disapproving, but most were indifferent or even nodding hello. Senator Hathaway was all polite formality but did not show himself especially friendly to the Nazi. I supposed as a government official, he had taken the proper route. I didn't know if I could be so polite.

It was time I went to join Sammy.

The little hall that led past the kitchen held a small display of mounted insects and arachnids — butterflies, moths, iridescent beetles, and spiders of all sizes. I had seen some of these bug collections around Amber House before but had never wondered where they'd come from or who had made them. I paused to read the white card pinned beside them. "From the extensive work of the early entomologist Sarah-Louise Foster Tate."

Sarah-Louise, I thought, *and her twin brother, Matthew*, the names coming oddly easily to my mind.

Mom had hung the gallery with quilts, including one detailed and edged with green appliqué shaping a symmetrical maze — I guessed in honor of the real maze behind Amber House. *Treasure in its heart*, I thought, reaching out a hand to touch it.

Richard walked up behind me. "Talented line of women you come from."

I was startled and a little pleased. *He followed me.* "Too bad none of it trickled down to my generation."

"I'm sure one or two gifts found their way into your chromosomes. You just have to wait and see what they turn out to be." He gestured with his head toward the front hall. "Come on. We're supposed to be in there."

Oh, I thought, disappointed. *Didn't follow. Came to fetch.* I trailed after him, wondering what was coming next.

The entry brimmed with people who'd filtered in from the adjacent rooms. Richard caught my hand and tugged me up the stairs a little to stand with his parents and mine. Speech time — and Richard and I were part of Senator Hathaway's backdrop.

The senator talked about the Amber House exhibit that would open in New York City on New Year's Eve. He kept his spiel short, punctuating it with some decently funny jokes. I felt hideously uncomfortable being part of the official grouping, but I fixed a smile on my face and tried not to focus on anything or anyone in particular.

He came to a close: "I know you all were hoping for an announcement tonight of my 'plans' for the coming year, but we've decided to save that news for the unveiling in New York." The crowd groaned and booed. The senator laughed. "Well, y'all should come on up and join the party — it promises to be a good one."

A wall of hands reached out to the senator once he finished — everyone wanted to wish him good luck. I faded back up the stairs to the first landing to wait it out, taking a seat on the bench beneath the mirror. I longed to be sitting with Sam and the desserts and the TV but couldn't imagine how I'd get through that block of people. *I could go around — take the stairs in the conservatory*, I thought, rising, turning away, and very nearly escaping.

"You must be the young Miss Parsons I've heard spoken of," he said in that perfectly clipped English I'd heard earlier.

I looked back into the face of our uninvited guest, smiling at me with easy friendliness. He was maybe thirty-five or -six, and a poster child for the Aryan ideal — strong jaw, long nose, tousled blond hair. He wore the black woolen jodhpur trousers of the SS uniform tucked into glossy boots, coupled with a black tie and a white silk button-up shirt stretched over muscular shoulders.

"Why 'must' I be the young Miss Parsons?" I realized my entire face was tight with dislike, but I did nothing to change that.

He continued to smile, as if my revulsion were entirely appropriate. Or entirely unimportant. He ticked his logic off on his long fingers. "A member of the senator's group, but not his child, for he has only one son. While, on the other hand, the owners of the famous Amber House, Dr. and Mrs. Parsons, have one daughter about the age you appear to be. *Ergo*: Miss Parsons."

"Famous?" I said.

"Oh, yes," he said, leaning forward confidentially. "Tell me, are the things people say about this place true?"

Like a wave pushed before a ship, his scent reached me — a mix of leather, smoke, and bay rum. Against my every inclination, I found it attractive, which made me even angrier. "I don't know," I grated. "Why don't you tell me what you've heard?"

My anger seemed to amuse him. "Amber House has a certain — *reputation*, shall we say? You may be aware German science is interested in some of the more *esoteric* branches of knowledge. Etheric energies. Temporal anomalies. It has been hypothesized that this house is located on a confluence of ley lines and that it therefore has the potential for enormous amplification of energetic abilities."

I smiled in incredulity. "*Who* hypothesized that?"

He ignored my question. "Can you not feel it?" he said, holding out a hand. "The electricity in the air?" His gestures were graceful and relaxed — like a snake that could mesmerize. I gritted my teeth and shook my head dismissively. He dropped his hands, clasped them behind his back. "I take it, then, that *you* have not experienced any amplification of abilities?" He smiled, as if complicit in my disbelief, but he looked suddenly — hungry. Predatory.

Out of the corner of my eye I saw that Claire Hathaway was watching my conversation with the Reichsleiter. She tipped her head to one side quizzically when our eyes met. "No. I haven't experienced that," I told him. "But I'll be sure to let you know when I start levitating, or moving objects with my mind."

He laughed heartily. "Very good, Miss Parsons. I have enjoyed talking with you." He ended with a promise: "We will talk again." Then he excused himself. I was happy to see him go.

Claire came up as he went down. She stood at the landing rail, admiring the tree. Tall and slender, dressed in a cream cowl-necked sweater-dress, she looked beautiful against the backdrop of evergreen lit with tiny white lights, like an angel ornament that had escaped from one of its branches. I wondered if I was expected to join her at the rail, or if I'd be intruding. She looked over her shoulder at me and smiled. "I always loved your grandmother's solstice parties, and your mother has certainly upheld the tradition beautifully. I think it's so fitting," she added, facing me, "that our two families could finally unite in one cause, don't you?"

"Mm-hm," I offered, while I repeated in my head: *Finally? Fitting?*

She made a move to go, but then turned back, offhandedly. "By the way, dear, what did the German attaché have to say? Anything the senator should know about?"

So this was why Claire had come to talk to me — for the answer to this question. And I didn't know why, but I didn't have any inclination to give her what she wanted. I made my face blank. "No," I said, shaking my head. "He was just clarifying who I was. Since I'd been standing with you guys on the stairs."

"Ah," Claire said, regarding me a moment more. "I guess we should have introduced you formally so he didn't have to come prowling."

Prowling was what he'd been doing, all right, I thought. "I'm glad you didn't. This way I didn't have to smile and be polite."

From the living room, we heard the pounding of some attention-getting chords on the baby grand. Someone had apparently decided that Christmas carols would be just the thing.

"Shall we join them?" Claire said.

"Not me," I answered, feigning regret. "Tone-deaf. Not allowed to sing." Which wasn't exactly accurate, but Sammy, TV, and desserts were all still waiting for me.

She looked slightly confused, as if an inability to sing was too odd to be true, but then rallied with a smile. "So nice talking with you, dear." She gave my hair a small stroke and glided away gracefully.

Most everyone had migrated to the living room, so I decided to cut through the now-empty hall. Which was a mistake. My mother spotted me from the dining room, where she was helping Rose clear the used china and silver. She called me in. I grabbed a stack of dishes and followed her into the kitchen. "I was wondering," I said, my voice a little overbright, "why you let that Nazi into the house."

"The Wexlers brought him as their guest," she said, busy unloading her hands into the sink's hot, soapy water. "He's a political representative of the GSR, a foreign emissary. For Robert's sake, I didn't think throwing him out would be the right thing to do. Or, for that matter," she added, "for your sake, or Sammy's."

"For our sake?"

She turned to look at me. "We stand out more here, Sarah. I don't want to make you two targets for any — animosity."

I reflected on the levels of meaning in that statement, all of them awful. In Astoria, it was fine for our entire family to be publicly anti-Nazi, but here in the ACS, our political views had to be — sanitized? So that Sam and I would be safe?

In the background, a somewhat tuneless group effort at "Silent Night" came to an end and I heard the opening chords of a new song. Then someone began to sing in a pure and unwavering tenor: "*O Tannenbaum, O Tannenbaum, Wie treu sind deine Blätter!*"

Disbelieving, I crossed the hall to squeeze in behind the crowd surrounding the piano. The Reichsleiter was standing beside the pianist, working his way through the German version of "O Christmas Tree." The audience was rapt; the man had one of those achingly sweet voices. When he finished, his listeners burst into applause. The Nazi smilingly shook off their praise as he melted back into the crowd, which was substantially less hostile to him than they had been earlier.

He spotted me watching him and nodded. I turned and fled, back toward the empty gallery at the rear of the house. Richard caught up with me just as I was rounding the corner out of sight. "Parsons."

I stopped, looked back, trying to soften the angry lines in my face into a smile. He looked a little uncertain, a little shy. It was — charming. The smile produced itself.

"I just came to say good night," he said. "Dad has a five o'clock call tomorrow morning for a TV interview. My parents are probably already in the car."

"Thank God," I said without thinking.

"Ouch," he chuckled ruefully. "Give me a break here, Parsons. I'm bleeding."

"Oh, no," I said. "I only meant — if you guys are leaving, everyone else will go home too." I thought of the Reichsleiter, but opted not to mention him. After all, it wasn't Richard's fault the Nazi was there. "I'm just exhausted."

"Ah," he said. "I'm glad it's not me."

"It's not you, Hathaway."

"In that case," he said, stepping closer, "allow me to point out —" His finger tipped up at something above my head.

I looked. We were standing in an archway that had been decorated with a clump of ribboned mistletoe.

He leaned in for a kiss. I smilingly turned my cheek toward him, tapping the spot with one finger.

He hesitated, then his lips softly brushed my cheek.

"Night, Parsons."

I recognized afterward that most boys would have felt dismissed by that maneuver, but I didn't figure Richard's ego would suffer too much. I was certain he knew how insanely attractive he was. He probably thought I was just being coy. Which wasn't it at all.

I didn't know why, but somewhere along the line, I'd made such a big deal out of having my first kiss that I'd never actually had it. In middle school, the dating thing had all been so messy and juvenile, it was easy to avoid. But once I started high school, I'd agreed to a couple dates with nice-enough guys — only to retreat at the last minute, when they were moving in for the kiss. In my mind, I'd been waiting so long, it needed to be something special. Not something grabbed in the front seat of a car with the stick shift jabbing into my ribs. And not some joke kiss delivered because of a piece of parasitic plant life, with my parents maybe watching around the corner.

Frankly, I wasn't sure if I wanted whoever it was to be Richard Hathaway. I mean, the guy was gorgeous, and pretty nice besides, but there was just . . . *something* about him that made me uncomfortable. I had no idea what it was.

My prediction about the party's speedy demise proved accurate; after the Hathaways departed, people started leaving by the carload, including the Wexlers and their guest. I was called back to help find coats and man the door. When I finally was able to join Sam in the sunroom, he was asleep on the couch in front of the static-filled eye of the TV. Leaning against Maggie, who had fulfilled the promise I'd broken.

She smiled at me. "I'll carry him up and get him tucked in."

Huge pang of jealousy.

I followed along behind them to the front hall. The guests were all gone. The black-garbed waiters hired for the party were busy corralling the remaining party mess on trays. My parents were sprawled on the couch in the living room, looking hugely relieved and totally exhausted.

"I hate parties," Dad said.

"I hate high heels, forced smiling, and keeping an eye on Mrs. O'Brien to make sure she doesn't pocket one of the knick-knacks," Mom answered.

"Really?" I said. "That part about Mrs. O'Brien?"

"Oh, yeah," Mom said. "Your gramma was forever making surprise visits to her after parties so she could steal things back again." She shoved to her feet, groaning slightly. "I am going to change out of this dress and into something old and soft."

"Me too," Dad said, rising to follow her.

"Good night," I said.

"Sweet dreams, honey," Dad said, kissing my forehead. "You looked beautiful tonight, by the way. I noticed Robert's son was following you all over."

I rolled my eyes. "I was the only other person at the party his age."

Since I'd spent most of the party on the staircase, I took a couple minutes to peek into all the rooms and take a look at the displays: entomology, poetry, needlework, centuries of prominence in the community. *Seems like a pretty good family to come from*, I thought, wishing again I had some particular talent to contribute.

A display of ribbons and trophies filled a table near the front, beside a photo of my grandmother. She'd been a champion horse rider and breeder. My mom told me once that Gramma had always wished she could have ridden in the world Olympics, before they'd ended those games after the Second European War.

Two long, fabric-covered bulletin-board-type things stood in front of shelves in the library, hung with my great-great-grandmother Maeve McCallister's tintypes. Maeve's efforts to document the lives of the women, children, and blacks who lived in this area had been the starting inspiration for the museum exhibit — *The Women and Minorities of the South*.

I inspected the photos' subjects. Frozen-faced people stared out at me, caught unnaturally in the long exposure time of my distant grandmother's camera. The last tintype in the small grouping was a picture of Maeve herself, with a little girl. *Maeve McCallister and an unidentified child*, the card read. I bent to look at Maeve closely. And stopped dead, staring.

The little girl in the white dress held in my great-great-grandmother's arms was a dead ringer for someone I'd seen before. Someone I knew. The same sweet face, the same halo of soft curls.

She looked just like Amber, my childhood imaginary friend.

It was jarring. It was as if I'd been playing with a ghost all those years.

I gathered frantic thoughts: I must have seen this picture when I was little. Seen Maeve's little companion and adopted her as my pretend friend. That was the rational explanation. It was the *only* explanation.

Time for me to go to bed, I thought. *And pull the covers up over my head.*

Maggie was leaving Sam's room when I went up.

"Something happened," she said, more a statement than a question.

"No," I answered. "I'm just — tired."

It seemed as if Maggie wanted to say something more, but she let it go. She said instead, "You remind me so much of your mom when she was your age."

I brushed my teeth, changed into my pajamas — but I could not make myself turn out the light. I sat for a while bunched up against the headboard of the bed, staring at the closed door to my room until I realized I was waiting for it to open. At that point I got up, grabbed the green paisley blanket that was folded over the chair by the desk, and snuck into Sammy's room.

The light in the Nautical Room was out, of course, but the little star night-light Sam kept on, coupled with the soft sounds of his snoring, were enough to make things more bearable. I sat with my knees pulled to my chest in the chair next to Sam's bed and compulsively tucked the blanket all around me. I waited for what seemed like an eternity, unable to drift into sleep. Sometime after eleven, I guessed, I heard my parents and Maggie saying their good-nights. For a while, I heard faint sounds of doors, whispers of voices. Then all fell quiet. Even the sound of Sam's breathing ceased.

When I was younger, I'd refused to sleep without a light. It wasn't that I was scared so much as I was too aware of what the darkness did to my perception of things, how it affected my senses. My hearing became too keen, my sense of touch too pronounced — if I thought about it, I would suddenly itch in a thousand places and hear the thuds of my own heart thumping in my chest.

Sitting curled up in that room that night was like when I was little. But it wasn't my ears or my skin that was suddenly attuned — it was some other part of me, some part that had no name. Some part that waited silently, there in the dark.

She walked barefoot and silent as a ghost down a hallway blue-gray with predawn light. It was cold enough to turn her breath to clouds; no one had wakened yet to stir banked coals to new flames. She pulled the paisley blanket a little tighter around her and up over the top of her red curls. Her mouth formed unuttered words; her fingers tightly gripped the pen she carried.

She turned into a bedroom with pale lavender walls and sat low on the far side of the bed. Then she started to scratch at the walls with the pen, shaping letters, forming words. She whispered as she worked: "Sorrows . . . Bruised . . . Mystery . . . Past and future . . . Fate is in thy hands. . . . Heal the wound. . . ."

She scribbled faster, whispering a little louder. "Hast thou . . . a chance . . . to choose it all . . . again . . . then take . . . the path . . . that leads to . . ."

I woke as I spoke aloud the final word. "Otherwhen."

CHAPTER TEN

I opened my eyes to the same gray light that had filled my dream. Darkness bleeding into day. The longest night of the year was over.

For a moment, the confusion of waking in the wrong place dominated my thoughts, until I remembered falling asleep in the chair in Sammy's room. I forced myself to sit still so I could hold on to the fragments of my dream. A mad woman walking. Scribbling on the wall. Red hair — *Fiona?* I could picture her clearly then, and the rest of the dream took shape around her. Writing a poem in a lavender room.

I rose, following my dream, my bare feet padding, oblivious, over cold floorboards. Across the compass rose, into the west wing. Finding the door on the right that *she* had entered. Turning its handle.

But the room was not lavender. *Of course not,* I thought. *It's white, all white, except for the wallpaper's pattern of tiny sprigs of flowers.*

I went to the stretch of wall where Fiona had written, low down and next to the double window letting in the rising light. I ran my fingers over it, wishing I might somehow be able to feel the words right through the paper. I needed to see what was there. I needed to know if my dream was true.

A curl of paper beneath the window snagged my eye. Seeping moisture must have eroded the glue, loosening a patch. I peeled it back. There was indeed lavender wall beneath it. And marks. I peeled a little more, bent closer. They were handwritten words. Slightly smudged, but still legible. Repeating, over and over, a poem.

We chase the turnings of a maze confused,
Drawn on by hope, pursued by history.
By fortune we are soothed, by sorrows bruised,
We stumble on, purblind, toward mystery.
Yet Time hies round thee, hushed, on unshod feet,
Lest hearing, thou should wake to Her, and rise
To seek the point where past and future meet.
Though choice seems chance, though happenstance belies
Intent, learn thou that fate is in thy hands.
Discern the joint that shatters Time, that bends
Her flow, Her heedless whim, to thy commands.
Thus heal the wound; thus make all good amends.
   Hast thou a chance to choose it all again,
   Then take the path that leads to Otherwhen.

All my random phrases locked into place in the poem I'd known was there. The words settled into my brain like a virus, taking hold, infecting me, multiplying, crowding out every other thing.

My thoughts whispered, one on top of the other, building, until a wind keened inside my head. My hand ached in the center and I felt spread thin — so thin I might disappear. I remembered a gold dress, too beautiful to be real, and running through the maze, twigs clutching at the silken gown like fingers. A boy was there, at the maze's heart, waiting for me. I knew him. I could almost see him.

I pressed my palms to my eyes and tried to recover that sight. But the wind whipped all around me, a funnel of noise, a flood rising, a train coming at me, pinning me with its roar. Unshaped memories speaking with voices that echoed one over the other, clamoring, bellowing, pulling me in, pulling me under.

Then a sudden mercy of stillness when a pebble hit the glass.

I lifted my head, opened my eyes, almost surprised by the daylight falling through the window. I looked out.

She was standing in the snow under the oak tree, her little feet bare, her gauze dress all she had to keep her warm. But I understood the cold couldn't reach her.

It was Amber. My imaginary friend. And she was staring up at my window.

I ran for the nearest stair — the spiral steps in the conservatory. My feet beat the rhythm of the phrase from the poem: *the chance to choose, the chance to choose.*

What did I feel? Not fear. Something more avid. A hunger that had terror in it. Whatever Amber was, she was my only hope for answers.

I shot out the conservatory door, my bare feet screaming at the cold stone beneath them. Dashed around to the front of the house, my feet saying less and less, growing numb. When I got to the tree, she wasn't there anymore.

Movement.

She was at the far edge of the front porch steps. When I spotted her, she started off again, running toward the kitchen, disappearing past the front corner of the main house.

I tore after her. I saw, as I raced across the light snow on the flagstone walkway, she had left no footprints.

I took the turn and continued on to where the path bent again along the front of the east wing. And found myself alone.

No trail. No little girl. No answers.

I felt the cold, suddenly. Like freezing water outside and in. I stumbled on numb feet through the nearest door, the one to the kitchen.

Jackson was inside, writing something at the table. "I was just leaving a note saying Gran can't come to —" He glanced at me, broke off. "What on earth?" He took his coat off and wrapped me in it, then led me to the built-in bench seat by the fireplace. I sat unmoving while he put the kettle on the stove, got out a mug and tea bag, sugared it slightly, then brought me the tea to warm me from the inside out.

"Drink it," he said, and I obeyed.

"Did you see her?" I asked dully. My feet were burning with the rush of returning blood. I could feel a flicker of heat spreading from my center.

He crouched beside me, taking my hands in his to warm them. He looked up at me cautiously. "See who?"

"The little girl," I said. "Amber."

He shot to his feet abruptly, bumping his head hard against the mantel. He lifted his hand to his temple and brought away fingers wet with blood. Then his head jerked backward as he crumpled to the floor.

"Jackson!?"

He gasped as his spine arced up off the ground. The cords in his neck stood out. His left arm and leg began to shake, and a trickle of blood oozed from his nose.

"*Oh, my God!*" I screamed. I pushed open the door to the hall and shrieked as loud as I could, "*Dad!*"

Jackson's body trembled and slowly stilled. I bent over him, not knowing what to do. I heard running. My father, still in his pajamas, slid to a halt in the doorway and swore under his breath. He rushed to crouch beside Jackson, whose eyes opened slightly. Jackson moved his head a little. He groaned softly.

"There's so much blood," I said with a pale voice.

My father gave me a stern look. "Everything's fine," he corrected. "Everything's just fine, Jackson. You have a little cut. Head wounds bleed like the dickens, but it's just fine."

Then why is he bleeding from his nose? I wondered, but remembered not to speak it out loud.

Mom pushed open the door and stopped still, moaning a little. Something about medical emergencies left her weak. "Go back to bed, Anne," my father ordered. "Sarah and I can handle this. Everything's fine."

She nodded and let the door swing shut again.

Dad helped Jackson rise to sit in a chair pulled near the fire. "Get him a glass of water."

I jerked into motion and quickly handed a glass to my dad, who held it while Jackson took a sip. Then he helped Jackson to his feet, and led him to the living room couch. He pulled Jackson's boots off and made him lie back. "Get my bag from the front hall," he told me.

His doctor's bag. Of course. I stumbled to fetch it.

Dad started in on his medical thing, wrapping a blood pressure cuff around Jackson's arm. I went back to the kitchen to give them some privacy.

It was absolutely necessary I keep busy to prevent any sliver of reflection about anything that had happened that morning from creeping into my consciousness. Jackson's blood had spattered the stones and wood all around the fireplace. I got a bowl of soapy water and a rag to clean it up. I started with the mantel, then mopped my way down the stone face to the hearth. The rock crevices resisted giving up their stains, but I persisted methodically, stoically. I changed the water in my bowl and knelt again to get the last of the blood — some stray marks Jackson had made with his fingers on the plankwood of the floor.

But when I bent over them, I thought that maybe they weren't stray at all. Maybe he'd *written* something. If I mentally filled in the places where the marks thinned — a curve here, a line there — I could imagine letters.

J A N U S. In the black-brown color of drying blood.

I felt the word inside me like a lump behind my collarbone. I couldn't bear the sight of it, the sensation of it. I stared a moment more, then scrubbed hard and made the marks go away.

Dad came back to the kitchen. "It's half past eight. I'm going to change and drive him to the clinic in town so he can get a couple stitches in that cut and they can check him over a little more thoroughly."

"I want to come."

"You should just stay here, honey. He's going to be perfectly fi —"

"I want to come," I repeated.

I hurried upstairs and threw on some dungarees and an oversized sweater. And stared at my unslept-in bed. I understood what had happened. *Oh, my God, of course.* I'd fallen asleep sitting up in Sam's room — I must have been sleepwalking. Dad did it; Sammy did it. It explained everything. I hadn't woken up until the cold finally penetrated my sleep. I felt better, saner, calmer. Now I only had Jackson to worry about.

When I went back down, Dad was helping Jackson toward the front door, Jackson's arm draped over Dad's shoulders. I stomped my feet into boots, pulled on a coat, and shut the door behind us.

A pretty little vintage New English convertible was ripping down the drive, with Richard Hathaway behind the wheel. The top was down despite the cold. "Parsons!" he called, waving. His brilliant smile faltered a little when he saw Dad supporting Jackson.

"Stay and talk to him," Jackson said thickly.

"I want to go with —"

"I don't want you there," he said.

It hurt. He'd just been so kind to me, so gentle. Why couldn't he let me help him? I guessed I simply wasn't needed. Not by Jackson. I backed away and let Dad drive off without me.

Richard was leaning on the open door of his car, patiently waiting for me. I remembered then that I hadn't even combed my hair. I must have looked insane. I *felt* insane. Running my fingers through my tangles and twisting them into a knot behind my head, I made myself walk over to him.

"I'm sorry," he said humbly. "I'm a git. I hate drop-in visitors, especially —" He looked at his watch. "God! It's so early. I'm sorry. I was just excited and wanted to show you —"

I tried to smile. I touched a red-lacquered curve on his fancy little car. "Nice wheels, Hathaway."

"Christmas present. The dealer dropped her by," he said. "I'm taking her out for her maiden voyage and wanted to ask you to come. But . . ." He trailed off. "Another time, huh?"

"Another time," I agreed.

"He all right?"

"Yeah," I said. "He just — hit his head really hard. Needs some stitches."

"Cuts on the head bleed like crazy," he said. "He looked dizzy."

"Dad said he'll be fine," I said firmly.

Richard's face held a tiny frown of hesitation. "Can I —? That was Harris, wasn't it? Jackson Harris?"

"Yeah."

"I've got nothing against him — I've never heard a single thing bad about him, except —" He broke off, then plunged ahead to his point. "Except I heard my mother say once that she was warned about him. That he presented a danger. I don't know why." He looked embarrassed, apologetic.

"I'm not afraid of Jackson."

He shrugged. "Like I said, got nothing against him. Just thought you should know." He put a smile back on his face. "So, just to get this clear — you owe me a rain check, right?"

I nodded and tried to imitate his smile. "Yes. A rain check."

"Great!" he said, then seemed to realize I wasn't really mirroring his enthusiasm. He paused a little awkwardly. Uncertain of himself yet again. "Go back inside," he said finally, gently. "You look a little dizzy yourself." I nodded again, the smile still pasted on my face. Richard folded himself back into the tiny car, revved the engine, and shot away.

I let my face fall and went up the front steps on legs hardly willing to move anymore. Sleepwalking evidently didn't allow for much rest.

My thoughts buzzed like hornets in my head, a thousand unexamined questions flying madly. And behind them, under them — *He didn't want me there.* He didn't really like me anymore. Somehow, somewhere along the line, I had grown up into a person Jackson didn't like.

I was so tired. Drained. Confused. And, I realized, still afraid. I turned the knob, ice-cold to the touch. My hand found the table by the door, keeping me upright, I stood in the entry, wavering.

And saw someone climbing the stairs.

She was a young woman in dark blue denim pants unlike any I'd seen before. She was a mess — her clothes and skin grimed with dust and dirt, her hair veiled with spiderweb trailings.

"Hey," I said. She didn't turn. Her legs kept climbing mechanically. She frightened me.

I forced myself to follow after her. *Like moving against a current,* I thought. *Like walking into air that rejects your presence.* The girl above me glanced at the mirror on the first landing, but didn't pause. I saw her face then.

Gray with a pall of illness. Tear-streaked. Frightened.

I knew that face. I knew her.

Her features were backward, lopsided, distorted. Not the girl from the mirror — not the girl I'd always seen. I felt inside out.

The girl was me.

Chapter Eleven

She was a Sarah I had never been. I'd never climbed those stairs looking like that. Pushed beyond endurance, sagging forward, skin chalky.

I shadowed her, in sync with her footfalls, numbed legs bending and straightening, bending and straightening. Following. The other Sarah paused at the top, as if listening, then turned to climb to the third floor. When I reached the upper hall, she was passing through the farthest door, to the long garret room on the end.

I stopped. Unwilling to go farther. *Of course she'd lead me into the old nursery. The place where the monster lives.*

Darkness milled in the hall, and the windows of the smaller rooms shone silver from the light of a full moon. It was night here, though it was daytime in my world. *So what world is this?* I wondered.

The nursery appeared candlelit, but I saw no candles. The other Sarah was kneeling before a trunk, speaking in a low voice.

I made myself enter the room, to get a better look. My skin crawled, as if I was losing all my heat. I stopped behind the girl so I could hear what she said: "Can you see yourself in the mirror?"

She had pulled a small, polished wood box from a pack, had placed it on the trunk. She was shaking her head. "You're asleep," she said slowly, with a clumsy tongue. "You have to wake up."

I felt relief. *Yes, of course*, I told myself. *That's all this is. I never woke up. The purple room. The little girl. The poem, the blood, the crimson car. A dream. A nightmare.*

The other Sarah struggled to speak again. She said, "I came to find you, Sam."

The words jolted me. Something seemed to shift sideways. And suddenly I could see — two children, sitting side by side behind the trunk. Sammy, his sweet face gone slack. And a little girl not much older, with the fine features she shared with her sister, my mother. Maggie.

I knew what would happen next. Sammy was going to jump up and run out of the room, and then Maggie would say —

"It's dark in the mirror."

Yes. Yes. I had seen Sam's face trapped in the mirror once. Hadn't I? Until I found him in a dream. And Maggie with him.

I groaned — the kind of noise you make when you want to scream in your sleep, but you can't.

The night attic vanished. I staggered and almost fell, catching myself on an upright post. I stood alone in a dusty storeroom dimly lit by winter morning light.

Not a single thing I'd seen made any sense at all. I clung to the post, trying to sort it out.

If I'd been dreaming all of this — the purple room, the little girl, Jackson, Richard, the other Sarah — then when had I changed out of my pajamas? Why was I wearing a sweater and dungarees?

Not a dream. I'd had some kind of — vision — of *me*, doing something I could swear I hadn't done, except that I seemed to have some actual memory of it. But how could I remember something that hadn't happened? Or forget something so crazy? My little brother — trapped inside a mirror.

I was crazy. That was the only answer.

The light seemed to dim. I had a nauseating feeling someone else was in the room with me, someone standing in the far corner, in the shadows.

I turned and ran.

At the foot of the stairs, I hugged the railing to steady myself. *Gramma's mother was crazy. It's in my genes.* I was sucking in air as if I had been holding my breath for a long time.

I heard Sammy running up to me, laughing. I struggled to get hold of myself, to face him with a smile. But when I turned, it wasn't Sam.

I watched an auburn-haired child dart past and through the arch to the west wing, her pale blue dress fluttering behind her.

I squeezed my eyes tightly shut. "Please," I whispered. "Please make it go away." But I could hear the girl's footsteps slow to a stop. And voices farther down the hall.

I inched toward the hall entrance. A few feet down, the girl stood facing away from me, listening to a woman crouched in front of her, pleading. The woman looked like my grandmother from three decades before.

"You promised me you would stop doing this. Don't you understand, sweetie? I almost lost you. I thought I had lost you. I could see you in the mirrors, but I didn't know how to get you out."

"In the mirrors," the girl repeated, and so did I, silently.

"It's just too dangerous. We mustn't listen to them anymore. They don't need our help." She reached up and took the girl's chin in her fingers. "You've got to promise me — *promise me* — you'll stop seeing, stop hearing. Promise me, Magpie."

"Maggie," I said.

The woman and child disappeared and another woman stepped into the space where they had been. "Sarah-too," my grown aunt answered.

Maggie led me to a bench and made me sit. She crouched in front of me, as her mother had with her. "Tell me what you saw."

I realized I was crying noiselessly. I wiped my cheeks. I tried to find some starting point for answering my aunt's question. "Gramma. From a long time ago. Telling you — to stop 'seeing.'"

My aunt nodded. "Yes."

"Yes, what? You mean it happened?" I said. "In real life?"

"Yes," she said. "It happened."

I couldn't bear the way my head felt. I just kept reaching new levels of — incomprehension. "I don't understand," I said. "You don't seem — *surprised* that I saw that. Why is that?"

"I see them too. Your gramma called them echoes."

Echoes. The word itself seemed to resound in my mind as if I'd heard it before. "Is that what Gramma wanted you to stop seeing?"

"Yes," she said. "She thought they were to blame for my coma. And maybe they were, a little."

Maggie could see them. It had all actually happened. I didn't just make it up. I wasn't crazy.

"Wait," I said again. "How did Gramma know about them?"

"She could see them too. A lot of the grandmothers could."

Wonderful, I thought. *I've finally discovered the family gift I inherited. I'll have to tell Richard.* Some part of me felt like giggling. I took a ragged breath instead. "You have to explain it a little better, Maggie, 'cause this is freaking me out. 'Echoes.' What are they?"

"It's like replaying a piece of the past. A moment played over again. Like a scene from a movie. But only certain people can see them."

It was as if I'd fallen down some kind of rabbit hole. Words didn't seem to have the same sense they used to. And yet it was all somehow terribly, achingly *familiar*, as if I'd known it all along, had experienced this before. The past, replaying itself.

"Why haven't I ever seen an echo before now? You could see them when you were little."

"It doesn't happen the same way for everybody." She shrugged. "And your mama worked pretty hard to talk you out of seeing them at all."

The creepies, I thought to myself, and then said, shocked, "Mom can see them?"

"She used to, before Gramma made her promise to stop. Maybe she still can, but she just doesn't tell. Like me."

"Why did Gramma make you both promise?"

"I got stuck," she said, "until you reminded me to wake up."

That other thing I'd just seen. "In the attic," I said.

"Yes."

I woke Sam and Maggie up. They'd been asleep, and that other Sarah — *I* — had been talking to their — *what?* Their *dream* selves? Their *souls*?

"Why don't I remember doing that, Maggie? If these visions are echoes of the past, how come they showed me doing something I don't remember doing?"

Maggie looked confused. "I don't know. I always figured it hadn't happened yet, for you, but if you saw it —"

I mentally finished her sentence: *If I saw it, it must be in the past.* But I would swear on the Bible I hadn't done it. "Maybe I saw an echo from the future?" I said.

Maggie shook her head. "As far as I know, that's not what happens for our family."

"Sarah?" My mom was calling up the stairs.

What would Mom say when I told her about this? Why hadn't she ever just told me?

Maggie answered for me. "What is it, Annie?"

I forced myself to stand, to go out to the rail.

"Your dad called." She stood at the foot of the stairs, smiling up at me. "Jackson's good to go, no problems. The folks at the clinic even let your dad sew him up, which is lucky, because no one makes neater stitches than he does."

"Thanks, Mom." I was managing to keep my voice level. Light, even.

"Would you give me a hand for a little bit, hon? I have to get the rest of the exhibit stuff packed up."

Good Lord, please no, I thought, but said, "Sure. Be right down."

Maggie stopped me with a light hand on my elbow. Her voice was low, pleading. "Don't talk about this with your mom."

"Why not? Why shouldn't she know?"

She shook her head a little, trying to find the right words. "She won't like it. And there's stuff you have to see."

"Stuff I have to see?" It just kept coming. One crazy idea after another. "What do you mean?"

She looked resigned. As if she knew she sounded lunatic. "Sarah, that's what the house does. That's what it's for. Just — give it a chance."

She said it so matter-of-factly. I wondered if she understood what she was suggesting. "Maggie," I said, "it's just a house. Just bricks and wood."

She answered patiently, "I don't think anything is just anything, Sarah. Seems like everything has a piece of soul in it. Only we don't know it, because mostly we can't feel it. But in Amber House, the women of our family can."

I didn't answer her. I didn't know how. I just turned and left.

Mom and I spent an hour or so packing up the exhibit pieces we'd had on display at the party. I wanted to spill my guts, but each time I started, I shied away from it again. Some part of me was unwilling, as if it wanted — needed — to hear what Maggie's "house" had to say.

So I channeled my thoughts away from what I'd seen and learned. I tried to be "normal." For once in my life, I forced my

mom to chat. Which by itself should have clued in Mom to realize that something was wrong

We got everything packed, all padded and secure. Then I
taped the boxes while Mom stuck on address labels and huge
arrows beside the words THIS SIDE UP.

"I wanted to remember to ask you," she said, "what did that
man talk to you about?"

"What man?"

She reddened a little. "That — German. At the party."

That Nazi, I thought. "He just introduced himself. Said he
heard that Amber House was haunted."

"What did you say?"

"No ghosts. Just zombies who eat Germans."

She grinned and rolled her eyes. "Where were they when we
needed them?"

I grinned back. It felt good. It felt normal.

"You know what he said to me?" A tone of disbelief had filled
her voice. "He asked if we would sell Amber House. Can you
imagine? He said he could pay in gold."

"What did you say?"

"I said that Amber House would never be for sale under any
circumstances."

Yes. Never for sale. But then it seemed to me it might have
been. Once.

Mom started to laugh.

"What?" I asked.

"Good thing your gramma wasn't there."

And I started to laugh too. "Oh, my God," I said. "*Such* a good
thing."

She laughed harder. "Remember when that realtor came
knocking on the door?"

"She didn't know what hit her. Gramma was so outraged.
'What do you mean, if I ever decide I want to sell Amber House?!'"

"That Nazi wouldn't have known what hit him either." She was wiping tears from her eyes, laughing so hard. "We wouldn't have needed the zombies."

"Oh, my God," I wheezed. "Gramma would have chewed him up and spit him out." We laughed a little more, then tapered off to smiles.

My mom said, "You won't forget her, will you? You'll tell your children?" More tears were in her eyes. Different tears.

"I'll tell them, Mom. I'll remember everything."

She nodded. "Good."

Then I asked her the same question I'd asked Maggie. "Do you remember your gramma? Fiona?"

She looked off, distantly. "I guess I haven't told you much about her." She looked back at me. "I remember her. She always scared me a little — maybe that's why I don't talk about her much. She —" Mom searched for the right words. "She never seemed happy to me. I knew she loved Gramma and Maggie and me, but she always seemed a little — distanced from everything. Maybe it was because of the things they did to her when she was young. She might have been schizophrenic — they didn't know about that back then. They gave her electroshock treatments, and other things. . . . I suppose they were trying to help her."

"Do you think she was crazy?"

"Sometimes I thought my mother did. I guess I did too. I tell you, it's no fun growing up convinced that insanity runs in the family." She shook her head a little. "But then, it's so easy to paint a woman crazy. She was a dreamer. In her own way, a remarkable individual. A writer. A poet. She published several volumes, you know."

Insanity runs in the family. Maybe Maggie was right — I should wait a little longer before I told my mother I was seeing things.

We gathered together the packing tape and scissors to return them to their kitchen drawers. Without Rose in it, the kitchen was cold. I stirred the coals with a poker and threw another couple logs onto them. I noticed I'd missed a smear of blood when I'd cleaned up. It reminded me of the word I thought Jackson had scrawled.

"Mom, you ever heard of a 'janus'?"

"Jay-nus," she said, correcting my pronunciation. "He was a Roman god."

"Really? God of what?"

"Janus was the two-faced god," she said. "One face was supposed to be of a handsome boy and the other of an old, bearded man. Symbolically, the old guy looked into the past; the young one, into the future. He was the god of beginnings and endings. The god of time. January is named for him. Why do you ask?"

"Jackson — mentioned him," I said. "Impressive Roman god expertise, Mom. Thanks."

Dad came in.

"Where is he?" I asked.

He looked puzzled for a half second. "Oh. I drove Jackson straight home."

"He's all right?"

"Yeah, he's fine, honey. Jackson has had seizures since the accident. You know that. He's learned how to handle them."

Yeah, I had known about Jackson's epilepsy. Years before, Dad had sat me down and tried to prepare me for if he ever had an attack while he and I were playing together. But in the span of a decade, I'd never witnessed one before. The violence of it, the blood — what an awful thing to have hanging over his head. It was terrible that someone had to learn how to "handle" something like that.

Mom drafted Dad to carry our sealed boxes to the car. "I have to get them in to the freight office before five o'clock," she said, "so they'll be shipped in the morning."

I waved them off. When I went back inside and closed the front door, thoughts of the echoes, the attic, slammed back down around me. I lifted my eyes to the stairs. Maggie was standing there.

"Did you tell her?"

I shook my head. "Not yet."

"Just try to wait," she said. "See what happens."

There was an insane question that I realized I'd left unasked since she'd first mentioned the attic.

"Maggie, if you were dreaming when I found the child-you in the attic, how could I have talked to you? That wasn't an echo, was it?"

"You were seeing the past, so it was an echo for you."

"All right," I said. "But what about you?"

"I was dreaming the past — a dream echo."

"You can go to the past in your dreams?"

She nodded and shrugged a little. "Sometimes you're just watching, but sometimes you're right inside the person, thinking their thoughts. Have you ever had that happen?"

Yes — I realized, I had. Maybe my dreams about little Deirdre and Fiona had actually been echoes. Except — "How come we could talk, could see each other?"

She shrugged again. "I think, maybe, psychic experiences have something to do with energy. I guess, wherever we were, your energy could see my energy, and vice versa." I must have looked dubious; she struggled to explain. "You know what I learned once from a science teacher? If the nucleus of an atom was blown up to the size of a pea, its electrons would be the size of pinpricks orbiting that pea — *at the width of a soccer field.* Can you imagine that? A pea, pinpricks shooting around at the edges of a soccer field, and all the rest just empty space."

I shook my head, waiting for the punch line.

"See, we think of ourselves as solid stuff" — she slapped her arm — "but we're *not*. We're really mostly empty. What makes us *seem* solid is the energy holding us together. That's what we are. We *are* the energy. And energy isn't ruled by time or space. It's all part of spirit. In the attic, we'd *both* gone back to the same moment in the past. We were *in* an echo, but neither one of us was *part* of the echo. So we could see each other, and talk to each other. Maybe."

Yeah, maybe, I thought. Maybe I didn't need to know the exact answer. But there was something I did need to know: "Can the echoes hurt me?"

"I don't think so. Some of them aren't as nice as others, but I don't see how they can hurt you."

"What would have happened to you and Sam if I didn't wake you up?"

She stood there, silent a moment. "I don't know. We would have woken up ourselves sooner or later, I guess."

CHAPTER TWELVE

Even after all of Maggie's explanations, I still wondered: What had I seen in the third-floor garret?

The question would not let go of me and would not be answered. If an echo was something that came from the past, why couldn't I remember having been there, having said and done those things? The events I had witnessed certainly weren't something someone could forget, yet before today, I hadn't had any memory of it at all. But I also recognized that, as I'd watched, I did have the feeling that I *almost* remembered. That I knew what would come next. That sense of knowing in advance — did that suggest that I could see the future even though Maggie couldn't? I hoped not. That would mean I still had the events in the old nursery to look forward to.

And I didn't want to be that Sarah. Ever.

At the top of the stairs, I spotted Sam at his worktable, disemboweling an alarm clock. I sat down beside him.

"You all right, Sarah?" he asked as he focused on twisting out a screw.

No, I thought but didn't say. "Bud? Can I ask you something?"

"Sure you can," he answered. He put down the screwdriver and gave me his full attention.

"Do you . . . remember when I . . . found you?"

"You're always finding me."

Hotter, Colder, I thought. Maybe that had something to do with Maggie's *energy* too. "This was in the attic," I said. "In a nursery."

"Oh, the nursery," he said, concentrating on a gear he'd picked up. "I remember."

"I don't."

He considered. "Gramma said that you would need to remember."

Gramma?

He put the piece he was holding back in its place. "I don't remember it all exactly good either, Sarah."

"Tell me anything you got, Samwise."

"Well, I went to the pretend nursery that Mama made, where Maggie was before she got big. Only I forgot it was pretend, so I couldn't get back. And then you finded me, and you told me I had to remember, and showed me I wasn't in the mirror. So I said, 'You're my Jack,' and then I could go." He held out one little hand, palm up, a platter of clarity. "You see?"

And oddly enough, I did see. When I shut my eyes, I could see a red and white nursery full of toys. A music box. Sammy, not knowing who I was or who he was. But I had made him remember.

I'd been afraid, so terribly afraid, that I wouldn't be able to do it. Find him and wake him. "What would have happened, Sam, if I hadn't found you?"

He shrugged it away. "You *always* find me, Sarah. That's what was *s'posed* to happen. You fixed it."

"Can it happen again?"

"No," he said. "You fixed it. You made *her* remember. It won't happen anymore."

"I made Maggie remember."

Sam nodded. "Uh-huh."

"How come *I* didn't remember about being in the attic until today? How come I can't remember anything else about it — how I got there, what happened before or after?" *How come I'm asking my six-year-old brother?*

He was poking in his clock again. "I don't really remember much about what happened *before* either. How could we, Sarah," he asked in a reasonable voice, "when you made it all different?"

"Made *what* all different, bud?"

He spoke as if I was failing to understand the simplest thing. "You woke up Maggie," he said. "You changed what happened."

I wasn't quite sure how I escaped from Sammy's room. Everything I'd seen and heard that day had been nearly impossible to believe. But that last thing Sam'd said hit me so hard I couldn't think. It kept ricocheting in my head. *You changed what happened you changed what happened you changed what happened.*

When I'd woken up my aunt, I'd changed the *past.* Which had changed everything that came after. Our present. Once there had been a *time,* a history, that just wasn't anymore.

I couldn't process the idea, couldn't wrap my mind around it. Where did the other time go?

When I made myself quiet and stilled the thoughts scampering around inside my head, I could even remember pieces of that other past. That other time, when Maggie had been dead.

I went into my room, leaned against the closed door and slid down it until I connected with floor. I let more memories come. When Maggie was little, she'd fallen from the tree fort in the old oak — that had always happened, that had never changed — except in the other time that was gone now, Maggie had *died* instead of waking up from her coma. And her death had hurt everyone in ways that never healed. I remembered. Gramma had blamed my mom, and Mom had blamed herself. She'd never painted again and kept herself distant from everyone, even Sammy and me. Gramma had died from liver disease because of drinking. My parents had separated.

The images rose in my mind, one after the other — a parade of misery. Shifting and not quite in focus. Like photos under water.

All of us had been *different*. We'd started out the same, but ended up different. Even me. That other Sarah had been — less happy, maybe. More alone. But stronger. I thought of that girl I'd seen struggling to climb the stairs. She'd been bitten by a Good Mother. She'd been poisoned, maybe was dying. But she'd finished. She'd saved Sammy. She wasn't me. I couldn't have done that. I didn't have that kind of strength.

I knew now, finally, why I'd felt I'd been missing pieces of myself. I'd been missing *her*.

I sat in the gathering darkness, every part of me too drained to move ever again, trying to remember what it had felt like to be that other Sarah.

My parents returned home with Chinese takeout. Sammy came to my door and slapped the wood. "Come, Sarah. We're gonna eat with sticks."

I found a smile somewhere and put it on to go down the stairs with my little brother.

They laughed and chatted — my parents, my aunt, and Sammy. My parents agreed: the contents of our cardboard cartons weren't as good as the real thing "back home," prepared by Chinese immigrants who'd fled the Japanese occupation. Maggie and Mom traded in-jokes that went over my head, but that Dad seemed to get. Sammy sat contentedly spearing fried pork with his chopsticks. All of us comfortable and happy in one another's company, a family, united. Not like the family of that other Sarah. It felt like part of her sat inside me, marveling at how easy we were together.

Sammy passed out the fortune cookies, one to each person. "Read mine, Sarah," he said, waving it in front of my face.

I trapped his hand. "Okay, bud, just hold it still." I flattened it out. "It says: 'You will surprise people with your many hidden talents.'"

Sammy smiled and made one firm nod. "What's yours?"

I cracked the cookie and pulled out the little paper. "'Confucius says, It does not matter how slowly you go as long as you do not stop.'"

"Oh, Sarah," my brother said sympathetically, putting his head in his hands, "you always get the crappy fortunes."

We headed down to the sunroom with bowls of ice cream, to watch *A Christmas Carol* on the TV. It was nice. It was normal. I forced myself to relax into the familiar rhythm of it, to enjoy it — until the ghost of Christmas Future pointed its bony finger at Scrooge's grave. That upset me for no reason I could understand. I guess I had taken all I was able to endure for one day. I excused myself and went back upstairs.

On the second-floor landing, the light changed. I could feel that thickness in the air, as if I should not enter. *An echo.* My stomach went hollow and the desire to be back home, in our little yellow house, bit so sharp I felt tears starting. But I forced myself to look — to *see* — whatever it was the house wanted to show me.

A young black woman in a long cotton skirt walked down the hall with an armful of bed linens. She seemed as real, as fully fleshed, as Sam or Maggie walking the same route. I followed her. She entered the Tower Room, only the room that I saw had no tower — just four straight walls. I realized that where the woman was, *when* she was, no tower had yet been built.

It was a child's room, soft with pale fabrics, but the surfaces all held scientific paraphernalia. Neat displays of labeled, dead insects covered the walls. The black woman set the linens on the bed and went to stand beside a little pale girl in a blue silk dress, her chestnut curls held back from her face with matching ribbon.

They were looking at something in a bell jar. "The sac will open soon," the girl was saying. "She'll loosen it from her back and attach it elsewhere, lest the babies kill and consume her. We must take her to the woods before then."

I drew closer. Inside the bell jar, on a web woven in the fork of a branch, perched a honey-colored spider. A Good Mother. She carried a gray orb on her back, where the bulb of her abdomen joined the legged part of her body. I loathed her.

"Maybe ought to kill her, Sarah," the woman said. "Crush the sac."

Sarah. My seven-times-great-grandmother, Sarah-Louise Foster, for whom I was named.

"Dangerous thing to try," Sarah said. "The sac is very tough and the babies very small. I've heard tell of men who stomped a Good Mother and were made sick or even killed by the bites of the hatchling spiders. Hard to crush them all."

"Drown them in boiling water, then."

"Because they are venomous? They eat many times their weight each year in noxious pests — flies, mosquitos. And there are so few left. This Good Mother is the first I've seen in my whole life." She smiled. "She shall go free, Nanga."

"Nanga?" I repeated, struck by the name. I knew it. I'd heard it before. "Nyangu."

Something opened between me and the woman. Her eyes got wider. *She sees me,* I thought wildly, crazily, wanting to hide.

And then the scene shifted to the present. I was standing alone in the room, with night beyond the tower's windows.

I fled back down the hall.

Had Nyangu seen me at the end? How could that be if the echoes were just remnants of the past? Yet, when I considered it, it seemed to me that I had *talked* to Nyangu once upon a time.

The other Sarah had done it, I thought. Sarah One. I really was Sarah Two.

I put on my pajamas and brushed my teeth for bed. The girl I saw in the mirror had changed. She felt more like me. I was scared, a little, and confused. Uncertain what to do or think. But the girl in the mirror felt right. Stronger. Bigger. I thought maybe I would do what Maggie asked. Try to wait. To see what happened. To give it — *the house* — a chance.

It is dark and I'm afraid of the dark. I sit up in my bed, wondering where I am. Then I see the flowers climbing up the slanted ceiling. "Oh," I tell myself, "at Gramma's." We are leaving today to go home, so I will be back in time to start school. Remembering that gives me butterflies. I hope my teacher is nice, like Mommy.

Someone calls my name: "Sa-a-a-rah. Sa-a-a-a-rah!"

Mommy says I am not supposed to get out of bed in the night. But I slip my feet out from under the covers and jump down.

"Sarah," the voice whispers. I run on tiptoes to follow.

I think it is Amber. I see someone run into the other hall, and I think she is playing hide-and-seek. So silly. In the middle of the night. I am a little cold, but I run to follow.

The first door is partway open and I see Amber's hand on it, disappearing inside. I go push the door open all the way.

The moon is so bright I can see everything. Amber is hiding, but another little girl is sleeping in the bed. She is very pretty. She has beautiful princess hair that spreads all over the pillow. Shiny, like a new penny. She opens her eyes and looks at me.

"Who are you?" she asks.

"Sarah. Who are you?"

"Fee." She jumps out of bed, but part of her is still there, sleeping. She says, "Want to see something? Come on."

We sneak down the stairs and through the library, and outside through the sunroom.

She runs across the patio and the grass, into the bushes, and I follow. It is very exciting to be running outside in the nighttime. I feel wicked. We creep along a dirt path, bent over beneath the branches. It is dark under the bushes, but I can see her white nightgown. She stops and pushes a branch away to make a hole. "See?" she whispers.

I peek through the hole. A woman in raggedy clothes is stepping out of the bushes. More people are there, but I can't see them good because they stay in the bushes. The woman is walking across the grass. She is holding her side. There is a dark spot on the back of her coat.

Another woman is on the patio, lifting up a light. She is tall with brown hair. She is wearing a pretty nightgown and a bathrobe. She is trying to see in the dark. She says, "Who is there?"

The first woman walks into the light, and I see she is a black woman. She says, "Miss McCallister? We need help." Then she falls down.

The other woman sets down the lantern and gets on her knees next to the black woman, turning her over a little. "You're bleeding," she says.

The black woman says, "Got shot. But I trusted we'd be safe at Amber House."

"You were right," the tall woman says. "You will be safe." Then she says, "Come on out now and help me get her in the house."

And I think she is talking to us, so I start to go forward, but Fee giggles and says, "Not you, goose." I see five more raggedy people come out of the bushes.

"How did you know to come here?" the tall woman asks. "Do I know you?"

The black woman shakes her head. She says, "Amber House knows me."

Chapter Thirteen

Sunlight slanting through glass woke me.

My first thought: *Why did I dream that?*

I lay quiet, giving myself time to reconstruct my nighttime adventure. It was like I had had the dream before. When I was little. Only now I was thinking maybe it hadn't been a dream at all. Maybe it had been one of those things Maggie had described — an echo. An experience that the child-me had interpreted as a dream because nothing else was comprehensible. I wondered if I had been seeing echoes all along, without ever realizing it.

But if my dream had been an echo, then the pretty red-haired girl must have been my great-grandmother Fiona, showing me an even earlier grandmother. Maeve McCallister, perhaps, although with her hair down, in the darkness, it was hard to match the dream face with the one I knew from sepia tintypes.

The really eerie part, though, was that Amber had been there in the dream, playing hide-and-seek, as she always did. Not a creature of my imagination, but something else. If she was the same child in the photographs with Maeve, what did that make her — a ghost who had played with me and Jackson? And ten years later led me on a chase through the snow?

I knew Amber wasn't an echo — she'd *interacted* with me. I wondered if Jackson had ever actually seen her, or if he had just pretended to. For that matter, I wondered if she'd ever appeared to anybody else. The Fiona in my dream had spoken of a mixed-race child. The letters on the dedication plaque at the hospital wing — *A.M.* The A could be for Amber. It was possible that Fiona had seen my ghost-friend too.

The white light bouncing off the snow outside drew me to the window. The world was dusted in diamonds under a cloudless sky, every detail sharp in the cold air. I could see across the river to the sweep of hills beyond — a sketched landscape of charcoal trees holding up a sparkling lace canopy, each shard of light piercing me.

The moment passed. My thoughts resurged, filling my head with tangles, a child's furious scribblings, crossing and knotting.

Why was I seeing all this? What was the house trying to tell me?

Maggie's way of thinking had infected me.

Downstairs in the kitchen, Sam was busy fixing animal pancakes with Maggie. "Hi, Sarah-too," she said with a sweet smile. "Want a mouse or an elephant?"

"Elephant," I said, on the theory that it would be bigger, which turned out to be wrong. Sam sat down happily with a mouse head made of three giant pancakes and a manic blueberry smile.

"How are you doing?" Maggie asked as she set my plate in front of me.

"I'm —" How could I even put it into words? I couldn't. I shook my head a bit and shrugged. "I'm — trying to wait. Like you said. Giving it a chance."

"You'll see," she said, smiling, nodding. "It'll work out."

"You sound so sure about that."

She dipped her head and caught my eyes reassuringly. "This old house has kept our family safe and warm for centuries. Don't you think it wants what's best for us?"

I stuffed a pancake bite in my mouth. I didn't want to answer that question — didn't want to start guessing at what *the house* might want.

To thank Maggie for my breakfast, I did the dishes, standing at the sink, thinking about Fiona. It seemed like the entire time we'd been here, since moving in, Fiona had been trying to say something to me. The poem fragments. The dreams.

Well, maybe not to me, exactly. Maybe just someone, anyone, from the future who could hear her. Who could help her. She'd said, "Something has gone wrong." It seemed like it was my great-granddaughterly duty to find out what, exactly, she thought that *something* was.

Mom had told me Fiona published "several volumes" of poetry. After the last dish was dry, I headed for the library. I figured there had to be copies of the books in there. This *was* Amber House, after all, where nothing was ever discarded or lost.

I found them in the shelves below the brass plaque FICTION, alphabetized by author. Under *W* for Warren. A few little dusty leather-bound books embossed with gold vines leaned against a larger volume by the same author. I took them all to one of the tufted leather armchairs.

The big one was pressed with ornate lettering: *Amber House.* The publisher's information on the back of the title page announced: "McCauley Printers, Ltd., 1 of 100," which meant it had been self-published, with a run of just a hundred copies. I suspected the other 99 might be hidden in a sealed box in the attic.

The second page bore a "Note from the Author" beneath a photo of Fiona, in her sixties, perhaps, but still beautiful.

"Forgive an old woman her foolish notions," she had written. "As some people conceive the future — a branching path with a multiplicity of possibilities — so I conceive the past. Only in the present moment are we unified, congealed. This book is a testament to that vision."

After the photo page came a poem. Not my bits-of-phrases poem, which I'd mentally titled *Otherwhen*. This one was called something else just as odd. *Neverwas*.

> But Time turns round, and turns round once again,
> A restless hound intent to make her bed.
> Indiff'rent to the happenstance of men,
> Unheeding of the grieving and the dead.
> One chance there is to bring this bitch to heel,
> To wind back all the hours and the days
> And hand in hand uncover what is real —
> A pas de deux, a dance inside the maze.
> What life, what light, what truth there is in Time
> Derives from what is whispered heart to heart,
> The hand that pulls us onward in our climb
> To find again the place where we must start.
> > And if she glances backward as she does,
> > She'll see it's just a dream that neverwas.

People had thought my great-grandmother was insane, writing poems like this. But perhaps she hadn't been at all. Perhaps she'd just been more sensitive than everyone else. Understood what they didn't. That time could *change*.

In that dream I'd had of her trying to explain things to her father, she'd been convinced history had taken another path. It didn't seem as if she could see it, like I could. She just *sensed* it. I wondered how. And wondered what it meant. Because, really, my saving Maggie couldn't have changed time for Fiona, a half century before I woke my aunt.

Maybe others had figured out how to use Amber House to make things happen differently. Fiona thought of the past as branching, changeable. Maybe that was what Fiona had been obsessed with, why she'd been desperate to find Amber McCallister.

Maybe she'd discovered that Amber had made time change —
for the worse.

I flipped through the book's pages, recognizing small reproductions of the oil-painted ancestors who hung on the house's
walls. I stopped on the chapter dedicated to Maeve McCallister.
The picture under the chapter heading showed the tintype I
knew — the one of Maeve holding the "unidentified" child.
I studied the little girl in her white cotton dress. She evidently
had not been able to sit still for the sixty seconds needed to make
the photograph. Her image was more blurred than Maeve's. But
she looked like my Amber — a sweet-faced child, with large
eyes and a halo of dark hair.

I didn't know what to think about it all. No matter which way
I approached it, the puzzle Amber presented was disturbing and
impossible to take hold of.

They'd decided Fiona was insane, I thought. *How can someone actually
tell if she's going crazy?* Every single thing I'd experienced —
Amber, the dreams, the poetry, the echoes, even Maggie's part
in it — could have been made up in my head. How could I be
certain that it hadn't?

I put the poetry back on the shelf, but I kept the Amber House
history, hoping maybe Fiona would give me some answers.
Bedtime reading, I thought. I carried it up to my room and hid it
in a drawer. I didn't want to have to explain to anyone why I'd
taken it.

On the way back downstairs, I veered off. I paused at the foot
of the staircase up to the third floor. Fiona's old writing office
was up there. I felt like I should poke around, see whether
there was anything to see, but I doubted whether I could make
myself climb those stairs again

The memory of Sarah One stumbling up those same steps
shamed me into it. I hated to think she was braver than I was.

I only had to go as far as the first door on the right — a small-ish room overlooking the hedge maze and the river. It was sparsely furnished: a desk, a little cabinet, a chair, a lamp. I didn't know what I thought I'd find. Journals, maybe, telling me all about Maeve and the mysterious little girl. But the shelves, the drawers, were empty.

I did find a second door in the rear inner corner of the room. I'd spent so little time on the third floor, I'd never seen it before. As far as I could remember.

It opened into the attic over the west wing. Small dormer windows let in enough light for me to see the space, filled with boxes and old furniture so thick with dust their outlines were softened, like a landscape under snow. I had no desire to disturb these pieces of the past.

I turned to push the door shut again when the light shifted.

I looked back to see a girl — the other Sarah, not me — poking through a box of what I recognized as my mother's early paintings. And Jackson was there, watching, in the light of Fiona's oil lamp.

Sarah One looked upset, betrayed. I could remember feeling that, and I knew why too. I — *she* — hadn't ever known that Mom was an artist because Mom had hidden it away.

Why was Jackson there? What had we been looking for? *Treasure.*

I closed the door.

As I left Fiona's office, I heard a voice behind me. "Are you watching?"

There is a terror that leaps up from the knowledge that some-one is speaking to you from an empty room.

I made myself pivot. *A moth on a pin.*

Fiona was sitting there. She was perhaps in her middle twen-ties, her russet hair bobbed short and set in finger waves, her

fine features frowning a little in concentration. She wasn't looking at me. She had a drawer inverted on the desktop and she was
working to squeeze something into a corner of the carved slits
that held the edges of the drawer bottom in place.

I walked closer — so close I could see the faint dusting of
freckles on her ivory cheeks. Then she looked up at me, but
blindly. I knew I wasn't visible to her. She pointed to the envelope she'd wedged in the drawer's grooves. "Do you see?" she
asked me. Me. The one she knew would come.

I gasped slightly, and my great-grandmother disappeared.

Moving mechanically, I slid the same drawer out of the desk.
When I turned it over, the envelope was still there, still fixed
in its place. I pressed on the wood of the drawer bottom to
loosen it and tugged the yellowed paper free.

The envelope held a card with a paragraph written in ink, in
my great-grandmother's graceful script:

> *I let them believe they cured me with their pills and shocks
> and "analysis." But I still know the truth. Things are not as
> they should be. The girl is connected to it, somehow, but I
> have never been able to discover in what way. I believe she is
> my grandmother's mixed-race adopted daughter, who disap-
> peared so long ago. I will search until I find her. I will leave
> her story behind me, so you will know. So you can make
> things right.*

I put the card back in its envelope. Wedged the envelope back
in its place. Put the drawer back in the desk. Closed the door on
the room.

Everything in Amber House had a place, I thought, as I walked
numbly down the stairs. A place in which it rested patiently, bid-
ingly, until it was needed once again.

CHAPTER FOURTEEN

On the second-floor landing, I saw her. Looking up at the window I was looking out. She stood in the entrance to the maze, dressed, as always, in the gauze of summer. *Amber.*

I turned, hurried down the stairs to the front hall closet, and pulled on boots and a coat.

Amber House's hedge maze was a famous landmark all by itself. The entire continent of North America had only four hedge mazes. Ours was small compared to the others, but cleverly made and relatively ancient. My mother hadn't particularly liked it when Jackson and I played in there when we were little, but that never stopped us. The place offered an irresistible combination of sunlight and mystery.

It also offered a challenging puzzle, very possible to get lost in — if you didn't know the key. Right, skip, right, left, skip, left, right, skip; then left, skip, left, right, skip, right, left, skip. Followed faithfully, the pattern would lead you directly to the heart. But it seemed this time that was not where I was headed.

The entrance to the maze opened onto a long straight corridor. The plants that formed its walls were so old and thick that, even stripped for winter, one could not see through them. The snow lay on the hedge tops and maze floor, an unbroken foam of white. No footprints ran after the little girl who stood at the corridor's end.

The ghost of Maeve's lost adopted child.

She turned and darted left behind the hedge. And I went after her. As I knew I must.

At the corridor's end, the passage continued both left and right. I cut left and ran to a corner that bent left again. Halfway down the next corridor, two passages crossed, and looking right, I saw a flash of movement. I dashed after it and hit another choice of turns. A left took me to a dead end.

I'd lost her.

I walked back, following my footsteps, when a little bit of color peeking from the snow caught my eye. I bent to pick it up. A mottled green pebble. I'd held it before, I realized. In this same spot. Only then the hedge had been dressed in leaves turning gold. I even knew what I'd find around the next corner —

— a summertime maze with hedges no higher than my head.

An echo. A marble bench stood in a small alcove in the maze, and on the bench sat an old black woman. She looked toward me, squinting, and a smile spread across her face. She spoke. "Sarah, girl, here you are again."

As if I'd been punched in the stomach, I felt short of breath. *An echo who* knows *me,* I amended. And some part of me was completely unsurprised.

I made myself inhale, then I made myself speak. "You're from the past, right?"

She laughed, warm and throaty. "Feels mighty present to me. But yes, your past, I guess."

"How come you can see me? How come we can talk?"

"Not sure," she said. "I can see the future, like you can see the past. Somehow our sights meet."

The ability to see the future — that was a scam, wasn't it? But if I could see through time to the past, why shouldn't this woman be able to see the opposite direction? I thought of what the Nazi had said — that Amber House had been built on a special spot, where "ley lines" came together. Maybe sensitive people were *more* sensitive in this place. "How do you know my name?" I asked.

She looked confused then. "We've talked many times afore now." *Sarah One*, I thought. "How could you not know me, not know that we know each other?" she said, puzzling it out. "This ain't the first time we met — 'cause I remember that time. You can't have two first times." A queer note had crept into her voice.

I restrained myself from blurting an answer. I had no reason to trust this woman with my secrets except a gut feeling left over, I supposed, from Sarah One. Yet I *wanted* to talk to someone. I decided to take a chance. "I think maybe you can," I said.

She looked at me keenly. "Tell me," she said.

"My brother —"

"Sammy," she said.

"Yes. Sammy got stuck in an echo while he was unconscious, but I was able to find him and wake him up. Except my child-aged aunt was with him and —"

"And you woke Maggie too," she said.

"Yes." This was the part that was hard to say. "But I can remember a different time when she never woke up. When she died."

The woman pressed her hands to her cheeks as if to hold herself together. "You did it," she whispered. "You changed things." Her eyes glinted, moving as if seeing a multitude. "She said it was possible, but I did not actually believe it. I could not see the path. But she can."

"Who?"

She ignored my question. "Do you remember the time before? The time that is no more?"

"Seems like I'm the only one who does. Sam and Maggie remember me waking them up, but they don't remember what happened before that. Not in the other time."

"They remember the change because they were there."

The change. The word was unbearable somehow — it made me feel tenuous, as if I were spreading out thinner and thinner.

I felt irritation that I was giving this woman so many answers and she still hadn't even told me her name. "I'm sorry. Who did you say you are?"

"They call me Nanga."

The woman in the vision with Sarah-Louise and the Good Mother spider. Older, but still recognizable. Looking pretty good for someone dead and gone about two centuries.

Her head turned, as if she saw something I didn't. "Here she comes now. My little friend. My solace. I thought her one whom I had dreamed. But she grows clearer. Each time she comes, she grows clearer."

She looked toward me again, but I didn't think she could see me anymore. She spoke blindly. "You go find Jackson. Now."

The bubble of time that had held us dissolved, and she was gone. But not before I noticed a small trickle of blood from her nose.

I stood there a moment more, in a maze turned back to winter poverty. I felt unwilling to move, caught up in some game I didn't know the rules of. It didn't seem fair. I didn't want to play.

Then I turned and backtracked my footprints out of the maze, dropping the green pebble where I'd found it. I was going to go find Jackson.

Nanga's words kept turning over in my head. *The change. The time that is no more.* There were ugly possibilities in those phrases. *Was I responsible? And had I made things worse?* But that was absurd. Maggie was alive, I told myself, over and over. Everyone was happier. Things were better.

I went inside through the kitchen heading for the stairs. But then I heard the voices of my parents, coming through the swinging door to the dining room. Loud and angry. My mother, practically snarling: "Let's not even plug money into the equation, Tom. Maybe I just think it'll be important to Sarah, someday, to look back on this party in her family's house. How come it never occurs to you that I might be thinking of someone besides myself?"

My dad, heavy with sarcasm: "Maybe because that's how I've experienced our life together."

"Oh, great," my mom came back at him. "Let's just open up all the old wounds, shall we? Rehash it all. Because I'm not the one who betrayed our marriage."

I realized the voices didn't belong to my real mom and dad — they belonged to the other ones, the ones that didn't exist anymore. Sarah One's parents. But I pushed the door open anyway. Just to make sure.

The dining room was deserted. But I was relieved to have heard, remembered, that argument. Things couldn't be much worse than that was.

I heard three quick raps on the door I'd just closed behind me. I turned and saw a young version of my father entering, his hair absurdly long and unruly, a big grin on his face, dressed in dungarees and deck shoes.

"Lord, Parsons, you here again?" my mother said. I looked toward the table. She was sitting there, her hair long and curled at the bottom, her mouth turned up in a teasing smile. She wasn't much older than I.

"I just wanted to give you another chance to knock me into the bay with the boom."

"You're putting the blame on me?" my mother said, lifting her eyebrows, making her face innocent. "Half the boats on the river heard me yelling 'Jibe ho!' You're supposed to duck, Parsons. But I always heard New Englanders don't make very good sailors."

"You just dunked me because I criticized your anchor hitch knot."

"Maybe," young Mom said, reaching up and grabbing hold of my dad's shirt front. "But I'll never confess." She pulled him down until their lips met in a kiss that made me look away. When I turned back, they were gone.

It was as if Amber House was trying to set my mind at ease. Things were better.

But I wanted the visions to stop.

I sped up the stairs two at a time, ran a brush through my hair, put on a bit of mascara and lip gloss, and then ran back downstairs and out the front door. I was glad to go look for Jackson. I needed a break from that house.

Just as I had before, I followed my sense of Jackson, and just as before, it led me back to the same clapboard church. Where I found him waiting for me, standing outside the door with his arms crossed.

"How'd you know I was coming?" I asked.

"Didn't you promise not to do this?"

Yes, I had promised, I thought with some resentment. *You insisted I promise because you want to keep secrets from me.*

"Someone told me to come," I said defiantly.

"Who would that be?"

"Nanga. Her name is Nanga."

I didn't know what I expected, but the effect that name had on Jackson astonished me. He looked stunned, and yet — *hopeful*. Confused, maybe even calculating, but trying to contain it all, keep it all inside. Finally he said, "Then I guess you'd better come in."

I wasn't all that surprised that it wasn't actually a Bible study meeting. It looked more like something — political. The Asian girl I'd seen with Jackson before turned around as we came through the door. She shot me a suspicious look. At the front of the room, a New Englander in a suit was addressing a mostly black crowd.

". . . a new encryption code that Jewish Intelligence hasn't cracked, but the sheer number of communications with German agents in North America indicate that the operation is major and imminent — a high-magnitude threat. We are encouraging all of our allies and activists to be watchful and as prepared as possible for an incident that may involve a large number of civilian casualties."

I thought I must have misheard. I turned to Jackson. "Did he just say 'a large numb —'?"

Jackson shushed me with his hand; he was trying to listen. A member of the audience rose with a question: "Wouldn't such an incident be considered an act of war?"

"J.I. says the Nazi action will be directed toward destabilizing and-or sabotaging the Unification movement. Whatever occurs will be masked in such a way as to throw suspicion on another group. The action almost certainly is not intended to precipitate war. As far as we are able to discern, neither the Germans nor the Japanese Empire are yet prepared to resume a policy of military expansionism."

I plucked at Jackson's sleeve a little frantically. "Is this guy for real?"

He looked at me with something like exasperation. "It's all for real, Sare. I don't want to scare you, but like I keep telling you, time is running out."

"Time for what?" I asked, but he'd turned back to listen. The black minister I had met two days before — Pastor Howe — had risen and was shaking hands with the speaker.

"Thank you, Rabbi Hillel." The pastor took over the podium. "It doesn't appear that either the New English government or our own is releasing this information to the general public, so spread awareness where you can. We do not want to promote panic, but we do want to promote preparedness. We also want people to know that Germany is actively trying to undermine the Unification movement, which means the Nazis must perceive it as a critical threat. Which makes its success of critical importance.

"I want to remind you that our Christmas Eve candle service and remembrance begins at ten P.M., but do try to get here early. The inspiring Diane Nash will talk about the days when she and our own Addison Valois" — he gestured toward Jackson, and people turned to nod — "worked together to build the liberation movement in this area." The pastor noticed me then, standing next to Jackson. He concluded, "And I want to welcome all new visitors to our Bible study group" — this provoked a smattering of chuckles — "and encourage them to come again. We need the participation of all people of goodwill."

With that, the meeting ended.

Jackson tugged me into the stream of departing people, working his way against the current. He told me, "I want you to meet someone."

I followed reluctantly. I had a pretty good idea who that someone was, and I wasn't all that keen on meeting her. "Haiyun!" Jackson said over the crowd.

The Asian girl turned and smiled. *She's lovely*, I thought, a bit resentfully. Jackson tugged me in closer: "I want you to meet my best friend — Sarah Parsons." *Best friend.* I was a little surprised that he'd meant me. "Sarah, this is Kim Haiyun."

"Helen," she corrected him. "Helen Kim. Sounds more Confederate." She smiled at me. "I am very happy to meet you." She extended her hand.

I took it. "And I'm pleased to meet you." I couldn't help but smile back. "Kim — is that a Chinese name?"

"My family is from the place once known as Korea."

She had the accent — very slight — of a non-native speaker. Which meant that she and her family had escaped the Empire. I had met quite a few refugees back home and heard their stories. I knew that successful escapes took a small fortune in bribes or incredible luck or heroic daring, and most often some combination of all three. "The Confederation is fortunate to have you."

She smiled again, and nodded. "Thank you. I wish the government shared your opinion." She turned to Jackson. "I will see you Friday?"

"I'll be there," he said. "You need someone to walk you home?"

She shook her head. "My brother is picking me up, but thank you." She slipped past us, saying as she went, "Good night, Sarah."

Jackson bent to gather his possessions from the pew. Which confirmed he *had* been sitting next to her. I must have seemed a little miserable, because he looked at me quizzically. I shook my head slightly and put on another small smile. "I guess you can walk *me* home, then."

"Yep."

I was second-best now. But that was all right. If I actually was still Jackson's best friend, I guessed I could get used to it.

CHAPTER FIFTEEN

Outside the church, the clear sunshine of the morning was gone; clouds from the Atlantic had blown in. My brain was a welter of questions. About Jewish Intelligence and fake Bible study groups and a lovely Korean girl. Not to mention — "How is it you know Nanga?"

He glanced around at the other people still gathered near the front doors. "Let's start walking," he said. When we reached the end of the road and set off across the field, he picked the conversation up again. "I don't know Nanga," he said. "I know *of* her. She's my great-grandmother about eight times removed. Dead one hundred and eighty years. The more interesting question is, how do *you* know her?"

I thought about lying. Passing it off somehow — a joke, a reference in Fiona's *Amber House* book, something or other I'd seen in the house that could explain why I'd used that name to justify my hunting Jackson down. Because I didn't see how I could tell him the truth without making him think I was a lunatic.

"May I guess?" he asked calmly. I nodded, thinking I'd love for him to give me an explanation that would get me off the hook. But then he said, "She talked to you in an echo."

Oh, my God. I stopped dead still. "You're telling me that you already know about the echoes?" *And that I'm not delusional?*

He stopped too. "Yes, I already know."

I felt relief. And excitement. And confusion. *Wait a minute —* "How long have you known?"

He was studying his shoes. "Maybe ten years."

"For God's sake, J. Why didn't you tell me about them?"

He looked up at me, shrugging just a little. "I didn't want you to think I was a lunatic."

And I had to smile at that. "Fine," I said. I started us walking again. "How'd you find out about them?"

"Someone told me."

"Who?"

His forehead had a little furrow in it. Like this was going to be hard to say. Or maybe hard to hear.

"You did, Sare."

I just shook my head. "What are you talking about?"

He looked off, trying to find words. "I have to tell you something," he said, and I was hit again with that too-familiar feeling of déjà vu. He'd said that to me before. We'd been standing on the Amber House river dock. He'd been afraid that time too. Afraid to tell me the next thing, to tell me —

"You have a gift too," I said.

He looked disconcerted. "Yes."

Family gifts, I thought. I had mine and he had his. Passed down to him from the woman whose name had started this conversation. "You know about echoes because ten years ago you saw *me* telling you about them, because you had a vision of *this* conversation," I said. "Because you can see the future."

This time he stopped short. "How could you know that?"

I stood there considering what I could say. The silence between us filled with the sounds of snow dripping from the tree branches, the quarrels of cardinals searching for food, the far-off hum of cars on the road that wound its way past Amber House. How was I supposed to explain to him that he told me about his gift on that river dock, in a time that ceased to be? "I know it," I said carefully, "because you told me once before."

"I think I'd remember telling you something that important," he said.

I lifted my eyebrows all the way and shook my head a little. This had to be the most insane conversation of all time. I forced myself to say the words, one at a time. "You don't remember telling me because you told me in a *different* past — a past that doesn't exist anymore."

I thought I'd get disbelief maybe, even laughter. But what I saw in his face was — excitement. He reached out his hand to steady himself with mine.

"You don't know," he said, "you can't possibly know how *incredible,* how *amazing* it is to hear you say that." His hands went to his face; he shook his head; he seemed barely able to contain himself.

I must have looked as stupefied as I felt.

"Sarah," he said, "it's amazing because all my life, ever since I was little, some of the things I've foreseen — the *best* things —" He looked around to see if we were still alone, but the park that stretched between town and home was deserted. He started walking again, long rapid steps that reflected his excitement, and I trotted after him to keep up. "The best things I've foreseen," he repeated, "could only happen in a different future, a future you can't get to from here."

A future you can't get to from here. More words I'd heard before, a memory from that other past.

He was looking up, away, smiling. "I always, *always,* thought I was hallucinating or something. But if you can see a different past, Sare, maybe I actually *can* see a different future.

He seemed — changed. In an instant. Just like that. He seemed *bigger* somehow. Calmer. Stronger. All the years I had known him, I had never seen the secret he'd hidden — that he was afraid he was genuinely out of his mind. Not connected to reality. He'd tucked it away inside himself. How could he do that? Keep a secret so big, from me? Day after day, watching everything he did and said, to make sure no hint of it ever slipped out. *He must have so much self-control,* I thought. I'd known about the echoes for fewer than two days and had already told him everything.

"What is it you see?" I wanted to know. "The future you can't get to from here?"

He looked at me, and there was regret in his eyes as he said, "I can't tell you, Sare."

He was still keeping secrets. He didn't trust me the way I trusted him. Which was probably my fault. "Fine," I said down to the ground.

"Hey." He took my arm and turned me to face him. He bent down. "I want to tell you, but —"

We'd reached the edge of the road near Amber House, and a familiar car slowed and pulled up next to us. I glanced over and saw my mother in the passenger seat, rolling down her window. A small frown pinched the space between her eyes, but she said with a smile, "You guys want a ride?"

It would only save us the walk across the front pasture, but we both recognized that was hardly my mom's intention. We got in and Dad drove past our driveway to take Jackson to his house.

But what? I wondered how Jackson had been planning on ending that interrupted sentence. I wouldn't like what he saw? I'd do something to mess it up? I noticed Mom was watching me out of the corner of her eye; I turned my face away and stared out the side window.

Dropped off at his own front door, Jackson duly thanked my parents and headed inside.

I kept wondering about that "different future" on the drive back from Jackson's house. I could feel a memory from the time before trying to break through, but I couldn't quite take hold of it.

"Are you listening, honey?" my mother said.

"I'm sorry, Mom. Was thinking about something."

"I could tell," she said, smiling. "You and Jackson seemed to be having quite a serious conversation. Everything okay?"

"Everything's fine," I said. "What is it you asked before?"

"I need you to come with me to Annapolis to help me pick up a few last-minute gifts."

I held in a sigh. I didn't want to go shopping. I wanted to hunt down Jackson and finish our conversation. *Not going to happen.* I said, "Sure, Mom."

I went upstairs, changed into something a little more presentable, then trotted back downstairs dutifully, resigned to a two-hour shopping trip. I heard my parents talking through the door to the kitchen. I hesitated, remembering the shouting match in the dining room between the other Sarah's parents.

My dad was mid-sentence: ". . . don't have anything against their friendship, Annie, but she's got to understand how it might look to other people around here, people whose good opinion she's going to need."

"Not to mention what Jackson himself might be thinking," my mom added.

I thought it was about time for me to interrupt, so I shoved through the door. "For your information," I said, "Jackson has a girlfriend named Helen. She's a refugee from the Empire, and she's really beautiful. So I don't think you have to worry about him." They both had the good sense to look embarrassed. I took some satisfaction in that. "Shall we go, Mom? We want to get there before the stores close."

My mother drove us to her favorite antique shop on Main Street, to look for a gift for Richard's mother. Something striking yet fairly innocuous, since Mom said she and Claire had never been close. She settled on a little tole-work metal box, festive with stars and birds, dated 1793. I peeked at the tag tied to its clasp and my eyes widened. Mom may not have been very fond of Mrs. Hathaway, but she was prepared to get her something expensive.

"Did you get a gift for Richard?" she asked me.

"Mom, I hardly *know* Richard. Why would I give him a present?"

"Well, you can't go to his house empty-handed."

Go to his house? My face must have telegraphed my thought. Mom said, "Dad was supposed to tell you — they invited us for Christmas Eve dinner. Claire insisted, really. She was very — sweet. Talked about building 'bonds' between our families."

I rolled my eyes, and knew my mother would too, if she could. I didn't want to get a gift for Richard. It seemed too personal, like an admission that I wanted something to be going on between us. "Can't I just give all the Hathaways a present — a box of fancy chocolates, maybe?"

"Well" — my mother shrugged unhappily — "I know he got something for you."

How does she know that? I wondered, understanding from this tidbit that I was fully condemned to go to the dinner. With a gift for Richard in hand.

I saw something in the glass case I'd been resting my hand on — a pocket watch from a century or more before. Its case was etched with twining lines; its face showed graceful numbers beneath delicate asymmetrical hands. A masterwork of Time. The salesclerk noticed my interest; she slipped it out of the case and onto a black velvet tray before I could stop her. I picked it up. "Nice price," my mother commented, "if it works." I twisted the knob on top and held it to my ear to hear its whisper. *Tick-tick-tick.* "You think Richard would like that?" she asked.

"It's not for Richard," I said with sudden clarity. "It's for Jackson."

"I already got both Rose and Jackson two very good gifts from the family, honey, to go with their Christmas bonuses." She sounded anxious again. "You probably shouldn't give him such an expensive thing."

Fine for Richard, I thought, *but not for Jackson?* "It's not *that* expensive," I said. "I'm fairly certain I just heard someone call it a 'nice price.'"

I handed it back to the clerk along with a one-hundred-dollar note — the remnants of my Astoria babysitting money that I'd had converted into Confederation currency. Mom tightened her mouth but didn't say anything else.

When we got home, Dad was busy frying up crab cakes from the seafood place in Severna. Rose was still not feeling well, so we were fending for ourselves. We ate in the kitchen, like we used to in Seattle.

Dinner was tense. I could see my parents were decently unhappy at being cast as racists. And maybe I was being unfair. They clearly thought there was more going on between Jackson and me than being best friends, and maybe they wouldn't have had a problem with that if we were still in Seattle. Things were different here. Perhaps they were only trying to protect me. But I was a big girl. And I didn't want that kind of protection.

I headed down the rear hall toward the conservatory after dinner. I needed a break from my parents, and needed to think, to process.

I needed to talk to Jackson.

In all the time I'd been visiting my gramma's house, whenever I was lonely or grumpy or bored or just needed someone to talk to, I'd go to the conservatory and, magically, Jackson would be there, waiting for me. I used to think it was because we were such good friends that we were kind of in tune. But now I realized it was because Jackson had foreseen somehow that I needed him and had generously consented to appear.

Just one of an endless number of kindnesses he'd shown me over the years.

But this night, when I reached the koi pool, Jackson wasn't waiting for me. I guessed someone else needed him more than I did. It hurt a little.

I sat on the edge of the pool and looked up at Fiona's statue. For a moment it wasn't Pandora I saw but another weeping young woman with six bloodred stones on her outstretched hand. *Persephone*, I remembered. The lost child.

I felt the atmosphere change, shift, and I heard voices behind me. I turned to see an old woman walking toward me, holding a little girl's hand. I realized they were Fiona and my child mother.

"But she's so sad, Grandmama," the girl was saying. "Why didn't you pick someone happier?"

Fiona was remembering. "It had to be Pandora. The girl who let troubles loose in the world."

"I don't like stories that blame the girl. I don't like the one in the Bible either."

"I used to think that too, Annie. But then I thought, what if we should be grateful to Pandora and Eve instead of blaming them? What if they did exactly what God wanted them to do — to choose *choice* itself? To bring change and chance into an orderly world."

"But Mama always says to keep my things orderly. Isn't order a good thing?"

"It is when you create it for yourself. It is not such a good thing when someone tries to make it for you. Believe me, child, I know. Many people spent many years trying to make me live according to their ideas of order."

"But didn't Eve do a bad thing?" my mother persisted. "Didn't she make Original Sin?"

Fiona smiled. "So the ancient patriarchs would have us believe: Man could have lived in paradise but for the wickedness of Eve. And yet I think," she said, looking at Pandora, "that paradise is not a home you can be given — it is a destination you must reach by fighting for it." Then she looked in my direction, as if she knew I was there, listening. "By choosing and choosing yet again. Do you see?" she said.

I turned and fled up the metal stairs to the second floor. I did not see. I did not believe. I did not want to participate. And I did not, under any circumstances, want to be my crazy great-grandmother's Pandora.

CHAPTER SIXTEEN

I need to finish my conversation with Jackson.

I went to sleep thinking this, and woke up thinking this. I decided to find him.

I did my Hotter, Colder routine and could feel the warmth of him somewhere close by. I pulled on some outdoor clothes and went out to finish my search. My sense led me down the path to my grandmother's stables. I unlatched the door and went in.

It was dark inside — not the darkness of shadows, but of night. A lantern threw orange light against the whitewashed walls of the central corridor. I saw a man sitting on top of a horse, lolling drunkenly, while another, younger man tried to help him down, both laughing raucously. They wore clothes from another era, another century. The younger man's were finer, trimmed with gold braid and buttons in a military style.

The man in the saddle came down in a sodden lump, nearly carrying them both to the stone floor. "Steady as she goes," the younger man grunted, trying to balance the older on his feet.

The drunken man slid down the wall to sit sprawling on the straw spread over the stone. "Give it here," he said.

"Wait," the younger man said, opening a stall door.

The man on the floor waved an arm. "Give it —"

"I said wait!" the younger man ordered. "This animal performed well and deserves its rest." He led the horse into the stall and came out a moment later carrying the saddle and the bridle.

"Jes' wanted another drink," the older man said. "Didn't mean no offense."

The younger man handed him a flask. "What a lucky man Dobson is," he muttered, looking around enviously, "to have all this."

I could see his face clearly then. A beautiful face. Fine bones, a sensuous mouth, eyes both blue and dark.

"Deuced lucky," the man on the floor agreed.

"But deuced brilliant too, to do so well. They say of him that his ships always come through, even when all others are lost."

"Jus' lucky," the drunken man sneered. "He makes every decision on a coin toss."

"A coin toss?" the younger said, sitting beside the other. "Surely not."

"Swear to God," the other slurred. "He calls it . . . 's lucky coin. Always tells him true. And so it does."

"His lucky coin," the young man repeated thoughtfully, and smiled. And I thought irrationally: *What big teeth you have.*

A touch on my shoulder made me jump, but then I heard Jackson asking, "You all right, Sare?"

I looked up at him, squinting a bit in the sudden full daylight. "I'm fine."

"Echo?" he guessed.

I nodded, but did not elaborate.

"Come on back. I'm in here." He entered a stall and finished forking fresh hay across the floor. I stood at the siding and watched him work. "Can you grab a square of alfalfa?" he asked, gesturing behind me.

I turned to where he pointed, went and broke a few inches off the green bale I saw there, and handed it over the siding. He tossed it into the feed bin. "You do this every day?" I asked. "Even holidays?"

He smiled tolerantly. "I tried to persuade the horses to be more reasonable, but they still insist on getting hungry every day." He shrugged. "I don't do it three hundred and sixty-five days a year. Once the grass is up, they don't need it as often, and during the winter, if I can't come over, I have a buddy who'll come in and cover for me." He set his pitchfork outside the stall in the corridor, then opened the exterior door to lead the roan back inside. She moseyed over to the feed bin. He rubbed and patted her neck as he unclipped her lead. "I kind of like doing this today. Making the animals comfortable and warm. Feels Christmasy to me — Christ was born in a stable, you know?"

It was a very Jackson-ish kind of sentiment — practical, but sort of poetic too. I'd forgotten it was actually Christmas Eve. Somehow slipping through time made ordinary hours and days harder to keep track of. I took a moment to breathe in the smells, this other scent of Christmas. I noticed he was watching me again. "Look," I said, "can we talk some more about — the stuff we were talking about yesterday?"

"I kind of think we have to."

"I told you I see pieces of a different past — do you have an idea *why?*"

He leaned on the fork's long handle. "I figure, Sare, that someone did something in that other time that changed what happened — that made events turn out differently." He looked at me, waiting, but I didn't leap in. I was busy wrapping a stray piece of twine around a finger on my left hand. "You know who that was?"

"Maybe," I said.

"Maybe?" He seemed slightly amused. "If I had to guess, I'd say it was you. Was it?"

"I don't know," I answered a little defiantly. "Maybe. I suppose so. I woke up Maggie. She was supposed to die in a coma in that other past, but I found her in the mirror world and I woke her up."

"Whoa," he said, letting that sink in. "You remember a time in which Maggie died?"

"Just bits and pieces. Not real well." I felt I had to explain, to excuse myself. "I didn't *mean* to change things. I was just trying to save Sammy."

"Maybe," he offered gently, "you woke her up because she wasn't supposed to die."

That was oddly comforting. It meant I was just someone who had fixed a mistake, mended a broken piece.

"So," he continued, "you woke up Maggie, and the present that *used* to be isn't anymore. That's —" He paused, marveling. "Jesus," he said again. "You're kind of like a superhero, you know? Who does something like that?"

And that was oddly *dis*comforting. I didn't want to be a superhero. I liked being an accidental mistake fixer better. I went back to my finger wrapping. "Maybe," I said, "this kind of thing happens all the time, only we don't know it because we can't remember the other pasts." I clung to the thought that Fiona had been convinced that it had happened before, decades prior to Maggie's accident.

"But *you* do. Remember a different past."

"Like I said — just little pieces."

"Like I 'remember' little pieces of a different future."

"But how do you know it's a different future? Maybe it's this future, the one that's already coming."

He shook his head. "You can't get there from here."

"How do you know?" I said again.

"Well, for one thing," he said, and stopped, a trace of some kind of hesitancy in his voice. He started again, pushing forward, "For one thing, I'm not scarred in that future."

I had to bite my tongue from saying, *That's impossible.* Jackson saw a different future because it came from a different past. A past where he hadn't been burned in the accident that killed his parents. A past where, maybe, his family hadn't been in an accident at all.

I understood then why Jackson had seemed so reluctant to talk about this. It was because he wanted to get there. To get to a time where his parents didn't die and he hadn't been scarred and — life was better for him. Who could blame him? Who wouldn't want that?

But the other thing I understood, in the same instant — he thought I could make it happen for him. Because I'd done it once already.

It gave me a sick feeling inside. How could I tell him I couldn't — wouldn't — do that? I wished I could help him, but — I couldn't change time again. Not on purpose. In the first place, I didn't know *how* to do it, and in the second, what if I saved his parents but simultaneously made things worse for everyone else? "I have to go," I said abruptly, moving toward the door.

"Where are you going? Don't we have to talk about this?" He was hurt. I knew it, but I couldn't do anything about it.

"I can't talk about it, J. This is all just crazy. You think I can do it again — change time — but what I did was an *accident*. I don't know how to make that happen, and I wouldn't want to be responsible for it if I did. I don't even want to think about it."

"Sare," he said, stopping me with my hand already on the wooden door latch. "I know you have no reason to believe this, but this isn't the way the world is supposed to be."

I lifted the latch.

"Sarah," he said again. His voice held disbelief, but he was trying to keep it in. "You're the only one who can fix it."

I went out the door without answering.

The kitchen was deserted when I went inside. I was glad. There was a chill inside me I felt I would never be able to get rid of. I sat down on the bench by the fire, leaned back, closed my eyes, and let the heat soak through my skin.

How could I ever make Jackson understand? He just wanted his parents back. He thought I could make things better, but I was afraid that if there actually *was* a way for me to change time again, I could just as easily make things so much worse.

"May I offer you a cup of coffee?" A woman's voice, not one I knew.

The house again. I kept my eyes squeezed shut. *Go away*, I thought. *Leave me alone.*

"Thank you, missus," a man with a New English accent answered.

I groaned and opened my eyes.

The light had changed again — become the yellow ochre of an autumn dusk. Fiona set a cup and saucer on the table before a small man with an oversized mustache, dressed in a brown plaid jacket and trousers.

She poured him a full cup, then nudged a sugar pot and creamer closer to him as she sat. "Tell me," she said.

The man opened a notebook on the table and referred to it. "The name of the child's uncle was Josiah Burnes. A black seaman living in the township of Acushnet outside of New Bedford. He owned a small house there, up until the year 1877. The records show an Amber Burnes was enrolled in the local school from 1874 until 1876." The man handed Fiona a loose page from his notes. "Josiah Burnes is listed deceased, lost with all hands on the *Charles R. Morse* on January 14, 1877. His house was taken by the bank. Had a hard time tracking the girl after that."

Fiona nodded at him to continue. He smoothed the halves of his mustache, warming to his subject. "Spent considerable time combing the area, checking every orphanage, but most of 'em didn't take black children. Some places were long gone, so I was fearful the trail might have gone cold. Went as far as Providence, but they told me the child would have been kept in state. Finally found her again all the way up in Boston — Sisters of Charity school and orphanage. One Amber Burnes listed resident there until 1880."

"Poor child," Fiona murmured. "My grandmother never could learn what became of her. Better for Amber if the uncle had left her here."

"Don't know how she spent the next four years, but in 1884 she married one Peter Cooke, giving birth to two children in three years, Peter Nathan Jr. and Adella Maeve."

"Named for both of her mothers." She teared up slightly. "Go on," she said.

"Death certificate for Amber Cooke dated 1889, sepsis related to childbirth. Death certificate for Peter Cooke dated 1897, factory accident. The younger Peter was old enough to find employment and kept his sister with him until her marriage in 1904. Peter died childless in 1923. Located one Adella Cooke Martin in Stoughton, employed as a factory worker, mother of two: Addison and Lucy." He looked up at Fiona expectantly.

"You did well, Mr. Farnham, thank you. The daughter's name confirms your findings." Her voice was low, strained.

"You want to go forward with the trust for the grandchildren?" Fiona nodded. "You still wish to remain anonymous?" She nodded again. "I'll have the lawyer send the papers, then."

He rose to leave. She looked up at him, a puzzled look on her face. "And there was nothing else? Nothing strange? Nothing worthy of remark?"

He lifted his eyebrows. "No, missus. They seemed like very ordinary lives and deaths."

She nodded, looking down. "Poor child," she said. I saw two wet drops hit the table.

Then the swinging door to the hall opened and I lost the connection — Fiona vanished.

Sam stood in the doorway looking outraged. He held the Advent calendar, all its little windows gaping.

"This isn't right, Sarah," he said. "There aren't enough doors."

"Yes, Sam," I said. "You open the last door today, Christmas Eve, because tomorrow's the big day."

He was almost shouting. "Nope! It's not! You know, don't you? Tomorrow's not the big day!"

"Yeah, bud," I said, walking toward him, reaching to hug him up, "tomorrow's Christmas."

"That's not it!" he shouted and hurled the calendar to the floor. He dodged away from me and ran out the door.

When I turned back, Fiona was with me once more. She sat at the table, old and bent, pulled in on herself. "I'm sorry," she said.

A young black woman was seated across from her, posture rigid, her face frozen in bitterness. It was Rose, maybe thirty years younger.

Fiona continued. "It was I who asked him to come, asked him for help with Mark's illness. I thought giving him the land — I don't know what I thought. That Amber's only surviving grandchild was supposed to be here. That his being here would finally help things turn out right. That his being here was necessary for the ones to come." She was weeping and the words were coming out hard. "I should have known what would happen, I should never have brought him here. I'm sorry, Rose."

Rose spoke stiffly. "Wasn't your fault, Fiona, and we don't blame you. Addison wasn't the kind of man to back down or turn away. I knew they would stop him. I knew this day would come."

"He was strong man, a good man."

"He was grateful for what you'd done for him and his sister. The schooling. The chance you gave him to design that hospital wing. A black man, in this country. His workers were so proud."

Her chin trembled and a tear spilled down her cheek, but she kept her face set.

I thought, as she faded into the past again, that part of Rose had turned to stone that day. In that other time, life had wrapped my mother's heart in chilled fingers and turned part of her to stone. In this time, it had been Rose.

CHAPTER SEVENTEEN

The Hathaways' estate was Amber House's direct neighbor — the boundary marked by a twisting rivulet that bent and coiled down a cleft between the properties — but nevertheless, we drove to dinner. The distance in crow-flight terms was less than a quarter mile, but evidently the inhabitants of the two estates had never been friendly enough to install a gate between them.

The house was a three-story redbrick Georgian trimmed in black, with a columned entry and stretches of balconied porch along its two-story, mirror-image wings. It was all very symmetrical and correct-looking, unlike the silhouette of Amber House, and every window in the main house glowed golden in the darkness, a lit candle centered in the bottom of each.

"Be good, kiddo," Mom reminded Sammy. "Remember what I told you about eating what's on your plate. And always say —"

"Please and thank you," Sammy recited dutifully. "Tell Sarah too."

Mom was clutching a bottle of wine with a wax seal. My gramma hadn't been a big drinker, but she owned a somewhat legendary collection of wines. Dad handed me the gift-wrapped package for Claire that Mom and I had bought in Annapolis. Sammy was assigned to carry the family gift — chocolates imported from a province of New England that was now home to significant numbers of the last century's Swiss immigrants. Dad brought up the rear with the small package for Robert and my large one for Richard.

I wished I were in more of a holiday mood. Instead I felt wound impossibly tight by all the demands tugging at me. As I picked my way across the herringbone pattern of the Hathaways' brick walk and up the porch steps, I concentrated on relaxing the muscles in my face so that the smile I fixed there would not look maniacal. I hoped it was working.

Robert ushered us in. "Welcome, welcome," he was saying.

Claire stood in the entry, her slender frame poured into the sleek lines of a pair of black wool pants with matching tuxedo jacket, a loosely knotted black silk tie dangling above the plunging neckline of a white blouse. I gritted my teeth in envy.

Like Claire, the house mixed classic lines with modern, underplayed drama. The furniture was all antique, and vaguely European, in impeccable, never-been-touched condition. Lots of dark wood. The backdrop for all this polished perfection, the space itself, was *crisp* in a way that Amber House wasn't — recessed lighting, a palette of pale gray and faint beige and soft white.

"I love what you've done with the place," Mom announced.

"We remodeled just last year," Robert said. "Claire knocked some walls down, lightened things up a bit."

"Didn't knock down *too* many walls," Claire said. "But Father did some ghastly stuff to the place back in the sixties. I tried to *revise* the revisions, really."

"It's very subtle," my mother said.

The four adults gravitated to the sideboard, where a nice bottle of wine was already breathing. Glasses were poured and clinked together. "To the success of the exhibit," I heard Robert say.

"To the success of the purpose *behind* the exhibit," my father amended.

Richard gestured for Sammy and me to follow him to the large color-coordinated Christmas tree in the living room. He crouched down and found a small green package that he handed to my brother. When I nodded permission, Sam tore the paper off, revealing a small wooden box.

"Wow, Richard," Sam said, "I love it!"

Richard laughed. "No, bud," he said, using the pet name I always used, "you have to open the box."

Inside, nestled in tissue, was a perfect little black horse made of cow hide, fully fitted with leather riding gear.

"*Wow*," Sam said.

"This was the first old thing I ever owned, Sam. My mom gave it to me when I was your age. I wanted you to have it now. It's *almost* as old as Amber House, give or take a century, so you have to be *gentle* with it."

Sammy took it out of the box as if it were made of glass. "I can be gentle, Richard."

"It's not really to play with, just to put on a shelf to look at, but I hope you like it anyway."

"I *love* it," Sam insisted. Then he looked stricken. "But I didn't get anything for you."

"Yes, you did, Sammy," I intervened. "Are you forgetting?"

Sam looked confused. "Maybe."

"You go get that really *heavy* package you helped me wrap." I pointed helpfully. "The red one."

Obediently, Sam trotted toward the side table near the front door. He popped back a minute later, straining under his burden.

"Goodness," Richard said. "What's in it, Sam?"

Sam shrugged his shoulders. "We can unwrap it and find out."

"What Sam means," I said, "is, just open it."

"Yes!" Sam said. "Open it!" He plopped it heavily in Richard's lap, and Richard let Sam help him unwrap it. It was a complete illustrated history of sailing — about fifteen pounds' worth.

Richard started to flip back the cover, but I shot out my hand. "Give it here first." He passed the book over. "Got a pen?" I said. He handed me one from a side-table drawer. I opened the flap and added another five words to the message I'd already written on the flyleaf. I capped the pen and handed the book back.

He reopened it and read aloud, " 'For the guy with the second-prettiest sloop on the river, Merry Christmas, from Sarah. . . . And her first mate, Sammy.' " He looked up and smiled. "I have to admit: eighty years old, handcrafted by a sailor — your *Liquid Amber* is hard to beat for beauty. Now, if we were talking *speed* —"

"Is that a challenge, Hathaway?"

"I believe it is, Parsons," he said. I was grinning at him and he was grinning at me.

Sammy stepped in between us. "Now," he said, "where's Sarah's present?"

I sighed and shook my head.

Richard reached into his jacket pocket and pulled out a small package. "Got it right here, Sam. Shall I give it to her?"

I let Sam pull off the paper, but I flipped open the velvet-covered box myself. It held a little Victorian snowflake necklace, worked in silver and hung from a black velvet ribbon. On its back, an etched quote: *Not a snowflake escapes His fashioning hand.*

"Wow," I said, echoing Sammy. "Thank you." Richard gave me one of his patented just slightly crooked smiles.

"Put it on!" Sammy urged. I swept my hair off to one side and awkwardly tried to tie the ribbon myself.

"May I help?" Richard asked. I wondered, strangely, why it felt familiar to have him standing behind me, his fingers lightly brushing my neck. And I could not shake the thought I should be wearing a gold leaf.

⚜

Mrs. Hathaway came in to tell us, "Time for dinner." She smiled when she saw I was wearing Richard's gift and reached a languid hand to touch it. "That's a pretty little thing, isn't it? Delicate, like you."

Claire called it just a "family meal," but two maids in matching long-sleeved dresses brought the courses out on silver trays. Round after round, they circled the table soundlessly, holding the trays as each of us served ourselves. First an appetizer, then a salad, and finally roast beef and caramelized potatoes.

Just before dessert, I realized I'd been watching Claire Hathaway for most of the meal. The way she held her knife. The way she chewed her food. The way she tossed her head when she laughed. It all reminded me of my mother.

Richard seemed to notice my staring. He said with a low voice, "They move a lot alike, don't they?"

"Yes."

"Your mom was three years ahead of mine in high school and then again at Notre Dame College. Freshman-senior awe, I'm thinking."

After dinner, Robert asked my parents to his study to show them the draft of a press release on the exhibit. Richard pulled Sam to a telescope to look at the "man in the moon" through a break in the clouds. I was following after them when Claire called to me. "I want to introduce you to someone, Sarah," she said.

I trailed Claire to the living room, wondering if another guest had just arrived.

Claire gestured to a pair of mirror-image portraits mounted above the mantel. The man was dark and angular, with a pair of old-fashioned muttonchop whiskers. The woman was fair and fragile-looking, dressed in pink silk. A husband and wife, I guessed. "Relatives?" I asked.

"My ancestors. Gerald Fitzgerald, and his wife, Camilla. Portraits painted three years after her presentation at the Royal

Court." Claire walked over to stand before them. She and the woman shared the same blond beauty — marble planes set with sky blue eyes and a full mouth.

"She's beautiful," I said.

"She resembled her father. There was a portrait of him too — he was invited to sit for a famous painter, in honor of his loyalty to the Crown during the 1776 uprising."

"What happened to it?"

"Some of us are not so lucky as you, my dear. Our pasts are scattered, like ice in a river. These" — she gestured to the mantel with a long white hand — "are all I have."

She touched the pink satin shoe of Mrs. Fitzgerald. "Her mother, Lydia Crawley, was an heiress, English, titled. But Lydia eloped with a naval officer of no standing, and was disowned. The couple fled to the Colonies. Lydia's husband tried to restore his beloved wife to her life of privilege through a bold gamble, but his ship was seized, and it took more than a year for him to return to Maryland.

"When he returned, he was told Lydia had died in childbirth, and their daughter, Camilla, had been sent to a pauper's orphanage. It was amazing the girl was still alive when her father finally found her."

"What happened to them?" I asked.

"He learned the waters of the Chesapeake and the Atlantic seaboard, and rose to the rank of captain. And one day he was approached by a man — Thaddeus Dobson — who needed a partner. Someone clever enough to smuggle cargo from Africa to the Americas."

"Cargo?"

"The two things of greatest value stolen from the dark continent: people and diamonds."

"He was a slaver," I blurted.

"Indeed. So he made his fortune. Eventually, he married his

partner's daughter, although by then Dobson had died. Her name was —" She smiled at me. "Can't you guess?"

I could. "Deirdre." Who married Captain Foster, and bore him two more children — the twins, Sarah-Louise and Matthew.

Claire nodded. "You and Richard are cousins," she said.

"About a hundred times removed." Richard had snuck up behind me. "Does this mean I get to call you coz?"

"If you start counting cousins that far removed, I expect you could call half the Confederation 'coz.'" I turned back to Claire. "How did you find all this out?"

She led me to a glassed-in display case set before a window. "Captains keep meticulous logs, you know. Joseph Foster chronicled his entire life, whether on sea or on land. All in notebooks identical to that one." I saw a leather-bound volume, its pages tipped in faded gold. Beside the notebook lay an ancient pistol.

"The gun also belonged to Captain Foster," Claire said. "An unusual piece because of its double-barrel. It was the first gun Camilla ever owned, and was the start of her interest in weapons. But even though she became a famous marksman, she never fired this gun. She preserved it just as the Captain left it, with one shot still loaded. It has been sealed in this case for two hundred and fifty years." She smiled. "Did you know it will also be a part of the exhibit? Because, after all, Camilla was once a part of Amber House too."

The gun was a work of amazing elegance — golden-red wood inlaid with etched silver, all of it done in curving sinuous lines except for a single darker silver circle set into the sloping rounded handgrip. I stared at the circle, unable to quite make sense of its crevasses of tarnish, until they suddenly resolved into a face embossed in the metal.

"You've noticed the coin?" Claire said.

"It's an ancient cheat," Richard said, "a two-headed coin."

"I hardly think it was a cheat," Claire said. "It was the Captain's good luck piece."

"Very good luck," Richard said. "He lived and the other guy died."

"How do you know it has two heads?"

Claire smiled. "I peeked." She tipped her head, appeared puzzled. "Is something wrong?" she asked, touching the back of my wrist. "You have gooseflesh. Someone's walking on your grave."

Yes, I realized, something *was* wrong, but I couldn't identify what it was. I was missing something here — something I should know. I wondered who the gun had killed.

I could feel Claire still watching me curiously, but then my parents entered the room with Robert following behind them. Claire shifted her attention to them. "Are we meeting you at St. John's for Midnight Mass?"

Her innocuous question proved to be one irritant too many. Once again my future was being planned for me without my input when I'd had something else — something *important* — I'd wanted to do. "Wait," I said, and instantly wished I hadn't. All eyes turned toward me.

Claire purred helpfully, "What is it, dear?"

"Um," I said. "There's this — service tonight in Severna. . . ." I trailed off. "Well, you know how you guys are always talking about the theme of the Amber House exhibit —"

"Yes?" my father prodded.

"I thought maybe we all ought to go by the Good Shepherd Church tonight instead of St. John's. They're having a kind of Christmas remembrance for some of the people who led the black equality movement around here."

"Sarah," my mother said, "perhaps you ought to run those kinds of ideas past me before you —"

The senator cut her off. "I think that's a wonderful idea, Sarah." And Richard agreed, smiling, approval in his eyes.

A half hour later, we all climbed the gray steps of the little clapboard church.

There was something of a stir when we walked in. Seemed like everyone in the church turned around to stare. Jackson turned around too, and noticed me standing close to Richard.

I could see the question on his face, and I almost shook my head no to answer it, but just then Helen tugged his arm so she could whisper something in his ear. I found myself tucking my hand into Richard's arm. Which made Richard turn toward me and smile. I stood there, trying hard to listen, while meditating on how many emotions one person could feel almost simultaneously: jealousy, gratitude, awkwardness, guilt, amusement, and embarrassment. And I was probably missing a few.

The evening's guest speaker had risen to the pulpit. "Diane Nash," Richard said with surprise and respect. Everyone knew Miss Nash, who had labored bravely and tirelessly for the cause of civil rights since the 1970s. Astorian schoolbooks devoted a few pages to her life and work.

She was a small woman, in her mid-sixties. A photo near her on the stage showed her as she had been when she'd begun her life of activism — slim, fine-boned, with large solemn eyes. Her voice was deep for a woman, and smooth, strong. I stopped thinking about Jackson or Richard, caught, finally, by the power of this woman's words.

Near the end of her speech, her eyes sought and found Jackson, "Addison Valois was, like me, from New England, but deeply committed to his adopted country and to the cause of bringing change." I realized she was talking about Jackson's grandfather. "When I learned of his death, I almost quit the fight. But I knew that the only way to honor his memory, the memory of all the martyrs to our cause, was to continue to fight to bring change.

"Change is a strange thing," she said with a small sorrowful smile. "It demands a price, sometimes in blood, and you may not even realize that it's begun until you're halfway deep into it. It takes courage, but not the courage of leading the charge. Just the quiet everyday courage of taking the next step, and then the next, even though you're afraid, even though you want to quit. Seeing it through to the end. We're still fighting, all of us, to reach that end, still taking those next steps. As long as we keep moving, we are not defeated, and we must, finally, inexorably, inevitably, prevail."

The applause was thunderous, as much for the person as for her words. A quietly courageous individual. I wished I could be more like her.

When the service ended, the senator was mobbed, as usual. My folks and I slipped out. Sam was asleep on Dad's shoulder. I wished I was still little enough to be hanging there safe and limp in Sam's place. It felt like months since we'd moved in. Years. I was exhausted.

She — I — heard Papa talking to a man with a pleasant baritone voice. I walked near to the library door to listen. The man was asking Papa for a position on a ship. I pushed the door farther open to see.

He was very handsome, with vivid blue eyes and full lips. He stared at me, startled by my entrance.

"My daughter," Papa said.

"Forgive me for staring," he said with a little bow in my direction. He explained to Papa. "She is so like unto my late wife, except raven-haired, where my Lyddie was flaxen." He turned to me again. "She was a great beauty."

My cheeks warmed at the compliment.

He spoke again to Papa. "As to the matter of the position?"

Papa smiled genially. "Your own ship lost to the Crown for smuggling? You must see where that might make me question the wisdom of turning one of my own over to your captaincy."

The man nodded stiffly and gathered his hat and gloves to go. But Papa fished into his watch pocket and produced his lucky coin, holding it up for the man to see. "Will you bring me better luck than you found for yourself? Shall we submit the question to the judgment of chance?"

Papa flipped the shining coin into the air, where it seemed to hang, spinning, before it dropped. The man shot out a hand and caught it before Papa could. Then he chuckled nervously, as if to apologize for his impertinence. "Reflex," he said. He made a show of slapping it onto the back of his hand, but I saw his fingers twitch as he did so.

He lifted his hand off the coin. I could see the coin's happy young face, not the old grieving one, staring up from the man's tanned skin.

My father said, "Fortune smiles — you have your ship, Captain Foster." Then he picked the coin off the man's hand and returned it to his pocket.

I wondered if I ought to tell Papa that the handsome man had secretly reversed the coin before he revealed it. I wondered if I wanted to.

I sat up in the darkness, reconstructing the pieces of my dream, knowing there was something there I needed to see, to understand. The old face and the young one, alternating dizzyingly on the spinning coin.

"Janus," I said.

CHAPTER EIGHTEEN

"Get up, get up, get up," my brother trilled far too early the next morning, Christmas Day. "I already woke up Mommy and Daddy and Maggie, and you're the only one left. Get up!" He hurled himself up on my bed and found an arm to tug on.

I lay there a minute trying to recover some notion I'd had in the middle of the night, but it refused to surface. I finally decided that I probably should get up.

Sam paced outside the bathroom door until I reappeared with clean teeth and combed hair. Then he pulled me along by two gripped fingers. "Hur-ry UP! There are so many PRESENTS!"

I dragged my feet the whole way. I'd decided long ago it was part of an older sister's job to torture her younger brother a little bit on Christmas.

The tree in the parlor had a wide apron of ribboned gifts around it. My parents always tried to tread the line between "magical" and "overindulgent" in their gift giving, but they tended to err on the overindulgent side. Sammy tore through a mountain of carefully wrapped packages — a herd of resin dinosaurs, puzzles, a model railroad, and construction blocks. For me, there was an antique cameo, a camera, a signed first edition of my favorite book, a foldout case filled with cosmetics imported from New York, and a gift certificate for the department store in Baltimore.

We did family gifts after Saint Nick's. Sammy was excited to watch me open mine from Maggie and him.

"Maggie's first," he directed. Still mindful of my duty to torture, I carefully untied the organdy ribbon and worked up the tape, until I heard him growling a hurry-up noise. I smiled and opened the box.

"So beautiful," I gasped. It was a vintage black *peau de soie* evening bag.

"Your grandmother gave that to me when I was sixteen," Maggie said with a shy smile. "I hope you like it."

I gave her a big hug. "It's gorgeous, Maggie. Thank you!"

"Now mine," Sam said, handing me a large box. "Faster."

Grinning, I unwrapped it to find a half-dozen smaller wrapped gifts inside. The little compass from the Advent calendar. A cigarette lighter. A simple can opener. A brass token for the New York City subway. A pack of chewing gum. I noticed after I had unwrapped a few that Sam was tucking each item inside the black purse. "Oh, no, Sam," I said, glancing apologetically at Maggie and reaching for the bag, "those don't go in there."

He swung his arms to one side, keeping the bag away. "Yes," he said firmly. "They do."

I looked again at Maggie and she was nodding her head. So I let him be. I unwrapped the last item — a pen-sized flashlight — and passed it to him.

"You're welcome," he reminded me.

"Thank you, Sam," I said, catching him and giving him a backward bear hug. "What a great bunch of stuff!"

He beamed. "Yes!" he said. "They're, um, what was that word she said again?"

I looked at him quizzically. "I'm not sure, bud. Who?"

"I 'member," he said. "*Needful*."

It prickled in my mind. *An echo.* I shoved it to one side. I did not want to be thinking about that this morning. "So, did you end up having a good Christmas, Sam?"

"It was great!" he said, with a little jump.

"Well, see?" I said indulgently. "I told you today was the big day."

"Nope," he said. He stared intently at his fingers as he put up one after another. He finally turned to me, holding out both hands, three raised fingers on one and four on the other. "It's in this many days."

I did the calculation. "That's — New Year's, Sammy."

"That's right!" he said. "I *knew* you knew." He nodded enthusiastically. "It's new years!"

Mom, Dad, and Maggie went in to rustle up our brunch while Sam and I bagged torn wrapping paper. When we were done, there was only one small present left under the tree. Sam picked it up and shook it. "What's this, Sarah?"

I pried it from his fingers. "It's a present for someone else, Sam. Stop shaking it."

"Who?"

I felt embarrassed. "It's for Jackson," I said.

"How come you didn't give it to him yet?"

"Well, Sam," I tried to explain, "I'm not sure he got me anything." *Probably didn't get me anything*, I thought to myself, since he'd most likely sunk all his spare change into some nice thing to hang around Helen's neck. Like a snowflake, maybe.

"That's silly, Sarah. He doesn't have to give you something back. Christmas isn't about trading."

I nodded. "You're right, Sam." I tucked it in the pocket of my robe. "I'll give it to him later." Hard to explain to a six-year-old that it wasn't about trading, but about embarrassment. Jackson's and mine.

At brunch, I had a helping of everything on the table: eggs, sausage, bacon, hash browns, corn bread, blueberry muffins, and orange juice. I had just hauled my stuffed self to my feet to help with cleanup when the phone rang. "I'll get it," I said. Maybe a touch too fast.

Richard was on the other end of the line.

"Merry Christmas, coz."

"Merry Christmas, Hathaway."

"Sorry to disturb your holiday, but would it be all right to cash in on that rain check you gave me? Come with me on a little trip tomorrow? I have to go down to Richmond, actually. Pick up some video film for my dad. I could sure use some company."

I felt reluctant and I didn't know why. This guy actually seemed to *like* me. And it wasn't like I was attached to some-one else.

He heard my hesitation. It hurt his feelings. "Look, I know it's pretty far away and this is the last second and all." He was mak-ing excuses for me — it was just so nice of him.

"Pardon me, Hathaway. You don't get to retract the invitation before I even finish asking my mom if I can go."

"Oh," he said, sounding happier.

"And I can," I said, making that executive decision for myself.

"Great," he said, restored to his normal level of utter confidence.

I adopted an exaggerated tone of resignation in response. "A debt is a debt," I sighed. "Your rain check to cash." I had the sense that girls didn't tease Richard Hathaway anywhere *near* enough.

And perhaps I was right, because I could hear him grinning through the phone. "You're a stand-up guy, Parsons. Ten o'clock sharp."

I felt reckless as I hung up. I'd just committed to an all-day road trip without a by-your-leave from either parent. I didn't know what had possessed me. But it would get me out of Amber House for a day, and I was thinking I needed a little break from Amber House. Maybe some sightseeing, a nice lunch.

I pushed open the swinging door to the kitchen. Three adult faces turned toward me with expectant looks. Waiting, I guessed, for some account of who I'd been talking to. And I just didn't want to share.

"Hey, I just remembered something I have to do that will take about a half hour. I'll be back," I ended, turning immediately and letting the door swing shut behind me.

I ran up the stairs, my hand on the package in my pocket. Sam was right. Christmas was about giving, and this was Jackson. My oldest friend. I shrugged mentally. I could give my oldest friend a present if I felt like it. It was allowed. Even if he did have a girlfriend.

I threw on a sweater, some dungarees, and a pair of boots, anxious to complete my escape. I grabbed my coat and gloves and paused on the compass rose to decide my direction.

It made me happy that I could still find Jackson using Hotter, Colder. Even though Jackson had moved on, he couldn't unilaterally break my connection to him. I could still call up my image of him, still sense his warmth. And the warmth was telling me that right then he was where he was supposed to be: at home, with his grandmother.

I took the path on the bluff that led to Rose and Jackson's little house by the river. I made my way carefully — the slush of snow on the ground beneath the trees made the footing dangerous. There were places where the trail came right to the lip of the cliff that dropped down to the river. I had always been afraid of those spots.

Rose's small, tidy home was, in its own way, as full of history as Amber House. Its front rooms were nearly two hundred years old. Its squared-off logs were gray with time and chinked with more modern sealers than mud, but spoke of the care with which the house had been built in that long-ago time.

I knocked on the wood-plank front door and heard Jackson yell, "Come in."

The "Merry Christmas" on my lips died half uttered. The house was quiet and dark — the only hint of holiday was a tiny tree set on a table, hastily decorated. Jackson came out of the kitchen, carrying a tray with a bowl of soup and a bottle of prescription medication. He headed to the rear of the house without stopping. "Give me a few minutes," he said.

I sat at the table and waited, realizing I should not have intruded this way. I was just making up my mind to leave when Jackson emerged. "What are you doing here?" he asked.

What *was* I doing there? "I'm catching you at a bad time," I apologized, standing up to go.

"No," he said, shaking his head and pulling out a chair to sit. "I'm sorry. That came out really — unwelcoming. It's just that Gran is worse than usual today. I gave her some painkillers. She'll sleep for a couple hours."

I sat back down. " 'Worse than usual'? What's wrong?"

"Gran didn't tell you guys?"

"She didn't tell me. I don't know if she told my parents. They never tell me anything."

He smiled. "That's because they know you can't keep a secret."

"I can keep a secret," I said, indignant.

He shook his head, still smiling. "You never have and you never will. It's just not in your skill set. Sooner or later the truth always comes spilling out of you."

Is that why you stopped telling me things?

"Gran was always a big smoker," he said. "Even though she knew it was stupid. She has cancer."

"Oh, my God. I'm sorry," I said, not knowing anything else to offer.

A memory from the other time welled up in me. That Rose hadn't had cancer. She hadn't been Gramma's housekeeper either. She'd . . . I struggled to remember. She'd been a nurse at — Johns Hopkins.

Why? I wondered. I felt confused. Why would my saving Maggie have changed things for Rose? And changed them for the worse?

"Don't say anything to your folks. I don't think Gran wanted them to know." He stood. "I'll walk you back," Jackson said. An invitation to leave, but at least it was a nice invitation.

Jackson went ahead of me up the narrow path, turning at times to make sure I was keeping clear of trouble spots. I had to work to keep up with his long strides. The present in my pocket was weighing heavier with every step. What if Jackson misunderstood? It really was too expensive a gift between friends. I didn't know what I'd been thinking. I should have listened to my mother.

I raised the subject of Helen, lightly, to show him I knew and it didn't matter. "How long have you and Helen . . ." I trailed off. *Stupid.* Started again. ". . . have you and Helen been — part of the movement?"

He turned and held out a hand to help me up a large rock step, then pulled me up level with him. He was watching me. He seemed amused.

"I've been going to meetings since I was fourteen. Helen's only been coming a few months."

"Oh," I said. Letting go of his hand. Taking the lead. "She seems very nice."

"She is," he said. "Very gutsy too. She's organizing opposition to the government's policy of Asian deportation."

"Wow," I said, wondering why he still seemed amused.

We walked clear of the woods, coming out on the grassy bluff to the west of Amber House. As we neared the fenced-in graveyard holding generations of my family, Jackson turned aside to open the iron gate. "Let's sit a minute and you can tell me why you came by."

I busied myself brushing the snow off the bench just inside the gate, stalling. I arranged my gloves on the seat to keep my rear end off its cold stones. I tucked my hands into the opposite sleeves of my coat, like a muff. Then I finally looked up. He was waiting, his eyes on my face.

"Why are you always doing that?" I said. "Why are you always watching me?"

"I want to know what you're thinking."

"Is it written there? Plain as day?"

"Pretty much," he said, hiding a smile.

"Lord," I said, embarrassed. "I'm like a five-year-old. Can't hide a thing."

"Not 'can't,' Sare. You just don't. I think it's really brave. I wish I was more like that."

"Yeah?" I said, turning a little pink. Pleased.

"Yeah," he said. "So, now tell me, Miss Forthright, why the Christmas visit?"

I laughed. He'd trapped me into coming clean. I shook my head a little. "Well, two things, really. The first is to say I'm sorry for running out on you like that yesterday —"

He stopped me before I got any further. "I get it, Sare. I understand. You don't think it's right to play God. Forget it."

"Yeah?"

"Yeah."

I doubted either one of us would forget it, but at least we could put it aside. "Second, I wanted to give you your Christmas present, only —"

He lifted his eyebrows.

"It's a kind of crazy gift, but I saw it and —" I pulled the box from my pocket and handed it over. "I don't know why, it had your name on it."

He untied the bow, pulled off the paper, and opened the box.

I rushed on to explain, "Sammy got you that really great old thing —"

"The stethoscope."

"Right," I said, "and I thought this was something else a doctor might need —"

"A really great old pocket watch to go with it."

"Exactly," I said. "You know, to keep track of your appointments and everything."

He smiled. "It's perfect, Sare," he said, easily, lightly. "I love it. Thank you."

There. He loved it. Why had I thought that was going to be such a problem? He twisted the little knob, winding it, and pushed back his sweatshirt hood to hold it to his ear.

I saw the neat row of thread Xs my father had put in his forehead.

"Oh, my God," I gasped. "I remember what I wanted to tell you."

"What?"

My dream. The young blond man. The spinning coin.

"That word you wrote on the hearth, when you bumped your head —"

"I wrote something?"

I nodded. "Janus."

"The Roman god?"

"That's right," I said. "And I found it. The thing connected to Janus."

I wasn't prepared for the blaze of hope I saw in his eyes. "What is it?" he said.

"It's a coin. A really old coin. Not Amber House old. Like ancient. It has two faces on it, one young and one old, although I've only seen the young one —"

"*Where* did you see it?"

"Well, I saw it in a dream. An echo dream last night. According to that, it used to belong to an ancestor of mine named Captain Foster, and to his wife's father before that. They both thought it was lucky. But I also saw it in real life. Yesterday. At the Hathaways'."

He stood up, his face excited, intense. He walked away from me, deeper into the graveyard. He was holding his head. He turned back, pressing one side of his nose with his sleeve. "We have to get it," he said.

"Why? Why is it important?"

"It's the key," he said. "That's why I saw it, in my vision."

"The key to what?"

"To changing time again."

CHAPTER NINETEEN

No.

I realized I was shaking my head. *No.*

He'd said *forget it*, but of course he hadn't meant it. And I understood. Honestly, I did. He wanted to save his parents. If your friend has the superhero power of changing time, why shouldn't she do that for you? I'd want him to do it for me.

But the very thought made my insides shriek with anxiety. *I don't know how. And what if I screw things up?*

"Look," Jackson said, "I'm sorry I won't let it drop, but if you knew what I know, if you'd seen what I've seen —"

"I haven't," I interrupted. I tried to calm down, to explain myself again. "I told you, I don't even know how that — time-changing thing — happened before. I can't just *make* it happen because I want to. Plus, and maybe more important, I have nightmares about my great-grandmother saying something went terribly wrong. She spent her whole life trying to track down someone who changed *her* time. Some little girl who made everything go wrong for her. What if I tried to change time and just made everything worse?"

"Saving my parents is going to make everything *worse?*"

"You change one little thing in the past, and the whole world could end up changed."

"Did saving Maggie make the world worse?"

"I don't know. I didn't set out to save Maggie. It just *happened*. And I don't know what else I did. I don't know what price we *all* paid for that. You don't know either."

"Sarah, the future I see is *better* than this," he said softly. "What if this is your chance to make everything better?"

I was still shaking my head. I felt my cheeks getting wet. I wanted to help him — I really did. Jackson was — I shied away from putting a word there. Important. He was important to me. He looked so bewildered and disbelieving. I couldn't bear it. I stood abruptly, "I'm sorry. I have to go."

I started running, out of the gate and down the path home, and didn't slow down until I hit the spiral stairs in the conservatory. Behind me, Pandora wept into the pool. I understood her tears. I hid in my room until mine stopped.

When I went down to the kitchen, my parents were standing shoulder to shoulder at the kitchen sink. Talking, laughing, preparing our Christmas feast. Christmas was another one of those holidays when it seemed necessary to fix a small mountain of food — not as bad as New England's Thanksgiving Day, but pretty close. We always had goose with mashed potatoes and all the trimmings, finished with a choice of three desserts.

I watched my mother deadpan a joke that made my father laugh out loud. And thought about Jackson sharing Christmas with his dying grandmother in a darkened house.

A lump began to form in my throat, so I forcibly pushed the thought from my mind. I would think about it later.

My mother had noticed my arrival. She said, "Richard called while you were out." She raised one slender eyebrow. "He asked me to tell you he wants to leave a half hour later."

Oh.

She went on, "In the future, please remember that you are not allowed to plan cross-country trips without consulting us first. You're not quite an adult yet."

Maybe not an adult, I thought, *but sixteen* is *old enough to plan a day trip*. I sighed. I wondered if Sarah One had had this kind of overprotective mother.

"That being said," my mother added with a smile, "how exciting is this?"

I found it hard to believe my mother would be this starry-eyed about Richard Hathaway asking me to accompany him to Richmond. "What's so exciting about it?"

"Richard told you why he is making the trip, didn't he?" my father asked incredulously.

I shrugged a little. "To pick something up?"

My father looked at me disbelievingly. "President Stevenson called and told Robert he would give him a taped endorsement to play the night Robert announces his candidacy."

"That's — great?" I said.

"Sarah, honey," Dad said patiently, "you evidently don't *get* how important this is. Unprecedented, really. Stevenson is so well loved in the ACS that he has held the office of the presidency your entire life. And now he *is crossing party lines*" — I swore Dad said this with italics — "to endorse Robert as his successor. It's unheard-of! That kind of thing just doesn't happen! This will make Robert a shoo-in! *Every*body is going to take his message seriously."

"Why is Stevenson doing that? Backing Richard's dad instead of his party's guy?"

"Because Stevenson understands how important it is, now more than ever, to pull together the UOA. He knows it will take a man like Robert — someone with a reasoned and liberal attitude toward race relations — to build up stronger alliances."

"The UOA?"

"The Union of the Americas."

"They said something about that the other day, at Jackson's church. That the Nazis were going to try something to sabotage the Unification movement."

"Who said that?" my father asked.

I shook my head, trying to remember. "Some New English man. A rabbi. He said he'd been told by Jewish —" I searched for the word.

"Jewish Intelligence," my dad finished for me. "They know more about the Germans than anyone else. Did he say what the Nazis were going to do?"

"He didn't say anything specific. Something about being prepared for a lot of civilian casualties." I felt stupid. I should have taken notes. And maybe should have mentioned it to my parents a little sooner?

"You think —?" Mom was concerned. "Should we tell Robert?"

My father shook his head. "If Pastor Howe knows, I'm sure Robert's also been informed."

"Why would the Germans want to do something like that?" I asked.

"Tom," my mother interrupted, giving Dad a pointed look, "we don't need to be too — graphic."

"You said yourself only a minute ago, she's almost an adult. She still can't do much to change things, but she should understand." My father put his hand on my shoulder. "You know that the Reich has had more than sixty years to solidify its hold on Europe and North Africa."

"So?"

"And the Japanese Empire has done the same in the Pacific. They took Australia almost thirty years ago now."

"I passed world history."

"Well, sweetie, who do you think is next on their agenda?"

To tell the truth, I hadn't thought about them having an agenda. Didn't they already have what they wanted? It hadn't occurred to me they thought they needed more.

"The time has come to strengthen our position globally by uniting in common cause with the other American countries —

North and South. We've got to make these aggressive regimes think twice before taking us all on."

That was a lot of information I hadn't considered before. And it didn't sound good. "Does Richard know all this?"

"I'm guessing he's probably better informed than your typical seventeen-year-old. Anyway, honey, now maybe you can understand a little more why we thought it was so important to come back to Amber House and do what we could to help get Robert elected."

Mom kind of slipped in between me and Dad then. "Enough about politics!" she said cheerily. "And no talk of this at the dinner table in front of Sammy. Some things are too scary for a little guy, especially this one —"

Who doesn't think about the world the way most kids do, I finished mentally.

My dad pulled open one of the ovens. "Goose is about done," he reported. "Be on the table in about ten minutes. Can you round up Maggie and Sammy?" he asked me.

"Sure."

My mother linked her arm through mine. "You're going to have fun in Richmond with Richard. Do you have any idea what you're going to wear?"

I mentally rolled my eyes. Yes, of course I did. I nodded and pushed out the swinging door to the hall.

The way my parents thought about Robert Hathaway, I could understand why they'd seemed to be pairing me up with his son. They looked at Richard and saw an important man in the making. But, Lord, I wished my mother would stop pushing.

Cleanup from dinner was an hour-long ordeal, but when it was done, I was glad to put Christmas behind me. Seemed like it had been going on forever. I felt so much *older* than I had only a week before.

Up in the Flowered Room, I fussed over the clothes I would wear to the city in the morning. Something that would travel well — three hours in the car at least — but would look grown up and ladylike.

I noticed I had left the little dollhouse partially open. I pulled the front back and picked up my old pieces of poem.

If you have the chance to Choose it all again —

It was like a snake had bitten me. I threw the scraps in the trash.

A familiar tap sounded on the window. Jackson was out there, standing in the cold, his breath puffing little clouds.

For the first time I could ever remember, I was reluctant to go meet him. I was afraid he would begin again with the subject I wanted very much to avoid thinking about. But I nodded and pointed toward the conservatory.

He was waiting for me by the statue, sitting on the edge of the pool. "This time I came to tell you *I'm* sorry," he started. "I shouldn't have pushed at you that way. You can't see what I see, so you couldn't possibly want to change things as much as I do."

"What do you see?" I asked.

He shook his head. He wasn't ready to tell me. He reached into his pocket and held something out for me. "I also owe you a Christmas present, I believe."

"I don't think *owe* is the operative word," I said. He dropped a little bow-tied box onto my palm.

It held a military medal. A British medal of valor.

"It was my dad's," he said. "He fought for the last colony against the Japanese. They gave it to him for charging a machine-gun nest when his platoon got pinned down outside of Melbourne. He took a bullet, but he cleared the nest. Whenever I've felt too discouraged to go on, I say those words to myself: 'Clear the nest.'"

"I didn't know your dad was British."

"His parents left England just before the end of the Second European War. Then, when Australia fell, he got out and went to New England. That's where he met my mom."

"You can't give me this, Jackson."

"I want you to have it." He searched for words. "Sare, I know something about you that you don't seem to know about yourself."

"What?"

"You're a really brave person. I've always thought so, from the very first. You're fearlessly honest, and I've never seen you back down from any challenge or anything you thought was right, even if you were scared out of your mind. So if you don't want to" — his voice dropped lower — "try to change things again, I have to respect that. All right?"

My nose stung. He was too generous to me. He'd always been that way. "Thanks," I managed. "I'm sorry."

He shook his head. "Maybe someday I'll be brave enough to tell you what I see."

"I still can't take this from you," I said, holding the medal out on my palm for him.

He curled my fingers around it. "It's the only thing I have to give you. And it's the thing I want you to have."

He smiled at me gently, then went back out into the night.

Someone is calling my name: "Sa-a-a-rah. Sa-a-a-a-rah!" I slip my feet out from under the covers and jump down.

"Sarah," the voice whispers. I run on tiptoes to follow. I see someone run into the other hall.

The first door is partway open and I see Amber's hand on it, disappearing inside. I go push the door open all the way.

The moon is so bright I can see everything. An old woman is sleeping in the bed. She has white hair that spreads all over the pillow like spider silk. She opens her eyes and looks at me.

"I know you," she says. "What's your name again?"

"Sarah. What's yours?"

"Fee. Remember?" She pushes back the covers and gets up out of the bed, and suddenly she is a little girl. Like me. And I do remember. She says, "Want to see something? Come on." I look back as we leave and the old woman is still there, sleeping.

We sneak down the stairs and go through a trapdoor in the kitchen closet. Down again on secret steps. Two women are at the bottom. A pretty black woman lying on the bed and a tall white woman sitting beside her. I've seen the two women before, that other time I went with Fee.

There is a little squirming bundle tucked into the nook of the black woman's arm. She seems very tired. She is having a hard time speaking. "You'll keep your promise."

"I will," the tall woman says. "If it comes to that, I will raise her and love her as my own. But it won't, Della. You are young and strong. This won't kill you."

"It will," she says dully. "I've seen it. No matter. You tell her . . . I was willing to pay the price."

The baby starts to fuss then, and the tall woman picks her up and gently bounces her in the crook of her arm. "Shh, shh, shh," she says.

Fee crooks her finger at me. "Come closer."

We creep up right next to the woman, but she doesn't notice us. We're invisible. "Look at her eyes," Fee says to me. "Do you see?" I stand on tiptoes to look.

The tall woman says to the other, "What is her name?"

The black woman says, "Call her Amber."

I am excited. So this is Amber, I think, looking right into her large brown eyes. And then I see and feel that Amber is looking back into mine.

CHAPTER TWENTY

As I got ready the next morning for the trip to the capital, I mulled over my dream. Like the other time I'd dreamed of the child Fee, it all seemed familiar to me. Perhaps that was what had inspired my imaginary Amber . . . if Amber *was* imaginary. I wondered why old Fiona had wanted me to see the baby's eyes. And why I'd had the sense the baby could see me. Maybe it meant she could see the future, like Nanga. That might explain why Fiona thought Amber had been the one responsible for making time go wrong.

When I finished dressing, I gave myself the once-over in the full-length mirror, I felt oddly disconnected from what I saw. I knew that the Sarah who'd used this mirror in the other past would not approve of my outfit: a high-waisted plaid dress with coordinating wool coat. Gloves. A beret. It was all too — *compliant*. That other Sarah was never compliant.

Which may be why, when Richard pulled up, got out, and walked around the hood as I came down the steps, preparing to open the passenger's side for me, I quickened my pace to beat him to it.

He smiled. "You really take all this equality business seriously, don't you, coz?"

"Yeah," I said. "I guess I do, *coz*. Will that pose a problem?"

He shook his head emphatically. "Not at all." He turned around and went back to the driver's door to climb in. "Think the dress just confused me a little. Forgot who I was dealing with. You look nice, by the way."

"Nice and girly," I grumbled.

He grinned.

A memory tugged at me, playing out like a scene in my head. Richard and I were sitting in a different idling car, and he was apologizing: "I don't know why I lied to you like that — it was stupid, okay? It's just — I just didn't want to have to say it out loud, you know? That she up and left us."

Claire, I realized. In that other time, she had left Robert and abandoned Richard. But this time around, she was a picture-perfect wife.

And there was something more to the memory. That other Richard — he'd leaned over, put his index finger beneath that Sarah's chin, and kissed her. Kissed me. I'd let the other Richard Hathaway kiss me that night, and I'd liked it very much.

I wondered if I'd like it again.

"Forget something?" Richard asked.

"N-no," I said, a little too quickly. "I remembered something, actually."

"We have time."

"For what?"

He laughed. "If you want to go back inside to get it. We have time. You can."

"Oh. No. It's fine."

"Then we're off," he said, and revved the engine. We shot out of there like a bullet.

"This car has no seat belts," I said with a rising note.

"Nope," he said.

We turned south across a bridge over the Severn, with Richard going as fast as ever. "How far is it to Richmond?" I asked.

"About two hundred miles."

"How long will it take?"

He slowed, downshifting. "About thirty minutes."

"Not even *you* are that fast," I said.

He hung a right through a gate. When we cleared the trees, I saw where we were.

"Yeah, Parsons, I'm that fast."

A small airfield spread out before us, with a pretty little Messerschmitt twin-engine plane on the tarmac, ready and waiting.

He parked the car next to the hangar. A mechanic was there, wiping his hands on a rag. "All gassed up, Mr. Hathaway."

"Um." I'd noticed something missing. Some*one*. "Where's the pilot?" I asked Richard.

"You're looking at him."

"Oh, no," I said. "Nuh-uh. I've seen the way you drive."

He laughed and opened the door on the right side. Then he took my arm, guessing correctly that some physical encourage-ment was going to be necessary to propel my body onto that plane. "Been flying since I was twelve. Got my license when I was fifteen. Whenever my dad and I go south, I'm the pilot. Believe me, Dad would never trust his life to me if I weren't competent."

I reminded myself that Richard Hathaway was more than competent at everything he did. I climbed up into the seat.

Richard settled himself, turned the engine over, then started flipping switches and checking gauges like he knew his business. "Safety belt," he directed, and snapped his closed. He pulled a stick of gum from his pocket and started chewing with great concentration.

"Wait a minute," I said. "Shouldn't we have parachutes or something?"

"Suck it up, coz. Your fate is entirely in my hands." He grinned again, that wicked, crooked grin. "Enjoy the flight."

He eased the throttle forward and the plane lurched into motion. We taxied onto the runway, started to pick up speed.

Within seconds, the wheels had left the ground. "The most dangerous parts of flying are takeoff and landing," he told me. "You're already halfway there."

I nodded my head toward the windshield. "Just pay attention, all right?"

We flew due west before circling south. Flying was different in this small plane — the ground was closer. I leaned my head to one side and watched the country sliding in and out of view below — the gentle hills, the rivers, the towns, the great estates like Amber House.

Then the tops of the trees got closer and Richard was talking into his headset. "Thank you, tower." I saw a hangar and a lot of pavement coming up fast. I gripped the arms of my seat and closed my eyes.

The wheels hit pavement with a little shrieking sound, bounced and hit again. We bobbled into a steady roll. I could hear Richard flipping switches, then the motor whined as he throttled back.

"You can breathe now, coz. We're here."

I opened my eyes and realized I had indeed been holding my breath. I exhaled as quietly as I could. "Nice landing," I offered.

He laughed. "Next time, you'll have to try to keep your eyes open." He taxied into a hangar and shut the engines down.

"Now for the really dangerous part of the trip," he said. He gestured over his shoulder with his head. "John is driving us into Richmond."

I looked and saw a black man in a chauffeur's cap standing next to a gleaming Mercedes limousine.

Again that charming smile. He swept his arm out grandly, and said, "*Après vous.*"

❦

We went straight into the center of the capital — massive stone buildings with columns and Grecian pediments, huge flights of marble steps and crowning domes. Four of these structures flanked a long central park of grass and trees and fountains. Richard acted as tour guide.

"The congressional building is on the west side. On the south, the president's mansion. The east, the Supreme Court, and the north, a monument to the heroes of the Confederation."

John deposited us at the bottom of a lengthy flight of stone steps at the western end of the park. At the top, Richard was greeted politely by the guards. He led me to his father's office, a suite of rooms filled with mahogany desks and leather chairs, brass lamps and oil paintings. A pretty raven-haired secretary bubbled over to offer us coffee or tea.

"The film reel been delivered yet, Stacey?" Richard asked.

She blinked. "Didn't somebody tell you? President Stevenson has that waiting for you across the street."

Richard kind of startled at that. "God. I had no idea."

"What's going on?" I asked.

"The president is expecting us," Richard said.

We were escorted to President Stevenson's mansion — a white-washed brick building in the Greek Revival style. We didn't use the front door; a guard led us around to a businesslike side entrance. A man in a charcoal suit and yellow tie came out of nowhere and rushed forward to shake Richard's hand. "Right this way."

Thick blue carpeting ran down the length of a wide hall flanked with what might have once been bedrooms but now were busy offices. People looked up from their work as we were ushered past. Most of them sat in front of TV screens attached by snaking cables to banks of metal cabinets punctuated with winking lights. Computers. Of course the president would have the latest technology.

Up an elevator, down another carpeted hall, closing in on the "executive residence," as the charcoal-suited man explained. Our pace was brisk, but I took in as much as I could, peering up stairwells, down bisecting corridors. The complex was massive, palatial, with arched doorways, elaborate crown molding, and paneling on the walls. All of it painted butter yellow, or sky blue, or mint green. I wondered if Claire Hathaway would "revise" the color scheme when she became first lady.

Our guide led us to a sitting room. Its windows overlooked the central park of the governmental buildings. From here, in wintertime, it all looked unpalatably gray.

"He should be ready for you shortly," the man said.

A crowd stood outside the iron fence at the end of the sweeping lawn. They waved signs and chanted. Many of them wore red armbands marked with an interlocking black figure. *Swastikas.*

"Are they Confederates?" I asked Richard.

A hoarse voice answered me: "Unfortunately, yes. A small but growing part of my constituency, I'm afraid. Fools looking for a 'stronger' government."

I turned. President Stevenson was making his way over to the window, leaning heavily on a cane. I hardly recognized him from the photos I had seen — he had the same lion's mane of white hair, the same shrewd eyes, but his face drawn, lined, weary. He snorted his disgust at the demonstrators. "Lunatics. More and more of 'em every day."

He held out a gnarled hand to Richard, who stepped forward to take it. "Richard, is it?" the president said.

"Yes, sir."

He smiled, but it didn't reach his eyes. "The young prince in line for the throne. Your father's smart to be training you." He regarded me. "Who's this?"

"My neighbor, actually, Mr. President," Richard said. He gestured ever so slightly with his head for me to step forward. I honestly didn't know what was expected — was I supposed to curtsy or something? I stuck out my hand.

"Sarah Parsons, Mr. President."

The man in the charcoal suit seemed to materialize from nowhere, stepping forward to whisper in the president's ear. "Ah. The heiress of Amber House," Stevenson said, taking my hand in his. "Suitable," he commented.

Suitable for what? I wondered as he released me. Fixed with the weight of Stevenson's stare, I found myself wishing I hadn't come.

Richard broke the silence: "On my father's behalf, I'd like to thank you, sir —"

"Your father's a shrewd man." Stevenson put an empty hand out to Charcoal Suit, who swiftly filled it with a small film canister. "Don't much like his politics. Never did. But he's the right man for the job in front of us."

He held the reel out to Richard, who stepped closer to take it. "Thank you, President Stevenson."

Stevenson didn't release his hold on the case, pinning Richard in place. "Don't thank me, boy. I'm not sure I'm doing your father any favor. Just tell him he has to act fast. Time's running out. I'm too old and set in my ways to do it myself."

"To do what, sir?" Richard asked.

The president let go of the canister. "To prevent a world war, of course." He turned and started back out of the room, done with us. I heard him mutter, "Time for a change."

Charcoal Suit led us back out. He also had a message for Richard to give to Senator Hathaway. "Your father should be careful. Jewish Intelligence says the Reich isn't happy with him, and our own agency agrees. They'll stop him if they can."

John was waiting with the car just outside the side gate. He held open a briefcase when Richard reached him, and Richard put the movie reel in it. Then John locked the case and put it in the trunk of the car.

We climbed in. Richard was quiet. After a moment, he shivered involuntarily. "Creepy old man. Did you feel the power radiating off him?"

Maybe I had. "Do you think he's right?" I asked. "Do you think there'll be a war?"

"Stevenson's nearing eighty. He's going senile."

"What a comforting thought. Dotty old man running a country."

Richard shrugged, almost shaking off his glum mood. "Well, you heard what he said, didn't you? 'Time for a change.' At least he knows it's time for him to step aside."

I wanted to ask Richard whether he thought his father could handle the responsibility. Whether he could really do what Stevenson hoped he could.

Change the world.

Chapter Twenty-One

Richard had a couple of things to pick up, so we swung by the Hathaways' capital residence, in a nearby neighborhood of dignified homes looming over manicured lawns. The Hathaways' was brick with black shutters and a gray slate roof. I guessed at least two hundred years old. "This won't take long," he said. "You can wait in the car if you like."

And miss the chance to see the inside of that house? My curiosity must have shown on my face.

"Come in," he laughed as he climbed out of the limo. "Look around."

While Richard hurried upstairs to fetch a pair of "lucky" cuff links his father wanted to wear when he announced his candidacy, I wandered into the living room. Claire's telltale minimalist aesthetic was present yet again. That soothing palette of neutrals. My eye was drawn to a wall of framed black-and-white photos. A swathed baby in a bassinet; a pearly-toothed toddler being pushed in a swing. The same towheaded boy building sand castles on the beach, running through fall leaves, putting the finishing touches on a snowman. In many of them, a blond woman stood off to one side, watching fondly — Claire Hathaway admiring her perfect son.

But in that other time, she left him. Why was it different? What had Fiona wanted me to see in baby Amber's eyes?

"Um." Richard had appeared in the doorway, just in time to notice my path forward to get a closer look.

"You were a pretty cute kid," I said.

He smiled at that. That winning hybrid of Claire's tilted smile and Robert's square grin.

He took me to a bistro for a late lunch. Richmond had an enclave of French refugees who'd fled the Nazi occupation in the forties and fifties, but had not wanted to join their compatriots in the much different geography of the nation of Louisiana that stretched north and west of the Mississippi River.

Richard knew exactly what to order, which saved me the embarrassment of trying to sound out the menu in my worse-than-mediocre high school French. He quickly figured out I was not able to keep up with his patter about the menu, at which point Richard had the happy notion of engaging the waiter in a untranslated conversation about the "mademoiselle." *"Mais oui,"* the waiter kept answering, bowing his head in my direction, *"assurément," "tout à fait."*

"What, what?" I kept asking, but Richard shook his head and held a finger to his lips to ensure the waiter's silence. I supposed it was fair payback for all the times I had teased him, but I thought he was taking *way* too much enjoyment from it. Finally the waiter said, *"Permettez-moi,"* and explained in accented English that Richard had asked him whether or not the man found me the loveliest young lady he had seen all day. I blushed and rolled my eyes and smiled. They both laughed.

He seemed a happier and more earnest version of the boy I remembered from that conversation in the car, in that other time. I supposed having a mother to grow up with might cause that difference. Perhaps my saving Maggie had had something to do with that. Perhaps it had been a good thing for more people than just my little family.

Afterward, we drove back through the capital's center on our way out of town. Richard must have noticed the longing on my face as we passed the Jackson Memorial, because he asked John to stop.

We climbed the smooth steps slowly. The spot was nearly deserted now, so late in the day. A chill wind blew in from the west, buffeting me from behind, sending my skirt dancing around my knees. Inside the monument, the wind rose to an audible sigh, whipping through the open spaces around the stone columns. The high pitch of it seemed to catch in my ears as I focused on the pale, carved seated statue before me.

It was — all wrong, somehow.

The blind eyes gazing out through the columns to the future of the country he helped to build. The gentle craggy face, slashed by a long scar. The beloved first president of the ACS, Andrew Jackson. Behind him, etched in the marble walls, a roll call of the Confederation's cherished fallen, the soldiers who died in the brief, successful revolution against England in 1833.

I thought, *Someone else should be sitting in that marble seat.*

John secured the briefcase in the Messerschmitt, then we powered up and taxied to the runway. "I want you to keep your eyes open this time, coz. I special-ordered this sunset for you."

We took off and flew west-northwest into a pink-orange sky darkening to purple. Richard acted as tour guide. "That's Charlottesville down there on the left. Several of the most important leaders of the colonial revolt came from there. The guy who wrote the document that they sent to King George — he lived a little to the southeast of the town. His estate is still standing, although it was confiscated by the Crown. He called it something like Montevideo or —"

"Monticello," I murmured.

"Yeah, that's right. You've heard of him, then."

No, I hadn't. I hadn't ever heard any of this. Had I?

"It's really a neat place. Beautiful architecture. We should go see it sometime."

"Sure," I agreed.

"Outside of the colony of Massachusetts, Virginia had the greatest number of insurrectionists, most of them really wealthy landowners. And most of them probably related in one way or another to your ancestors."

He banked north. Ahead, the land was split by a wide river that bled, shining, into the Chesapeake — the Potomac. We were nearing home.

"Another one of the old estates, maybe even bigger than Amber House, off to the left there, near Alexandria. It's still standing because the property actually belonged to the wife. Her second husband — I forget his name — was one of the rebels wiped out by Loyalist agents in the 1770s, at the beginning of the insurrection. The house was called —" He thought a moment. "Mount something."

"Vernon." It swam forward, unbidden. Mount Vernon, the home of — I remembered his name — George Washington. In Sarah One's time, the owner hadn't been some failed rebel officer. He had been called the father of a country.

Washington, Jefferson, Hamilton, Franklin, Adams — the names came to me. What had become of these men? What had become of their revolution? Why had it failed this time? And how could that have had anything to do with me? That last question was an agony I couldn't bear to consider. How could that have had anything to do with me?

Near Annapolis, Richard stopped chatting to focus on his landing. I was grateful for the silence. It had become impossible for me to follow his conversation. I was hunting — searching the spaces inside me for traces of another world, another time that — what? Never was? I was gathering embers that I piled one next to the other in the hope their heat would build until my mind was filled with it, until it was a roaring flame that would light every corner.

I hardly noticed Richard's landing. The wind was harsher here, farther north, sweeping in off the Chesapeake after its race across leagues of cold gray ocean. When I opened the passenger door, my hair rose like snakes, whipping at my nose and eyes and ears.

Richard put an arm around my shoulders and hurried me to the car, helping me in, closing the door, stilling the wind that blew outside. He climbed into the driver's seat. Ever so gently, the tips of his fingers swept the wild pieces of my hair back behind my ear. And lingered on my neck.

"You all right?"

"I don't think so, Hathaway. I have to get back to Amber House. I have to get home."

He was stung, but there were ashes and embers of another Richard inside me too. I couldn't deal with seeing the shadow of Richard-past in the Richard who was watching me with such concern. I needed to go back.

The closer I drew to Amber House, the worse the double-image chaos in my head became. Bright, hot images from the dead past casting light perversely on all the things of now that hadn't been before. I remembered ripped jeans and a palm-sized phone and a black president of the American nation. Not corseted dresses. Not a dying Rose. Not a segregated movie theater. Computers and the nations of Europe and a very different end to the second World War. Not Reichsleiter Jaeger and the Japanese Empire and the Thousand-Year Reich.

Of course the change hadn't been because of Maggie. It was too huge; it went back too far. But that meant it wasn't because of Amber either. Fiona had been mistaken. She'd followed the wrong trail.

So what had happened? *How* had it happened? Since I was the one — the only one — who remembered that other time, I was sick with the conviction that, somehow, it was because of *me*.

Richard eased the car to a stop. He was staring at his grip on the steering wheel. "Hey, Parsons, did I do something? Say something wrong?"

I recognized the tone of his voice — the same brittle tone he'd used to describe Claire's abandonment, in the time before.

"I'm sorry, Hathaway. It wasn't you."

"Then what?" he said. "It's always like this, Parsons. Just when I think we're starting to — I don't know — connect, you go somewhere else."

He was upset, and I guessed he had a right to be. He had no idea that every conversation I had with him involved not just we two, but the other Sarah and the other Richard. It was crowded in the front seats of that little car.

"I'm sorry," I said again. "I saw something on the trip that left me really upset, but I can't explain it right now. Forgive me?"

And he did, of course he did. Because, whatever the shadow-Richard had been like before, this Richard was perfect.

Richard drove away as I started up the front steps. But I couldn't go inside. I realized I needed to go somewhere else. I needed to go *to* someone else.

I took the path to the river. The frozen grass crunched beneath my feet, faster and faster until I was jogging. The air I sucked into my lungs burned, but I didn't slow down. Careless of my clothes, careless of my safety, I fled down the sloping path to Jackson's house.

And he answered the door without my even having to knock.

I took a step back, startled. He looked pale, thin, exhausted. His skin had an ashy cast, and there were dark circles under his eyes. "J, are you all right?"

"I'm fine," he said. "Come in." He stepped aside. "Cocoa?" He pointed to two cups steaming beside the stove.

I realized a cup of cocoa would be just the right thing.

Had it been this way all along? Jackson always knowing exactly what I would want before I did myself?

We took our cups and settled on the couch. I wrapped my fingers around my mug, feeling it too hot, but wanting the warmth that spread inward from the contact. Jackson waited for me.

I watched the frothy film on the surface of the cocoa swirl clockwise.

I wanted to apologize, wanted to tell him how right he had been, that things needed to be changed. But now that I was sitting there, I couldn't find words to say what I had remembered about that other time. That better time. Not better for me and my family. Or Richard. But for everyone else. I bent over my cup so that my hair hid my tears, and struggled to swallow the knowledge that had lodged like a stone in my throat. And still Jackson waited.

I found my voice again, and I started to talk. I told him everything I could remember about a different world, where things had been more advanced — science, medicine, technology — and everyone had been more liberal, more equal, blacks and whites, men and women. When I finished, I said, "I'm the only one who remembers that other past. I think that must mean something."

"Maybe," he said.

"My great-grandmother, Fiona, thought the change involved her grandmother and the little girl she adopted, but it didn't.

They took Amber away from here and she never came back. She died in New England. Young."

"The child in the picture with Maeve McCallister."

"Yes," I said. "And really, she didn't live long enough ago to have caused all the changes I've seen."

"Because they started in the seventeen hundreds."

"Yes. With the failed revolt. It didn't fail in that other time." Which, oddly enough, I was beginning to think of as the *real* time, before I'd messed it up somehow. "There's something else you should know. In that other time, your parents still died. The accident still happened."

He closed his eyes, his face constricted. "That's a terrible thought, isn't it? Like they suffered twice."

"What are we supposed to do? Try to change it back?" I said.

"I don't think we can change it back," he said. "But — maybe we can change it again, to something else."

"I'm afraid," I said. "Look at what happened last time. What if there's something worse than this?"

"I *see* something else, Sarah. Something *better*. A lot like the world you describe, but better."

"Better how? Can't you tell me?"

He considered it. I could see that he wanted to. Then he shook his head. "It's still not the right time. Can you take it on faith?"

Faith in Jackson? Yes, I could. "What do we have to do?"

I heard his breath catch, then he smiled so kindly, so gently, it nearly made me cry. After a little nod, he said, "Seems to me, first things first, we need to track down the point where time changed. We need to search the house, hunt for memories from the other time."

A treasure hunt, I thought. "You'll help me?" I asked.

"Of course," he said.

Of course.

We agreed we would begin in the morning. Somewhat comforted, I walked back to Amber House.

My mother descended on me when I entered the front door. "Didn't I hear Richard's car a while ago? Is everything all right?"

I smiled and nodded and told her it all went exactly as planned. "I just went for a walk. I needed to think."

"To think?"

"I'm not feeling well, Mom. Can we talk in the morning?"

"I saved you some dinner."

I shook my head. "I can't eat."

There was worry in her face. But she let me go.

I stopped in the library before I went upstairs. There was something I had to do, something I had to know. Someone I had remembered.

The woman's voice on the other end of the telephone line was bright and cheerful: "Information. May I help you?"

I asked for a Seattle listing. I dialed the number. "Hello? Mr. Wanderscheid? Can I please speak to — Jessica? Jecie?"

But he didn't have a daughter. Or a wife whose name had been Deborah Goldman. When I called information again, they didn't have a listing for her either.

The Reich had been so thorough, I thought bleakly. There weren't many Jews left in the world. Including the girl who once had been Sarah One's best friend.

CHAPTER TWENTY-TWO

Mom and Dad were waiting for me when I went down in the morning. They were drinking coffee, chatting, making alterations to a list — but still obviously waiting.

My mother looked up with a carefully neutral smile. "You never gave us your full report, hon. How was the capital?"

I turned for the refrigerator, busied myself with pouring some juice. "The whole thing was kind of" — *Unbelievable?* — "amazing." I put the juice away. Went and sat in a chair. Took a sip. "Yeah. Amazing. Did you know Richard is a pilot?"

My mother's face fell. "*He* flew you there?" She turned to my father. "When Robert said they'd fly —" My father held up a hand to stop her train of thought. He turned back to me.

"Yeah, a really great pilot, as it turns out," I said. Another sip. "And you know who handed Richard that tape? Stevenson."

My father: "The *president?*"

"I know, right?" I nodded with widened eyes. "He shook my hand. That was pretty — amazing too."

They both of them leaned back a little in astonishment. "So why did you seem so upset last night?" my mother pressed.

Another sip. "Well," I said, my eyes searching down and to the left for an answer to that one, "he said some kind of disturbing things. The president."

"What did he say?" My dad.

"I'm really bad with remembering conversations," I hedged.

"What did he say?" My mom.

"Like, 'time is running out,' and he was too old to 'do what had to be done,' and . . ." The phrases smacked me like slaps. I recovered my line of thought: "He said Senator Hathaway had to stop another world war."

This did not seem to surprise my parents. They looked at each other, even while my father said, "Don't worry, honey, it's not going come to that." He reached out and gave my hand a little squeeze, then he and Mom stood to go.

She pushed a list toward me across the table. "A few pieces of the furniture are going north to help decorate the exhibit — I need you to empty the stuff inside them into boxes. Please?"

I sat staring at the notebook page after my parents left, thinking glumly that real superheroes — the ones in comic books — didn't get handed a list of chores just before they were supposed to save the world. It was almost nine o'clock; Jackson would be arriving any minute. I was supposed to be trying to change history. I didn't have time for chores.

I went to find Maggie.

She was curled up with a book in an armchair in her room. She looked up at me when I stuck my head in, her usual simple smile in place. It froze me for a moment. I recognized I hadn't thought through what I was going to say to her.

She helped me. "You've seen more, you've remembered more."

I went in and closed the door behind me. I sat in her desk chair. "Yeah, Maggie, I have."

She closed her book. "Tell me," she said.

So I told her. The short version of the whole thing. The terrible changes. And the fact that I needed to change things again.

She sat very still when I was through, staring at her folded hands. "It's all right," she said quietly. "I don't mind, really."

I was confused. "Mind what?"

"I'm grateful I had this chance to grow up," she continued in a soft voice. "But it's all right if you have to undo it. I won't disappear totally. The house will remember me. You'll remember me."

I couldn't speak for a moment. The pain in my chest was terrible. Maggie was willing to be *erased* to make things right.

I shook my head. "No," I said. "no. The world is better with you in it. I won't lose you. Jackson's going to help me figure it out. How to make things right. And right includes you, Maggie, you hear me?"

Maggie said she and Sam would empty out the stuff stored in the furniture so I could work with Jackson. I left the list with her and hurried to the conservatory. He was waiting by Pandora's pool. I sat next to him.

"Where do we start?" he said.

"I don't know. It seems like the one change to the past that I know I caused happened when I went to find Sam. Maybe we should begin there, in the attic. In the nursery."

He smiled at the grim look on my face. "Your favorite place." He stood and held out his hand. I reached up and took it. His was so much larger than mine, warm and smooth and strong. He pulled me to my feet. "Let's get started."

The last door in the third-story hall was closed. When I wrapped my hand around its knob, lantern-lit darkness settled around me and I saw another hand where mine was. A man's hand, brown and strong beneath a fringe of lace. I stepped back to see.

The man was leaning his blond head against the door, pressing against it as if he needed it to hold him up. I heard a woman's voice coming through, soft at first, but getting louder: "Are you listening? Can you hear me?" The words seemed familiar to me, as if I should remember them.

The woman's voice went on, louder. "You know I cannot be trapped here. You know I can leave this place any time I wish. You know you cannot stop me." I felt fear bubbling up inside me, but I wasn't sure why. The man — *the Captain*, I thought — covered his ears with his hands.

But the voice was nearly a scream now. I knew he could hear her even through his hands. "You think you are safe? You think I can't hurt you? I can. I can get you. I can find you in your dreams." And I knew who she was — knew the other Sarah had witnessed her — mad Deirdre shrieking out her promise of vengeance against her hated husband.

He turned then, this ancestor of mine, and of Richard's. I stared at his handsome face. Full of fear.

Jackson's voice broke the spell. "What is it?" he said.

Dim daylight reasserted itself, reaching us through the open door to my mother's studio. I shook my head. "This room was where the Captain locked Deirdre away. She scared the bejeezus out of the other Sarah, the one from the other time. I think that might be why I've always hated the attic."

I followed Jackson into the middle of the long room, looking at its dusty contents, wondering how to make something — anything — happen. I spotted an old crate that seemed familiar.

"Can we move this to the middle?" I said, starting to tug on a handle, trying to drag it.

Jackson stopped me. "Let's try to be as quiet as possible." He lifted the whole crate and set it carefully, silently, where I pointed.

I knelt down before it and placed my hands on its surface. Nothing happened. I felt like an idiot, a fraud. I looked up at him. "I don't know how to force it."

He crouched down by me. "You can't force it," he said. "You just have to open yourself up and let it happen."

I nodded. His gift was different, but in some ways the same. He knew.

I tried to relax, sitting back against my heels, closing my eyes, letting my arms, my fingers, go limp, resting on the crate. I felt something coming on — a different space that I pushed into, like a stick being forced into a marshmallow.

It closed around me. I opened my eyes to candlelight, the night I'd gone into the mirror world. They were there before me — those two dear little faces. Sam and child-Maggie. "Sarah too," she was saying. I listened to myself trying to reason with them, trying to convince them that their mirror lives were a dream and that they needed to wake up.

I saw my hands holding the box that had been the key to changing time in that other past — the box Sarah-Louise's dead twin brother had made, which had contained the two things I'd needed to wake both Sam and Maggie: a mirror and a brooch.

Sammy stood and trotted off on sturdy legs, fading away as he went. And I felt a wind rising, as if my hair should be lifting. But nothing moved. The other Sarah set the brooch on the crate, and Maggie too stood and disappeared. Then Sarah One fell sideways.

I stood over her, observed her. She'd been bitten — *I'd* been bitten — by a Good Mother spider. She was dying. The roaring of a tornado filled my senses, but she just lay there, unmoving, in the dust.

Her eyes cracked open — she was looking at someone else. *Who?*

Hands. I saw soft white hands stroking the other Sarah's face. Hands that belonged to a woman with long iron-gray hair hanging in tangles around a sweet but ravaged face.

"I am sorry for you," the woman said to the girl on the floor, "but I have to go now. Sarah-Louise needs me." And she too disappeared.

Leaving just the other Sarah. "Oh, my God," I said. Gray daylight hit my eyes.

"What?" Jackson asked.

"I woke up someone else," I said. "I woke up Deirdre Foster."

Thaddeus Dobson's daughter. Captain Foster's wife. The mother of my namesake, Sarah-Louise, and her twin, Matthew. The little girl who'd once saved Nanga on the docks. Deirdre. According to family lore, when her little boy died in 1775, she'd slept and dreamed, semi-comatose for more than a year. Her dreaming self must have found Maggie and Sam, and believed they were Sarah-Louise and Matthew — and in the world of dreams, she'd been able to convince my aunt and brother to believe it also. Until I woke them out of the mirror world and sent them back to the land of the living. And then, for good measure, woke up Deirdre too.

So she could change history. I was an idiot.

Deirdre had lived during the time of the Revolution — long enough ago to cause all the changes I'd seen. My waking Deirdre could have done it. Still . . .

"How could saving one crazy woman have changed *everything*?"

"I don't know," Jackson said. "I can't imagine. But we're going to have to figure it out."

I was ready to leave. The attic had returned to silence, a mere repository of the flotsam of the past, at rest beneath its blanket of dust. It had lost that feeling of threat it had always held for me.

On the way down the stairs, I saw a man descending before me — a black man in simple cotton clothes. He was carrying Deirdre limp in his arms. *Another message from the house.*

I hurried after him. When I reached the landing, I spotted Captain Foster and Nanga waiting by the door to Deirdre's room. The Captain's face was hollowed with fatigue, his eyes half-circled with dark moons of shadow. He said to Nanga as Deirdre was carried inside, "She has a fever. Fix it. And keep her awake at night so I can —" He broke off mid-sentence; Nanga tipped her head just slightly, as if she wished to hear the end of his thought. Anger twisted his features. "Move!" he roared.

Nanga turned away, a suggestion of a grim smile on her lips.

A very pretty blond girl, perhaps as old as thirteen, stepped out of the doorway to the Captain's suite.

"Why not let her die, Papa?" she asked. "I do not know why you've kept her around this long."

The Captain stood looking in at the woman on the bed. His jaw was knotted. "She is my son's mother, Camilla."

The girl lifted one eyebrow. "Your son is dead. He does not need her anymore."

The Captain turned and regarded her. "You look like your mother, but she never would have made such a suggestion." The girl shrugged. "A practical answer, then, for my practical child. If she dies, none of this" — he gestured generally, to the house — "will come to me. The house passes, has always passed, to the eldest daughter, if there is one."

"To Sarah, then," the girl said. "As good as to you. She is easily dispensed with."

"No," the Captain said, emphatic. He grabbed her arm and made it clear. "Do not even think it, girl. I want no accidents. Understand that if Sarah-Louise . . . does not *survive*," he spoke the word delicately, "there is a female second cousin who inherits. I would still not take the house. And I must keep the house."

"Sarah!" My mother's voice. The vision dissolved. Mom had climbed the stairs to find me. "Why are Maggie and Sam doing the work I gave to you?" She noticed, then, Jackson still standing on the steps to the third floor. "And — what is Jackson doing here?"

I looked at her blankly for a moment. Too many shifts — I felt disoriented. My thoughts coalesced. "He came to help move the boxes Maggie and I filled, Mom. I'm putting the stuff upstairs." She did not look appeased. "And Maggie and Sam volunteered to help," I added.

"I'm sure Rose needs Jackson's help more than you do," she said. "And next time I check on the work, I want to find you there. Working."

"Your mom's right," Jackson said, slipping past her down the stairs. "I really should go check on Gran. See you, Sare."

I was frantic. I didn't want him to go. "Um. Thanks for the help. See you *soon*," I added, hoping he'd take the hint. But he didn't look back.

My mother could have that effect on people. Still, I remembered the other Sarah's mother, and realized it could have been a lot worse.

I found Maggie and Sammy in front of a tall pewter cupboard — Maggie busy with actual packing, Sam with finding things he'd never seen before.

"Look at *this*, Sarah. A mechanical clown who eats pennies!"

"I told your mom to leave you be," Maggie said, "but she never did listen to me. Little sister and all."

"It's all right. Maybe I needed a break."

"Find anything?"

"Yes. Someone else was there in the attic with you and Sammy."

"Mama," said Sam, making the clown toss another penny in its mouth. I realized he'd said that before. It occurred to me I ought to listen more closely to the things Sam said.

"It was Deirdre Foster. She lives in the seventeen hundreds." I noticed after I said it that I used the present tense.

"You saved her too?" Maggie said. "You're so kind, Sarah."

"Kind, maybe, but it was a stupid move. I changed the past *way* back. God only knows how many things it made different."

"The house knows too. It will show you. Be patient."

I smiled at that. "I'm still waiting, Maggie. Still giving it time."

Because I'd made up that story about Jackson helping me take the boxes to the third floor, I couldn't ask for more help getting the job done. I ended up having to carry them all up myself. Five trips.

On the last climb, I stopped on the second landing, to rest the box on a sideboard and ease my exhausted arms. Space shifted and I saw the little black-haired girl who had been Deirdre Dobson standing by the windows that looked toward the river.

A young black woman limped up behind her. Portions of her face were swollen as if from blows, and she looked like a scarecrow, loose skin over bones. She was the woman I had seen in a dream, lying half-dead on a dock in Annapolis. She'd recovered enough for me to recognize her — Nanga.

"I wish they would not do it," Deirdre said, looking at something happening below.

"What they do?" Nanga said, not yet fluent in English.

"Papa is burying the little house. It makes me sad. The first grandmother and grandfather built it. It is called Heart House."

The vision dissolved in my excitement. I *remembered*. A secret tunnel. A buried house. Maggie was right. One piece at a time, it was all being shown to me. Everything I needed. I just had to be patient.

I carried the box as far as the first turn in the upper stairs, then ran to my room to get my coat. I snuck into the kitchen to get a screwdriver from a bottom drawer. I needed to make it outside before my mother could happen upon me and stop me.

Right, skip, right, I recited, racing through the turns of the maze. Remembering — *remembering* — having done it before. Done it for this same purpose. To find the secret passage.

The center of the maze held a little octagonal gazebo shaped of wrought iron, guarded by ancient wisteria vines that dripped purple blossoms in the spring. My destination.

I turned the last corner —

Jackson was there, of course. Waiting for me. Because he could see the future like I could see the past.

Chapter Twenty-Three

He was holding a crowbar, a flashlight, and a broom. I looked at the puny screwdriver in my hand and laughed at myself. He had always known what I wanted, what I needed, before I did.

"They're here, aren't they?" he said, gesturing to the gazebo. "The tiles you want to pry up."

"Yes," I said. "We have to hunt for some odd-looking grout."

He spotted the loose tiles quickly and levered up the marble squares, making sure not to crack or chip them. I watched him work, noticing his efficiency, the lack of wasted movement, the care. *How long has he been like this? This careful?* So long I could not remember him any other way.

With the tiles removed, the trapdoor was revealed. Jackson looked at me with wonder in his eyes — unlike me, he could not remember having found this door once before.

He planted himself firmly, grabbed the ring handle, and pulled. The last time, in that other time, I remember he had oiled the hinges. This time he was fighting both rust and ice. He groaned between clenched teeth with the effort of it. But he pulled until it gave, until the hinges squealed surrender and the door creaked open for the first time in a century. Again.

He stabbed a flashlight beam into the darkness. I saw him twice over — once in the winter afternoon, and once surrounded by autumn night. He descended the stairs, my double vision continuing. He asked for the broom, again, and kindly swept the stairs for spiders. When I climbed down after, he said, "Just keep an eye on your footing, because the rock's a little uneven."

I smiled, even though it gave me a feeling like pain. "You said that to me the last time. Word for word."

"Did I?" he asked, startled.

"It was a ploy. You didn't want me to look up and see the crickets."

He smiled and nodded. "Smart guy."

The buried house was waiting for us, just as before. The house, I remembered, that my many-times-great-grandfather Liam O'Malley had built for his bride, Sorcha: "Everything my heart has ever wanted," she had told him. When Jackson found the oil lantern left filled on the main room's table by the last visitor to Heart House, I knew already that he would make it light.

Maggie had promised me that Amber House would show me what I needed to know. So why was the house showing me this other Jackson, so like to mine that his words and thoughts and actions were identical? That other Sarah . . . She was like me, but not me. Some things about her were a little bit better — some things, maybe, a little bit worse. But Jackson was Jackson.

"See anything?" he asked as he set the lit lantern back on the table.

"Besides one long *Heart House Discovery* rerun?" I shook my head. "Not yet."

The stone cottage, like Jackson, was the same as before: from Liam's massive brick fireplace to the rotted rope-strung bed in the corner, to the built-in cupboards and bricked-in windows. The cottage's single adjoining room was also just as I remembered it. A ruined child's bed, a trunk, a crude rocking horse. I remembered something else, and stepped to the farther wall. I found and pushed a hidden lever. A secret door swung open, and I felt a coil of darkness unspool from above.

"Shall we go up?" Jackson said, shining a light in at the web-draped stairs. His voice was eager. "We could use the broom to clear the webs."

I shook my head. "It only goes to the kitchen, and it's probably blocked." I rubbed my hand. "Besides, it's full of spiders."

We went back to the main room. He dusted a chair with his coat sleeve and offered it to me. I sat, and sudden sunlight streamed into Heart House once more.

A girl walked through the door — young Deirdre. "Look what I found, Nanga. Papa's purse." I saw then the black woman sitting at the same table as I. I thought again how beautiful she was. Fierce and intelligent, and broken with sorrow. "Look at what he keeps in it," Deirdre continued. "His lucky coin."

She held it up in the sunshine falling through the door. The two-headed coin gleamed as if it had fire inside it. Something tight passed over Deirdre's face. She said, "I want it."

Like a striking snake, Nyangu's hand flashed out and slapped the coin from Deirdre's grasp. It fell onto the packed-dirt floor, the aged face of grief looking up. Nyangu bent her head and said in a low voice, "Miss Dee-da-rah must not touch this thing."

For a moment, the little girl looked angry enough to hit the woman — it was an ugly thing. Then her anger broke, and she stepped closer. "Why, Nanga? Why mustn't I touch it?"

"Miss knows things can hold . . ." She stopped, unable to find the word.

"Memories," Deirdre said. "Memories of the people who touched them."

"Yes. Memories." Nyangu peered into the little girl's face. "Some things . . . this thing. It holds worse."

A shudder loosened me from the vision. I looked up and saw Jackson watching me, a question in his eyes. "I saw the Janus coin," I said.

He nodded. "It always comes back to that coin."

We went back out the way we had come. Jackson closed the trapdoor and set the four harlequin tiles back in place. I was doubtful anyone would come here in the dead of winter and find our discovery, but thought perhaps he had a need to seal the past away again. I understood it. Like closing a coffin.

We ducked back inside the conservatory and found Sammy waiting for us. "Mommy sent me to find you, Sarah. To tell you 'time for dinner.'"

"Does she know I slipped off?"

He shook his head. "Maggie said you were carrying up more boxes."

I knew he was unhappy because of the lie. I lifted his chin. "She was trying to help, bud. Because what Jackson and I are doing is important. But we just can't talk about it with Mom and Dad right now. You understand?" He nodded. "Shall we go up those" — I pointed to the iron stairs — "and come down the main ones so it'll look like Maggie was telling the truth?"

He nodded again. He was willing to do that for Maggie.

I turned to Jackson. "Will you — can you — come back? Later?"

"I'll come back."

We were still eating Christmas for dinner. Leftover goose, potatoes, and gravy. I felt them all watching me: Dad, Mom, Maggie. I put a smile on my face and tried to act normal. I talked animatedly to Sam about going crabbing.

My father asked, "Where did you learn about crabbing, Sarah?"

For a moment, I couldn't remember. And then I could.

"Jackson taught me," I said. "Some time ago."

After dinner, I attempted to continue the hunt alone.

I climbed the stairs, wondering where to look next, questions forming and re-forming in my head: Why was the coin relevant? What had Deirdre done?

I went to the small room I knew to be Nanga's. Perhaps she would have some idea, some clue, some help to offer. I didn't know why I hadn't thought to ask before.

I opened the door into the room and found myself standing beside the Captain, so close it seemed he must be able to feel my breath. He was dressed in shirtsleeves — no jacket or vest. Though I had never before seen him anything but perfectly clean-shaven, his face was rough with stubble. He wavered slightly on his feet, and I understood he was drunk.

His cheek was marked with three parallel red stripes. He put his fingers to them, then looked to see the tips wet with blood.

Nyangu was pressed into the corner of the room. She too was bleeding, from a cut on her lip. "Kill me!" she yelled at him. "I have no wish to live as a slave. And I would rather die than let you touch me."

"I will kill you one day," the Captain promised, "you and all your line. An old hag warned me long ago to beware a black witch and her witch seed." He grabbed something hanging around his neck, hidden beneath his shirt. "So every day I ask, 'Is today the day I can kill her?' And every day it tells me, *No*. But one day," he said, "one day — our luck will change. And until then, I have use for you."

He started forward, and I backed out fast, not wanting to see. Wishing I could help her.

And I remembered then. Nanga had told the other Sarah — Jackson was also descended from the Captain.

I changed my mind about hunting alone. I hid in my room and waited. I heard Maggie bring Sammy up to bed. I heard my parents talking as they went room to room, turning out lights. I heard the house grow quiet and still.

Then I slipped out and down the halls to the wrought-iron landing, the spiral stair, the pool in the garden. To find Jackson, as always.

"Where to?" he said.

"That hidden stair in Heart House reminded me that there are more." I turned and started back, leading him through the conservatory to the door that opened on the west wing's ground floor.

"Yeah?" he said, following.

"You never foresaw us doing this?" I whispered, once inside the house.

"No," he whispered back. "I don't see everything that is going to happen in the future. Just like you don't see everything that happened in the past. It's hit-and-miss."

"So," I said, struggling to get clear, "you don't know for a fact that what we're doing is going to work."

"I see that it *can* work, Sare. We *can* get there from here. But the future is never fixed. We make choices and the future changes. The future can go in a million different directions."

"Better ones?"

He was silent a moment. "Some of them."

That was *so* not what I wanted to hear. "Then," I said, "we *could* be making things worse."

He stopped before the turn that would take us to the rear gallery behind the library and kitchen. "We still have to choose. Every choice changes the future. We just have to do our best to choose unselfishly. 'Act in good faith,' as Gran says."

I didn't want noble advice; I wanted certainty.

"Look, Sare, one thing I can tell you: If you don't act, if you don't choose, what lies ahead is *not good* for a lot of people. I know you're scared, but I think we just have to keep going. We'll never get there if we don't keep going."

If he could see the future, I wanted him to tell me that everything was going to turn out the way it was supposed to. I swallowed hard and started forward again. There wasn't any way around it. We just had to keep going.

In the kitchen, I went to the strange little built-in, waist-high cupboard next to the closet. It opened onto a panel full of latching drawers, each drawer shaped to hold a specific piece of silver service. I felt blindly along the molding on the top of the cupboard. "There's a catch or lever hidden up here," I said. "You found it last time."

"Weird," he said. He thought a moment, then reached up and shifted a small piece of wood with a *click*. The top edge of the panel of drawers popped a crack. We then were able to pull the whole set of drawers forward and down on the hinges hidden on the bottom edge. The backside of the drawers inverted to become steps, leading up to an entire staircase, concealed in the recess of the wall beside the rough bricks of the kitchen and dining room fireplaces.

"Weird," Jackson said again.

I steadied myself on the wall to start to climb, but then I saw Fiona, white-haired and bent with age, pushing up the stairs ahead of us, a bag over her arm. We followed her up, pausing to trip the lever that would close the cupboard behind us. Ahead, Fiona hauled herself up onto the first landing and continued on to the next, and then passed silently into the hidden attic Jackson and I had found before in the other time.

When we opened the old brass-bound door, I found Fiona kneeling in the shadows, before an open trunk set on a faded rug. The hairs on my arms rose. I remembered that trunk. It had held memories better left forgotten.

Fiona put things from her bag inside. When she was done, she closed the lid but didn't lock it. She lifted her head, looking into the darkness where I stood. "Do you see? It is everything the house showed me to bring."

"Shall we open it?" Jackson said from behind. My great-grandmother disappeared.

"It's full of bad things," I told him. Partial images of echoes rose in my mind, one after the other: blood splattering from the scourging of Nanga's back; a girl in blond ringlets forcing a baby underwater; Deirdre driving a blade into her husband's chest. The memories burned.

But still I knew I had to see and touch the things that had been hidden inside.

"Open it," I said.

Jackson bent and lifted the lid. I made myself kneel where Fiona had, in front of the trunk.

I couldn't remember precisely what had been in the box before, the last time, but I knew the objects had been different. I saw a moth-eaten military jacket. A dagger. A goblet. A rosary. I squeezed my eyes shut. I didn't think I could make myself touch them. It didn't matter that I didn't remember any of them specifically. I knew what they were. Evils locked in a forbidden box.

I sighed and looked again. A baby's blanket, a soft knitted thing, peeked from the tangle. I gritted my teeth. I pulled it free.

The sense of thicker air; the change in light. I saw two pale hands shake the blanket out. Deirdre's hands. She was sitting by the hearth in the kitchen, spreading the blanket on her lap. "Give her to me," she said. "She and I shall sit by the fire while you fetch some dry clothes for her."

Nanga was there too, holding a wet and dripping baby. A baby who had just been held down in a bucket of water. A baby who a little girl nearly drowned, while the other Sarah had watched helplessly, before Nanga stopped her.

Both women worked to strip off the wet clothing. "She tried to kill my child," Nanga said. "She knew what the gypsy told the Captain. They will kill her. We will not be able to stop them."

"I have a little money, Nanga, and friends in the North. I can send you both to safety."

Nanga began to sob, a deep, wrenching keening that brought me to tears. She gasped out words — "I cannot. I cannot. But you will send her."

"Both," Deirdre protested.

"Do not tempt me," Nanga moaned. "I cannot. You will send her."

I let the blanket go and closed my eyes and made the vision stop.

"What was it?" Jackson asked.

"Nanga had to send her baby away." I shook my head. "But she wouldn't go with her."

I turned to the trunk again. I saw a hat pin, gold and onyx, jabbed through a piece of velvet. I slipped it loose from the cloth.

The vision that came had happened at night. Outside on the front porch of Amber House. A black woman, already noticeably pregnant, crept by me, holding the pin. I had seen her before, twice — guiding a group of slaves north to freedom, and giving birth to the baby in her womb.

I looked left and saw where she was headed. A man had Maeve pinned against the wall. She was struggling to get away from him, but he had her arm twisted up behind her back. He kissed her. Hard. A possessive, violent gesture. He leaned back far enough to grip her bodice and tear.

But then Della had her arm around his throat and the hand with the pin in it up against his ear. "You feel this point sticking, Mister? Best you don't squirm, 'cause if I jab a little deeper, you aren't ever gonna be the same."

The man let Maeve go and held very still. Maeve ran past me to the front door. She came back with a shotgun. "You can let him go now," she said, and Della backed away. "I should kill you, Ramsay. Just know if I ever see you on my property again, I will shoot first and swear you tried to rape me later."

The man snarled at Della, "I'll catch up to you one of these days," and then left.

Della slumped down, and there was blood on the floor beneath her. Maeve helped her to her feet. "We must get you back home, to your husband and safety."

"He's dead," Della said. "I will be too, soon, after this one is born. I want her born here."

"'Her'? You cannot know —"

"I know. My grandmother's grandmother came here a slave, and died here free."

"Nanga," Maeve and I said together. The vision faded.

"Tell me," Jackson said, but I shook my head.

"Hold on. I think one more."

I reached into the trunk at random and pulled out the goblet. I saw a man's hand holding it steady as he poured it full of red wine. The hand fascinated me — tan and strong, the nails perfectly trimmed, the fingers decorated with rings. My vision widened. It was the Captain, reaching inside his jacket for a small paper packet, the contents of which he dumped in the wine. I thought to myself, *That's what they do when they poison someone in a movie.*

The Captain lifted the glass, turned, and carried it to the dining table where Deirdre's father sat, smoking a cigar. The Captain held out the wine.

"Thank you, Foster," Dobson said.

The Captain sat down facing Dobson, watching him drink deeply. The older man smiled, enjoying the wine. "Let me say, Foster, that you've acted the gentleman in all this. It was not easy to refuse you. You know I like you, and you're my best captain. But Deirdre is my only child and will inherit everything. She should marry one of her own kind."

"So said the father of my first wife," the Captain said.

"And he was right. Your lives together were harsh. A father wants better for his daughter."

"As I want for mine." He was still watching Dobson. Waiting.

A puzzled furrow shaped between the brows of the older man. His hand reached for his collar, pulled at his cravat. His face started to redden. I could see *understanding* fill his eyes.

The Captain observed him curiously. His head nodded slightly. He said, "I will marry Deirdre. Mrs. Dobson will need a strong man to run the business — and will be glad to trade Deirdre for safety. But she won't live long after that." He reached into Dobson's watch pocket and pulled out the two-headed coin. "A woman my Lyddie had treated kindly told me I must do two tasks to assure the future of Lyddie's child. I do not know when I will be faced with the second, but the first I accomplished today — to take the two dearest treasures of my enemy, and today I have accomplished that."

". . . enemy?" Dobson gasped.

"When my ship," the Captain said quietly, "when *all* the ships in our convoy were seized by the Crown, *your* ships made it through." He held the coin up, dangling from its chain. "Because you *knew* where not to be. And yet did not warn anyone else." He finished his explanation patiently, even though Dobson was no longer listening. Only I. "You were responsible for the loss of my ship, the death of my wife — alone, in poverty, the misery of my infant daughter in a hellhole of an orphanage. You were responsible."

The sins of the fathers, I thought. I released the goblet back into the trunk.

"More?" Jackson asked.

I shook my head. "I think I'm done for tonight. I feel like I've seen what I needed to, what I was supposed to. Let's close it up and go."

On the way down, I described for Jackson what I'd seen. "The Janus coin again" was all he said.

On the second-story landing, I remembered that there was another exit. Jackson had found it in that other time. *Using his future sight*, I realized. "You found a sliding panel here, last time. When I asked you how, you told me, 'It seemed logical.' It was before I knew you could see the future."

"I've never liked hiding things from you, Sare. I bet he didn't either."

Strange, I thought, *for Jackson to use the third person to refer to himself*. "It was up there, on the top edge — some kind of catch." He felt until I heard the small click. A section of the wall, from chair rail to ceiling, popped inward a few inches so that it could slide on a metal track behind the neighboring piece. We climbed out the opening to the hall near my room, then pulled the wall back into place.

I walked with Jackson toward the conservatory. We didn't use the flashlights, finding our way in the suggestion of moonlight that fell through the windows of the upper gallery. I slid my fingers on the chair rail to keep myself on track, searching with my hand for the balcony banister when we reached the main hall.

My fingertips touched wood; a fan of light spilled from beneath Deirdre's bedroom door.

"Jackson," I said, but he was not with me anymore. I had gone somewhere else. Somewhen else.

I wished it wasn't Deirdre's room, but I made myself go to it. I heard — a man and a woman. I turned the knob and opened the door.

The room was lamplit. Deirdre lay propped up with pillows in bed. Her hair was shot with iron gray and her once-beautiful face had been pulled into harsher angles and looser skin by hardship and illness. She looked much like the sickly Deirdre from the other time who had lured two dreaming children to a fantasy nursery.

This Deirdre seemed to be somewhat healthier, perhaps recovering her strength. She had a tray over her lap, set with paper, a quill, and an ink pot. She was pulling at her shawl, speaking to the Captain, unhappy, confused. "But why should I write to him? Our connection is so distant. Why would you have him come?"

"I explained this already, Wife," the Captain said. "He has influence among the colonials. He can get me a commission." He stepped closer and took her by her wrist, twisting it slightly. "Would you deprive me of this opportunity? Shall I send you back to the nursery?"

"No, no," she said, tugging her wrist loose, fumbling to take up the quill. She dipped its tip in the ink. She began to write, slowly and carefully, *Dear Cousin* —

"Sarah."

The room fell dark.

Jackson touched my elbow. "I lost you. I didn't realize you'd stopped. What is it?"

I shook my head a little. "Nothing. I don't know. The Captain wanted Deirdre to send an invitation."

"To whom?"

I shook my head again. "I don't know. Her cousin." I pulled the door shut.

A new crack of light flared, this time coming from beneath the double doors to the Captain's suite.

"Another one," I said grimly. The house just wouldn't stop talking to me. I opened the door.

The Captain sat behind his desk, one of his leather-bound logs open before him. I saw him flip a coin, a silver coin — *Dobson's coin* — and slap it on the table. *Thunk.* Then he checked the coin and made an entry in his log. He did it over and over again.

Thunk.

I walked closer and slid in behind him. I needed to see what he was writing. He used the long feathery script of the era, so I had to work to decipher the words.

At the top, *Advancement.* Below that, *British* and *Colonial,* with the first word circled and the second crossed out. Below that, many words with neat lines drawn through them: *Navy, Army, Smuggling, Finance, Espionage, Sabotage.* The word *Assassination* was circled.

On the next page, a list of names that I knew — names I had studied in history class in that other time: *Dickinson, Shipley, Mason, Hamilton, Varnum, Pickens, Jefferson,* and more. Several names had been crossed out; as I watched, the Captain drew a line through yet another. Then he flipped the coin again.

Thunk.

I understood. I stepped back, appalled. In order to make his fortune, the Captain was deciding who to assassinate to prove his value to the Crown, by flipping Dobson's lucky coin.

The room fell dark. I felt my way to the lighter rectangle of the door.

"I saw something," I said as I reached it. "It's —"

"— the coin," Jackson said. "It always comes back to the coin."

"You know what I'd like to understand —" I started, but another voice interrupted. A voice from the shadows near the stairs.

My mother's voice.

"I'd sure like to understand why the two of you are creeping around up here in the dark."

Chapter Twenty-Four

We met the next morning in the stables, because we figured it was a place where even Sammy wouldn't find us. It wasn't that my mom thought Jackson and I were doing anything *wrong*. She just didn't like the way I started to stammer and evade when she asked for an explanation. Which I could understand.

I told Jackson everything I'd seen about Deirdre and the Captain and Nanga, but none of it pointed us to exactly what had caused the massive changes or what could we do to intervene. The house had fallen silent just when I needed to see more. But it seemed like the coin might be able to lead us to some of the answers.

"The gun's probably already in New York," I said. "We won't have a chance of getting the coin until they send it back."

"No," Jackson said. "We can't wait. We need it here on the first."

"The first?" I said. "Now there's a time limit on this?"

Jackson nodded. "I've seen it."

"How are we supposed to get that coin here by New Year's?"

"We'll have to steal it from the exhibit."

I started to laugh. Then I saw he was completely serious. "Come on," I said. "Maybe I can just ask my mom if we can borrow it."

"How does that conversation go?" he asked me.

How would it go? What could I possibly say to Mom to let me walk off with Claire Hathaway's family heirloom? *"Um, the house needs it, Mom. Jackson asked me to get it."*

What about asking my dad? Or maybe asking Claire?

I just sat there shaking my head. Any of those conversations would be crazy, but to *steal something from New York's Metropolitan Museum*? That was even crazier.

"Sarah," he said to me, "we can steal it. We do steal it. I saw it last night."

"You saw it?"

He nodded. "You were wearing a long red dress."

The Marsden. An item I hadn't shown or even described to him. I thought about that vision: Jackson had seen us stealing Dobson's lucky coin from the Metropolitan. Successfully. Which meant — didn't it? — that it *could* be done. Which meant that we *had* done everything that *needed* to be done to make that possible. Starting from this moment. Didn't it?

It was just too scary to contemplate. The whole idea gave me a shrieking anxiety that turned my stomach and scrambled my brain. I wasn't ready for any of this.

Then I thought of the consequences of changing time the last time. The Japanese Empire. The Thousand-Year Reich. The continuation of slavery into the twentieth century.

I was *Pandora*, I thought. *And I needed to put all the bad stuff back in the box.*

A sound escaped me, half sigh, half sob. I shook my head. I wanted to throw up. "Tell me," I said, "what we need to do."

We had only one day to figure out how to break into a museum neither of us had ever visited, in a city neither of us had ever seen, to steal an object whose exact purpose we did not know. But further planning would have to wait. Jackson needed to go home to take care of Rose. "I'll be back as soon as possible," he promised.

I decided to walk into Severna. I wanted not to have to talk to my parents. I wanted some cold fresh air and physical activity to clear my head. And I wanted to see what the Metropolitan looked like. I headed for the public library.

My path took me past the hardware store and up the street to the Palace Cinema. Two stores down, a woman wrapped in a dark green velvet cloak was trying to scrub painted graffiti off a front window.

Exodus 22:18.

She caught me looking. She rolled her eyes. "Fundamentalists. Or maybe the Confederate Nazis. Getting to be a lot of them."

"I'm sorry?"

"Exodus twenty-two eighteen," she said. " 'Thou shalt not suffer a witch to live.' The joke is, I'm Catholic."

I noticed, then, the store's name: The New Dawn Metaphysical Bookshop.

"Person can't help it if she can see things other people can't." She'd gone back to scrubbing; she was mostly talking to herself. But she looked back at me again, pushing her hair out of her eyes. "Do we know each other?" She was peering at me as if she were having trouble focusing.

"I don't —" I shook my head. "No."

But I had the sense, a memory, of a night sky filled with a thousand floating lights.

The woman took my hand, lifting it. The unexpected contact startled me. "May I?" she said. I nodded and she spread my palm flat. "What's this mark on your hand?"

"What mark?" I looked for some kind of smudge or stain, but she was pointing to the two pinpricks of red that had been in the center of my palm my whole life. "Oh. Those. Just some kind of birthmark. I've always had them."

She stared a moment more, puzzled. "It cuts your life line into three." Then: "May I read your cards?"

Tarot, I thought. She looked concerned suddenly, as if she might have blundered. "I hope I haven't offended?" she said.

"No. I" — *how do I say this politely* — "don't have any money on me, so —"

"No charge."

I did know this woman. I remembered her from a fabulous birthday party — *my* party. In that other time. In Sarah One's world.

She pressed me. "I think it's important. I don't think we met by accident."

I let her tug me into the store. She shook a cloth out on a glass countertop. She pulled a deck of cards from the shelf below her cash register. She set it facedown on the cloth. "Cut the deck," she directed, and so we began.

First card — a man surrounded by a fence of sticks. "The nine of Wands," she said. "This is your issue. It has to do with a need to finish what has been started."

Yes. I nodded. I knew that.

The second card laid across the first: "The three of Wands, reversed." It meant that someone or something, the psychic told me, would try to prevent me "from finishing what must be finished."

Each card spoke of what I already knew. The distant past — the Moon: illusion and deception, hidden enemies, plots, dreams. The Captain, of course, doing whatever he thought would get him more money and position.

The recent past — the Queen of Cups: a psychic or a dreamer who helps others realize their talents. *Maggie.* The near future — the Knight of Pentacles: someone who assumes responsibility, someone who can be counted on. *Someone named Jackson.*

I watched all this as if from a distance. I listened to her speak the words and saw the colorful images on the cards, but part of me heard echoes of her voice, as if I had heard it many times, repeated endlessly, like the images in two facing mirrors, on and on into infinity. The thought left me hollow.

The last card in the diamond around the central pair: the far future, the two of Cups. "It speaks of partnership, maybe even true love. Soul mates."

And I wondered, *Who could or ever would love Pandora?*

"Just four more to go," the woman said, flipping another card to the right of all the others. "The seven of Cups, reversed, which means a loss of hope. The cards are telling you, don't despair, keep on going until you" — she tapped the nine of Wands — "finish what needs to be finished."

She flipped another card above the last. "The seven of Swords." I saw a man sneaking away from a camp with swords in his arms. "This usually means theft or guile, the use of deception, but it can also speak of a journey overland, possibly in secret."

She set another above those. "The Page of Wands. How other people perceive your situation or maybe how they see you. A person who is surprising, exciting, consistent, and faithful."

"The last card — the most likely future outcome of your issue." She flipped it. I looked at it, strangely unsurprised. A skeleton rode a pale horse across a night landscape scattered with bodies.

Death.

The woman hurried to reassure me. "This is actually —"

I interrupted her, speaking in a flat voice. "— a good card that means the end of an old way of life and the beginning of a new way of life."

On and on into infinity.

"Yes," she said, surprised. "How did you know that?"

"I was wrong. I did have my cards told once before." *The first time I turned sixteen.* It was much too hot in that little shop. She needed to let in some fresh air. I felt faint. "Thank you," I managed. "I have to go."

The library was nearly as warm as the fortune-teller's shop, I supposed because the thermostat was under the control of an elderly librarian. But I wasn't going to stay long. I found the alcove that housed the card catalog. I started in the Ma-Mom drawer, looking for "Metropolitan," but was redirected to the Mon-Mu drawer for "Museum, Metropolitan." I flipped through the cards, searching for something on the museum's design.

Growing discomfort between my shoulder blades made me stop — it felt as if I were being watched. I turned, but saw no one's eyes on me. I went back to the cards, still uncomfortable, grateful when I found a reference to a multivolume set on New English architecture that promised four pages of photos of the museum, along with a floor plan.

I followed the Dewey decimal numbers deep into the stacks, into the silence convoked by muffling walls of books. A neon light overhead made humming and cracking noises as it decided whether to stay lit or become permanently burnt out. I ran my eyes along the book spines, bending over to make out their letters and numbers in the failing light.

I heard — something. And smelled some trace of vanilla, maybe. I peered through the gaps in the books to check other aisles, front and back. I scanned the numbers faster, looking for a matching four-book set. Finding it. Pulling out the correct volume and starting back. Darting into the main aisle where the rustles and murmurs of other patrons reached me once again. I felt ridiculous for my attack of nerves. But relieved to be heading back toward people.

I begged paper and a pencil from the librarian, and settled at a table. Laboriously I worked to re-create the lines of the Metropolitan floor plan to offer to Jackson as a reference. I hadn't inherited my mother's artistic abilities, but the drawing wasn't too bad. It gave one a general idea of where the main rooms and halls were.

That smell. Not vanilla, but something else, something close, mixed with citrus and herbs.

"You are interested in architecture, Miss Parsons?"

I jumped. *Bay rum.* The smell was bay rum and smoke. Karl Jaeger walked around the table into my view. "May I see?" he asked.

I looked up into his blue eyes and rudely flipped my drawing facedown. "Sorry," I said. "Not much of an artist."

He smiled. As usual. He leaned to see the original in the book. I closed it. His smile widened to show teeth. All perfectly white and even. A phrase — so familiar I could practically taste it — got stuck to the tip of my tongue.

"Evidently you don't think the architect was much of an artist either," he said mildly. "Fortunately for Mr. Hunt of the Metropolitan Museum, the rest of the world does not agree."

I found his interest distinctly unpleasant. As he intended, no doubt. "My little brother doesn't get to go to the Amber House exhibit. He wanted to know what the museum looked like."

"Such a solicitous older sister," he said, tipping his head. He looked a little puzzled. "It was strange. When I met you in Amber House, you seemed almost to have an aura around you." I made an involuntary dismissive noise. "I have been trained," he said a little acidly, "to observe people closely."

Trained to observe? "What's your job?"

He smilingly wagged his finger at me, as though I was making an improper suggestion. "Attaché," he said. "Embassy staff. It is even printed on my cards. At any rate, now I can see in the bright daylight of this fine Confederate library, you are a very ordinary girl after all. Aren't you?"

I stood, picked up my book and paper, coat, and bag, and shoved my chair back in place. I looked him in the eyes. "A *very* ordinary girl," I said, adding as I walked away, "who doesn't like Nazis."

Out on the street, I wanted to be — *home*. I felt, suddenly, exposed and alone. The thought swam forward: *What was he doing here?* Then another thought, wilder and more suspicious than the first: *Is he following me?*

After the heat of the library, the cold had more bite. I quickened my steps, to warm myself and to shake the feeling I was being pursued. I was nearly jogging when I reached the park at the edge of town. I made myself slow as I wound through the naked trees, taking care not to stray from the path that ended just across the road from Amber House.

A black Mercedes idled on the road's shoulder in front of the estate, smoke oozing from its exhaust.

I hurried across the road, well east of the car, heading for the small gate, but Jaeger stepped out of the trees, much closer than his car. I stopped in my tracks, standing in the center of the road like a startled deer.

He said nothing. He was a silent presence, tall and wide, wrapped in a heavy black coat trimmed in silver. My scarf dangled from the hand he held out toward me. His other hand was hidden in his coat pocket.

He spoke finally. "I found it left behind, beneath your chair."

I took two small steps forward, but could not make myself go farther.

"How interesting," Jaeger said. "Here in the shadows of

Amber House, I can see my first impression of you was the correct one. There is something quite special about you after all. Your energetic emanations are quite vivid." He cocked his head. "But perhaps, I just see more clearly here. What do you think, Ms. Parsons?"

All the while he held my scarf out, daring me to come closer. I didn't budge.

"Did you know," he continued, "that I made an offer in gold to your mother for the property? She was insulted." He smiled. "But she should have taken it, because sooner or later I will have that house, and my price will only go down from here."

He was still smiling as he started toward me, his footsteps falling swiftly and silently on the frozen ground. And the phrase I could not bring to mind in the library finally surfaced. I thought, suddenly, wildly: *What big teeth you have.*

The sound of a gun cocking made him stop short.

A voice spoke from my right. "My dad was in London when the Nazis reduced it to rubble." *Jackson.* "I don't like Nazis very much." I saw him then, partially hidden behind a rock, with a shotgun aimed squarely at Jaeger. I could have wept, I was so glad he was there.

Jaeger had turned at the sound. "If you know what's good for you, you will go now. What happened to your grandfather might turn into a family tradition."

"I've heard," Jackson said coldly, "a shotgun blast leaves a pretty big hole in a man. Want to try it out?"

Jaeger dropped my scarf in the road, walked stiffly to his car, and opened the door. "Jackson Harris, is it not? I wish to get the name correct in my report."

"Two *R*s," Jackson called to him.

"We will meet again," the Nazi said, smiling before he disappeared behind the dark glass of the car.

Jackson trained the gun on the car's windows as it pulled away. It roared to the crest of the hill, where the hum of its engine faded. Jackson sagged down against the rock he'd been using as a shield. I scooped up my scarf and ran through the gate to kneel beside him. "You all right?"

He gave a weary chuckle. "Surprising how exhausting it is keeping that thing pointed at someone. It's a big chunk of metal."

"That was incredible. You were incredible," I said. "Where'd you get that gun?"

"The barn. Was your grandfather's." I helped him to his feet. He broke open the barrel and showed me. "It's not even loaded."

I just shook my head. "I believed you."

He smiled. "Good thing *he* believed me."

"What was he trying to do?" I said.

"He was trying —" Jackson started, then stopped. He put an arm around my shoulder and started us walking back toward the house. I thought to myself that the arm was partly support for him, but partly support for me too. "I don't want to scare you, Sare. But he wanted to make you disappear. Whatever kind of sense he has that makes him good at what he does, Amber House makes it a whole lot stronger. When he looked at you, he saw a threat to his Thousand-Year Reich. And he was right to see it. Because you're going to make *them* disappear."

Poof. No more Reich. Could it be that easy?

"I still have no idea how we're going to pull that off." I stopped walking and pulled my sketch of the museum out of my pocket and unfolded it. "I had some thought this might help, but it's pretty pathetic."

Jackson pulled a wad of papers from his pocket and handed it to me. "We'll match yours against mine and see how it all stacks up."

I opened his. Page after page of notes, some with times jotted in the margins. Flecked with — "Blood," I said. "You've been forcing visions? No wonder you can't stand up."

"We need to know what to do." He shrugged. He took the pages back. "I'm not done yet."

"Jackson —" I started. He tried to silence me with a look. I wouldn't be stopped. "*If* you need to do this again, I want to be there with you."

He started to shake his head, but then said, "Fine. Maybe it will help."

"*After* my parents leave," I said.

"Sure."

"Anything else we need to handle?"

"I need to get a train ticket to New York."

"I'll drive you into town — you're not walking. You don't look like you'd make it."

"Will I make it with you behind the wheel?" he teased.

We'd reached the house. My mom stuck her head out the front door. "I've been looking for you, honey. Where did you vanish to? I need you for a couple things. Come on in as quick as you can." She started to duck back inside but turned back to speak to Jackson. "Is Rose getting over that bug?"

"Yes, Mrs. Parsons. She told me to thank you for the soup."

"My pleasure. I know it wasn't as good as she could make."

"She enjoyed it very much. It was really nice of you."

"No problem. You tell her we miss her, all right?"

"Sure will, Mrs. Parsons."

I watched my mother disappear, then turned back to Jackson. "Bug?"

He shook his head a little. "She didn't want them to know. She didn't want your mother fussing over her. Don't tell her or your father. Or Maggie or Sammy either."

"She's going to need help, J."

"No, she's not." He stopped me when I started to answer: "Come Saturday, we are going to fix time, and then she won't need any help."

He sounded so confident. "Did you see us do it? Succeed?"

He thought about his answer. He looked into my eyes. "You know I wouldn't, couldn't, lie to you, Sarah. I've seen it go a lot of different ways. There are a lot of things that can go wrong. But — I *have* seen us succeed. We just can't quit. Neither of us. We have to see it through to the very end."

Like his father, I thought. *Clear the nest.*

We agreed to meet again at five o'clock, near the front gate, to go buy Jackson that ticket to New York.

It was really happening. We were going to break into the Metropolitan Museum to steal a two-thousand-year-old coin so we could —

Save the world.

Chapter Twenty-Five

At 4:57 P.M., I slipped out the front door, quietly lifting the car keys from the tray on the table as I went.

Not quietly enough.

"Hey, hey," my mom called after me. "Where are you going with those?"

"I asked Dad," I said, closing the door before she could squeeze off another question.

Jackson was waiting just out of sight at the driveway entrance. I pulled over and he climbed in.

"You didn't tell me what you saw," I said as we drove off. "All those notes."

"I want to get it all worked out first."

"They looked pretty detailed."

"I've got pieces of it — I've got *most* of it. We'll have to memorize it all, right down to the minute. I'm going to be responsible for part of it and you're going to be responsible for part of it."

"Wow," I said, nodding, "sure." I could do that. But still — "Can you tell me the big picture? So I have some idea how we're going to do this? Because it would make me feel a lot more settled."

So he told me, briefly, how we were going to manage. "You'll go to the exhibit party with your parents," he said, but added that I was going to have to sneak away early. "We'll break in about a half hour before midnight," using a key that we didn't have yet, In fact, he wasn't sure exactly what the key looked like or even where we'd get it — "I just know that we'll find it in time." When I asked him how, he shrugged and said, "It'll come to us." He'd worked out a specific escape route that "you have to memorize, Sare, because that's the part you'll be in charge of."

He made it sound real. He made it sound like we could do it. Maybe.

The train station was on the far side of Severna. Its parking lot was full of the cars of commuters who worked in Baltimore or Arlington; a trainload of them were exiting the station when we arrived. Making our way inside was like swimming upstream, but by the time we entered, the long room full of benches was nearly deserted again, awaiting the next train's deposit.

Aside from the trip home from the Baptist church, I'd never been out in the world with Jackson before. Our friendship had always been bounded by the estate or the twists and curls of the river. As I walked by his side into the station, I saw that we were drawing stares. I didn't know whether it was because they didn't like a young black man escorting a white girl, or if they were gawking at Jackson's scars. I honestly just didn't notice the scars anymore — they didn't have anything to do with who Jackson was. But when I looked through strangers' eyes, I could see they were still vivid enough to provoke morbid curiosity. Jackson looked straight ahead, evidently used to the unpleasant attention.

The man inside the ticket window tried hard *not* to stare, to the point he would not even look Jackson in the eyes. He kept himself busy with paperwork and making change. I had brought along money to pay for the ticket, but Jackson beat me to it, pulling out a wad of cash held together by a taut rubber band. My eyes boggled at its thickness.

We were leaving when a pale redheaded guy sitting on a bench called out, "What happened to you, boy? Half a lynching?"

Jackson did not even glance his way, which the creep seemed to take as a personal insult. "Hey, I'm talking to you, boy. Hey!

Can a man just ask you one little question?" He was grinning now, warming to his topic. "Is it Halloween already, or you always go around scaring the women and kids?"

I started to turn, but Jackson covertly pulled on my coat sleeve and said, "Just keep walking."

"Holy Jesus," the redhead added, "I just about lost my lunch looking at you."

I stopped, tugging my sleeve loose from Jackson's fingers, and walked closer to the bigot. "Mister," I drawled sweetly, "can a girl ask *you* one little question?"

He knew I wanted to murder him, but he just purred, "Sure, sugah, a pretty little thing like you. G'wan ahead."

I saw it then, just under his jawline on his neck. A tattoo. A swastika. *One of President Stevenson's "constituency."*

I smiled and spoke up loud enough for the onlookers to hear: "If yo' mama and papa got a divorce, *sugah*, would they still be brother and sister?"

The ticket counter guy busted out laughing, and snickers spread through the small crowd. The redhead narrowed his eyes. He answered in a murmur, just loud enough for me to hear: "You think I don't know who you are? You think that fine house on the river's gonna keep your kind safe from what's coming? You best think again."

I shook my head. "No," I said, meaning it to my core. "No. *You're* the one who's going back in the box." Then I made myself turn away.

I fell into step beside Jackson, who had never stopped walking. He said mildly, "For someone trying to avoid drawing attention to herself, you sure don't go about it very well."

"*Some*one needed to tell that Nazi creep to keep his white-trash mouth shut."

He said with a certain amount of irritation, "You think I *need* you to defend me? You think I haven't been hearing garbage like that on pretty much a daily basis for the last thirteen years? Does calling that man out for being white trash make either of you a better person?"

I dropped my chin. "I'm sorry," I said miserably, feeling like a five-year-old. The truth was, Jackson was just a better person than I was, more mature, more certain. I thought, *Helen is probably like that too.* I would bet she was, but I hoped it wasn't true.

We got back in the car. "Look, Sare," he said, "I appreciate you trying to help me. I do. You're a good person." I started to shake my head, but he insisted. "Yes, you are. I'm not saying you're perfect" — he smiled — "but you're way ahead of the rest of the crowd. Not once in all the years I've known you have you *ever* made me feel that, when you looked at me, you saw the scars instead of the person. Not even when you were little. And that's helped a lot."

I started the car, put it in motion. I thought, if I did nothing else in the rest of my life worth noticing, it was good to know I had at least helped Jackson.

I pulled over just before the driveway to Amber House to let him out. "J, what is with that roll of bills in your pocket? Where'd you get all that money?"

"I've been saving it."

"What for?"

"It's my college money," he said quietly.

"You can't spend that. I have a rainy day savings account. Let me use *that* money for this."

He smiled and shook his head a little. "You just don't believe this is really happening, do you, Sare? You don't really think we're going to fix time and save the world."

"I believe it," I said.

"No, you don't," he said. "Because if you did, you'd realize I am *never* going to need that money to go to college. If I have any future at all, it won't be here, and it won't depend on the roll of cash I had stuffed in a coffee can."

He was right, of course. If what we did worked, he wouldn't need that money. *And* — I *didn't* really believe we were going to fix time and save the world. It just was so preposterous.

How can I do it, I thought, *if I don't really believe it?*

Jackson had pulled out the money roll and was contemplating it. "You know what I'm going to do with this money when I get to New York?" he asked, with a small smile of pure pleasure.

"Tell me."

"I am going to buy myself some new clothes, head to toe. I am going to rent a room in the nicest hotel I can find. I am going to get myself an enormous steak for dinner, and maybe one of those giant crawdad things too."

"A lobster?" I said, smiling.

"One of those. And I am going to buy just as big a breakfast, and leave huge tips everywhere I go. I am going to spend that money like —"

"Like?"

"Like there's no tomorrow. Because there won't be."

Back at the house, I staved off Mom's curiosity with "I needed a couple of things from town for the trip." She and Dad were leaving the next day with the Hathaways, and they were taking the bulk of my luggage with them — Mom wanted to get my dress pressed by the hotel staff in plenty of time for the party, or so she said. It might have been she just didn't trust me to get to New York on the right train arriving at the right time with all my luggage in tow. Which might have been a fair assessment.

We had a kind of farewell dinner for Sammy's benefit, since we would not be celebrating New Year's with him. It was the final remnants of our Christmas goose — as always, shredded and shaped into cakes with the mashed potatoes, then sautéed to golden. It was my favorite leftover meal, both because it was the best and because it was the last. The goose's swan song.

Sam was uncharacteristically gloomy. I asked him why, later, on our way upstairs. He said, "That was our last dinner until after new years."

"That's only a few days away, Sam. Mom and Dad'll be back sooner than you think."

"I know," he said. "But I love them so much. I don't want them to change."

"They're not going to change, bud." He got such strange ideas in his head. "They'll be back. Exactly the same."

"I hope so," he said.

I packed my suitcase for New York after dinner: sightseeing clothes, PJs, shoes, all the necessities. It weighed half a ton when I zipped it up — I was glad Dad was going to wrestle with it instead of me. I dragged it downstairs and left it near the front door. The long garment bags full of formal wear for Dad, Mom, and me were already hanging over the edge of the front closet door.

My mom spotted me. "You sure this is all right, hon? Going up without us? You feel fine about it?"

"Mom," I sighed, exasperated. "It's a four-hour train ride. Maggie will drop me off at the station. Richard will ride with me. You'll be in New York when I get there. What could go wrong?"

She smiled, smoothed down my hair a bit, and kissed me on the forehead — a silver kiss. "Sometimes I forget how grown up you've become, sweetie. Dad and I are off to sleep. See you in the morning before we go."

Snow was falling past my window again, white puffs caught in the lamp's light against the black beyond. It felt good to be inside, warm and cozy — a house hug.

I curled up on my bed and looked over a list Jackson had given me to memorize — part of the steps I was to be responsible for: "12:02 Turn left to north museum exit. Follow dirt path through trees — DO NOT USE SIDEWALK. Just before fountain, turn right up hill, come out on street. Cross at light. East three blocks to subway entrance. 12:15 Transfer at Lexington to the line to Penn Station. Take 1:00 Baltimore train." It didn't say what happened after that, but I figured Jackson would have it handled.

He had foreseen this stuff down to the last detail. It was going to work. Predicted and guaranteed in advance.

At least, I hoped so.

CHAPTER TWENTY-SIX

My parents left just before noon. Mom got all misty. Even for just a day or two, she didn't like leaving Sam. Which I could understand.

When we went back inside, Sammy opened the drawer in the front hall table and took out my black silk purse, the one Maggie had given me for Christmas.

"Sam? I packed that for New York. I wanted it for the party. Why'd you get that out of my suitcase?"

"You have to keep it *with* you, Sarah," he said severely, handing it to me.

"Jeez, Sam," I said, opening it, "you put all that junk back inside it."

"It's *not* junk. She said it was good stuff. And you *promised* you'd leave those things in there. You can't break your promise, Sarah!"

His little eyes were blazing. I had never seen him this furious. "Fine, all right. I'll keep it with me. I'll leave it stuffed. I'm sorry."

"You have to *promise*."

I rolled my eyes, imagining myself clanking around the New Year's gala with a can opener and a lighter in my evening bag. "I promise, Sam. Honest to God."

I was restless, ill at ease. I couldn't find a place to be quiet. I felt that I still hadn't remembered enough, learned enough. I couldn't imagine everything working out.

If we were *insanely* lucky enough to steal the coin, and get away with it, what then? I had no idea what we were supposed to do with it. Use it, maybe, to summon an echo that could tell us how things could be put right? Because I still had no clue what exactly Deirdre had done to change the course of time. And no matter how I poked and prodded, the house wasn't telling me any more of its secrets.

I bundled up warmly and went outside. The cold air felt good on my face. It made me recognize I wasn't in a dream. This was all real; this was all happening.

I saw the rungs of the ladder that went up to the tree fort in the oak. I had not climbed them for at least a couple years.

The simple plankwood steps nailed into the tree were slimy from all the snow that had been falling on and off since we'd got to Amber House. I started to climb, making sure of every step. Halfway up, I remembered seeing an echo in which child-Maggie had fallen past me — the tumble that led to her coma, and being trapped in the mirror world.

She was there when I got to the top — the real, grown Maggie, sitting on the bench under the tree fort's partial roof.

"I'm sorry," I said, starting to back down again. "I didn't know you were up here."

"Come," she said, patting the space next to her.

I hauled myself up onto the tree house floor and went over to perch beside her. We sat silently, listening. Even with the tree naked of leaves, the wind sighed through its branches. Accumulating water dripped off the twigs above us to fall in random rhythm on the wood floor. *Voices*, I thought. *So many things have voices we never listen to.* The sounds soothed me. It was a moment of peace.

Maggie finally spoke. "You remember it all yet?"

"The other time?" She nodded. I shook my head. "More and more, but not all. Some of it — most of it, was better than this time. But not *all*. No matter what, Maggie" — I took her hand in mine — "I'm glad I was able to wake you."

She squeezed my fingers. "Me too."

"Why aren't you going to New York? You're one of the women of Amber House."

She smiled, looked down, considered. Then she looked into my eyes levelly. "You're going to make this happen, Sarah-too. You're going to succeed. And I would rather spend every last moment up till then here, at Amber House."

I understood that Maggie still expected she might not exist after time changed again.

"Besides," she went on, "you might need someone's help when you come back. I want to be here for that."

Maggie would be here to help me even if it meant she would be erased.

"I wanted to ask you, Sare — do you remember the other person who was there in the attic?"

"Deirdre?"

"No, not the mama. The other person. He was there at the end. Watching you."

"What did he look like?"

"I don't know. Where I was, I wasn't seeing the outsides of people. I was in dream time," she explained. "I was seeing who I understood people to be. Sammy was my twin brother and we were the same. You were like a flame, Sarah, radiating light that darkness fled from, but your light was growing fainter all the time. I felt bad, because I knew you were going to go out."

I remembered thinking that too.

"And this other person — well, he was all soft golden light. Steady, calm. I thought maybe he was an angel. A guardian angel."

"You thought he was your guardian angel?"

"Not mine, Sarah. Yours."

Mine.

I realized then who it was, who it must have been. I could even picture him there. He had followed me upstairs. He had held my hand and kept me from slipping away.

Jackson, of course. He had stayed with me until the very end.

I wondered where he was. He'd promised to let me be there when he tried going into the future again — to finish figuring out how to steal the coin and, Lord help us, save the world. If he wasn't going to find me, I guessed I'd just have to find him. I brought his image to mind and searched for his heat.

I sensed him in the vicinity of the stables. I smiled. That was just like him — he was still doing his chores even though he expected all of time to collapse. I supposed, when I found him, he'd tell me, "The horses still have to eat."

But when I opened the stable door, I saw him on his back on a pile of hay on the floor, his limbs rigid from a seizure.

"Damn it!" I ran to crouch beside him. He was cold, his skin ashy — there was no heat in the stable. He'd been wrapped in a blanket, but had shaken free of it; I pulled it back around him. Then I lifted his head to cushion it on my lap. "I'm here," I whispered.

The tightness in the cords of his neck, the muscles of his face, his arms, his spine, his legs, began to ease. I could see his eyes moving rapidly beneath his closed lids. He was panting, and there was a catch in his breath, as if he was terrified. I took his hand in mine. "I'm here," I said again.

The light changed. I had entered a vision, but it wasn't mine. A place of fog so thick I couldn't look beyond. The wind was blowing, whipping past in all directions, shrieking, pulling the thoughts from my mind. I could see Jackson ahead of me, partly solid, partly light, both parts blurred and spread by the wind. He was following a path marked by a silver thread. He strained forward, staring. Where he looked, the fog thinned. I thought I could see something. Some*one*. Small. Dressed in white. *Amber*, I thought, but then told myself no, for she was of the past. Jackson turned back and saw me. And smiled.

I heard him gasp and felt him stiffen. Then found myself sitting on the stable's stone floor in pale daylight. Jackson had opened his eyes and was wiping away the blood seeping from his nose.

"You promised me," I said.

"I don't think I actually *promised*," he said, "but I wish I had listened to you. You helped."

"Did you see what you needed to see?" He nodded. "You going to tell me?" I said.

He nodded again, but said, "Not yet. Soon."

"You promise?" I said.

"I promise," he said.

I shook my head. "You look terrible. You look like a little girl could whup you one-handed. You need some hot food. We've still got a ton of leftovers for dinner. You want to join us?"

"Thanks," he said, "but no. Going to have dinner with Gran. I want to say good-bye to her."

"Good-bye?" I repeated. It sounded so morbid. "It's not like you'll never see her again."

He smiled, shook his head a little, and pushed himself up to sitting. "No matter what, Sare, I just can't turn you into a true believer. If this works," he said, "if we succeed at what we're trying to do, this Gran will be gone. I *won't* ever see her again. And . . . that's probably a good thing, since she's been suffering a lot the last couple months, with more suffering ahead of her. In the future I saw, she was a nurse. Too smart to smoke."

I remembered. "She was a nurse last time too."

"Anyway," he said, "I want to be with her."

I understood. We walked back in silence, parting at the end of the east wing, he heading for the river and I for the front door.

When I touched the railing by the steps, I saw two children I remembered from another lifetime — Sarah-Louise and her twin brother, Matthew. They were young, plump-faced. It looked like a summer evening, full dusk. The two of them had nets and canning jars — they were capturing fireflies.

Nanga sat down between them. "We had many of those in my homeland. Different colors, different patterns of glowing. My brother and I also liked to catch them, though we had no glass to put them in."

"You miss that place?" Matthew asked.

"Yes. Oh, yes. Every day. That place. My home. My people. My family. My husband. Every minute. When I reached this land, I wished to die, but your mama wouldn't let me." She paused to remember. "You know what she said to me when I asked her why?"

"What did she say?" Matthew asked, listening intently.

"She was not much older than you. A little girl. Headstrong. She said, 'You touched my boot and spoke my name. So I knew we were alike. The same kind. I knew you belonged here. I knew Amber House needed you.'"

"I think she was right," Matthew said.

"The house," Nanga said quietly, "and the ones to come."

The phone was ringing when I went in. It was Richard.

"Dad called. They're at the museum, working on the setup."

"Oh, good," I said.

"Shall I swing by around noon tomorrow?"

"'Swing by'?"

"With the limo. Give you a lift to the station. Patrick's driving me. I thought we could go in together."

"Oh," I said. "Thanks, but Maggie's driving me in. She and Sam want to wave good-bye."

"They can ride with us too," he said cheerfully. "Sam would like the limo."

"I bet he would. That's so nice of you, but" — the fatal pause, why couldn't I *think* faster? — "I think Maggie said something about wanting to run some errands in town after. I'll just meet you on the train."

"Oh," he said. He sounded a little confused. "All right." He brightened his tone, excusing my lame lies. "Meet you there, then. Good night."

"Good night, Richard."

I thought, as I returned the phone to its cradle, that Amber House needed all of us. Deirdre and Nanga. Maeve and Fiona. Gramma and my parents and Maggie and Sam. Even Richard, somehow. We all belonged to this place because Amber House needed us.

Chapter Twenty-Seven

Jackson came through the kitchen door at eleven thirty the next morning. He crouched by the fire to warm himself after the walk from his house. "Gran was still asleep when I left," he said. "I didn't tell her I was going. I decided to leave that to the neighbor who is coming by to take care of her until — while I'm gone."

"Want something to eat?" I asked. "We're just doing cereal, but I could get you some oatmeal, help warm you up."

He shook his head. "I'm good."

I didn't have much of an appetite either. We were a somber group climbing into the car — all except Sammy, who was back to being his usual cheery self. "Be happy," he said. "New years are coming!"

"Is," I corrected automatically.

Thanks to my mom and dad, my only luggage was a light pack in which I didn't have much more than the black silk purse, a book, some money and my mother's written directions as to where they would meet Richard and me in New York. Jackson carried a substantial backpack full to bulging.

Maggie parked the car so she and Sam could walk into the station with us. They stopped just inside the door. Sam hugged Jackson around the waist while Maggie pulled me close. She said softly into my ear, "See it through."

Then Sam threw himself on my waist while Maggie shook hands gravely with Jackson. "Cheer up, Sarah," Sam told me. "It'll be good, you'll see."

We all waved good-bye as Jackson and I walked around the benches to the farther door. Jackson reached to open it for me, but a sheriff stepped forward to block it before I could go through.

"Sarah Parsons?" he asked.

"Yes?" I said.

"How old are you, honey?" he said in a drawl.

I was confused. "I'm sixteen, but my parents know I'm taking this trip. I'm meeting them —"

He wasn't listening to me anymore. He'd turned to Jackson. "I'm afraid you're gonna have to come with me, boy."

"What?" Jackson said. I could see by his face that whatever he had foreseen of this trip did not include his being arrested by the local sheriff.

"We still have laws in the Confederation prohibiting a colored boy transporting an underaged white girl out of the country for illicit purposes."

"No!" I said, disbelieving. "We aren't even traveling together." I tried to step between them.

"Missy?" the man said. "You want I should take you in too?"

"This is ridiculous," I said. "I'm traveling with Senator Hathaway's son. Jackson is just my neighbor. We gave him a ride." My voice kept rising. I couldn't stop it.

He grabbed my wrist then, and pulled me in close. I could see the pits in his skin, the stains on his teeth. The tattoo beneath his jaw — a swastika. "I know who you're traveling with, girl," he gritted out in a low voice, "and unless you want to cause the senator a world of embarrassment, you better back off."

I stepped back then, not knowing what to do. I looked toward the entrance. Maggie was still there. She had seen. She moved her mouth silently, shaping words.

Be ready?

She took Sam by the hand and pulled him out the door, bending to speak to him as they went. The sheriff put cuffs on Jackson and started to lead him out. I followed after helplessly. Jackson turned his head to speak to me over his shoulder. "Get on the train, Sarah. I'll get there, I swear. I don't know how, but I'll get there."

"He's right about you getting on the train, sugar," the sheriff drawled. "I understand the senator is expecting you. But don't be looking for this boy to join you. He'll be safe in jail till tomorrow evening."

They'd reached the front curb and the sheriff's car, with everyone looking. He handled Jackson into the backseat, tossing his backpack into the front. Then he climbed into the driver's seat.

Where is Maggie? I wondered, looking about wildly. *What am I supposed to do?*

The sheriff's car pulled away from the curb lazily, starting the long circle through the lot to the exit.

I spotted Maggie then. She was standing near the front of my parents' car, which was stopped just before the exit. The driver's door was open; I saw Sam's head above the car hood just before he disappeared. I started to run between the parked cars in the lot, taking the shortest route to the exit, keeping low, trying to avoid the sheriff's notice. I got to the end of the last of the parked cars just before the sheriff did. Sam lay on the ground in front of my parents' car, his limbs splayed out like a broken doll's. Then Maggie was waving her arms and screaming.

The sheriff stopped of course. "What in hell?" he said as he heaved himself up out of the car.

Maggie was babbling, shrieking, about the little boy shooting out from nowhere, dashing in front of her car, so she couldn't stop, it wasn't her fault. "Is he dead? Is he dead?" she screamed.

Jackson leaned forward to look at me through the window and gestured with his head — *Come.*

Oh!

Crouched over, I dashed to the sheriff's car, but someone else beat me there. A young black woman wearing a yellow scarf. "Get the keys," she hissed as she opened the rear door and helped Jackson up and out.

I snatched the keys from the ignition and snagged the strap of Jackson's pack, still keeping low, watching the sheriff and my aunt. I'd just heard Maggie exclaim, "I don't know what in the *Sam hill* he was doing," when Sammy leapt up and started sprinting down the sidewalk. His name must have been a signal.

"Come back here, boy! Come back here!" The sheriff started after Sam as Maggie whirled around to climb back into her car, and the young woman, Jackson, and I ducked down between a row of parked cars.

"Give me the keys," the woman ordered, then quickly sorted through them to find a little silver one she used on Jackson's cuffs. I heard Maggie's car squeal away. I heard the sheriff yelling, "Stop, dammit! You come back here."

Jackson said to me, "When I tell you, run like hell for the tracks to the right of the station and don't stop for anything. Thank you," he told the woman, clasping her hand. Then he grabbed the pack, took my elbow and started moving. "Run," he said. "Run!" And I did.

Behind me I heard the sheriff's voice. "Stop those two! Stop 'em." Two nasty-looking men near the station entrance instantly started running to cut us off. The sheriff pounded after us, his heavy footfalls gaining ground. I wondered hysterically if he would shoot.

We reached the tracks. My train was gone. I could see its caboose just disappearing around a bend. Where were we supposed to go? What was Jackson's plan?

A freight train was charging in from the opposite direction, hardly slowing. Jackson grabbed my hand, pulling. "Faster!" he said.

The men were behind us, all three of them, putting on speed, sprinting to catch us.

I realized then what Jackson meant to do. Put that freight train between us and our pursuit. It was almost on us, a wall of moving noise. Its engineer had spotted the two mad teenagers trying to outrace his locomotive and started yanking on the whistle. Its shriek went on and on. "No, no," I sobbed, but did not slow. I had to look to leap the rails and keep my footing — I couldn't watch the train, but I could feel it coming. Noise and heat and thunder in the ground. I jumped another rail, singing with vibrations. *Oh God, oh God, oh God*, my brain whimpered as I struggled to gain footing on the gravel between the ties. Jackson yanked my hand hard, pulling me up, over the last rail. The train's wake of wind blew my hair high as we staggered to stay on our feet on the other side.

All I wanted was to sag to the ground, but Jackson was still pulling. *"Keep going!"*

Ahead of us, another freight train was beginning to move, to build up speed, going in the same northerly direction as our missed train to New York. An open door to an empty car went past before me; Jackson tugged us right, toward that door.

"Oh, no," I moaned. I had a stitch in my side, I was sobbing for breath, and the floor of the freight car had to be at least chest height. I would never be able to get inside.

We pulled level with the open door. Jackson heaved his pack in. He shouted to me, "I'll get in and pull you up. Keep up with me. Don't stop."

"Yes," I gasped, watching the ground, trying to run on the thick wooden ties. Jackson jumped, grabbed a metal handhold, and pulled himself up out of sight.

"Take my hand!" he called to me. I raised my arm in the air, reaching blindly, afraid to take my eyes from my footing. "Look!" he commanded.

I lifted my eyes and swung my arm toward his. My toe hit the edge of a tie. I started to go down.

But he caught my wrist and held it fast as he pushed himself upright, pulling me into the air. My feet found the floor of the boxcar. I straightened up into his arm, holding me steady, holding me safe.

"Oh, my God," I sobbed between breaths. "I can't do this. I want to go home. I'm not strong enough. I'm not brave enough. I'm not *anything* enough for this."

"Stop it!" he said. He held me out so he could look me in the eye. He shook me a little. His voice was harsh and unrelenting. "Too many people have suffered because of what happened —"

Because of what I did.

"— and more people are going to suffer before this is done."

No. Please, no.

"You can do this, Sare. You can make it to the end. You have to promise me that you won't give up, no matter what, or all that suffering will be for nothing."

I squeezed my eyes shut. The tarot card — the nine of Wands: *"Finish what has been started."*

I was still sobbing, but I nodded my head. "I promise."

Jackson did what he could to make us comfortable, closing the sidings, pulling a couple sweaters from his pack for us to sit on. Even with the doors closed, it was still freezing. We braced ourselves next to each other against the rear wall, the sweaters beneath us, our packs wedged on either side, my coat over our legs, his wrapped around us and tucked up under our chins. The light in the boxcar had been reduced to dusk, with random beams falling through chinks in the walls.

"It isn't all going to be like that, is it?" I asked.

He shook his head. "I didn't bother to see us leaving from the train station. I had no idea we'd have a problem. Wonder why we did."

"The sheriff had a swastika. Just like that creep when we went to get your ticket. Maybe they were connected to Jaeger?"

"Maybe. But they didn't stop us. We can still make this work." He put his arm around my shoulder to keep me warm. "You were pretty impressive back there, Sare."

"I was scared out of mind back there, J," I said. I didn't want to think about it. "Who was that woman who helped us?"

"I don't know." He shook his head a little. "Just a yellow scarf, trying to help."

"A yellow scarf?"

"Someone in the movement. We all take an oath to help other yellow scarves."

I'd kind of figured it was something like that. "You have any idea where we're headed?"

He shook his head. "The tracks branch in four different directions a little north of here. One line toward New York, two into Pennsylvania, and one west. No way of knowing till we get there."

I remembered something. I fished Maggie's silk purse out of my pack, peeked inside, and pulled out one of Sam's Christmas gifts. I held it out on my palm: a little functional plastic compass. "Think this'll help?"

"That ought to. If I know which way we're headed, I can figure out how and where to catch the train back to New York in the morning."

" 'In the morning'? Are you kidding me? My parents are going to be hysterical."

"We'll figure out something you can tell them before we get there."

"I'll be seventy-two before they let me travel by myself again."

"Day after tomorrow, they won't remember a thing about it," he said.

The rocking of the train combined with the exhaustion of the day to fill my mind with a craving for oblivion. My head found Jackson's shoulder. I felt safe there, tucked inside his arm. What I'd been through was — impossible. But Jackson would make it work. I was safe with Jackson.

"Sarah," he said.

"What?" I jerked awake, remembering in a rush where I was sitting and how frightened I was.

"Shhh," Jackson said. "You were having a bad dream."

"I've been having a bad day. Where are we?"

"Pretty much at the end of the line."

"We coming to a station?"

"Nope. We hit a long climb. We've slowed way down. We're hopping off."

"We're hopping off a moving train?"

"You can do it," he said, and I heard the smile in his voice. "It's a lot easier than hopping on."

He yanked open the side door. Frigid air rushed in. I put my coat on, slung my pack over my shoulder, and forced myself to walk to the edge of the car. The moon was down to a slim crescent, but it cast enough light to show that the train was running along a narrow ribbon of leveled ground that fell away sharply. "No way," I said.

Jackson came up next to me, zipping shut his backpack. "I'll get out, you toss this down to me, and then you jump. I'll catch you. It'll be all right." In an easy movement, he crouched, planted his hand, and disappeared over the edge. His head popped up after a couple seconds as he jogged beside the door.

"The pack," he called. I tossed it to him and he transferred it to the ground. "Now you," he instructed, but I couldn't make myself. "Sit on the edge. Then push off. I'll catch you. I promise." Still I hesitated. "Got to hurry, Sare. This thing is going uphill and I am running out of steam."

I sat. I braced my hands. I pushed off.

He caught me and held me as my feet slid in the gravel at the edge of the slope. I clung to him, remembering a similar moment, a similar feeling from the time before. He was always catching me.

I forced down my panicky feelings. "What do we do now?"

Clouds threatened to extinguish what little light we had from the moon. The air was substantially below freezing, and a light snow dusted the ground, with more drifting down lazily.

"We're walking back down the tracks about a half mile. There's shelter there. We're going to be all right."

We set off between the rails, his arm linked through mine to keep me steady. He took up his pack as we passed it.

A sharp wind blew up the gap the tracks made in the trees on either side, burning my cheeks with cold. It had grown so dark, I had no idea where we could be headed. Aside from the moon and the wind, there was not a hint of light or sound anywhere around.

Jackson kept us centered between the two rails, using the dull gleam of moonlight on the metal as a guide. "This is the way people get hit by trains, you know," I fretted.

"Not to worry," he said cheerfully, tugging me to the side. "We're here."

Chapter Twenty-Eight

Jackson helped me down a slight embankment. A small shack materialized from the darkness. "What is this?"

"A place for railroad workers, I think. My sense is, it isn't used much." He bent down, felt along the ground, then stood with a large rock in his hand. He climbed the steps. I heard him hammering on something metallic, then the sound of metal sliding on metal. "Come on," he said. He pushed open the door and we went in, out of the wind.

I heard his hand patting the wall, looking for a light switch.

"Wait a minute," I said, slipping my pack off my shoulder. I found Maggie's black purse, opened it, and searched the insides by touch. I fumbled for a second, then "Voilà" — a small blue flame sprouted from the lighter in my hand.

"You're good," Jackson said. "Exactly what we needed again. What are you — psychic or something?"

"As a matter of fact, I am, but not very competent with the future," I said, "Sammy insisted I take this. The compass too."

"Huh," Jackson said. "He's an odd little guy, isn't he? And I mean that in the best possible way."

I smiled and agreed, "He's an odd little guy. But as far as I know, not a fortune-teller either."

"Just someone who believes in being prepared?"

"I guess," I said.

We set to work trying to make ourselves comfortable. I located and lit a lantern. Jackson pulled the drapes closed over the single window. "Keep out some of the cold."

The room was maybe ten by ten, containing a table, four chairs, a Franklin stove, a set of hanging shelves with some canned goods and folded blankets, a bag of old newspapers and a pile of cordwood. A door in the back wall led to a lean-to add-on that held a functioning toilet and sink.

"All the comforts of home," I said.

Jackson chuckled. "If you live in a freezer."

It was true I could see my breath. Pennsylvania was a lot colder than Maryland, and outside air spilled in through gaps in every surface. We went to work building a fire.

As the stove heated, it took the worst of the chill out of the room, but it was still far from comfortable. Jackson shook out two of the blankets, and draped one around me. He spent a few minutes stuffing some of the worst cracks in the walls with newspaper. Then he poked through the things on the shelves. "A few cans of food up here. There must be a can opener too, but I'm not seeing it."

My hand dove back into Maggie's purse. Triumphantly, I held up a simple pointed opener.

"Sam again?" he said.

"Pretty strange, right? But come to think of it," I said, frowning a little, "I don't think it was him. I think he said 'she' told him."

"She?"

"Yeah. *She* said I had to have this stuff with me."

"Maggie?" he suggested. I shook my head. "Then Nanga, maybe?"

"Maybe."

We pulled two chairs close to the fire, with one corner of the table between us, and set about prying some food from the cans.

I hadn't eaten since — I couldn't remember when. A few spoonfuls of cereal.

Jackson handed me a can he'd opened with a full circle of V-shaped cuts, together with his multi-tool pocketknife swiveled open to a two-tine fork. "Ladies first," he said.

I looked inside the jagged opening and saw the orange plumpness of peach halves in heavy syrup. I speared one into my mouth. The sugar hit my tongue — cold, wet, and blissfully satisfying.

The act of eating made me realize how ravenous I was. I could have sucked down the whole can. I made myself hold it out to Jackson with the fork. "Your turn."

He shook his head. "Got my own," he said, holding up another can of the same.

I shoveled three more into my mouth, one after the other, hardly bothering to chew.

"Save room for some real food," he said. He pulled a sandwich out of a pocket in his backpack. "Meat loaf. Gran's recipe, prepared by yours truly. Naturally refrigerated all day."

"I hate stealing your food," I said.

"We're in this together, Sare."

I accepted half the sandwich and took a healthy bite. It was *so good*. Exactly the right combination of meat and bread. "*You* made this?" I said around a full mouth.

"Yes, ma'am," he said. "Don't sound so incredulous. Cooking is just chemical formulas you can eat."

"Right," I said. "Science geek."

"Yes, ma'am," he repeated.

I shoved in my last bite. I was beginning to feel better. Warmer. Not so empty. "Then I guess all this ESP stuff must kind of weird you out," I said.

"Doesn't weird you out?"

I smiled. "It weirds me out, J, but I'm not the one who expects the world to be all logical and scientific."

He shook his head a little. "I figure it must have a scientific basis. We just don't know what it is yet. Maybe energy patterns some people are more receptive to. Or time as a function of perception rather than a constituent part of reality. Something like that," he said.

"Huh," I said.

"What?"

"All these years I've known you, J," I said teasingly, "I never had you pegged for the bona fide brainy type."

He shrugged. "All these years I've known you, Sare, I never had you pegged as the bona fide perceptive type."

I laughed out loud. It felt good. Stuck in the middle of nowhere, in a drafty cabin in arctic weather, halfway between Nazi-loving cops on one end and the attempted burglary of the Metropolitan on the other, it felt good to be able to laugh.

We had to be out of our minds, the both of us.

"You seem so — calm — about all of this. I am so scared all the time I can hardly stand being myself."

"I'm scared too," he said.

"You don't seem like it."

He gave me another of his little shrugs. "I'm scared for your safety, I'm scared for mine. I'm scared about what happens if we don't succeed. I'm scared about what happens if we do."

"If we do?"

"We just have to keep going. Do what makes sense in the moment. Get the job done. See it through to the end." He said it quietly, even somberly. It gave me a chill. He caught my eye. "I have faith in you, Sare."

I felt a sudden sting of tears. I looked away and blinked them back.

"Hey, now," he said. "Enough of this. I think I saw —" He stood and fished something from the back of the shelves, then turned, victorious. "This." He was holding up a cheap portable radio as if it were a trophy. "Think it works?"

I summoned something like a smile. "You're always an optimist, J."

He started turning knobs. First it coughed out static, proving it still had batteries with some juice. Then he zeroed in on a couple of semi-audible signals — local news, some very fuzzy classical music, an oldies station, and one pretty clear channel playing upbeat jazz. "That's what I'm talking about," he said, grabbing my hand and tugging me to my feet.

"It's too cold to dance. And besides, I'm lousy at it." But I held out my hands obediently, one to reach for his shoulder, the other to take his hand.

He looked at me and shook his head sadly. "You got to be kidding."

"What?"

He took both my hands in his and lowered them to waist level, then began to saw back and forth in time with the music. "Now bend your knees," he directed, showing me, "and swivel your hips."

I straightened up and pulled back a little. "I don't know how," I said.

He tugged me back in. "Bend the knees. Swivel the hips. Get your shoulders into it." He demonstrated as he went along. "There you go, Sare. Doing the twist." He grinned wickedly. "Look at that white girl go."

I laughed. I stuck out my tongue. I leaned back like he was leaning back. I lifted one knee like he was lifting one knee. He was a good dancer. A lot better than I was. But it didn't matter. For the length of the song and the one that followed, I was doing the twist.

It was warmer after that or, I guessed, I was just warmer from the blood flowing. The stove had built up a nice bed of coals, so I added the biggest logs I could find, hoping they would burn slower and steady. We cleaned up our trash, made everything neat.

"It'll be colder on the floor," Jackson said, "but I really need to lie down for a while. I feel beat up. Everything hurts."

I knew how he felt.

We spread the newspaper on the floor as thick as we could. We put a layer of clothes on that, and a blanket on top.

Then he stood there awkwardly for a moment. "Look, I don't know how to put this exactly, but to stay warm while we sleep —"

"— we should spoon," I finished for him.

"That's what I was thinking," he said.

He opened the stove and added a couple more chunks of wood, then piled more within easy reach, to feed in during the night.

He blew out the lamp and sat down beside me. I curled up on my side, my arm under my head. He folded himself in behind me, tucking the last two blankets around us, leaning the backpacks against his back for a little more insulation.

I was grateful for the warmth of him. I felt — safe. I felt not alone. He was in this with me. To the end.

"You still on board, Sare? You going to be able to see this through?"

"Yeah, I'm still on board. It's my mess."

"It's not your mess," he said. "It's not your fault."

"I'm still on board, J," I repeated. "Thank you for sticking with me."

"I have my own reasons, good reasons, to want this to work, Sare, to want time to change. There's a better future out there, and I want that guy, that other Jackson, to have it. But even if I didn't have those reasons, I'd still have to keep going, right? I mean, in this other time, this other future, the Nazis lost. Slavery ended in the eighteen hundreds. Life will be better for a lot of people. We don't have a right to stop."

I realized I didn't really think about it that way. I was always focused on my own little part. *I* had made a mess that *I* had to clean up. As best I could, I had to put things right.

The fire crackled, filling up the silence that had settled on us. Outside, a winter wind hunted, looking for ways in. But I felt safe with Jackson at my back.

"What am I like," I said, "in that other future you see?"

"I don't know how to explain it, really. You're —" He struggled to find the words. "You're mostly the same. Snarky-funny, spunky, kind, observant, stubborn."

I savored the words.

"But you have this other thing. Something more grown-up, maybe. It's like you've known sadness, grief. You see the world with more compassion."

I could hear the admiration in his voice. For someone I *wasn't*.

"What did you mean," I said, "when you said 'that other Jackson'?"

"Well, it won't be me, will it? It'll be some other Jackson who lived some other life. He won't even remember me. I'll just be gone."

I felt tears start again. This is what he believed? And he was still going forward? I couldn't speak, but I wanted to tell him there was no other Jackson. He didn't change. He was constant. And *I* would remember him.

"It'll be all right," he said soothingly into my hair. "It'll be all right. Everything is going to be all right."

I fell asleep on those words, playing them over and over in my head. Words I wanted to believe. And they worked their way down to another level of me, the Sarah who had heard them before. Standing on a dock, brokenhearted, while this boy, this same boy, told me he'd known me before he met me, known me through visions of a future we would spend together.

Together.

I dreamed and woke, slept and dreamed again. A familiar dream of running in a dress of drifting gold. Flying down stone steps. Coming to the dock on the river, and finding someone standing there, silhouetted on the face of a pumpkin moon. When he turned, I saw it was Jackson.

"I have to tell you something," he said thickly. "My visions —"

"*My* visions —"

We finished together: "are all about you."

We danced, like floating on a floor of stars, and I wept on the shoulder of the boy who saw a future he thought could never be. A future where he loved me. And I loved him.

Again.

Chapter Twenty-Nine

I woke before dawn. Jackson had rolled onto his back sometime in the night. He was making the noise of dreaming. I turned quietly so I could see him.

His head rocked slightly in denial; the suggestions of winces flickered on his face. Despite the cold, I saw sweat on his forehead. His sounds were unborn groans. They rose in volume until he jolted awake.

"Hey," I said. "You were having a nightmare."

He looked at me, his face still taut. Slowly, his features softened and he smiled. A sad smile. "Was I? I don't remember." He rose. "We have a mile or two to walk. We'd better get moving."

I stood, straightening my clothes, the mess of my hair. I had not forgotten my dream. It made me feel out of place, ill at ease, unable to hide.

In that other time, I had loved Jackson and he had loved me. And the truth was, I still loved Jackson. He just didn't love me anymore. He had moved on to someone better suited to him — Helen. She was more serious, more committed. A gentle and decent person, just like he was. The one thing this whole mess had taught me was the fact that I didn't quite measure up as a mature, responsible, and compassionate human being. I was too quick to judge, too selfish, too soft. Not like him.

It must show, I thought. *He must be able to see this thing inside me, so enormous I can hardly breathe around it.* I wished I could tell him what I had remembered in my dream. But it wouldn't be fair to put that on him. This Jackson had Helen.

Jackson opened another can of peaches for us to fill our stomachs. "It'll take us at least a couple hours to get to New York."

I tugged a comb through my hair and longed for my toothbrush. Why hadn't Sammy packed me one of those? Then I remembered the pack of chewing gum. Spearmint. Clever devil.

We put things back the way we had found them. Jackson left a twenty-dollar bill on the shelf pinned under a can. Then we headed out into the bitter cold morning of the last day of the year.

As the world turned gray, we followed the double ruts of an overgrown dirt road to a local highway. We didn't speak. About a mile farther on, we reached the edge of a town. We bore left — north — toward the tracks we'd left earlier, and soon found the train station.

"You go in first, get a ticket to New York. In about ten minutes, I'll go in and get a ticket for someplace beyond. Don't look at me. Pretend you don't know me."

"You think that's necessary? Here, in the middle of nowhere?"

"Look, Sare. Someone was trying to stop me, stop *us*, back in Severna. Now I've escaped from a cop. It's just better, I think, if we're not seen together."

We waited in our own corners of the train station. We stood in line separately and boarded the train without raising an eyebrow. We sat in different cars, but after about ten minutes, I went and plopped myself down next to Jackson.

"Hey," he said. "I thought we agreed."

He was smiling slightly. Just that turning-up-the-corners thing he always did. I needed something light and airy to toss at him, to hide behind. "I don't think I *agreed* to anything. But if you've got something in writing —" I half lifted from my seat.

He cocked his head, amused. "I think they call this 'consorting with criminals.'"

I sat back down firmly. "When you put it that way, you make it pretty irresistible."

"If they come after me, I don't want you hauled away too."

"The thing is, J . . ." I got stuck again, tongue-tied. I made myself keep going. "If they stop you, then we'll just have to find some other way. Some other time. Because I can't do it without you. So I think we should just stick together."

He regarded me. I felt measured. I felt seen-through. He nodded. "We'll stick, then."

We talked about nothing things, stuff we had done together as kids, trouble we had gotten into, reliving the past, pretending for a little space of time that the future wasn't coming at us with the speed of a train. We also worked out a story for me to tell my folks.

All the while, I watched him from the corner of my eye and saw him like a stranger. Noticed how he greeted the ticket taker and thanked him. Noticed how he held himself still when he talked, until suddenly some bit of story would catch hold of him and make him paint pictures with his hands. Noticed again how much his hands were like my father's. *A surgeon's hands.* I wondered if Helen saw these things about him.

I wished — *wished* — I had the guts to say something to him. Something meaningful. Something *true* about the way I felt. But I was gutless. What if this Jackson just couldn't feel this way about me? What if this Jackson was so used to seeing me as his little friend, he'd never be able to see me as anything else?

At Penn Station, he pointed me toward a pay phone. "Call your mom and dad. Tell them the story we came up with. Get ready for tonight."

"Where're you going?"

"I'm going to check out the museum, make sure I saw it true. Then I'll find some place to rest and get cleaned up. Don't worry. Everything'll be all right."

I smiled a little. That seemed to be Jackson's refrain.

The man behind the front desk at the Park Hotel eyed me dubiously as I walked through the lobby between my parents. I wondered if I had any leaves stuck in my hair.

Mom couldn't stop peppering me with questions. "What town in Pennsylvania? Where did you stay? Why didn't you call? How'd you pay for it?"

I stuck to the story Jackson and I had worked out together. I got on the wrong train, which took me west toward Pittsburgh. I made it back to Harrisburg, but missed the last train to New York. So I spent the night in the station and took the first train out in the morning. I hadn't called because I couldn't remember the name of their hotel. It seemed to satisfy my parents, even though I could see a glint of doubt in my father's eye.

Mom was still obsessing as the elevator doors slid open. "We waited and waited for your call. We thought you'd been murdered or something."

A large group of people disgorged themselves from the elevator car, but one man in particular snagged my attention as he passed. He had his hat on and his face tipped down and away, his hand touching the brim, hiding his features. Still I knew the blond hair lying with straight precision in a blunt cut just above the collar. The Reichsleiter.

My parents, the crowd waiting for the elevator, swept me through the doors and he was gone.

I took a shower and shrugged into clean clothes from the luggage my parents had brought for me. Then I took a nap. My mother woke me after an hour — I had an appointment in the salon downstairs. "But first I want you to come across the street and see how nicely everything turned out."

She grabbed her coat and purse and went to the table near the door. "Tom? Did you move the exhibit key?"

My dad came out of the left bedroom of our suite. "No, hon. Last time I saw, it was there."

She looked in her purse, then looked at me. "You didn't move it, did you?" I shook my head. "Well, I suppose it doesn't matter for now. It's the middle of the day. The rest of the museum is open. We'll just have to get a security guard to let us into the Amber House exhibit."

A key, I thought. *The key Jackson said we'd need?*

The museum stood on a rise in the park across the street. As we climbed the front stairs, I realized I had been to the Metropolitan before, but it hadn't looked like this. It had been an entirely different building, yet still called the Met. I guessed as far as New Yorkers were concerned, in this time or any other, their city was *the* metropolis.

We found a helpful security guard who led us past the entrances to other exhibits, other wings: Ancient Egypt, the Impressionists, Modernists, Old Masters. The last name caught my attention. I remembered it written in Jackson's scribbled, blood-grimed notes. I turned to look in. Jackson was there, sitting, watching me. Our little group continued on past him, but I gave him a tiny nod.

The guard let us into the still-closed exhibit, using a plastic card with an embedded metal strip. *The key.*

We descended a flight of stone steps to the museum's central atrium. Its long rear wall of arched windows looked down on the gardens below the museum. The space was high and hollow and echoed queerly. It reminded me of the conservatory back home.

Mom had outdone herself with the exhibit — the rich wood tones of stray pieces of furniture harmonized with quilts and needlework, paintings and photographs. Three hundred and fifty years of artifacts. Three hundred and fifty years of family clutter. All of it spread out against freestanding Ls of stenciled walls, set up maze-like to force people to meander. Here and there the trees that lived in this garden room poked up above the walls, reminding me of a dream I'd had the first night we'd returned to Amber House.

I wanted to wander and admire my mother's work, and to locate the gun that Claire Hathaway had loaned to the exhibit, but I needed to make a quick detour. "It's amazing, Mom," I leaned in to say to her, "but I need to run to the ladies' room."

"Sure, honey. Hurry back, though. I wanted you to have the private tour before tonight." She turned to chat with a museum worker about one of the displays.

Jackson was still waiting for me in the Old Masters. We sat in front of a studied domestic scene from one of those intense Dutch painters. I told him, "I think I know what key we need, but I don't know where to get it. Mom's is lost."

"You'll find another," he said.

"Where?"

"I don't know. It'll show up."

That hardly seemed a satisfactory answer, but I let it go. I trusted Jackson. "How am I going to find *you*?"

"I'll be at the party."

"You need a special invitation to get in."

He shook his head. "I just need a white jacket." I gave him a look, completely confused. "Don't worry. I'll be there. I'll find you."

"I gotta get back to Mom. You good for now?"

He nodded. "It's a beautiful place." He looked around him. "The museum. The city. My dad met my mom here. I'm glad I got to see it."

He was sounding morbid again. "We're going to do this, J."

He nodded again. "Yes. We will. Because we have to."

I got a quickie tour from Mom when I returned. We walked at a near trot, but I veered to every glass case and cabinet, checking their contents for Claire's gun. And I didn't find it. "What about Mrs. Hathaway's contribution?" I asked Mom.

"Not here yet, but we saved a spot for it."

"Where?"

"Near the back on the east side," she said unhelpfully.

Which side, I wondered, *is the east side?*

On the way out, I spotted a photo of Fiona when she was in her early twenties. Her hair was piled on her head luxuriously, with curls trailing down her neck. She was caught in that same frozen pose that all early photographic subjects shared — but I liked the way the corners of her mouth were curved up, and the grace of her hand resting lightly on the chair back beside her.

I walked closer. My mother saw me and called an instruction: "Straighten those two frames, would you, honey? For some reason, they're always slipping a little."

I reached out to nudge the two askew side-by-side frames. They were poems. "Otherwhen" and "Neverwas." The fragments that had started me on this journey. Fiona's fevered visions of the path to a better place. Directions to follow for someone to come. *Me.* But I looked at the words again and thought, *Not just to me.* She had written, "*A pas de deux, a dance within the maze.*" Had she somehow foreseen me dancing with Jackson in my golden gown in that other time? "*The hand that pulls us onward in our climb.*" Fiona must have known it would take two.

I made the poems perfectly parallel to each other and perpendicular to the floor. And realized something else, something I should have seen before. Fiona had brought "Otherwhen" with her *from the other time.* It had leaked through somehow. She had penetrated the déjà vu to keep it.

Proof for Jackson that who we were continued from Time to Time. *Different but the same.*

The hair salon had its entrance in the hotel's lobby, but plunged down below street level. It had once been a gentleman's bar — all mahogany and crimson velvet and brass. I thought it was a space Fiona might have felt right at home in, surrounded by male admirers and a veil of cigar smoke.

Booths had been converted to individual stations, where stylists worked on hair, nails, what have you. Double doors that must once have led to a kitchen now enclosed a spa. Mom and I were led to adjacent spaces, introduced to the ladies who would be overseeing our transformations, and quizzed about our desired results. For me: loose half updo, please, red lip stain but otherwise neutral makeup, hide the bags under my eyes, don't bother with a manicure or waxing, thank you very much. The stylist — Isobel — offered to touch up the stray hairs on my eyebrows, but if everything went according to plan, I figured I wouldn't have to worry about those tomorrow anyway.

"I'm growing them out," I said flatly.

Isobel worked quickly, efficiently, and expertly. I assessed her finished product in the softly lit vanity across from me. You could hardly tell I had barely slept in two days. The hair was all gently curled and discreetly pinned. She'd made a point of tucking a stark-white camellia in my hair, which she'd evidently ordered special for her "Southern belle" client. I didn't have the heart to tell her I was not, in fact, a native of the South.

My mother looked incomparable, as always. Her auburn hair was pinned into a loose knot at the nape of her neck, with select curls seeming to slip naturally from the chignon to frame her high cheekbones. Her slanted eyes were rimmed with burnished copper, making her hazel irises glint. Sometimes she was so lovely, I had an impulse to stand on tiptoe to kiss her forehead. "You look beautiful, Mom. So beautiful."

She blushed. "You're a sweetie. Thank you."

"I love you, Mom."

It was one of those moments — tremulous, lit with peculiar clarity — that would stay etched in my memory. I hoped.

CHAPTER THIRTY

We took the elevator upstairs and changed into our evening clothes. Mom wore a column of green silk with the Amber House emeralds; Dad wore a razor-sharp tuxedo with a white bow tie. "You look like a spy, Dad," I said. He chuckled and looked pleased.

My Marsden was laid out on my bed with a pair of matching slippers, new in the box. And the snowflake necklace Richard had given me. I hadn't thought to bring any jewelry; I guessed Mom had thought of it.

Back downstairs, the spacious entrance hall to the hotel's largest banquet room was lit up and glowing. A pianist played in one corner, and people milled about. Waiters made their rounds with trays of appetizers and flutes of champagne.

We joined a queue of fancy-dressed men and women to deposit various pieces of outerwear at the coat check. I couldn't imagine the insanity when the entire party came back en masse to retrieve their things before walking across the street for the exhibit's opening.

The line moved forward. I glimpsed then, between the shoulders of those in front of me, the ballroom below.

It was one of those places you know exists, has to exist somewhere — but you very much doubt you'll ever get to see. One of those places for *other* people, with ceilings so high, you feel like Alice after she's sipped from the "Drink Me" bottle. Everything was polished and gilded and mirrored and, to top it all off, entirely saturated with holiday trimmings: garlands of silver-spattered lemon leaves that overlapped one another like a fish's scales, accented by gilt pomegranates clumped in bunches.

The room held a roiling sea of exquisitely dressed people — sparkling waves of gold and silver, crimson and forest green, shadowed with the black of tuxedoes. And the waiters in white jackets, weaving in and out, balancing their silver trays. I heard the faint strains of what I realized must be a full orchestra — strings, brass — mixed with the muted roar of hundreds of voices chattering.

All these people brought together because Robert Hathaway believed the world was sinking toward war and he could stop it. I guessed, one way or the other, I was here for the same reason. The dissonance between all the frothy gaiety and the seriousness of the evening made everything seem a little unreal.

"Your cloak, miss?" a pretty young woman said, holding out her hand. Suddenly the question hit me with terrible significance — did I leave it here now or keep it with me? It was cold outside — would I have time to come back for it?

Do what makes sense in the moment, I almost heard Jackson say.

I handed it over, with a thank-you. But after too much of a pause. Mom was looking at me oddly. "Are you all right, honey?"

"I'm fine."

"You seem so nervous." She clutched my hand. "Don't worry. Try to enjoy yourself. You look beautiful."

Dad touched my cheek, smiling one of those happy-sad smiles parents sometimes seem to make. "I'm sure Richard will tell you the same thing."

I smiled back, even though I felt near tears. My dad. A good man, a man with serious purpose, a gifted healer, kind, self-effacing. Parties weren't his thing. The crisp wool tuxedo already looked slightly rumpled on him, because he wore it with discomfort. Mom stepped close to him, quickly straightened his bow tie, and kissed him softly, briefly.

They were inseparable — in how they met life's challenges, and even in the way I pictured them in my mind, as a unit, as a pair. But in another time, an otherwhen, they had been so cruel to each other. I remembered my father in a different tuxedo, my mother in a different gown, with an unbridgeable distance between them. Broken beyond mending.

Would they be the same as they were now, after tonight?

A thought occurred to me. I turned back to the coat-check girl.

"May I have my own ticket for my cloak, please? In case I need to step out?"

"Of course, miss."

That made sense, right? I tucked the little card into Maggie's purse.

Dad slipped one arm through mine, and the other through my mother's. We walked together to the head of the stairs.

Back home in Astoria, my friends and I used to go white-water rafting. It involved a lot of floating lazily downriver to get to those spots where the water's channel narrowed and dropped, propelling rafters into a churning chute of roaring, foaming, bouncing speed. There was always a moment just before the chute when I could feel the current grab hold of the raft, viciously, eagerly, and suck it deeper. A moment when I recognized that there was no way out anymore except forward and down. Standing there at the top of those stairs, I felt the current take hold of me.

This was the start of it, now. The party would begin, the steps would be taken, and Jackson and I would have to pray that we did everything right at just the right moment.

One last time, I wished I was back in Seattle.

"Ready?" Dad asked me. I wanted to tell him no, not at all. But I nodded. We descended together into the celebration for the last night of the year.

It was impossible not to notice the many glances in our direction. Dad met my eyes and grinned. My mother was stunning.

You couldn't help but stare. I'm sure I would have too if I were below, watching her nearly float down the sweeping staircase, her featherlight dress trailing behind her. Staircases like these were made for women like my mother to descend.

But Dad tipped his head slightly toward my right, and I tracked the trajectory of his gaze. A cluster of young men — perhaps college-aged — were watching *me*. I blushed and looked away.

There was one long table at the head of the room, raised above floor level. The rest of the room was strewn with circular tables, arrayed with gold and silver florals worked around silver candelabra. The meal would begin at nine, with appetizers, soup, entrée, and then a round of desserts. I suspected they wanted people to be in the best possible mood before Robert Hathaway began to speak.

Mom was enveloped by a flock of guests — some curious about the exhibit, some praising her for her support of Senator Hathaway. The gathering crowd seemed to alert the staff to her presence; we were guided to a central table, seated facing out toward the dance floor.

Then Richard, his father, and his mother came down the stairs. They were besieged on all sides: smiling faces, outstretched hands. Their progress across the floor was measured in inches. Richard broke away and came to our table. "Dad wanted you to meet a few people," he told my parents.

So we stood and squeezed our way through the crowd. We trailed Robert as he was guided by aides to "the dowager queen of New England," "Prince George and his wife, Princess Theresa," "His Excellency Don Julio del Rio," "Prime Minister Benjamin Goldblum," "le Marquis d'Orleans." On and on, group after group — the cream of the aristocracy of the Americas. I hadn't realized I would be expected to drop curtsies and, apparently, neither had my mother, who did it stiffly — the only thing I'd ever seen her do without absolute grace. But we followed Claire's lead. This was the Hathaways' show.

After ten minutes, I excused myself, though I didn't think anyone heard, and wandered back to our table. Most of the attendees were also trickling to their seats. The orchestra began playing softer music. Mom and Dad finally joined me. The New English prime minister took his place behind the podium in the middle of the long raised table saved for the most honored guests; Robert and Claire stood to one side, poised, ready. Silence settled over the room.

The prime minister introduced Senator Hathaway to the crowd, then Robert and Claire moved center stage. He stood, smiling, glowing in the spotlight like some kind of movie idol as the crowd applauded a thunderous welcome. And I thought to myself, as the thunder rolled over me, that if anyone had a chance of bringing all the factions of the Americas together into one united force, it was this man.

"First, my family would like to extend our sincere thanks, to each and every one of you, for spending your holiday with us this evening," Robert said.

More applause.

"I'm not going to keep you from your dinners. But before we eat, I'd just like to offer a brief toast, if I may, to the coming year." Everywhere, people stood and lifted their glasses. "May it bring with it prosperity, strength, and tranquility to this nation, to its neighbors, and to all Americans, north and south. To our disparate pasts, and our shared future."

After a mass clinking of classes, "Hear, hear," and the obligatory sips of Champagne, the crowd settled themselves back in their seats. On cue, a small army of waiters emerged, carrying trays of the first course: classic Chesapeake crab cakes in a piquant sauce. As I puzzled out which fork to use and whether I would actually be able to make myself eat, I noticed a latecomer sailing gracefully down the wide stairs, resplendent in a short black dinner jacket worn over a white vest and white-piped trousers, flecked all over with silver buttons and insignia. My ubiquitous Nazi, Jaeger.

He walked toward a table in the back, where he was greeted by a blond goddess in black velvet. He must have felt my eyes on him, because he zeroed in on me across the depth of the room. And smiled.

As anxious as I had been up to that point, the Nazi's presence pushed me over the edge. I felt like a nest of hornets had settled in my brain. I couldn't think. I couldn't remember what was supposed to happen next. I wished I could talk to Jackson.

The salad course came and went. I don't know whether I ate any of it. I kept checking the clock on the rear wall, watching the hands crawl closer and closer to the end of the year. President Stevenson's footage would play sometime around eleven, followed by Robert's formal speech. The ribbon cutting for the exhibit was supposed to occur right at midnight. I would be long gone by then. I hoped.

If I found the key.

I wished violently Jackson had told me how to get in touch with him or where to meet him or how he was going to find me. *Why didn't he?* Several times I had to stop myself from rising and heading for the stairs, the lobby, the doors to the street. He said he'd be here. He said he didn't need an invitation. All he needed was —

— a white jacket. That finally penetrated my mental fog. I started searching and found Jackson almost immediately, one among the army of waiters, working on the far side of the room. He was refilling a guest's wineglass with all the confidence and flair of someone who did it every day of the week. He glanced up at me briefly, but I knew he knew I had finally figured it out.

Crazy man, I thought. Bunches of people here knew who he was. My parents, the Hathaways, not to mention the Nazi. What if they spotted him? But I realized that his white jacket was the perfect disguise. It made him invisible. No one ever looked into the faces of the waitstaff.

I forced myself not to watch him. But I felt instantly calmer. Everything was all right. Jackson had it all under control. I found I was finally able to eat some of the food that had been set before me, and I focused on that. It was going to be a long night. I would need all the energy I could get.

At some point, I thought to ask Mom if she'd ever found her key, but she hadn't. "Is there some other one we can use?" I asked.

"We don't need a key anymore, honey. We'll all be heading over together."

No key, no break-in, I thought. It was not an unpleasant prospect. But during the dessert, I dutifully bent my brain to the task of reconstructing the page of notes Jackson had given me to memorize. *12:02 Turn left to north museum exit. Follow dirt path through trees — DO NOT USE SIDEWALK. Just before fountain, turn right up hill, come out —*

"I mean, only if you'd like," Richard said.

I stared at him. Realized he'd been talking to me. I hadn't even noticed when he'd walked up. "I'm sorry, what?"

"Jeez, coz," he said with a rueful smile, "way to make me feel like a putz. I asked if you wanted to dance."

The brassy strains of an Orleans standard were winding through the room. Couples were slow-dancing in time with the music. I literally *hated* dancing. Aside from the twist.

I looked at the clock. 10:33. Still no key. I smiled and nodded, and Richard took my hand and led me to the dance floor.

He was an excellent dancer, of course. There wasn't a single thing Richard Hathaway wasn't good at. *Perfect* at. But the ritual unsettled me. When I closed my eyes, I thought of the other Sarah. The Sarah in the gold dress, dancing on the floor of stars.

Waltzing with Jackson.

Before Richard shoved us apart. Before Richard struck Jackson in the mouth.

I pulled back. That too-familiar look of hurt and confusion flashed across Richard's face. "Is something wrong?" he asked.

"I just — can we sit down?" I wanted off the dance floor.

Richard led me to a bench by the staircase. "Can I get you water? Are you all right?"

"I just need to sit a moment."

I felt sick that I had let Richard close to me. Again. That I was here, dressed up, dancing with him, instead of with Jackson.

Except — I thought of the trip to Richmond. The photos on the wall. He *was* different. Like my parents were different. The same, but better. It felt wrong to judge this Richard for the other Richard's mistakes. What a mess it all was.

"You wore the snowflake," he said. I could see he was touched.

"I love it — it was just the right accent."

He smiled and nodded. "Yes, it looks great with your dress. You look beautiful."

I tipped my head a little. "Thanks, Hathaway. A small helping of flattery for dessert — perfect."

"Not flattery." He sat down on the bench next to me. "Parsons? Can I ask you something?"

"Sure."

"How come you missed the train yesterday? I mean, I saw you in the station. I thought you were coming on board. Then the next thing I knew, the train was pulling away without you."

I looked at him without a clue about how to answer that.

He looked down, away. "I mean, I thought maybe you were just ditching me."

"No," I said. "No. You're a great guy, Hathaway."

"Yeah?"

I laughed a little. "Yeah. You know that."

He smiled. "You have a knack for making me doubt myself, coz." Then his face turned serious. Uncomfortable. "Can I tell you something?"

"Sure."

"You know that thing I told you my mom said about Jackson Harris?"

"That she thought he was dangerous?"

He shook his head a little. "She was *warned* he presented a *danger*."

"All right."

He looked me in the eyes, asking me silently to understand. "She told me the same thing about you."

I might have been offended but for the fact that I knew the warning was true. I did present a danger to Richard and his family. They were a happy family now, in this time. Who knew what would happen to them in another time? Or what would happen to any of us?

"I swear to you that I would never deliberately do anything to hurt you or your family, Hathaway," I said.

He smiled. "I know that already, Parsons. I just wanted to ask you — to be careful, I guess. Be careful."

"I'm trying," I said.

He flashed me a crooked smile. "That mistletoe didn't work, so I'm gonna be looking for you at midnight. I'm a superstitious guy." I blushed; he laughed. "Got to get back to my parents. It's almost time for the presentation."

My eyes leapt to the clock. 10:56. The time was almost up. Maybe this wasn't going to happen. Maybe Richard would be collecting on that kiss. I wondered how I felt about that. If Jackson couldn't love me, maybe Richard could.

"Oh, hey," he said, turning back. "I almost forgot. Mom wanted me to give this to your mom, in case she needed to go over early. She heard your mom's copy went missing, and my parents each got one of their own."

I swiveled my head to look at the thing Richard was holding out for me to take.

A plastic card key.

CHAPTER THIRTY-ONE

The sight of that card — that one thing, more than anything, made it all real for me. Jackson had said the key would come to me. And it did. Like magic. Like it was meant to be.

As soon as Richard disappeared into the crowd, I stood to search for Jackson. It took me a second, but I found him. He was already looking toward me. I nodded and briefly gave him a thumbs-up.

Concern filled his features; he shook his head a fraction of an inch. I glanced around the room to see if anyone had noticed our collusion. Movement of a blond head caught my eye — Jaeger turning to his companion. *What were the odds that he'd been looking my way just when I held up my thumb? And what would it mean to him anyway?*

I wondered what I was supposed to do next. *Leave*, I guessed. I thought of going to speak to my parents — some fuzzy notion about saying good-bye. But I realized that wasn't possible. Instead, I just started walking toward the stairs.

My mother met me on the steps, coming down as I headed up to get my cloak. "I think things are just about to start, honey. Come back to the table with me."

I found it hard to speak. "Restroom," I managed.

"Well, hurry, then. It was pretty crowded. You don't want to miss Stevenson's film clip."

I nodded, swallowing hard. She looked at me queerly, tucked one of my curls back into place, then returned my nod. And let me go.

❧

Jackson was waiting for me under a streetlight, with a duffel bag.

"I came as fast as I could," I said.

Jackson smiled. "You came plenty fast enough." He pulled out the pocket watch I had given him to check the time.

"Hey, it's coming in handy," I said.

"Like you could see the future," Jackson said.

I pointed at the bag. "What's in there?"

"Stuff we'll need."

"You and Sammy," I said.

I gave him the key. He stared at it a moment, almost like he couldn't believe it. Then he said, "Come on," and led me to a museum side door marked STAFF. "Let's see if this works."

The door lock was a box card-reader, just like the one on the gates to the exhibit. The card key changed a little light on the reader's face from red to green. Jackson turned the handle and the door opened. We slipped inside and he closed the door as quietly as he could.

We were in one of those hidden service halls the public never sees, painted the usual baleful yellow, made even uglier by the weak and greenish lighting. Jackson pulled out his watch again, then stood watching it. I leaned in to whisper, "Shouldn't we get moving?"

He put his finger to his lips, then held his hand palm up. Wait. Evidently, we were running in silent mode and Jackson knew what he was doing. I waited.

After a minute or two, we heard a door open and steps receding. Jackson took my hand and started moving with a quiet measured pace. I walked on my toes, taking several steps for each one of his. Midway down the hall, I heard a man whistling and heavy footsteps coming toward us. I tugged Jackson's hand to retreat. He didn't even slow down, just pulled my hand firmly to keep me heading down the hall.

The whistling, the footsteps, got louder. I could see the side hall the man would emerge from at any second.

Jackson guided me firmly into an alcove — the entrance to the restrooms. He cracked open the ladies' door, we slid inside, and he closed it softly, just as the whistling reached us and receded behind the opposite door.

Instantly, we were out and running lightly up the rest of the hall and the stairs at its end. That brought us to the main hall, near the Old Masters. Jackson pointed up into the corners of the space, where the black Cyclops eyes of several security cameras stared down on us. He whispered, "That guy we heard watches the monitors. We have a few minutes. We have to hurry."

At the entrance to the Amber House exhibit, there was yet another security camera. Jackson handed me his bag and pulled himself up onto the heavy chest-high wall molding. "All right," he said, "give me the camera that's in the bag." I passed up an instant-photo camera, which Jackson used to take a picture from as near the security camera as possible.

As the camera whirred and hummed, and then extruded a developing print from a slot in its front, I handed Jackson the other two items in the sack — a roll of tape and a metal basket. He taped his instant photo into the bottom of the basket, slid the basket over the end of the security camera, and then taped that in place.

Then I understood. Even after we opened the exhibit's gate, the security guy would still think it was closed, because of the photo filling the camera's view.

He jumped down, grinning. "Saw that done in a movie once."

He pulled our magic key from his pocket and used it to open the "Amber House" gate. He slid it open partway and handed me the card. "You hang on to this." I thought it not quite sensible — why not just tuck it back in his pocket? But I slipped it into the bodice of my dress to have it at the ready.

"Got any idea where the gun is?" he asked.

"Wasn't here when I came through. And I didn't see an empty spot for it. Mom said toward the back on the east side."

"Since this entrance faces southeast, I'm guessing she meant the right side, but I'm also guessing her sense of direction is a little iffy. We better split up and get looking." He checked his watch. "It's eleven eighteen."

We hurried down the steps; he headed one direction and I headed the other.

Right, skip, right played in my head as I tried to do a thorough job of checking every case, every nook, every corner. A clock was tick-tick-ticking in my head. I walked in circles, trying to make sure I missed nothing.

And finally, near the back, in a faux room set up with eighteenth-century furniture atop a Persian rug, I found it. The reason I hadn't seen an empty spot for the gun earlier was because Claire Hathaway sent along the whole glass-topped Chippendale sideboard that she kept it in at home.

I walked up to the little table. The gun was there, polished and gleaming. The coin in its handle seemed to possess a glow of its own. But the case, of course, was locked.

Someone grabbed me from behind. I almost screamed.

"It's me," Jackson whispered in my ear. "Is that it?" He stared down at the object of our hunt with fascination.

"The case is locked," I whispered back. "How do we get it?"

He looked at me, reached behind us, picked up a small marble bust of some one or other of my ancestors — and smashed the glass tabletop.

"Oh, my God," I hissed, as much for the destruction as for

the noise. I was from Amber House; I couldn't help being a preservationist.

Jackson stood a moment, inspecting the gun. "The Janus coin is held in by screws — we should just take the whole thing." He handed it to me, and I put it in my evening bag. "You get going. I'll meet you at the subway. There's one more thing I have to do."

I stood frozen, confused. *Leave? Without him?* "What if we get separated? I don't want to go without you."

"Do what I say! I'm the man with the plan, remember?"

I nodded and turned, winding my way toward the front. I looked back. Jackson had gone deeper into the exhibit. *Why?* I couldn't make myself go without him. It just wasn't possible. What point was there for me to leave without him?

I reversed course, running silently in his wake. I saw him stop at a mustard-colored trunk at the back of the exhibit, decorated with oxblood hearts and doves. He opened its lid and crouched down, studying its contents.

I sneaked up behind him, drawing close enough to see inside the trunk — wires snaking up and down, something with a blinking light. "What is it?"

"Why are you still here? I told you to go!"

"What is it, Jackson? What are you trying to do?"

A voice came from behind us. "I was just about to ask the same thing."

It was Jaeger.

We turned to face him together. "How'd you get in here?" I asked.

He patted his waistcoat pocket. "Your mother's key card." He held up a little box with an antenna on it and said to Jackson, "If you touch those wires, I won't need this to trigger it."

"You're going to blow up our stuff?" I asked. *Why?*

He chuckled. "No, Miss Parsons. Well, I guess, yes. But that is not my ultimate intent."

"Which is to blow up the people visiting the exhibit," Jackson finished. "He's just waiting for them to file over after the speeches."

Thereby killing many of the most powerful people in the western hemisphere, I realized, and remembered the Jewish Intelligence prediction: *Destabilize the Unification movement with one big boom.*

"Blow up, burn. Yes, exactly, Mr. Harris," Jaeger said amiably, "with two *R*s. I had everything arranged. But now here you two are — how is it you say it? Flies in the ointment."

"How did you know where to find us?"

"I saw you — both of you — at the gala. Saw you leave at almost the same moment." He mimicked my unfortunate thumbs-up. "Knew you were a danger. Excellent disguise, by the way," he said to Jackson. "I wonder how it is you managed to get here. I paid a sheriff to pick you up. Even told him when and how. Incompetent. I won't use him again."

"No," Jackson agreed. "You won't."

Jaeger laughed, incredulous and amused. "Is that a threat, Mr. Harris? But I fear you left behind your shotgun. And I have this." He held up the detonator. "And this." He pulled a small gun from the rear of his waistband.

"You're not going to set the bomb off while you're standing here," Jackson said. "You don't want to die." He stepped in front of me a little, partially shielding me from Jaeger, and spoke to me without taking his eyes off the Nazi. His voice was hard and cold. "You do what I tell you this time, Sarah. *Every*thing depends on it. You hear me?"

"Yes," I whispered.

"Then RUN!"

As he said those words, he leapt on the Nazi. I ran. Behind me, I heard the sounds of breaking glass, splintering wood. A gunshot. The thud of a fist on flesh. The sound of feet pounding after me.

I couldn't find the way out. The women of Amber House had me in their grasp. The exhibit was a maze and I was trapped in it.

I looked up toward the ceiling to find a direction, to stop running in circles. I veered around this wall, around that, but kept heading for the point in the glass web above that I knew was over the exit. And then there were the stairs, just ahead.

"Leaving, Miss Parsons?" Jaeger was just behind me. He was going to catch me. I made my feet go faster. I would have screamed, but I had no breath for it.

Oh God, oh God, my brain gibbered. *He is going to catch me.*

From the corner of my eye, I saw Jaeger go down as Jackson tackled him again. I staggered up the steps. Behind me, Jackson and Jaeger were still struggling. I looked back. Jaeger raised a hand, and a blade snicked into view. He stabbed it into Jackson. I saw the crimson of blood spreading all around the wound. The Nazi pulled his knife out and raised it up to stab Jackson again.

"Stop!" I screamed.

Jaeger glanced up at me, and started laughing again. I stood on the steps, gasping for breath, and pointed Claire Hathaway's gun at him. I tried, over and over, to pull the trigger, but nothing happened. Then I remembered — you have to cock old pistols.

Jaeger got up and started walking toward me, the bloodied knife in his hand. "You are so amusing, my dear Miss Parsons. Your family has such touching faith in its ridiculous heirlooms." I was struggling with the hammer, using both thumbs to try to make it move.

The hammer clicked into place. I pulled the trigger. The gun jumped in my hands, spouting flame and smoke, knocking me down.

Jaeger staggered back, sinking to one knee, his hand clapped to his shoulder. He brought his hand away to see; it was covered with blood. His moan turned into a snarl as he shoved back to his feet and started up the steps. A hole from an antique iron ball was not enough to down the consummate Aryan spy.

But somehow, Jackson threw himself at the Nazi yet again. "Run, Sarah," he groaned, "now!"

I made my legs climb the stairs. I turned left and left again, away from the entrance. I'd seen a case here earlier — a display of Japanese artifacts. I used the gun butt to smash the glass that protected them, grabbed a short blade, and started back.

And was knocked against the wall by an explosion.

The hall filled with dark gray smoke. An alarm was blaring, but I could hardly hear it over a dullness in my ears. I stumbled back to the exhibit gate. All around me, metal paneling was closing over paintings and tapestries on the walls — fire protection. I saw the entrance to the exhibit stairs just ahead of me. A grille of metal bars was descending across it.

Someone hurtled out beneath the dropping bars. He turned back and called into the exhibit: "You see, Mr. Harris, such a meticulous plan. I even triggered the gates to fall. And all for naught. But perhaps none of the guests are as important to eliminate as your little girlfriend. Yes? I promise you: I will find her." Without looking in my direction, he ran off toward the entrance.

I dropped the blade. Pointless now. I reached the gate and clung to the metal bars. At the foot of the stairs, Jackson was struggling to rise. A large bloodstain spread across the front of his shirt. He staggered up the steps to stand opposite me.

"How do I get this open?"

He shook his head. "You don't." His voice was muffled by the dullness of my ears, but still audible. "You have to hurry, Sare. If you don't stick to the schedule, you'll miss the train home. The guards will be here soon. They'll let me out. You have to get that coin back to Amber House."

"Are you crazy? I'm not *leaving* you here!" I looked around the room at the spreading flames. Was he insane?

"You've got to go or you won't make it in time. I promise — I will meet you back at Amber House."

"No — *no.*" I was sobbing. I must have been sobbing all along, because I was gasping for air, tears spilling down my cheeks. Jackson caught one with his fingertip, then traced his fingers down my jaw and under my chin, gently angling my face to meet his gaze.

"Sarah, listen to me. You have to trust me now."

"I do trust you. I do."

"I know. Listen to me — you have to finish this, all right? See it through to the end —"

"Clear the nest," I said.

He smiled. Set his teeth, and nodded.

"You remember that page I asked you to memorize?"

"Yeah. Yes."

"Good. That's good. You have to focus, Sare. That'll get you home, if you do it just the way I wrote it. Here." He tied his yellow handkerchief around my wrist. "Take this. It'll help."

"Jackson —"

"I told you, you have to hurry."

This was all wrong. I could hardly think — the alarm seemed to knock the sense right out of my head. "I can't."

"You *can.* I believe in you."

Jackson stepped close. His presence was like an anchor. A silent, stable place in the middle of the chaos roaring all around. One hand cupped my chin — my head pressed into the feeling of his palm, its smooth, cool certainty. His other hand traced down my arm and behind my waist, pulling me nearer, as near as possible with the bars between us.

I breathed him in. My breath became his breath. Strangely, I felt my heart slow — almost as though it were working to match the steady rhythm of Jackson's own. Above him, and behind, through the glass of the atrium ceiling, the sky blossomed golden, silver, and gleaming red. Fireworks, heralding the beginning of the year to come.

"I've seen this moment a long time," he said.

His lips met mine. Gently — so gently — but also fiercely. As if this belonged to him. As if he had waited for it. As if there was nothing in the world but that kiss. It could have lasted forever and it would have ended too soon.

My first kiss.

And then —

"Go," he pleaded. And I finally obeyed.

CHAPTER THIRTY-TWO

As I stumbled toward the doors of the museum, I repeated the litany of instructions Jackson had written another lifetime ago. North museum exit. Follow dirt path. Stay off the sidewalk. Turn right up hill before fountain. Cross at light. Three blocks to the subway. 12:15.

I wondered what time it was now. How many minutes, how many seconds were left.

I switched on my flashlight and pushed out the north exit. A new alarm started to blare. There was a cement walkway, but it led back to the front. *Where in God's name is the* dirt *path?*

I trotted up the walk, playing my flashlight over the ivy and bushes that bordered the cement. There was nothing — I couldn't find a dirt path, there wasn't any dirt path.

Suddenly, I realized I was standing in light. I had gone so far forward, I was within the reach of the streetlamps.

"Sarah?!"

Claire Hathaway was poised on the museum steps, staring at me, her mouth dropped slightly open. "Richard," she said, turning behind her, "I think she has my gun." She looked back at me. "That's my gun." She took two steps forward. "Why do you have my gun?"

But my attention was diverted by someone running toward me, someone tall and blond and dressed in black.

I turned and fled back up the cement walk, shoving the gun butt-first into Maggie's bag. *Where's that path?* A few inches of brown cut through the ivy. I gathered up my skirt and plunged through the branches, following that ribbon of brown. My slippers chattered down the dirt slicked with snowmelt turned to ice. Every rock jabbed up through shoe soles made for parquet dance floors. The bushes and trees grabbed at my clothes.

I heard Jaeger crashing through the bushes after me. I made an easy target. Flame red, with a flashlight beam shining out in front. I went faster.

The trees came to an end. Ahead I saw a plaza with a fountain. *Right, up the hill.*

I was breathing hard, and the air was too cold to be sucking it down in such big gasps. My throat hurt, my lungs hurt. But I kept running. *See it through.*

On the far side of the plaza, the hill rose sharply under a cover of trees and bushes. I pushed into the thick of it and switched off my light. I would shove up in the dark. I could see light from the street ahead. It wasn't that far.

Behind me, shoes pummeled the pavement. The sound stopped. He was looking around, listening. I kept going, tried to go faster still.

A stone wall rose above me. The top was shoulder high. *Oh God*, I moaned in my head. I switched on my flashlight. More light hit me from below. He started climbing through the bushes after me.

I found what I was looking for. I scrabbled to the right, under some low branches, placed a foot in the tree there, grabbed higher, and shoved myself up. With my skirts wadded in my arm with the flashlight, I placed my other foot higher still.

He spotlighted me then, an oversized cardinal perched in a tree. He crashed through branches, hurling himself toward me. I pulled myself up and pulled myself up until I put one foot on top of the wall.

A hand caught my other ankle. Without stopping to think, I kicked back toward it. My heel collided with flesh. Branches cracked and snapped as Jaeger fell back through them.

I pulled, shoved, dragged myself up onto the wall and dropped the few feet to the sidewalk on the other side before I was off and running again.

The road was full of fabulously dressed gawkers watching the flames above the Metropolitan. The circling lights of two fire trucks threw garish flashing shadows on the buildings around us. I reached the corner just as the traffic light turned yellow.

I ran out anyway. The light turned red. Cars lurched forward even though they had no place to go — the firemen had filled the road. I wove between bumpers. As I reached the other side, I glanced back and saw Jaeger, sliding across a car's hood, pressing forward, gaining on me.

For blocks, the traffic was at a standstill, with rerouted cars jamming the roads. The sidewalks were equally full of people running down to Fifth Avenue to see the fire. I felt like a salmon hitting the falls as I pushed and shoved through an oncoming river of humanity.

A hand caught my elbow; I felt myself swung around. I saw a glint of metal. I looked up into Jaeger's eyes. There was satisfaction in them.

His free arm slashed toward me but was stopped by two little bird claw hands belonging to a man so withered and shriveled he might have been a hundred years old. "Kelev," he rasped, his eyes burning as he clung to that arm with all his strength. "Rotseyekh! MURDERER!"

"Unhand me, you filthy Jew," Jaeger snarled, twisting his knife with a move so fast I couldn't follow it. His other hand still held my arm with fingers of iron.

I thought he would stab the little man right before my eyes, but his thrust was intercepted by an immovable grip.

A giant stood between the German and the Jew — a black man with a yellow kerchief in his jacket's breast pocket. His eyes touched briefly on the yellow fabric on my wrist. Then *his* free hand came up and slammed into the Reichsleiter's face. I felt the Reichsleiter's fingers slide off my arm, heard his blade clatter on the cement.

"I am a diplomat!" Jaeger shouted. "An attaché!" The pitch of his voice was rising.

"Nazi," someone growled, and I heard another blow connect.

"Murderer!" from someone else.

"I am a diplomat," Jaeger yelled again.

Then his face sank into the circle of backs surrounding him. The crowd seemed to swallow him. His protests ceased. The thuds of blows continued. I knew that he would no longer be following me.

I ran on. One block more. The subway entrance was just ahead. I rounded the end of the rail to the stairs down.

"Sarah!"

I looked back, hopeful, expecting to see Jackson.

No. Richard Hathaway. Chasing me for his mother's gun.

I started shoving my way down the steps. I could hear Richard above: "Let me through!"

I pushed harder. Just beyond the stairs I saw turnstiles. I kept running as I felt around the bottom of the bag frantically. *There.*

I popped Sammy's subway token in the slot and shoved the bulk of my skirts through the turnstile. The guard stepped forward, eyeing the crazed Cinderella slipping past him, but he did not stop me. I shot into the open doors of the subway car and whirled.

I saw Richard vaulting the turnstile, arcing through the air. I saw a clock on the wall, the second hand crawling to 12:15. Richard was going to make it. He was going to catch me. He was going to ruin everything.

His hand snagged my arm through the open subway door, his eyes full of confusion. I begged him, "You have to let me go, Hathaway. It's more important than you can possibly know. You *can* trust me. Please."

He held my eyes, as if he were trying to read something hidden in them. Then he smiled. Square with just a bit of crooked. And he let me go.

I reached Penn Station in time for the one o'clock New Year's special, heading for all points south. I'd brought enough cash for two tickets, but now I needed only one.

The train car held a fair number of passengers, many in evening clothes, most of them showing obvious signs of too much alcohol. It was a measure of how thoroughly all residents and visitors to New York had been indoctrinated to mind their own business that no one gave my torn, mud-stained cloak and gown a second glance. I shoved over to a seat by the window to hide my clothes as much as possible.

I huddled there, letting the rhythm of the train lull me. All I wanted was to look up and see Jackson magically rejoining me. Telling me what to do again. Making everything go right.

I remembered then I had never told Jackson about Fiona and her poem. I had never told him he was the same, time after time. The same Jackson — whom I loved.

I became aware of the staticky voice of a radio newscaster coming from a portable radio someone had turned up too loud. ". . . But reports confirm the blaze was started by an incendiary bomb and was confined to the portion of the Metropolitan known as the Atrium. Because the exhibit was an ambassadorial gesture by Robert Hathaway, who is widely predicted to become the next president of the Confederation, there has been some speculation that this was a terrorist attack. Again, the only known casualty is a negro youth who is presumed to have set the blaze. . . ."

I didn't hear anything after that. I sat alone, apart, absolute silence filling my ears.

I couldn't let the thought in. I couldn't face it, pick it up, let it be inside me. It was too horrible to accept it as the truth: *He had always planned to stop Jaeger. He knew all along he was never coming back.*

"Miss?" A hand on my shoulder made me turn, made me look up into kind eyes. A black porter. "Your stop is next." He watched me a moment, trying to decide if he should say or do anything more.

I nodded, brushing at tears. His words hardly made sense to me, as if they came from a great distance, difficult to hear. I moved obediently to the aisle seat to show that I was ready, that I would get up when it was necessary. That is what he wanted of me, wasn't it? I watched his pants, his shiny black shoes, move on.

The train lurched to a stop. I made myself stand. I moved legs I couldn't feel, walking in short, wooden steps. I made my knees bend to take the stairs, almost fell, caught myself on the metal rail, slipped and staggered the rest of the way to the ground. Then I started walking. My body knew the direction.

It was still dark, but the sky was growing gray. Dawn was coming.

I was cold to the center of me, an interior of snow and ice that hurt like fire. I didn't want to move anymore, but I didn't want to stop moving. I just kept walking and pulling in air through a throat squeezed tight. *I have to see it through*, I thought.

But I didn't know what that meant. I hadn't ever known what that meant.

At the edge of town, I began to jog. Down the trail through the park. That would take me back to Amber House. Where I would see it through. *Because Time without him in it must not be.*

Chapter Thirty-Three

The sky in the east, out beyond the Chesapeake, dreamed of day in shades of pink and plum. I didn't know how long I ran, stiff plodding paces in constant rhythm, on and on. My breath flew from me in cloud serpents. My velvet slippers were soaked through from the thin blanket of snow that held the world in quietude. My toes became dull things of ice.

I felt a stricken spot on my hip and recognized that the gun in the purse was beating upon me mercilessly. I drew it out and ran with it in hand.

He knew all along he wouldn't be coming with me. I reached the road that bordered Amber House. I had come home. The sky was shot with gold.

I shoved through the hidden gate, hardly slowing, onto the path that led across the fields.

I came out of the trees — and Jackson was there, waiting for me at the path's end. Sitting on the top rail of the fence, looking out over the hilltops. He held in his hand a yellow handkerchief exactly like the one I had tied around my wrist. He did not see me yet.

The joy I felt in meeting him again was so fierce it was pain.

"Jackson," I said, and a space opened around us, and then he saw.

He smiled. "I promised you I would be here."

I stood with my hand kneading my side, gasping white breaths. "You knew you were never coming back."

"I knew," he agreed.

"We should have found another way."

"There was no other way. It was me or all of them, including your parents."

I shook my head. It sat like a sickness inside me. How could he have made himself face death? *That* death, by burning?

I felt terribly cold. I wished he could hold me.

"I waited here to tell you that I love you," he said. "Seemed like you were a little doubtful at times." He exhaled, as if he'd been holding his breath for a long time. I watched him soften with that breath. I realized he was finally telling me the future he'd foreseen. As he'd promised he would. "I've always loved you, Sare. It's part of who I am." He slid down from the fence then and came close. His face had a sheen of prismatic light that testified to the gulf of time between us, that proved he was an echo, intangible. We could not touch, but he could meet my eyes. "I wanted you to know — the future that I've seen is worth fighting for. It's a better place. And you and I finally get to be together. I judged it worth dying for. Now you have to keep your promise and see it through."

"What if I fail?"

The smallest sad smile. "It's a possibility," he said. "I've seen that also. Where you become First Lady of a new nation."

"Richard," I said.

He nodded. "He loves you too."

I couldn't let myself think about that. There was something else. Something I had forgotten to tell him, something he needed to know. "Fiona — she remembered a poem from the other time. She found it in the déjà vu. It proves she's the same person. You are too. And I'll remember you. I'll tell you every detail."

"I know," he said.

"I love you," I said.

He smiled and nodded. "I know that too. I've seen you and loved you a whole lifetime's worth, Sare. *You* were worth dying for."

Pain filled my chest like an iron bar, cold and dull and heavy. "You have to go now," he said.

I forced myself to turn. I forced myself to walk on. When I looked back, the snow on the rail was undisturbed.

Sam and Maggie opened the door for me when I climbed up the front steps. The house was warm, so warm my skin burned with the rush of blood returning. "Where's Jackson?" Sam asked.

I started to sob. Maggie took me in her arms and I rested there. After a while, maybe a long while, I said, "I don't know what to do."

"You don't know yet what happened, what was changed?" Maggie asked.

I shook my head.

"The house will tell you."

"Why me?" I asked.

"Because you were the one who was chosen."

I shook my head again. "You say that like there's something behind all this, some intention, some reason. How do you know it's not all just random? How do you know I can do *any*thing to make it better?"

She hugged me close again and leaned my head against her shoulder. She stroked my hair to soothe me. "When I write stories," she said, "it's like chiseling a statue. I go back and find something deeper, layer after layer, until the story is all shaped, all laid bare." She lifted me away from her so she could take my face in her hands. "Maybe God is an artist. He saw something deeper. And you must be here to help Him lay it bare."

Sammy came up and slipped his hand into mine. "Jackson told me to make sure you remembered your promise."

I wiped my face with my fingers. I nodded. "I remember, Sam." I picked the gun up from where I'd let it fall.

"You'll make him come back, Sarah," Sam said.

I didn't know where to go, what to do, so I took the gun and started walking. Living room, library, gallery. Kitchen, dining room, hall. I would let the house tell me. I would *make* the house tell me. Ground floor of the east wing, back to the entry. Up the stairs to the second floor —

Where the light shifted.

Ahead of me, I saw the Captain hauling Deirdre to her room by one arm. She was protesting, "But I must prepare, Joseph. Make sure the luncheon is laid, put on a frock. He shall be here soon."

"No," he said, shoving her through the door. "He's not coming."

"He's not?" she said. "Did he write again? Send his regrets?"

"He's not coming," her husband said again firmly and pulled her door shut. As he walked past me, he pulled Claire Hathaway's pistol from his waistband and checked its touch hole for powder.

He was on his way to murder someone, I realized, dropping out of the vision. The man he made Deirdre invite to Amber House. The man whose name he chose on the flip of a coin.

Because I saved Deirdre, a man who wasn't supposed to die had been murdered by the Captain. And time changed.

It seemed inconceivable to me that one man's life mattered that much. That the entire course of history hinged on one death. I remembered my other father once saying something like that — how an infinite number of almost random events come together to push things this way or that, and if one little thing gets changed, the whole world could be too.

Who had the Captain killed? I had a suspicion, but I needed to know.

I rushed back downstairs with renewed purpose. "The Captain assassinated someone who wasn't supposed to die," I told Maggie as I continued past to the kitchen. She and Sammy followed me.

"Someone who came here," Maggie said, "because you woke the other mama up."

"Yes."

"Who?"

"I'm not sure yet," I said, "but I think I know how to find out." I scrounged a screwdriver out of a bottom junk drawer and sat down at the table with the pistol. I needed the coin free.

I gasped when I picked it out of its socket in the gun. It was cold in my fingers, and it seemed almost to *squirm*. My mind's eye exploded with telescoping images, one inside the other, each blooming out of the one that came before. I felt possessed, attacked. Faces ran before me down decades, down centuries, male and female, young and old, all made nearly inhuman by some kind of hunger. Violence surrounded them, every form of corruption, every kind of death, and I was drowning in it. Back and back, until the last face — the old man on the coin, lying in dirt among other pieces of silver, bare feet swinging in the air just above.

"Maggie," I cried, and she took my hand. My vision cleared. I dropped the coin. I was breathing raggedly, choking on evil, feeling fouled beyond endurance. The trunk in the attic was nothing compared to that.

"What happened? What is it?" Maggie asked.

"I don't know what it is," I said grimly. "Something cursed."

"Don't touch it again."

"I don't have any choice."

I wrapped it in a dishcloth. I took it and went back upstairs, into the Captain's front room.

I unwrapped the coin and held it again in my fingers. There was no replay of what I had seen before, just the chill of the metal and a sense of *wrongness*. I gripped it and concentrated with all my might, willing the Captain to appear. I went to stand behind his chair. Nothing. But I was certain this had to be it.

I balanced the Janus coin on the side of my curled index finger, atop the tip of my thumb. I flipped it into the air.

Another hand shot out to catch it. The Captain's. He checked its face — it was the grim old man. He used his quill to cross another name off his list. He flipped the coin again. The young and smiling god. *Yes.* The Captain circled a name in his log and sat back, contemplating. I leaned forward to see.

Of course.

Washington. The owner of Mount Vernon. The rebel general. The father of a lost nation in a time that didn't exist anymore.

The vision dissipated. I was back in my own time. The wrong time.

How could I stop the assassination of a man killed more than two hundred years in the past? Nyangu was the key. I could touch the past only through her. I needed to find Nyangu again. But I needed her from a specific time, the exactly right time. No other would do. How could I find her?

"Here, Sarah." Sam stood in the doorway, holding out his hand, palm up. On it sat the mottled green stone.

My sweet, strange little brother. Who knew things. And wasn't afraid. Who looked forward to the "new years" coming.

"You got this from the maze," I said.

"Yup."

"How'd you know where it was?"

"I was the one who put it there."

"How did you know to put it there, bud?"

"She told me to do it. So I did it."

" 'She'? Nanga?"

"Nope." He shook his blond head the slightest bit, almost impatient with me. "She loves you, Sarah. She looks after you."

"Who?"

"Amber." He patted my hand, tucked the stone into it. "And I love you too."

I leaned down and kissed the top of his head. "I love you too, Sam."

"See you later," he whispered. "Next time."

I went in search of Nanga. Deirdre's room, the Nautical Room, the Flowered Room, the Tower Room. I found her in the little eight-by-eight-foot chamber next to that. I heard her before I saw her, shifting in the chair in the corner, holding a piece of needlework. "Where you be, child?" she said, seeking blindly.

"Nyangu." And she saw me then, and smiled.

"You have need of me?"

"When I woke up Deirdre, everything changed. The world changed. For the worse. You have to help me fix it. So I can save Jackson."

"Jackson with you?"

I could hardly say the words. "He's dead. I have to finish without him."

She looked stricken, but she nodded. "He gambled on you to see it through," she said. "We mustn't fail him. Tell me."

"The Captain plans to kill a man who is coming to visit Deirdre — a distant relative. I don't know exactly when."

"That be today, child. Soon. The husband of a cousin stopping here on his way north. A military man from Virginia. Why would the Captain kill this man?"

"It was the coin. Dobson's coin. The Captain was using it to figure out how to make his fortune."

Nyangu nodded. "It is a thing of very old pain."

"We have to stop him. Without General Washington, everything changes. *You* have to stop him."

"How do I do such a thing? How can I save this man Washington?"

A new voice spoke behind me. "Why do you speak of my cousin?" Deirdre stepped into the room *through* me, raising gooseflesh, causing me to shudder. She looked something like the way I remembered her from the attic, prematurely grayed and weak. But she had lost much of the confusion — the *madness* — that had been in her eyes before. "To whom do you speak, Nanga? One of the ones to come? Is it the girl I saw in my dream?"

"Yes, Deirdre. The one named for your Sarah."

"Can she see me, hear my words?"

I nodded. Nyangu said, "Yes, she can."

Deirdre addressed the air. "Then I must thank you, grand-daughter, for waking me from that dream."

"She says we must stop the Captain."

"Because he intends to kill cousin George." She shook her head, thinking. "We cannot stop the Captain. But we might stop the general. Intercept him. Warn him. I cannot go — I would not make it half so far. But you or Sarah-Louise could."

"Why would he believe me?" Nyangu asked Deirdre. "He don't know me. Why would he take the word of a slave?"

"I will give you a note. Cousin George knows my writing."

She started out of the room with a decisiveness that reminded me of the little girl she had once been, headstrong and unstoppable. But where the hall joined the landing, the Captain stood waiting. "What are you doing wandering around in your nightshift?" he said with disgust. "Get back to your room." He grabbed her wrist and hauled her along by it as Nyangu watched, immobilized.

Deirdre twisted her arm, trying to break free. "But I must prepare, Joseph. Make sure the luncheon is laid, put on a frock. He shall be here soon."

I had seen this already, I realized. But I had seen it *differently*.

Deirdre had not been fighting the Captain's grip. Things had already begun to change.

"No," the Captain said, shoving her through the door. "He's not coming."

"He's not?" she said. "Did he write again? Send his regrets?"

"He's not coming," her husband said again firmly and pulled her door shut. And then he locked it. *Another change.* He pulled the pistol from his waistband, checked it and his watch. He leaned on the rail and yelled down toward the kitchen. "Fix me a plate. I'm in a hurry."

He went to his room and grabbed his greatcoat. Then he jogged down the stairs.

"What do I do now?" Nyangu asked.

"Take the page from the journal where the Captain circled Washington's name. If you show him that, he'll believe you."

"Captain will kill me if he finds me in his study."

"I'll keep watch."

She nodded. I could see she was scared half to death, but she set her jaw and started moving.

She went to the Captain's desk and opened the side drawers, searching through their contents. Nyangu lifted the leather blotter, opened the wooden box on the desktop. She shook her head, frustrated, then closed her eyes and leaned on the desk. A tremor shook her; a trickle of blood started from her nose. She whirled, stood on tiptoe, and felt on top of a cupboard. She stepped back, triumphant, a key in her fingers. She opened the center drawer and pulled out the leather-bound journal. Nyangu hissed to me, "Which page will it be?"

"It must be one of the last he wrote. It has Washington's name circled."

She flipped the pages from the rear forward until she found the right page. She ripped it out and tucked it in her apron pocket. Then she started to put the room back to rights.

I heard a chair scrape back in the dining room. I ran partway down the stairs. The Captain said, "Feed the rest to the hound."

I saw him emerge from the rear hall. He was heading for the door. Nyangu would be too late. But he stopped just short. He patted his pockets. He did not find what he was looking for. He turned back toward the stairs.

"Get out!" I yelled to Nyangu. "Now! He's coming!"

She ran on bare feet out the door and into the hall that led off to the left. The Captain heard the whisper of those soft running footsteps. He climbed up to the lower landing, craning his neck to see up to the balcony, then took the upper stairs two at a time. Even invisible, I shrank back from him. He crossed to his room and stopped in the door.

From where I stood at the rail, I saw Nyangu scurry farther down the hall. The Captain's head jerked forward; he'd noticed something. I walked closer as he took several steps into the room to stand before his desk. He leaned forward slightly, touching his finger to the surface. Then he held his finger up and rubbed the red spot on it against his thumb. Blood.

He trotted back out of the room, his gun raised. He checked the locked door on Deirdre's room, looked in the Nautical Room, and paused by the door beyond the stairs. Then he started down the steps, walking sideways and backward, keeping his eyes on the hall above.

He went all the way down to the lower floor, and I heard him push open the door to the kitchen. Then he came back to the lowest step and stopped, the gun still held high.

Nyangu had slipped midway down the hall and climbed on the bench there. Her fingers felt along the top of the crown molding, looking for the secret door.

"I know you're up there," the Captain roared from below. "Come out now and give me back what you stole, and you'll only get a whipping. Make me hunt you down" — the sliding panel in front of Nyangu popped open — "and I'll shoot you where you stand."

She eased the door open, so slowly it made no more sound than a sigh. The Captain took a step up, his ear tipped to hear. He took another and another.

"He's climbing up," I told her. She jerked and gave the panel a tiny shove. The wheels made a small metallic whir. The Captain began to run. I screamed, "Oh, my God, he's coming!"

Nyangu leapt up into the mouth of the hidden stair and slammed the panel shut. The Captain had reached the top of the stairs, saw the hall empty, and spun, cursing, to start back down. I ran after him. "We're on the stairs," I shrieked. "We're coming down."

At the lower landing, the Captain jumped past the remaining steps. I clattered down after him. I saw him pause in the door to the kitchen and lower the gun.

The muzzle spat smoke and flame; Nyangu screamed. I got to the door and saw her scrambling back up again the hidden stair. The Captain lunged and caught her foot. He yanked and she slid down, turning as she came. She reached out with claws and slashed his face. He swore and wiped his cheek with his sleeve, which came away marked with blood. She pushed upward, backward, and he lunged at her again. She grabbed the door frame and leapt up, jamming her bent legs forward to hit the Captain's midsection with her heels. He doubled over, gasping, and she jerked loose, scrabbling up and away. He snatched a knife from the table, then started after her, moving fast.

I could not follow. In my time, the hidden door would be sealed. I spun around and ran for the main stairs, winded and trembling and straining to cling to the vision.

When I got to the second-floor hall, the secret panel hung open. The bench below the door was on its side; paintings hung askew; a vase farther down the hall had been smashed on the floor. I heard the Captain roaring just beyond the corner, "Open this door, damn you! I'll beat you, daughter, if you do not unlock it!"

I reached the turn in the hall and saw the Captain heaving his shoulder against the door to Sarah-Louise's bedroom. It held solid. He pivoted and kicked up just under the doorknob. The rim lock gave way; the door burst in.

He advanced inside. I ran to the door, but I was helpless to do anything. The Captain held his knife low and tilted it back and forth, so that light played from its blade.

Sarah-Louise put herself in front of Nyangu. "Don't touch her, Father."

The Captain struck his daughter and she slammed against the wall and onto the floor.

Nyangu darted forward, screaming, a surgical blade in her hand. Lazily, the Captain blocked her swing and shoved her back. She staggered into the specimen table beneath the window; there was the crash of breaking glass as the bell jar with the Good Mother spider hit the floor.

Nyangu scrabbled away from the smashed bell jar, pulling a shard of glass from her forearm. She pushed to her feet, using the wall to brace herself. I saw her eyes dart down to the side.

The Captain took out his coin, his lucky coin. He held it out for Nyangu to see and flipped it. It arced, gleaming, end over end, head over head.

He caught it. He looked. He smiled.

"At last. Time to die, witch," he said with enjoyment.

In one fluid motion, Nyangu bent and grabbed a stick on the floor — the stick that had been inside the bell jar. She whipped it around and flicked it straight at the Captain. Something flew from it and landed on his lapel.

He looked. And laughed, his teeth showing. "A spider?" His hand clapped down on his lapel, smashing the thing.

But his laughter stopped, and he held up his hand to look more closely.

"No," he breathed, brushing his hands over his lapel, his shoulder. Slapping his neck, his face. "Help me. Sarah, help me, girl!"

Nyangu shot past him, grabbed Sarah-Louise's hand, and tugged the girl into the hall. The door slammed shut. The Captain twisted the knob and pulled, still swatting. I saw tiny spiders swarming his face. Hundreds of them. More. They filled the claw marks down the cheek. They crawled along the lashes of his staring eyes.

He sank onto his knees.

I could imagine how it must feel. A pulsing blossoming into pain, undeniable pain. Burning at the edges of everything. I *knew* how it must feel. My hand ached.

The storm had already started, I had no notion when. The hurricane storm of time changing. Darkness was creeping in from the sides, and the wind was rising.

I looked down at my hands, my fingers. Motes of me danced like embers, glowing, drifting, rising. They hurt as they broke away and blurred into a smoldering cloud. And each one of them carried a memory that grew fainter as it left: *The crushing defeat of the colonials at New York.*

It never was, I thought.

The Second Colonial Uprising of 1832. The victory of Nazi Germany at Normandy. The sacking of the Imperial City of China. The destruction of London. The invasion of Australia.

All of it, I thought: *Neverwas.*

And I was well satisfied. Part of me hoped, for Mom and Dad, for Sammy, for Richard and his family — but I would not stop this if I could.

I saw her then, in the way Maggie had once described. She was painted in energy: orange wrapped around violet that held a core of diamond brilliance. She was old, very old, but I knew her instantly because the light looked like who she really was.

"We did good, child," Nanga told me. "She's coming closer."

Who? I thought, and felt, more than knew, the answer.

I stood in the center, in the house, *with* the house, and Time spread out around us, all of it happening at once — past, present, and future. And the house showed me what I needed to see once more. Showed me things as it must see them: each moment intimately known. I *was* a grieving girl with blond curls who took a silver coin from a dead man's venom-swelled body. I *was* a young woman returned home, knowing some part of me was left behind in that place where they'd tried to cut away my visions. I *was* a mother who saw a fireball squeeze backward to become a car filled with her husband and child, saw the car fishtail away backward from the last apple tree of a century-old orchard. I *was* a slave woman who sent my child north because I loved her but loved as well all the grandchildren strung like pearls into the future. I *was* a woman seated in a sloop steered by a green-eyed man who smiled at our green-eyed little girl.

I was myself, nearly gone, blown away like smoke, and I was well satisfied. I thought with the last words left to me, *Time without him in it will not b —*

A hand took mine firmly.

"Wake up, Sarah," he said.

And I obeyed.

ACKNOWLEDGEMENTS

Our deep and sincere thanks to everyone who read and reviewed *Amber House* — your kind enthusiasm carried us through the battle of turning out this second book.

Our continuing thanks to our ever-so-clever agent, Jennifer Weltz, and her wonderful compatriots at the Jean V. Naggar Literary Agency: Tara Hart, Laura Biagi, Jessica Regel, and all the crew, building on thirty-five years of literary discovery and representation.

And our thanks to the person who can never be thanked enough — the amazing Cheryl Klein, our inestimable editor, whose clear-sightedness regarding all things literary leaves us constantly humbled. Our deep gratitude also to Elizabeth Starr Baer, our production editor.

A special thank-you to a dear friend who misspent his college years studying history at Yale in order to fuel an enthusiasm for alternate timelines. We asked David Leiwant to justify our "dead general" outcome and he provided us with a complete variant history, which we will be posting on the official Amber House website.

Finally, our thanks to our Gramma, Lore Moore, and our "Boy," Sinjin Reed, who read and suggest and encourage endlessly. Your turn is next, Boy. Love you.

This book was edited by Cheryl Klein
and designed by Whitney Lyle.
The text was set in Perpetua,
and the display type was set in Phiastos.
The book was printed and bound at R. R. Donnelley
in Crawfordsville, Indiana.
The production was overseen by Starr Baer.
The manufacturing was supervised by Angelique Browne.